GOLDEN STAR

PART ONE

TRIAL
OF
FROST

FAE BOUND
VOLUME
ONE

USA TODAY BESTSELLING AUTHOR
MICHELLE MADOW

TRIAL OF FROST
Fae Bound Volume One

Published by Dreamscape Publishing
Page edges by Painted Wings Publishing

ISBN: 979-8-9991625-1-9

SAPPHIRE

"THAT MAN LOOKS like he could use a drink," my best friend Zoey says, motioning to a startlingly attractive dark-haired man at the end of the bar who's staring into his water glass, brooding about something or other.

Join the club, I think, since I'm having a pretty terrible New Year's Eve myself.

But as the star bartender at the Maple Pig Bar and Grill, it's up to me to cheer this man up with whatever concoction comes to my mind as being the one he needs.

So, I walk over to him, and his gaze shifts to me.

His eyes are silver. An unusual color that holds an icy glint, like icicles pinning me down.

But I keep my cool. I've seen enough sad and mysterious eyes behind this counter to know how to deal with them.

Besides, there's something different about this guy. Something that makes me want to reach beneath that brooding exterior and touch his soul.

Something that makes all thoughts of my fight with Matt this morning disappear into the corners of my mind.

"Rough night?" I ask once I'm standing in front of him.

"You could say that." He keeps his eyes locked on mine, as if he's challenging me about what to say next.

"Lucky for you, I have just the thing." I pick up the shaker, getting ready to do what I do best. "This one's on the house."

It's what I always say to newcomers.

And, as always, my hands move like they have a mind of their own. Each ingredient flows into place, and there's a familiar soft hum beneath my skin, like the vibration of a note just beyond hearing.

"Aren't you a bit young to be serving drinks?" he asks as I work.

"I'm eighteen," I say. "I make the best drinks in Maine. So, as long as I don't *drink* the drinks, the restaurant lets me make them and serve them."

The finished product is a soft pinkish concoction—one that fizzes gently, like bottled warmth.

"Do I seem like a man who orders pink drinks?" He raises an eyebrow, not moving to take it.

"You must not be from around here," I reply, since he's right—he definitely doesn't strike me as the sort of man who orders pink drinks.

But my hands lead the way, and I obey.

So, pink is what he gets.

"I'll take it as a compliment that I don't seem like I'm from a small town in Maine," he says, sounding decently amused with himself.

"People come here from all over." I shrug. "But I always remember a face. And yours…"

Is beautiful, I think, although of course, I hold back.

"I lost my cat," he says simply. "Ended up finding him nearby, and this place seemed busy, so I figured I'd check it out."

"Your cat?" I repeat, since normally, people come to the Maple Pig for my drinks. Not for a *cat.*

"Correct." He smirks and leans back in his chair. "His name's Ghost."

"And where's Ghost now?"

"He's waiting outside." His eyes drop to my wrist—to the sapphire bracelet I never take off—apparently done talking about his cat. "That's a beautiful bracelet."

"My mom gave it to me," I say, and I force a smile, wanting to change the subject. "So, are you going to try the drink?"

"Depends," he says playfully. "Are you going to tell me your name?"

"I'm Sapphire." I glance down at my wrist again. "Like my bracelet."

"Except you're far more beautiful." He picks up his glass, and I stand there speechless as he gives the pink drink a try.

For a heartbeat, the chattering inside the bar fades. There's just the two of us, here in this moment, strangers on the verge of something I can barely understand.

Something I *want* to understand.

"What about you?" I ask when he places the drink back down. "What's *your* name?"

Before he can answer, the door slams open so loudly that everyone turns to look.

Matt.

My boyfriend—well, *ex*-boyfriend—strides in, his jaw set, his eyes blazing with that look that makes my stomach twist. Not in the good way it used to, but in that anxious, here-we-go-again kind of way.

"Larkin!" someone off to the side says Matt's last name—one of the guys who used to play on the Presque Isle football team with him. "You made it!"

Matt ignores him as he pushes through the crowd, barely glancing at the dark-haired, silver-eyed man as he steps around the bar to stand next to me.

"Sapphire." His eyes scan my body, as if he's making sure no one else has touched it in the less than twenty-four hours since we broke up. "We need to talk."

"Now's not really a good time," I say, but he reaches out and wraps his fingers around my wrist. Not hard, but with a possessive edge that makes my skin prickle.

"Please," he says, and there's a sort of desperation in his tone that makes my heart soften a bit. "It's the last few minutes before the new year. I don't want to end it like this."

I'm hyperaware of everyone watching us—the silver-eyed stranger, Zoey, Matt's old football buddies, and probably a dozen others.

"Fine," I say, yanking my wrist free. "Talk."

He pauses, as if he wasn't expecting me to say yes so quickly.

Then, he begins.

"I want us to have a fresh start." He leans closer, and his eyes are anxious—pleading. "Come home with me. Tonight."

"I'm not moving in with you," I say for what must be the hundredth time these past few months. "I'm not ready."

"You're *never* going to be ready." He slams his hand onto the surface of the bar, and I jump, and then there's a loud *crack* as water sprays out of the service sink.

"Great," I mutter, and I hurry to the sink, water getting all over me as I twist the valve, searching for that sweet spot to fix it.

"Let me help," Matt says, and then he's there, as if nothing happened, reaching forward to take over.

Before he can, I twist the valve shut, cutting off the spray. Water drips from my sleeves, chilling my skin, and I take a deep breath, steadying myself.

"I didn't realize how handy you were," he says in a strange mix of approval and irritation.

"It's been happening a lot lately." I wipe my hands on my soaked jeans, which doesn't do much to dry them off. Luckily, I keep a spare pair in the back, in case of incidents like these. "We really need a new sink."

His face softens a little, as if seeing me soaked and struggling pulls something sympathetic out of him. "You know I just want us to be together," he says, gentler now. "I love you. I always have, and I always will."

I love you, too, a part of me automatically wants to say—the part that's been saying it to him since I was a starry-eyed freshman, and he was the most celebrated senior on the football team.

He's waiting for me to say it back when the countdown begins, voices echoing through the room as people raise their glasses in excitement.

"Ten... nine... eight..."

Matt's eyes flick back to mine, and there's a look there—one that's almost pleading.

"Seven... six..."

"Sapphire," he whispers, and I can barely hear him over the rising cheers. "I don't want to lose you."

"Five... four..."

His hands are on my waist, the heat of his body closing in on mine.

"Three… two…one…"

He closes the distance between us, and there's a comfort in the familiarity of his lips pressing against mine. Memories rush back of the good times we've had together—our nightly phone calls when we were first getting to know each other, his making our relationship official by taking me to homecoming, the playful snowball fight we had before the first time he told me he loved me, and the walk around the lake the morning of my high school graduation when he told me how scared he was that he was going to be stuck in Presque Isle forever.

"Happy New Year!" The bar erupts into cheers, people shouting in excitement and clinking their glasses together.

I pull away from Matt and open my eyes.

But instead of focusing on him, I glance at the far side of the bar.

The silver-eyed man is gone.

A strange pang hits me. Regret, or maybe disappointment. I can't quite place it, but it makes my chest hollow with the undeniable feeling of loss.

Especially because I never even got his name.

SAPPHIRE

"I SHOULD GET BACK TO WORK." I step away from Matt, putting some distance between us.

"Maybe we could still go out tonight?" He looks at me with that earnest, boyish expression that used to make my heart flutter. "Everyone's going to the park near the mountains to see that meteor shower later."

"The meteor shower!" Zoey's suddenly here, bouncing with the excitement of someone who never turns down an adventure. "Yes. We're going."

It's true—we were planning on going.

But that was before we thought Matt was joining us.

"It's late. The park's closed." I frown, searching for more reasons to say no. "And it's freezing outside."

"We'll have each other to stay warm. And who cares if the park's closed?" Matt says. "It's not like anyone actually patrols it."

He's right—the cops don't bother patrolling much around here. Especially since tonight, their prime concern will be keeping drunk drivers off the main roads in town.

And I have to admit—I was looking forward to seeing the meteors.

"Fine," I say. "I'll come. But just to see the meteors. And if it's too cold, I'm leaving."

Zoey cheers, throwing her arms around me and giving me a squeeze. "That's the spirit! I promise you won't regret it."

"Hopefully not. But you know what I *would* regret? Getting fired for spending time with my friends instead of my customers," I say, squirming out of her grasp. "We close in a half hour. Think you both can wait that long?"

"Depends on what drink you're able to cook up for me," Matt challenges.

"Then it's a good thing I make fantastic mocktails," I say, grabbing a towel to dry the remaining water on the counter. "After all, you're driving."

He rolls his eyes, but he doesn't say no.

As I start mixing the drink, I glance at the corner of the bar again, where the man with the silver eyes was sitting.

"Hey," Zoey says, following my gaze. "You okay?"

"Just... wondering if I missed something important." I shrug, trying to make light of it, but the feeling lingers as I look away from the empty seat.

"If it's meant to be, you'll see him again," she says. "You never know how the stars will align."

I will if I don't get out of Presque Isle and end up bartending here for the rest of my life, I think, looking over to the door, as if the silver eyed mystery man is going to walk back inside at any moment.

He doesn't.

I'll probably never see him again.

The rest of the night passes uneventfully, and before long, the lights brighten in the universal sign for everyone to go home.

Soon enough, I'm in the passenger seat of Matt's truck as he leads three carfuls of his friends through the mountains. Zoey's in the back, and she talks for most of the hour long drive, which eases the remaining tension between me and Matt.

Finally, we pull into the parking lot. But the overhead lampposts cast too much light for us to see the meteor shower properly, so Zoey leads us deeper into the woods, to a small clearing.

Matt's friends lay out blankets, and someone passes around a flask, the sharp scent of whiskey mingling with the crisp night air.

"And now, the magic begins," Matt says, flinging his arm around my shoulders and pulling me closer.

"Can I have some of that?" I ask the girl next to me who's holding the flask—Mallory.

"I didn't know our star bartender drank whiskey straight." She gives me an approving smile and passes the flask.

"Only in emergencies. And it's getting so cold out here that I consider it an emergency." I take a sip of the whiskey, then glance up at the sky just in time to see a meteor zoom overhead.

The others are so caught up in chatting and drinking that they miss it.

They miss the next few meteors, too.

"I thought this would be more exciting," Andrew says with a frustrated sigh.

"If the stars don't hurry up and put on a show, I'm going back to the car," his fiancée Winnie says.

Zoey's chatting with Mallory, and even she's starting to look like she's ready to get out of here.

A few more minutes pass, and by the time another meteor zooms overhead, they're too caught up in deciding when we should leave to notice it.

"I think we've seen all we're going to see tonight," Matt's friend Kyle decides, standing up. "Let's get out of here before we freeze."

A murmur of agreement spreads through the group. Rhonda's already packing up her blanket, and Andrew pulls Winnie closer, both of them looking ready to make a run for the warmth of their car.

I start to stand as well, but Matt reaches for me, stopping me.

"I was thinking we could stay a little longer," he says. "Just you and me."

I pause, glancing at Zoey for backup. She's standing next to Mallory, blankets gathered, ready to go.

Matt stares her down, and she shifts uncomfortably, looking back and forth between us.

"You should stay," she finally says, surprising me. "Text me when you get back. Okay?"

Something's off. I don't know what, but I swear it is.

Matt's hand lingers on my arm. "It's the start of the new year, and I want to spend time with you," he says. "Here. Under the stars. Together."

Zoey's barely looking at me. I can usually get a decent idea about what she's thinking, but right now, I'm clueless.

And she's apparently not at all willing to fill me in.

"Fine," I give in to Matt, since I actually *am* enjoying watching the meteors. "I'll stay for a little bit longer."

And, as I sit back down next to him and watch Zoey and Mallory hurry to catch up with the others, I pray to the stars above that the new year will bring me clarity about what I want for my future.

SAPPHIRE

"Sapphire," Matt says after a few minutes of watching meteors together. "Look at me."

I do. And, as I do, I see a flash of the hopeful high school football star who chose me—a freshman—to charm and win over in only the course of a few weeks.

It's rare that I see this side of him anymore. Working long hours at the shop has worn him down over the years.

"I know things have been rough." He shifts, fidgeting, and removes his gloves. "I know you're unsure about where we're headed."

"I'm sorry," I say, even though I'm not sure what I'm apologizing for. "It's not you. It's just..." I trail off, the words tangling in my throat.

Before I can decide what to say, he reaches into his coat pocket and pulls out a small, velvet box.

No. No, no, no.

This can't be happening.

Please tell me this isn't happening.

"I want to give you the security you need—something solid." His voice breaks through the fog in my mind. "You don't have to be unsure anymore. We can make this official. You and me. Forever."

I'm frozen, watching as he opens the box, revealing a simple, sparkling ring that probably cost him over three months' pay.

"Will you marry me?" he asks, the hope in his eyes burning fiercer than ever.

Ice-cold dread rushes through me as he removes the ring and reaches for my hand, ready to put it on my finger.

"No."

I yank my hand back, and the wind picks up, as if it's trying to blow that ring right out of his fingers.

"What?" he asks, as if he didn't hear me right. Like maybe I'll take it back.

"No." Panic claws at my insides, scrambling my thoughts. "I don't want this. I'm not ready for this. *Any* of it."

The hurt in his eyes turns into something darker. A deep sort of pain that makes my chest tighten even more.

"We've been together for over four years," he says, not moving the ring away. "You're telling me that after all this time, you don't want this? You don't want *us?*"

"I'm saying that the reason I don't want to move in with you isn't because I *wanted you to propose to me first.*" I stand up, as if that'll clarify that there's no way he's getting that ring near my finger.

He should know me better than to think *this* was what I wanted. Especially since there's been no moment in our relationship when either of us has mentioned marriage.

"Andrew and Winnie have been engaged for three months," he says as he stands, as if she hasn't been showing off her ring every moment she can. "Andrew's the same age as me. He knows what he wants, and he's doing it. Why shouldn't we do the same? Why are we putting this off?"

"Because I don't want to be stuck in Presque Isle for the rest of my life!" I shout, and the wind surges, rattling the branches overhead and stirring the snow at our feet.

Matt goes still.

Then, his expression twists from confusion to anger, his eyes narrowing as he clenches his fists at his sides.

"You think I want to be stuck here?" His voice is sharp, louder than it's been all night, and he motions around the dark clearing. "That this is the life I dreamed of?"

I say nothing.

After all, I know how crushed he was when he didn't get the football scholarship he wanted. It was his only chance at paying his way through college, and he lost it to the quarterback in the next town over.

I just hit him where it hurts, and I feel terrible about it.

"I'm trying to build a life with you." He steps closer, as if he can convince me to change my mind by just talking to me for long enough. "But I'm offering you everything I have, and it's still not enough. It's never enough anymore. What the hell do you want from me?"

The crushed way he's looking at me makes my heart break.

"I don't know," I say honestly. "I just know it's not this."

He stands there, his face flushed with frustration, looking like he might say something angry. Something final.

Instead, he shakes his head and shoves the ring and its box back into his pocket.

"Fine," he snaps. "Good luck bartending your way to some great escape. Because we both know that while you're clearly too proud to admit it, you're as stuck in this town as I am."

With that, he stomps through the clearing, heading toward the trail that leads back to the parking lot.

Guilt and regret settle in my chest as he goes.

I shouldn't have lashed out like that. It wasn't fair.

But if I run after him, what am I going to say? Because I'm not going to take my decision back. And I know Matt well enough to know that he needs space.

A *lot* of it.

And, from the looks of it, that space is going to be permanent.

I should be devastated.

Instead, it's like the last bit of weight I've been holding onto through all our breakups this year has been lifted off my shoulders.

I sink down onto the blanket again, wrapping my arms around my knees, wishing Mallory had left some whiskey behind. I'm not the type of person to drink by myself, but I've also never been the type of person who's rejected her boyfriend's *marriage proposal* and then been left alone in a dark clearing in the middle of the mountains.

But I'm not getting back together with Matt. We're done. Broken up. For good now.

And I'm not going to drive back with him in what would be, without a doubt, the most awkward car ride in existence.

So, I pull out my phone, remove my gloves, and text Zoey.

You knew, I write, and then I add, *You knew he was going to propose, and you left me in the woods with him.*

I press send.

It doesn't deliver.

I stare at the screen, willing the message to go through. But there's nothing. Not even a single bar of service.

And as much as I'm dreading that car ride with Matt back into town, I'm also not stupid enough to stay here and freeze to death.

So, I get up and start down the trail, letting my phone's flashlight guide my way.

The heartbreak that should accompany a breakup like this doesn't appear. Not even when I think back on all our memories together. It's like the hole in my heart has been there for months, and I've been piling the dirt back into it this entire time without ever realizing it.

His proposal was the final press of the shovel to pack the dirt down for good, sealing it over like a grave I never wanted to dig.

And, as I continue to walk, everything feels wrong. Not just in my heart, but in my surroundings. The trees look the same in every direction. There's no clear path back to the parking lot. And every time I check my phone, there's still no service.

My breath quickens, and I ground myself, trying to calm the panic rising in my chest.

Then, I hear it. A bubbling sound, like water flowing over rocks.

A stream.

Relief washes over me. If I follow the water, it should lead me out of here. Streams always lead somewhere, right? At least, somewhere that's not a total circle?

Feeling more energized, I walk toward the sound of the water, picking up my pace.

Eventually, silver flashes in the distance.

A... tree? And in front of it, the stream.

I did it. That water will lead me home. Well, maybe not home, but at least out of the forest.

Hopefully. But given that it's the only solution I have right now, I keep going.

As I approach, a woman steps out from behind the tree, bathed in a soft, ethereal glow. Her silver hair glints like the stars themselves, and her face is pale, almost translucent, with eyes that shimmer like galaxies.

"Hello?" I call out, relief flooding through me at the sight of another person. "Do you live out here? Can you help me find my way back?"

The woman says nothing. And, as I get closer, I realize that something about her feels...off. Unnatural. Like she's there, but not entirely real.

I'm also not entirely sure it matters, given that she's the only person who might be able to help me get out of these woods before I freeze to death.

I take a cautious step closer and hold up my hands, not wanting to scare her away. "I don't have cell service," I tell her. "But if you have a house nearby—"

She moves, her feet silent against the snow, as if the night is moving with her.

I should back away. I should run. But I'm frozen, caught in the strange calm of her gaze, unable to move.

Her hand rises slowly, and before I can say anything, she touches me—a light brush of her fingertips against my forehead.

Pain shoots through my body.

It's like fire and ice at the same time, burning and freezing me from the inside out. My vision blurs, and I fall to my knees, the world spinning around me as I fight with everything I have to stop myself from collapsing into the snow.

The glow around the woman intensifies, growing brighter, until it's almost blinding. Spots dance before my eyes as the light creeps under my skin and becomes a part of me—consuming every inch of my being, all the way down to the marrow in my bones.

And then, just as suddenly as it started, the light goes out.

I collapse forward, catching myself on my hands as I gasp for air, my entire body trembling.

When I finally gather the strength to look up, the woman is gone.

Was she real? Or was I hallucinating from the cold?

Can people hallucinate from the cold?

I don't know. But one thing is clear—I have to get out of here. I will *not* pass out in the forest and freeze in the snow. Rejecting Matt's proposal will not be my death sentence.

Pain rushes through me again. Searing hot pain that starts from my forehead and rages through the rest of my body.

I need to cool down.

I need water.

With shaky hands, I crawl toward the stream, every muscle screaming in protest. All I can focus on is the burning—this unbearable fire surging through my veins, eating me alive. I've never felt anything this agonizing in my life. Not even during the sledding accident with Zoey when I was ten, when I snapped my ankle and passed out.

She dragged me all the way home on that sled. And, much to my embarrassment, my ankle ended up being totally fine.

I finally reach the water, and as I rip off my gloves, I catch sight of my bracelet. The string of sapphires on a silver chain that my aunt told me was a gift from my mother, wherever she is. It's the only thing of hers I have, and I can't help feeling like there's a part of her in the bracelet. Like somehow, she's watching out for me from the stones.

But my bracelet isn't going to save me. I need water. Now.

I scoop up a handful of icy water from an area of the stream that's wider and clearer than the rest of it and bring it to my lips. The first sip burns, but the fire raging inside me fades just enough to keep me from collapsing.

Then, the world tilts.

There's no time to scream—no time to catch myself—before I'm falling. Hard.

A sharp branch slices across my cheek as I tumble down, rolling over roots and jagged rocks. The world is a blur of trees, dirt, and silver leaves swirling around me like paint mixing together, each slam of my body into the earth driving the air from my lungs.

Pain explodes through my head as I crash into something—a rock, maybe—and land in some bushes at the base of a tree.

The last things I see are shimmering silver leaves before black haze creeps in at the edges of my vision, and everything goes dark.

SAPPHIRE

SOMEONE TUGS AT MY SHOULDER, rolling me over, startling me so much that I nearly jump out of my skin.

Suddenly, I'm not looking up at whoever found me in the woods.

I'm looking *down* at him. From up in a tree. Specifically, the silver-leafed tree that just tried to kill me.

Or... *did* it kill me?

Because right now, I'm looking down at my possibly dead body, and at the man crouched beside it.

Not just any man.

The man from the bar.

He's studying me—no, my *body*—his eyes narrowed in concentration as he checks for a pulse. I can't bring myself to speak, or to scream down at him to let him know I'm okay. Because I'm clearly *not* okay. My dead body at the base of this tree more than speaks for that.

Because that's what happened, right? The fall killed me? I hit my head and *died?*

I look down at my hands, and while they seem relatively normal, I swear there's a silver sheen to my skin. Sort of like the skin of the woman who tried to kill me, although not anywhere close to as intense.

As I continue to examine this strange ghostly form of myself, another figure moves into view.

Not a person.

A huge white leopard, its fur blending into the snow so perfectly that it looks like a creature sculpted from the ice itself. It prowls forward, toward the man from the bar, and panic surges through me.

It's going to kill him.

I have to save him.

Suddenly, I'm pulled back into my body like a snapped rubber band.

I sit up and gasp for air, and my arm flies out, as if trying to shield the man from an attack.

"No!" I scream, and water explodes from the stream, slamming into the leopard in a violent wave, knocking it back and drenching all three of us in the process.

The cold crashes over me, seeping through my clothes, and I crabwalk backward as quickly as possible to get away from the beast.

The man's also soaked. He's glaring at me, the calm, brooding expression from the bar replaced with something much colder.

Most alarmingly, he's holding a *sword* in front of him, and his knees are bent, as if he's ready to attack. And it's not pointed at the leopard, who's now retreated to his side.

It's pointed at *me*.

"You're in winter territory," he says, low and dangerous. "What are you doing here, summer fae?"

"What?" I push myself up to stand, my brain spinning, unable to keep up.

"Don't play dumb. I know what you are," he says, gesturing at the stream. "You just used your water magic."

"I don't know what you're talking about." I remain still, overly aware that if I make any sudden moves, this man might *attack me with his sword.*

Not to mention the *leopard* next to him, which he seems completely unconcerned about.

This is insane.

Absolutely, completely insane.

He steps closer, his gaze sharp, although my focus is mainly on the tip of his sword. "You revealed yourself when you attacked Ghost," he says.

"Ghost?" I ask.

19

"My cat." He raises an eyebrow, a flash of what might be considered amusement crossing his face.

"Your cat," I deadpan. "The one you lost, and then found near the bar."

"Correct."

"Your cat is a leopard," I say, unsure why this is surprising me more than his holding a sword and accusing me of using magic.

Not to mention the little detail about how I died and came back. And, judging by how I'm feeling right now, I'm completely unharmed.

"I was dead. I was up there watching you when you found me," I say, pointing to the top of the silver-leafed tree. "Then I saw the leopard—your *cat*—and I somehow came back. To help you."

"By drenching us with water?" he asks, and as ridiculous as this conversation is, I'm glad it's stopping him from lunging at me with that sword.

"I didn't touch the water, so I don't see how I could have splashed you with it," I tell him, although now that I'm thinking about it, I did feel… connected with the water when it came at them. "If I did something with it, I didn't realize it. Everything's a bit hazy right now. It must be a side effect from dying."

"You weren't dead," he says simply. "You had a pulse."

"Well, I sure looked dead from where I was standing. Well, sitting."

His expression hardens, all traces of amusement gone. "You're playing at something—trying to distract me," he says. "Clearly a spy from the Summer Court."

"Is this some sort of game?" I ask. "Run around with a sword and pretend the forest is a magical realm?"

"Everything's a game in our realm," he replies swiftly. "You, of all people, should be well aware of that."

Part of me wants to argue with him. To tell him he's insane.

But there's no denying there's something different in these woods. The snow sparkles unnaturally, like tiny crystals of magic have settled into it. The air hums with energy, and a shimmer weaves through the trees, giving the moonless sky a silvery hue.

It's magical. Completely, undeniably magical.

Just like the man with the silver eyes in front of me.

"I don't know anything about magic, or fae, or other realms," I tell him, desperate now—and wishing he would put away that sword. "I'm just a bartender from Maine, okay? I've lived there my whole life."

His grip on his sword's hilt tightens, his gaze locked on mine.

"So, you communicate with your kind from Maine," he decides.

"I have no 'kind,'" I say, unable to truly process how ridiculous it is that he's talking about me as if I'm some sort of alien. "I'm not a spy, or a fae. I'm a human. One who just had a rather dramatic breakup with her boyfriend, who then left her alone in the woods. I was trying to head back to the parking lot, but I got lost, and then I followed the sound of the stream..."

He says nothing, simply staring at me over the top of his blade, as if sizing me up.

As if *I'm* the crazy one here.

"You met me a few hours ago," I point out. "I'm a bartender at the Maple Pig. Why would I be working there if I was some sort of spy?"

"Spies can be planted anywhere," he says simply. "Including bars in Maine. In fact, bars are some of the best places to plant spies. Many secrets are spilled when people let their guard down over one too many drinks."

He's not wrong.

So, quickly, I wrack my mind for a way to prove I'm telling him the truth. "I can show you pictures of my life. On my phone. Just... don't come at me with that thing." I glance at the sword to make it clear what I mean. "Okay?"

"I don't need pictures," he says. "You clearly believe what you're telling me."

"Really?" I ask, stunned. "You believe me? Just like that?"

"Fae can't lie," he says, although he makes no effort to put away the sword. "We can only say the truth—at least what we *believe* is the truth. Which means you believe what you're telling me."

"I believe it because it *is* the truth," I insist.

"Given your demonstration of your magic just now, you're a summer fae," he continues, completely brushing off what I'm saying. "But you clearly don't know it. Which means you must be a changeling."

"I don't know what that is," I say, even though I feel like I should know what it is—like a fairy tale half remembered from childhood.

"You wouldn't." He chuckles. "That's sort of the point of it all."

I narrow my eyes at him and return my focus to his sword. "Will you please put that thing away?" I ask, as if saying it nicely will sway his decision.

"Sure." He slips the sword into his sheath, as if he didn't need it in the first place.

I start to thank him, but it should be a given that you don't go around waving a sword at a stranger who hasn't done anything worse than splash you with a bit of cold water.

He doesn't deserve my thanks.

"Much better," I say instead.

"My weapon might be sheathed, but unlike you, I've known for my entire life that I have magic," he replies. "I don't recommend making me demonstrate the precision of my training."

"Wasn't planning on it," I say, and he watches me, his eyes sharp, the air between us growing colder by the second.

Finally, he speaks again.

"Being a changeling means a fae went to the mortal realm and switched you out with a human child of the same age," he explains.

"No way. That's insane," I say, although… is it really?

I've never met my mom. And I felt that connection with the water. As if I was controlling it…

"What's going through that pretty blonde head of yours, Sapphire?" he asks, and it strikes me that this is the first time during this entire conversation that he's used my name.

But I'm not going to let the sudden familiarity shake me.

Because that's what he's trying to do, right? Catch me off guard so I accidentally spill something he thinks I'm hiding from him?

"I'm thinking that this might not be *impossibly* crazy," I admit. "Don't get me wrong—it's definitely crazy. But maybe not *impossibly* so. And I'm also thinking that I want to go home."

"Presque Isle isn't your home," he says, not seeming moved in the slightest. "It's just where you were placed."

"No," I insist. "It *is* my home."

"If that's what you say."

"Why were you there, anyway?" I ask him. "In my *home?*"

"Like I told you, my cat was missing." A flicker of amusement touches his lips, and he glances at Ghost. "I went looking for him."

"That's it?" I eye the leopard—who thankfully seems to be relatively tame—unconvinced. "You're telling me you wandered into my bar because your leopard went for a stroll?"

"It's technically not *your* bar," he says. "You don't own it. You just work there."

I clench my fists by my sides, and wind rushes through the trees. "That is so *not* the point," I say, somehow stopping myself from pouncing and trying to claw his eyes out.

Probably because he'd poke mine out with his sword before I could get within a foot of him.

"Then what *is* the point?" he asks calmly.

"The point is that you're accusing me of being a spy in your realm, yet there you were, hanging out in the town where I live, in the bar where I work. And you haven't even told me your name."

"I'm not *accusing* you of being a spy," he says. "I *accused* you of being a spy. Past tense."

Irritation courses through me, and the water in the stream rushes faster.

Maybe I could splash it at his perfectly smug face again.

But, as tempting as that is, I take a few deep breaths and control myself. Mainly because I don't want him bringing out that stupid sword again.

I also don't want his *cat* leaping at me and ripping my throat out.

"Fine," I say. "But you still haven't told me your name."

He pauses for a moment, and I wait semi-patiently, not wanting to accidentally say something that *distracts* him again.

"I'm Riven," he says, and then he tilts his head toward the leopard, who's still standing close to his side. "And, as you know, that's Ghost."

The leopard simply watches me, as if he's trying to figure me out as much as Riven is.

"Nice to meet you, Riven," I say, and leopard's tail flicks, causing me to quickly add, "And Ghost."

Ghost sits straighter, looking pleased—and undeniably majestic.

"He likes you," Riven says. "And I trust his judge of character. So, now that I've heard your plea, I'd like to offer you a deal."

SAPPHIRE

"A DEAL?" I narrow my eyes, still on edge even though Riven's possibly warming up to me.

Well, as much as a winter fae can probably warm up to someone.

"Yes," he says, studying me with those sharp eyes of his. "This realm isn't safe for you, especially if anyone else finds you here. You're a summer fae, and if anyone from my court discovers you, they won't hesitate to kill you."

A chill runs down my spine at the gravity of his words, and I instinctively step back.

"You're not exactly making me feel safe either, with all the sword-waving and accusations," I say, apparently willing to test the limits of his newfound warmth now that he's brought murder back into the picture.

"I put my sword away." He arches a brow, challenging me. "I don't intend to hurt you right now. But there are plenty of others around here who will. Which is why I'm offering you this deal."

I hesitate, crossing my arms, catching the intricacy of what he said.

He doesn't intend to hurt me *right now*.

It's not the same thing as not intending to hurt me *at all*.

"What's the deal?" I ask, since whether he'll eventually want to hurt me or not, I need to hear him out.

"If you agree to stay in Presque Isle for a year, then I'll bring you safely home," he says, and I blink, processing his words.

"I don't want to stay in Presque Isle," I tell him, remembering Matt's snide remark about how I was going to be stuck there for the rest of my life, just like he is.

"Then I guess you'll be staying here." He shrugs, as if it doesn't matter to him at all. "A summer fae, in the Winter Court, surrounded by deadly creatures who will kill you simply for existing."

I swallow hard, hating the thought of staying here, in this icy, deathtrap of a realm.

Maybe as much as I hate the idea of staying in Presque Isle for the rest of my life.

Actually, never mind. There's no way I could hate anything as much as the idea of staying in Presque Isle for the rest of my life.

"It's not exactly a dream vacation, is it?" he continues, apparently trying to drive his point home.

I frown, since unfortunately, I'm not well versed in "dream vacations." My aunt hates traveling. Most people in Presque Isle rarely leave the state. Minus Zoey, but she doesn't count. Her family's rich.

And while the thought of not leaving Presque Isle for another year stings, I've already survived being stuck there for my entire life.

I suppose I can survive another year.

I sigh, crossing my arms tighter around myself as the cold bites at my skin. "Fine," I say, hating that I'm saying it, but unsure what else to do. "I'll agree to stay in Presque Isle for a year."

Riven's eyes flicker with something unreadable—satisfaction, maybe, or curiosity—and he nods. "Good."

He extends his hand, waiting for me to shake on it.

Instead, I stare at it as if he's going to try to slap me with it.

"Relax," he says. "I'm not going to fling you to the ground, or push you into the stream, or do anything else that might be running through that pretty little head of yours. I just want to shake on it. Or else…" Amusement flickers across his eyes as he lets the sentence trail off.

"Or else what?" I ask.

"Or else we could seal it with a kiss."

My eyes drop to his undeniably tempting lips, and a rush of heat spreads through me, sharp and unexpected.

I should laugh it off, or scoff at him, or roll my eyes.

Probably all three at once.

Instead, my breath catches, and for some inexplicable reason, the idea of sealing the deal with a kiss doesn't feel like a joke. All it does is make my pulse race in a way it hasn't since... well, ever. Not even with Matt.

His eyes gleam with amusement, but beneath them, there's something darker. Something that tells me he doesn't expect me to take him up on the offer.

It might be fun to surprise him. Throw him off balance.

Just like how he threw me off balance when he waved that sword in my face.

"Okay." I straighten my shoulders, keeping my gaze locked on his. "Let's do it."

His amusement disappears, surprise taking its place.

Victory.

But he recovers quickly, tilting his head as a slow, lazy smirk spreads across his lips.

"As you wish," he murmurs, stepping closer, moving so slowly that it's like he's trying to tempt fate.

The closer he gets, the more tension coils in the pit of my stomach. His presence is overwhelming—cold and dangerous. But there's also an undeniable magnetism to him. Something that draws me in, despite every warning bell going off in my head that I should stay as far away as possible.

But I refuse to show any fear or weakness by taking it back.

He reaches out, his hand brushing a stray lock of my hair from my face, his fingers grazing my skin so lightly it feels like electricity.

"Are you sure about this?" he asks, his voice low, almost a growl.

"I wouldn't have said yes if I wasn't." I lean in, keeping my voice steady, even though my heart's trying to beat out of my chest.

He smirks again, and I can tell he's enjoying making me squirm. "You might regret this," he says, and I don't have time to respond before his lips brush mine.

His hand cups the back of my neck, pulling me closer as he presses his body flush against mine. A shiver spreads through me, every nerve buzzing with energy.

This is nothing like kissing Matt. It's more intense, more captivating, and more *magical.*

I don't ever want it to stop.

Then, I feel it. Something cold, physical, and alive brewing between us. Frost creeping along the line of my jaw, down my neck, and spiraling across my arms.

The kiss is no longer just a kiss. It's a channel for something far more powerful.

"Riven—" I try to speak, but the words die in my throat as the icy tendrils slip across my body, cold and invasive. They wrap around my wrists and ankles, invisible chains binding me to him, threading through my veins like frozen fire.

I try to pull away, but it's too late. The magic won't let me.

The spell is taking hold, whether I like it or not.

Finally, he pulls back, but not far. His face is still close, our breaths mingling in the icy air between us as he gazes down at me, fierce and predatory.

I'm too breathless to speak. Too overwhelmed by the cold seeping through me, claiming me.

Like *he's* claiming me.

"Ice magic," he says softly. "That's how the Winter Court seals its deals."

The frost shimmers along my arms and wrists, fading as the magic settles. It's inside of me now. A part of me. And while it doesn't hurt, the sensation is strange, like I'm connected to something I can't begin to understand.

"Is it done?" I finally bring myself to speak.

"Yes." His eyes flicker with amusement, or triumph, or maybe even desire. "The magic will ensure you honor your promise. You'll feel it if you try to break it."

"Well, that's ominous," I say, suddenly feeling like an idiot for jumping into a fae deal without more information.

All I could think about was getting home.

Plus, none of this feels real. I wouldn't be surprised if I woke up in the hospital soon. There'll be a doctor hovering over me, telling me they found me in the middle of nowhere after I hit my head, and that they brought me in as fast as they could.

"Keep your promise, and you won't have to worry about what happens if you try breaking the deal," he says. "Although who knows... maybe I'll stop by for another drink sometime."

"Really?" My heart races at the thought, even though I hate it for doing so.

"You're amusingly gullible." He chuckles. "My business in Presque Isle is done."

I glare at him—both for the gullible comment, and for the meaning behind his words. Because he clearly also means his "business" with *me* is done.

"That kiss was done to seal the deal," he reminds me, as if it would be pathetic if I thought anything else.

"I know. It was for 'business' purposes," I repeat what he told me —hopefully just as coldly. "Now, are you going to follow through with your end of the deal and get me back home?"

"I'll follow through whenever I want," he says. "After all, we never specified *when* I needed to get you home."

My stomach drops.

He's right. We never discussed exactly when he needed to bring me back. For all I know, it could be ten years from now.

But...

"You said you'd bring me back *safely* home," I remind him. "And, according to you, I'm at risk of being killed every moment I remain in this realm. So, it sounds like you should get me home sooner rather than later."

Ghost, who apparently sat down while Riven and I were having our *moment*, perks his ears up and stands.

Riven glances down at Ghost, then refocuses on me, sizing me up.

"An excellent point," he says. "Maybe you're not as gullible as I thought."

Anger courses through me, and before I realize what's happening, Riven's getting splashed with more water from the stream.

He doesn't flinch, doesn't move. He just holds my gaze with his increasingly intimidating silver eyes, daring me to try anything further.

"Careful," he warns. "Unless you want me to bring out my sword again?"

My cheeks flush, and I step back, putting some space between us. "Can we just focus on getting me home?" I ask.

He watches me for a long moment, as though weighing his next move. Then he gestures to the stream—the wider, clearer part of it that I was drawn to before. "Drink from that spot," he tells me. "It will take you back."

"Is this another trick?"

"When have I tricked you?" he asks in return.

Having no more patience for him, I huff, spin on my heel, and kneel before the stream.

It seems too simple.

Then again, I got here by drinking the water. Which means it makes sense that doing the same thing is the way to leave, too. And if it isn't... when did a little bit of water ever hurt someone?

Except when I splashed it at Riven. Although I doubt that actually hurt him. Maybe it hurt his ego, but physically, he's doing just fine.

"I told you that fae can't lie," he reminds me. "Which means I'm telling you the truth that the water will get you home. Now, stop sitting around, and drink."

SAPPHIRE

I HESITATE AT THE STREAM, even though there's no room for hesitation.

This is my chance to get home. I have no reason to think Riven's being honest about not being able to lie, but logically, it makes sense that this *is* the way home, since it's the same way I got here.

So, I bring the water to my lips. It's sharp and cold, and the world shifts beneath me, just like last time.

Unlike last time, I'm prepared.

Still, the landing is far from graceful. I stumble as my feet hit solid ground, and while I do fall, I don't roll over and over. Instead, I catch myself—hard—on my wrist.

It snaps, and burning pain shoots through my arm, but I don't have time to dwell on how much it hurts.

Instead, I run.

Not just run—I tear through the woods, the forest blurring as I pick up speed. By some miracle, I don't crash into the trees.

Also, by some miracle, my wrist is already feeling better.

No—not a miracle. It has to be because of *magic*. My body's healing itself, like it did after my near-death experience in the fae realm. And just like it probably did after that sledding accident with Zoey when I was a kid.

I have no idea where I'm going.

All I know is that I want to get as far away from that stream and silver tree—and from Riven and Ghost—as possible.

Branches snap behind me, and I push harder, but it doesn't matter. The initial burst of adrenaline is gone. My body feels heavy, and I'm slowing down, the exhaustion hitting me like a sledgehammer.

Before long, they're in front of me.

Ghost, as massive and calm as ever, with Riven perched on his back.

I skid to a stop, barely avoiding crashing into them.

"How did you…?" I glance around, confused about how they got in front of me so easily.

"I'm on a leopard," he says simply. "You're fast—impressively so—but he's faster."

I scan the forest, searching for an escape route, but it's useless. Ghost can easily outrun me again. And Riven doesn't seem like the type of guy who gives up once he's set his mind on something.

Right now, he's clearly set his mind on *me.*

"I thought you didn't want to see me again?" I ask instead.

"I told you that my business in Presque Isle is done. I never said I wouldn't return." He studies me like I'm a bird in a cage, and I shift uneasily in place. "Words, Summer Fae. You have to think about them—not just hear them."

I glare at him again—I seem to be doing a *lot* of that recently.

"I don't have time for this," I tell him. "If I'm not home when my aunt wakes up, she'll be furious."

"Then let me take you home," he offers. "After all, that was part of our deal."

I want to tell him no. That I'm not telling him where my house is.

But I feel that familiar, cold prickle on my skin. Frost. It's crawling over me, latching onto me, warning me.

If I don't follow through with this deal, it's going to consume me.

Plus, there's no denying that I'm lost. At the rate I'm going, I won't get home before sunrise—which is when my aunt wakes up—anyway.

"Fine," I give in, and then I tell him how to get to my house.

The threatening frost disappears as I do.

"Fantastic," Riven says, motioning to the place behind him on Ghost's back. "Climb on."

31

With a sigh of defeat, I step forward and awkwardly make my way up to Ghost's back.

The leopard's skin is surprisingly cool, his muscles shifting as he adjusts to the added weight.

Riven glances back at me, making sure I'm situated. "Now, I recommend you hold on," he says, and I wrap my arms around his waist, my pulse quickening as I feel the cold, hard planes of his body beneath my hands.

He doesn't react. He just nudges Ghost forward, and we take off, the world blurring around us as we speed through the woods.

My grip tightens around Riven's waist, and there's something about this moment—his back against me, the rush of the wind, the rhythmic pulse of Ghost's run—that feels oddly intimate. Maybe even more so than when we kissed.

No—*nothing* can feel as intimate as that kiss.

But this is close.

Eventually, the trees thin, and my house comes into view. It's modest—one floor, with wood siding and a thatched roof—and I assume it's unimpressive to Riven. But after everything that happened tonight, it's good to be home.

"It's safe to dismount," Riven says coolly, not even glancing back at me.

"That's it?" I ask. "No help down?"

"I'm an ice fae from the Winter Court," he reminds me—as if I need reminding. "Not a knight in shining armor."

"A surprisingly human reference," I tell him.

"I've been around for a while."

"Do you mean you're immortal?" I ask, and when he twists around to look at me, his eyes are so cold that my breath catches in my chest.

"Answering your endless questions wasn't part of our deal," he says. "I've brought you safely home. Now might be a good time to remind you that from this point forward, I can do whatever I want to you."

I swallow, since the things passing through my mind that I want him to do to me probably aren't what he's referring to.

Or maybe they are?

My cheeks flush at the thought.

"Get off," he tells me. "Now."

Annoyed, I shift my weight and swing my leg over Ghost's back, jumping down onto the ground. My boots sink slightly into the snow, and I brush some dirt from earlier off my jeans, the sting of Riven's dismissal prickling through me.

In a flash, Riven and Ghost disappear into the woods, like shadows swallowed by the night.

It's almost like they were never here at all.

But they were here. The tingling feeling lingering on my lips from his kiss proves it.

And now, they're gone.

Shaking my head—and trying to push down my disappointment at the fact that I'll probably never see Riven again—I turn toward my house, the sight of it grounding me. It's strange to think that just hours ago I was pacing around my room, angry and frustrated about my dead-end relationship with Matt. A difficult situation, but a normal one.

Now, nothing about me—or this world—feels normal.

But dawn will be here soon. So, I slip into my bedroom window —a skill I've perfected after many past-curfew nights with Zoey— and look around at the posters on my walls, my unmade bed, and the clothes strewn across the floor. Everything's the same as I left it.

There's only one thing in here that's changed.

Me.

And after tonight, nothing's going to be the same ever again.

SAPPHIRE

THREE FIRM KNOCKS on the door jolt me awake.

It opens before I can say to come in.

Aunt Martha gives me a hard stare, her arms crossed, her brow raised like she's been waiting for me to get up for hours.

"Late start," she scolds. "Didn't wake you at a respectable hour because of New Year's Eve. The only holiday where it's acceptable to stay out unreasonably late."

Reasonable.

That's the quality of hers she's most proud of, since it's what she says my mother lacks. She wears it with everything she owns and does, with her modest clothing, her sensible bun, and even her weekly grocery lists. No treats—just essentials.

"I definitely needed the sleep," I say, glancing out my window.

The sun is high in the sky.

I check my phone, shocked at the time.

Noon.

Aunt Martha let me sleep until *noon*.

It's crazier than falling into another realm, meeting a gorgeous fae man who claims I have powers, who then gives me a binding magical kiss and disappears into the woods on his giant leopard.

But most amazing is that after all of that, I feel surprisingly refreshed.

I'd think it was all a dream, if it didn't all feel so *real*.

"Lunch will be ready in five minutes," she says, yanking me out of my thoughts. "Steak and green beans."

With that, she gives my messy room a disapproving once-over and leaves without closing the door.

One of the major rules of this house is that when we're both home, we eat together. Which means I have five minutes to freshen up and get to the kitchen table.

In the bathroom, I run a hand over my face and glance in the mirror, half-expecting to see some visible sign of the magic—of *him*. But there's nothing. Just the same old me.

At least, the same me on the outside.

On the inside, I'll never be the same.

Aunt Martha glances at me as I enter the kitchen, her lips pressed into the thin line I've come to associate with her version of affection. She never says it, but I know she cares. In her own strict, no-nonsense way.

"Steak's almost done," she says, moving with precision around the stove.

I set up the table while she finishes up, my stomach growling when she places my plate in front of me.

Steak, barely seared, with green beans on the side.

It's perfect.

I dig in as if I haven't eaten for days, and that's when I see it. Or, more appropriately, I see the *absence* of it.

My bracelet.

It's not on my wrist.

My stomach drops, my food suddenly unappetizing.

How could I have lost my bracelet? I've worn it since it was able to fit on my wrist, and in all that time, it's never fallen off.

The last time I saw it was… when I drank the water that took me into the fae realm.

Maybe Riven stole it? He was transfixed with it from the moment he saw it. And who knows how long he was hovering over my half-dead body before the ghostly, in-limbo version of myself became consciously aware and was snapped back to life?

Then there was the kiss. I was so spellbound during it that if he was a practiced thief, he could have stolen it without me realizing it.

And let's not forget my tumble in the bushes. My clothes got pretty snagged up during the fall.

As for now, I can't let Aunt Martha see it's missing. She'll be furious.

So, I pull the sleeve of my sweatshirt as far down as possible, praying she won't notice, and eat as quickly as I can.

She doesn't force conversation. Despite all the qualities of hers that I'm not the biggest fan of, that's one I've always appreciated. And I appreciate it more than ever right now, since I'm not in the mood to rehash my breakup with Matt.

After everything that happened last night, my relationship with Matt is the last thing on my mind. Especially since deep in my heart, I know our relationship ended months ago.

It just took refusing his proposal to make it official.

"I'm going to Zoey's," I say after we finish eating and get everything cleaned up.

"All right." She takes a moment to study me—I can tell she knows something's up. But thankfully, she doesn't push. "Have a good time."

"I will."

Grabbing my phone, I text Zoey that I'm coming over, then hop in my car and head out. Luckily, Zoey drove us to the bar last night, so I didn't have to worry about getting my car home on top of everything else.

Zoey's house is on the edge of town, and it's easily the biggest in Presque Isle. Big enough that she and her brothers have their own rooms, along with their own bathrooms.

When I was younger, I used to wish I lived there. But over the years, I've come to appreciate the coziness of the home I grew up in, and the calmness of living with Aunt Martha.

Zoey opens the door, her dark hair tied up in a messy bun on the top of her head, before I can text her to let her know I'm here.

Her gaze drops to my left hand.

More specifically, to the finger that would have a ring on it if I said yes to Matt's proposal.

"You knew what he was going to do," I realize. "And you said nothing."

"I'm sorry," she says, and she genuinely looks it. "I just... it was

36

Matt's question to ask. You needed to hear it from him—not from me."

Even though I hate it, her point is valid.

"He asked me if he should do it," she continues, talking faster now, getting everything out before I can jump in. "Obviously, I didn't want to speak for you. I might be your best friend, but I'm not a mind reader."

"Come on." I roll my eyes, and we head up the steps to her room. "You know I wouldn't say yes."

"I told him he needed to do what he felt was right." She shrugs, guilt splattered all over her face. "Maybe this is for the best? You guys have broken up and gotten back together so many times these past few months that I can't keep up. It's clearly not working between you anymore."

"I know." I plop down onto her desk chair—the one I always sit on when we chat in her room—and she closes the door, making herself comfortable on the edge of her bed. "It was a disaster."

"He got angry when you said no," she guesses.

"He *left me in the woods.* And then…"

"And then what?" She sits forward and looks me over in concern.

"It's going to sound crazy," I say, not knowing how else to begin.

She smiles wickedly. "I love crazy."

"I can promise you've never heard anything *this* crazy."

"Try me," she challenges.

"Okay," I say, even though I'm completely unsure about how this is going to go. "But please just let me tell you everything, from start to finish? After I'm done, you can ask all the questions you want."

"Sure," she says, even though I know that with Zoey, quietly listening is easier said than done. "Go ahead."

So, I do, starting from the disastrous proposal and continuing from there.

There are a few times when Zoey wants to interrupt. But she controls herself and lets me talk, although I can tell by the way she's looking at me that she either thinks I've lost it or am making all of this up.

"And… that's all of it," I tell her when I'm done.

She says nothing. Which is more unnerving than any reaction I could have anticipated.

Zoey is the most talkative person I know, but apparently, I've shocked her speechless.

"You really believe all of this," she finally says.

My stomach drops. Because it sounds like *she* doesn't believe it. Not a word of it.

"I do," I reply, ready to fight her on this until she knows it's true. "Because it's what happened."

She presses her lips together, deep in thought.

"Do you think that maybe the woman pushed you down, and you hit your head, and that it knocked you out?" she finally asks, speaking softly, as if she's afraid that one wrong word is going to make me break.

"No. I drank that water. And then I ended up in that other place..." I trail off, unable to bring myself to say other *realm* again. It sounds so ridiculous. "Where I saw *him*. The guy from the bar."

Riven.

Just the thought of him makes my lips tingle from the memory of that kiss.

"Right. You saw him when you were a ghost hovering on top of a silver-leafed tree." She's clearly having a difficult time processing this, which I suppose is understandable. "With his pet snow leopard. Which caused you to come back to life and use water magic to attack them."

"Umm... yes?"

"Then show me," she challenges. "Use you water magic, so I can see it for myself."

"I'm not sure how much I can control it," I say quickly. "When I was there, I wasn't trying to do anything. It just happened."

"Then make it happen again," she says, as if it's that simple. "Because right now, I'm thinking it sounds like you hit your head pretty hard. You might have a concussion. Which means it's probably a good idea to see a doctor. It's New Year's Day, but the hospital should be open—"

"No." I hold my hands up, stopping her mid-sentence. "I'll try to do it again. But I need some water to work with."

SAPPHIRE

I STAND UP, make my way into Zoey's bathroom, and turn on the sink.

In the fae realm, the water responded to me like an extension of myself. But now, I don't know how to begin.

Zoey leans against the doorframe, arms crossed, watching me with a mix of curiosity and concern.

Pressure builds in my chest. I *have* to do this. If I don't, she's going to make me go to the hospital. It's probably the same thing I'd want her to do if the situation was reversed.

But last night was real. I'm sure of it.

So, it's time to show her that I'm not losing my mind.

I clench my fists by my sides, frustration bubbling under my skin as I stare at the water with every ounce of determination I have.

Nothing happens.

I try again, and still, nothing.

"Sapphire," Zoey says softly. "Maybe we should go back to my room?"

"No," I snap. "I can do this."

Her silence tells me she doesn't believe me, and my fingers twitch with the need to do something—anything—to prove I'm not crazy.

This is my chance. If I can't do it, then—

Crack.

The shower head snaps off, spraying water all around the bathroom.

"Crap!" I cry out, jumping back as cold water hits me in the face.

It's getting on everything—me, the floor, the mirror, Zoey.

Zoey gasps and scrambles for towels, trying and failing to stop the chaos. "What the hell, Sapphire?"

"I didn't mean to," I say, and I hurry over to the shower, jumping up on the bathtub ledge and fiddling with the faucet as best as I can through the water spraying out of it.

I can do this. It's just like when the sink breaks at the bar. The only difference is that this time, it's bigger.

Finally—and I don't know if it's because I got my magic back under control, or because I have experience with fixing broken faucets—I get it to stop.

Once sure it's most likely not going to explode again, I look around the bathroom.

The floor is covered with water, the rug is sopping wet, the walls and mirror are drenched, and Zoey looks like she just came inside from a rainstorm.

She's staring at me, wide-eyed, speechless for the first time in her life.

"I guess that was my magic," I say, wiping water from my face, my pulse still racing.

"Do it again," she says, and she's smiling in excitement, the soaked bathroom forgotten.

"You want me to break your shower again?"

"No—don't do that," she says quickly. "But maybe you can use this magic of yours to clean up the mess?"

I take a deep breath, taking in the situation around me. Water's everywhere. The idea of controlling it—cleaning it up—feels impossible.

Then again, everything that happened last night sounds impossible, too. And I'm *so* close to getting Zoey on my side.

And apparently, the way to convince her is by cleaning up her bathroom.

"Okay," I say. "I'll try."

I look around and focus, letting the memory of the stream flood my senses, remembering the way the water bent to my will.

Come on, I think. *Move.*

At first, nothing happens.

Then, I feel it. The smallest pull, like a thread of energy tugging at the air around me.

I have a grasp on it. Now I just need to...

Keeping my eyes laser focused on the puddle in front of me, I concentrate, willing a few droplets to rise from the floor.

They do.

Now, they're suspended in midair. It's like someone pressed pause during a movie, except everything other than the floating droplets is still playing.

Zoey's eyes widen, and she steps closer, poking at a droplet in front of her.

Immediately, it and the others fall back to the floor.

"Wow," she says, and this time when she looks at me, it's not with fear, or worry. It's with *awe*. "Can you really not lie?"

"Seriously?" I ask. "I made your shower explode and lifted water off the floor, and the thing you care about is whether or not I can lie?"

"You should test it out," she says, not bothering to answer my question. "Like you did with the water."

"Don't we have more important things to worry about?"

"Wow," she says, smirking. "You really can't lie."

"I can't believe this is what you're focused on." I shake my head and manage to raise more droplets up from the floor, so they move around me in what feels like a moment of pure magic.

"Just try it," she says, and I can't help it—I push some of the water forward, so it splashes on her.

She's completely unfazed.

"Lie. Right now," she continues, her smirk growing wider. "Tell me that... you wish you'd said yes to Matt's proposal."

"I definitely don't wish I'd said yes to Matt's proposal."

"You don't even realize you're doing it." She laughs. "You're just... talking around lying. Unbelievable."

I press my lips together and glare at her, suddenly aware of the truth of what she's saying.

Have I ever been able to lie? I don't know. I've never felt great about lying, so I guess I've just danced around it. It's always felt simple enough.

But when I try to tell Zoey that I've lied before, I can't. The words simply won't come.

"Fine," I admit. "Apparently, I can't lie. Happy?"

"Yes." She grins—looking *almost* as conceited as Riven. "I am."

I roll my eyes at her smug grin and refocus on the water around me, relieved when the magic comes to me way easier than it did during my first few attempts.

The water shifts and swirls, and I manage to pull some from the soaked rug, the mirror, and even Zoey's drenched hair. It collects into a ball in front of me, and I stare at it in amazement as it sparkles under the light.

It's like the magic is speaking to me. Telling me it's mine to command.

Confident about my abilities now, I step aside and guide the floating ball of water into the bathtub.

Halfway there, it wobbles and splashes to the floor with a loud splat, soaking everything again.

I curse in frustration, squeezing the water out of my hair.

Zoey bursts out laughing, wiping water from her face. "So, you're not exactly the fae version of a cleaning service yet, but still—that was amazing."

I rub my temples, a headache brewing. "I'm glad you're entertained."

She grabs a towel from behind the door and starts mopping up the floor, still grinning. "This is incredible. You have magic. Not to mention a gorgeous, male fae who apparently has some weird, magical bond with you and rides around the forest on a white leopard."

"We're supposed to be focusing on getting back my bracelet—not on Riven," I remind her.

She finishes wiping down the counter and tosses the towel into the sink. "So, we're heading back to the forest?" she asks. "To go to his realm?"

"Ideally, yes," I say. "But practically... Riven told me there were creatures out there. Ones that could kill us if we're not careful."

"You're sounding just like Aunt Martha," Zoey says. "Focusing on what's *practical* instead of on what's *possible*."

"I'm not like Aunt Martha," I say, irritated at the comparison.

"Since you're saying it, and you can't lie, then I guess you believe it," she says. "But you definitely sound just like her right now."

I sigh, knowing she's never going to let the whole "not being able to lie" thing go.

"We'll be fine," she continues, waving me off. "We're just going to look for your bracelet in the bushes, grab it, and come right back. We'll stick close to the stream. Plus, it'll be daytime. How dangerous could it be?"

She says it so casually, but I can tell by the gleam in her eyes that she's dying to see the fae realm for herself.

Of course she is.

She wouldn't be *Zoey* if she wasn't.

"You're not just interested in the bracelet, are you?" I ask. "You also want to go sightseeing?"

"Can you blame me?" She shrugs, not bothering to hide it. "You've been telling me about this beautiful place with magic and fae and hot men riding leopards. Of course I want to see it. And you want to get your bracelet back. Our interests are aligned. Isn't that why you rushed over here in the first place? To get my help?"

"You're forgetting one important thing," I tell her.

"And what's that?"

"Riven and I made the deal that I can't go back to the fae realm for a year."

She scrunches her brow, deep in thought.

We've already reached a dead end. Because I'm not going to be able to get my bracelet back. Riven's deal made sure of it.

I pretty much knew that before coming over here. But I also knew that I needed to tell my best friend what happened.

I didn't want to deal with this alone.

"Loopholes," Zoey finally says, and she goes back into her room, giving me no choice but to follow. "That's how you're avoiding lying —you're finding loopholes to step around telling the truth. Riven threatened using the loophole of how he never said *when* he'd get you back home. It was his way of getting around what the deal initially seemed to be. Maybe we can find another loophole now." She stops pacing, zeroing in on me. "What was the *exact* wording of the deal?"

I think back, combing through the memory.

"He said that if I agreed to stay in Presque Isle for a year, he'd bring me safely home," I say, sure of it.

"That's it?"

"Yes. That's it."

"I can work with that," she says, pacing around her room again. "He said he could get around his side of the deal by not *immediately* bringing you home. Because the two of you didn't specify timing."

"Yes," I say, curious about where she's going with this.

"I think *timing* is key here," she continues.

"How so?"

"Because he said you needed to stay in Presque Isle for a year. But did he say that the year needed to be all at once? Like… can it be spread out over time? A few weeks here, a month or so there? Can it just *add up* to a year?"

"I don't know." I smile, since as crazy as it is, she might be on to something. "But there's only one way to find out."

SAPPHIRE

Zoey pulls over at the sign that shows we're leaving Presque Isle and heading into the town just north of us, Caribou.

"Time to see if my loophole works," she says, and we hop out of the car, looking ahead.

"I guess I'll just walk?" I ask.

"Yes," she says. "That's generally a good way to cross from one town to the next by foot."

"Right." I take a deep breath and step forward, bracing myself for that awful frost to start crawling over my body.

Nothing happens.

I take another step, and another, and everything seems to be okay.

"We're out of Presque Isle," Zoey says next to me, looking down at the map she pulled up on her phone. "It worked."

"I can't believe it was that easy." I take out my phone to double check, and sure enough, I've crossed the line that separates Presque Isle from Caribou.

"Maybe Riven wanted you to come back," she says. "He just wanted you to prove that you were fae enough to think around the deal."

"Then he's going to be thoroughly disappointed. Because *you're* the one who was 'fae enough' to think through the deal. Not me." I put my phone away, ready to head back to the car and keep going.

"Anyway, we're going there to find the bracelet. There's no reason to think we'll run into him again."

"Do you want to see him again?" Zoey asks, teasing me.

She knows I do.

"Does it matter?" I ask. "He doesn't seem to want to see me."

"You really do an excellent job at dancing around lies," she says, walking to her car before I can say another non-lie. "Are you coming?"

"Of course I'm coming," I say, and an hour later, we're back in the clearing where we watched the meteor shower last night.

Where Matt *proposed* to me last night.

An ick feeling travels through me at the memory. I can't believe he thought I wanted that.

"Where did you go from here?" Zoey asks, looking around.

"That way." I point to the place where Matt left the clearing. The path is a bit left of where we came in, but he's always had a decent enough sense of direction that I'm sure he was fine. Especially because we didn't see his car in the parking lot.

"Then let's go that way," she says, and as we walk, she somehow manages to not chatter, so I can listen for the stream.

Eventually, I hear it.

"There." I point through the trees. "Do you hear it?"

She looks at where I'm pointing, listening carefully. "No," she says. "But I trust you."

"You're about to travel with me to another realm," I tell her. "I sure hope you trust me."

As I follow the sound of the stream, I realize how crazy this is. There are creatures in this realm who'd kill me for what I am. Zoey's human—assuming she also doesn't have any unknown magical heritage like I do—which means she has no powers to defend herself with, and no rapid healing ability.

Yet, here we are. Trying to go to the Winter Court so I can find a *bracelet*.

I do care about the bracelet and want it back. But truthfully, this is about far more than a piece of jewelry. Because I can't just continue with normal life after everything I learned last night. It's insane that Riven would expect me to. I can't just magically *forget*.

Well, for all I know, there's a potion or spell that could make me forget.

But I don't *want* to forget.

As for Zoey, she's always been my partner in crime. More than that—she's always been the one to *lead* the crime. Not having her by my side feels wrong. Plus, she's the one who figured out the loophole in the deal. Zoey may be human, but she's smart and strong.

I trust her with my life, and I know she feels the same about me.

I'm lost in thought when suddenly, there it is.

The silver tree.

Its leaves sparkle even more in the sunlight, shimmering so much that they almost hurt my eyes.

"We did it," I say, gazing up at the tree in awe. "We're here."

Zoey's using her hand as a visor to block her eyes, looking everywhere *but* at the tree.

"Where?" she asks.

"There," I tell her, moving closer. "Right in front of us."

"I don't see anything."

"It's *right* in front of us."

How can she not see it?

Losing patience, I move to stand behind her, grab her shoulders, and force her to look straight at the tree.

She flinches and curses.

Seconds later, she stills.

"Oh my God," she says, staring up at the tree in amazement. "How did I miss *that?*"

"Maybe because you're human?" I say, since it would make sense. "But it doesn't matter. You see it now. Come on."

Together, we hurry toward the stream and kneel beside it to peer into the water. It looks just as magical as I remember—crystal clear, almost shimmering, like it's lit from within by something otherworldly.

Zoey crouches beside me, staring at the water. "So, this is it?" she asks. "We just drink this water, and bam, we're in another realm?"

"That's what happened the other times I've done it." I glance at her, my heart pounding faster now that we're so close. "We should link arms when we do this, so we don't lose each other. And remember—the landing's rough. Be ready to brace yourself."

"Maybe it's best not to link arms," she says. "It'll be harder to land if we get all tangled up in each other."

"True." I don't like it, but her point is valid. "Let's just make sure to drink at the same time, okay? And be ready for the landing."

"I'm good at sports," she says, as if I didn't already know it. "Way better than you, even though you have supernatural abilities."

"I didn't *know* about those abilities until last night," I say. "I don't think I was using them anywhere close to my full potential before."

If I was using them at all.

"Fair point," she says. "But what I meant was—have a little faith in me. I've got this."

It's true. Of the two of us, she's always had better grace. And aim.

And I'm confident that means she'll be able to aim her body correctly to land in a way that *doesn't* give her a fatal head wound.

Well, a half-fatal head wound, given that I came back to life after it.

We share a nod of understanding, and then we each scoop up a handful of the shimmering water. It's colder than I remember, its icy chill biting into my skin as it trickles through my fingers.

"Ready?" I ask.

"Ready."

We drink.

The world tilts, the ground drops out from under me, and everything blurs in a dizzying rush. Then I'm landing on my back with a hard thud, knocking the air from my lungs and sending a rush of pain through my body.

Zoey lands on her feet, her knees bent, rolling into the fall as if she does this every day.

Not fair.

She reaches down to help me up, and I take her hand, fighting through the pain. It's already lessening, but the healing isn't immediate.

Once I'm up and generally okay, Zoey lets out a low whistle and looks around the forest. "Wow," she says. "It's more beautiful than I imagined. Eerie, too. A strange mix of both."

I nod, since it's different in the day. The sparkles on the thin layer of snow are more apparent, and there's a slight silver sheen on the tree bark. Not as intensely silver as the leaves on the silver tree, but it's still there.

Silver, like Riven's eyes.

Oh my God. I have to stop pining over this man. I'm not a freshman in high school anymore, and I should know better than to trust a guy who has a superior attitude and is cocky as hell. Not to mention the fact that he's a supernatural being from another world that I know basically nothing about.

"You're thinking about him," Zoey observes.

"How can you tell?"

"You get this dreamy, but also brooding, look in your eyes when you think about him." She gazes around the forest with her eyes glazed over and her brow furrowed, showing me what I must look like.

"How about we focus on finding the bracelet?" I say, since talking about how I can't stop thinking about Riven isn't going to *help* me stop thinking about Riven.

"Right. The bracelet," she says. "Where did you fall last time?"

"There." I point to the base of the silver tree, branches twisted and broken from my previous fall.

We hurry over, and I kneel beside the bush, pulling aside the branches and searching for a glint of sapphires among the leaves.

Zoey crouches beside me, poking through the bushes with a stick.

We search for what must be thirty minutes, the task feeling more impossible by the second. It's like trying to find a needle in a haystack.

The longer we look, the more hopeless I feel.

Suddenly, a low growl rumbles through the air, freezing both of us in place.

Zoey's eyes widen, and together, we turn slowly toward the sound.

A monstrous figure steps into view.

It's tall—taller than any human—with ashen skin stretched tight over emaciated bones. Its hollow eyes glow with an eerie light, and its teeth are sharp, jagged, and gleaming.

But it's not looking at us. It doesn't even seem to see us. Instead, it's walking toward the stream on its long, bony limbs.

I reach for Zoey's hand, squeezing it tightly, and we lower to a crouch behind the bushes.

If we can be quiet and still, maybe it will go away.

Time freezes. I can barely think. Barely breathe.

It takes another step, its claws scraping against the ground as it moves with unnatural grace. The worst part? It's heading straight for the specific part of the stream that acts as a portal, blocking it—therefore blocking us from making a run for the stream to get home.

The best solution seems to be to remain here. The bushes don't provide great cover, but it's better than nothing. If the monster doesn't look over here, we might have a chance.

But my heart's beating so loudly that I can hear it. Zoey's, too.

The creature tilts its head, like it's listening for something.

Then its eyes—those glowing, terrifying eyes—zero in straight on us.

SAPPHIRE

My stomach plummets.

The monster sees us.

Zoey and I remain frozen in place—as if we can make it somehow *unsee* us—when it lunges, faster than I thought something that thin and decrepit could move.

Its bony limbs stretch out, reaching for Zoey with its clawed, mangled hands.

Panic rushes through me.

Then, as if the universe can feel the intensity of my desperation, a gust of wind hits the monster, catching it unaware and making it stumble back.

It rebounds quickly.

Zoey picks up a fallen branch and holds it up like a weapon, as if she's an Amazonian warrior goddess.

The monster's eyes lock on her, and it lunges with a feral scream that makes the hairs on the back of my neck stand on end.

Fear for Zoey's life surges through me, and I call on the water, pulling it from the stream and forming a barrier between us and the creature.

It rises like a wall, shimmering and shifting.

The monster crashes into it. But while the water ripples, it holds.

I exhale, relief flooding through me.

Then, the monster rears back and lets out a furious growl, its claws slicing through the water like it's nothing.

I'm not powerful enough—or at least not trained well enough, given that I've never been trained at all—to control the water like I want to. Especially not with something this huge and feral attacking us.

I'm gathering more water as Zoey swings her branch as if it's a giant baseball bat, hitting the creature square across the face.

It staggers back with an ear-splitting screech, blood running down its face from its eye socket—its eye seemingly crushed from Zoey's swing.

"Let's go!" I tell her, but the monster lunges again, its claws outstretched and aiming for her throat.

Refusing to let the monster get to her, I thrust out my hands, and the water from the stream surges up like a wave, crashing into the monster and knocking it back.

The monster shakes it off as if it's nothing.

Fear shoots through me. But I push harder, drawing more water from the stream and using it to create a tube-shield thing that encircles me and Zoey, who's holding the branch with one hand and a particularly sharp rock in the other.

The monster slashes at the shield, threatening to tear it apart, and I glance around in panic.

The shield is keeping the monster back for now. But how long will I be able to hold onto my magic like this?

I have no idea.

Which means we'll have to outrun this thing.

Will we even be *able* to outrun this thing? I don't think so, but we're not exactly doing an A-plus job at killing it. And I have no idea how to drop the shield without giving the monster an in to attack us the moment it falls.

The barrier I created around us is both a shield and a coffin.

Horror tears at my throat.

But I'm not going to let us die like this. More importantly, I'm not going to let *Zoey* die because we decided the fae realm might make for a fun field trip.

It was so stupid. But the existence of monsters—*real* monsters—didn't seem real until one's staring me in the face.

Well, through a water shield. Same thing.

Zoey's still holding up the stick like a weapon, ready to strike if the shield breaks, when a gust of wind whips through the trees at an angle that allows me to use its momentum to *push* all the water that's part of the shield at the monster, throwing it so off balance that it falls to the ground.

Zoey throws her rock with all the strength she has, then grabs my arm, pulling me with her out of the clearing and into the forest.

I hold onto her as we bolt through the trees, keeping her pace even though I can run faster.

The creature roars, furious and relentless, its claws scraping the ground as it comes after us.

We're not fast enough.

It's gaining on us.

I reach for Zoey's hand, and the wind whips through the trees and pushes at our backs, adding speed to our steps as I pull us forward with every ounce of strength I can muster.

We turn a corner, and there, up ahead, is a massive pile of fallen trees.

A pile that might slow down the monster—if we're able to get over it.

It's an impossible jump. But we have so much momentum that we might be able to do it.

Either way, we have to try. It's either make the jump, have the monster catch up with us, or turn back around to fight it.

I don't like the last two options.

"Brace yourself!" I tell Zoey through the howling wind, tightening my grip on her hand. "We're going to jump."

"I hope you know what you're doing," she says.

"I don't," I say, and then we leap into the air, soaring higher and farther than I ever thought possible.

We clear the trees in one giant leap, using the momentum of the wind behind our heels to continue running without stumbling, weaving through the trees with more grace than I ever thought I had in me.

Eventually, we find ourselves in a clearing.

Zoey lets go of my hand, stumbling to a halt as she leans against a tree, her chest heaving, her cheeks bright red.

But we can't stop. The creature's crashing through the trees behind us, its guttural roar reverberating through the forest, threatening to rip us to shreds.

"Come on," I tell her, reaching for her. "We have to keep going."

I'll throw her over my back and carry her if I have to.

I'm about to do it when a deep, commanding voice cuts through the air.

"Get down!" he says, and I barely register the words before Zoey grabs my arm, pulling me down as Ghost leaps from the tree line, crashing into the monster with terrifying force.

The monster roars as Ghost's teeth sink into its skeletal frame.

Riven appears seconds later, flanked by four other knights, each armed with gleaming swords. They charge the monster, their movements fluid and precise, with the kind of grace only experienced warriors can possess.

I freeze, watching in awe as Riven's sword slices through the air, striking the creature's back with a sharp crack that makes it howl in pain.

The other knights fan out, surrounding the monster, cutting off any chance of escape.

Zoey grips my arm tighter. "Is that—?"

"Riven," I breathe, my heart skipping a beat.

The monster swings its claws at Riven, but he dodges with ease, sidestepping every attack like it's nothing.

His movements are hypnotic. Each strike is perfectly timed, every dodge effortless. Occasionally, he'll shoot a spear of ice at the monster, although the monster seems far more adept at dodging those than the sword.

It's beautiful to watch.

But before Riven left me at my house, he said he wasn't a knight in shining armor.

I'm not going to sit back, do nothing, and let him act like one.

And while there might not be a stream nearby, there's always moisture in the air. Humidity. Which means I'm surrounded by water—if I can figure out how to harness it.

So, I focus on the coolness around my skin—the mist lingering in the air—and pull on it with everything I have.

The water obeys, gathering in thick, shimmering tendrils around me. And, in that moment, I feel more powerful than ever.

But this isn't the time to stand around admiring my work. So, I thrust my hand forward, and the water surges through the air, striking the monster from the side.

The impact knocks it off balance.

Riven jumps onto Ghost's back, and they leap forward at the perfect angle for him to drive his blade through the creature's chest.

It screeches and falls to the ground.

Dead.

At least it *looks* dead, with its remaining eye glazed over, staring into nothing.

My heart's pounding, adrenaline coursing through my veins like wildfire. But I can't take my eyes off Riven.

He said he was well trained, but I wasn't expecting *that.*

Now, he's walking toward me, his sword dripping with the monster's dark blood, his gaze sharp and assessing.

"Surround them," he commands the knights, and they obey his order, forming a loose circle around Zoey and me.

All five of them are watching me and Zoey as if we're the next threat.

My happiness about our victory against the monster disappears in an instant.

"Your Highness," one of the knights addresses Riven. "It appears we've stumbled upon two summer fae."

"*One* summer fae," Riven corrects him. "The other one never used magic. We don't know what she is yet."

As he speaks, there's only one thing I can focus on.

"Your Highness?" I ask, keeping my eyes locked on Riven's, a million questions floating in those two words.

"Prince Riven Draevor of the Winter Court," he introduces himself, flat and matter of fact. "And you, Summer Fae, are trespassing on my lands."

I stare up at him in shock, waiting for him to take it back.

He doesn't.

"No." I shake my head, begging him to listen. "It wasn't like that."

"You used water magic in liquid form," he says coldly. "Summer magic. Which means you're a summer fae on my lands."

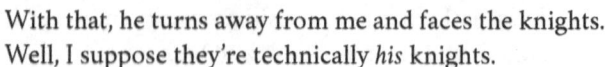

With that, he turns away from me and faces the knights.

Well, I suppose they're technically *his* knights.

"Blindfold the intruders," he commands. "We'll bring them back to the palace, so they can face my father, the king."

SAPPHIRE

"Wait—Riven—" I start, hoping to catch a glimmer of warmth, some hint of the man I met at the bar last night. The one who explained this realm to me, who made that deal with me to help me get home, and of course, who kissed me.

"You'll be silent," he orders, his silver eyes ice as they meet mine. "You're lucky you haven't been killed already. And you'll address me by my title—*Prince* Riven."

With that, the knight closest to me steps forward, places a makeshift blindfold over my eyes, and ties it securely.

The world plunges into darkness, and panic rises in my chest.

"Please, don't," Zoey begs, although she's quickly silenced.

"Zoey?" I ask, praying the knight didn't hurt her.

"Your companion currently has a blade to her throat," Riven—*Prince* Riven—tells me. "One step out of line—from either of you—and she'll be killed in a heartbeat."

I freeze, as if I'm the one with a dagger to my throat instead of Zoey.

"Understood," I say, ready to do anything they ask if it means keeping my best friend safe.

"You will not speak," Riven says. "Either of you."

I say nothing.

After all, that's what he just told me to do.

"Good," he says after a few painfully long seconds. "Now, we'll begin our walk back to the palace."

A heavy hand grips my arm, and I'm forced to move forward, stumbling over rocks and roots, my steps clumsy without my sight. I can hear Zoey being led somewhere close by, her breathing terrified and ragged.

We walk for what feels like hours. Each step disorients me further, and the hand gripping my arm never loosens, not even when I trip over root after root.

My heart pounds with every step. Not just from the physical exertion of using so much magic earlier, but with the overwhelming sense of betrayal and confusion.

Riven told me there were *others* in the Winter Court who would kill me for what I am.

He failed to inform me that he was included in those "others."

He also failed to inform me he was a prince.

But the one thing giving me hope is that if he wanted to kill me and Zoey, he easily could have back in that clearing. He didn't. I'm not sure what will happen when we talk to the king—I'm guessing nothing good—but at least we're alive.

For now.

Eventually, the scent of the forest fades, and we're walking on stone instead of the uneven earth.

"We're approaching the town," Riven says. "Do not speak. Make no sudden moves. The townsfolk respect me and my knights, but they're still winter fae at heart. Cruel and dangerous. If you want to live, do nothing to make them view you as more of a threat than you already are."

I hardly consider Zoey and I *threats*, but I keep my mouth shut.

Thankfully, Zoey does the same.

As we continue along the cobblestone, I hear whispers, shuffling feet, and gasps as we walk by. The sensation of eyes on me burns my skin, and while it's impossible to catch what most of them are saying, I do hear bits and pieces.

They don't look like warriors.

They must be prisoners.

Spies?

Are they the ones they've been hunting? From outside the border?

It goes on and on.

"Keep moving," Riven says from somewhere close behind me.

The knight guiding me fails to mention the steps ahead, so I stumble as he leads me up.

At the top, we stop.

"Open the gates," Riven commands, and I hear the heavy creak as the gates swing open in front of us.

The air changes instantly—cooler, crisper—and the whispers of the winter fae fade behind us. The sound of our steps bounces off the walls as we continue forward, through what I assume is a long hallway.

Not only does it feel cold—it *smells* cold. Like freshly fallen snow.

Then, suddenly, we stop.

"Tamsin," Riven commands. "Inform the king that we need an audience in the throne room immediately."

A deep voice answers—one of the knights we've been traveling with. "Yes, Your Highness."

Footsteps echo as he hurries away.

I hear Zoey shifting slightly, and I reach out, brushing my fingers against her hand to let her know I'm here.

She squeezes my fingers in return, a silent acknowledgment of solidarity.

Neither of us dare say anything. Not when speaking might end in death.

The wait feels endless. Silent. My senses have been stolen away from me, and all I'm left with is cold, overwhelming fear.

Eventually, the door in front of us creaks open.

"Move," a voice orders, and the knight gripping my arm tugs me forward.

I stumble over the threshold, my legs heavy and unsteady, as murmurs echo through what I assume is the throne room. I hear the rustling of fine clothes, the soft clinking of jewelry, and feet shuffling.

A crowd is gathered.

And while I can't see the king, I can feel his presence—power radiating through the room like a chill seeping into my bones.

"Father," Riven's voice cuts through the stillness. "I bring a summer fae and her companion, who have trespassed onto our lands."

A heavy silence follows, and I hear the rustling of the king's cloak as he moves, perhaps shifting in his throne.

My pulse quickens.

It was supposed to be so easy—get the bracelet, then go back home before anyone knew we were here. But I should have known better. I never should have come back here. And I especially shouldn't have brought Zoey with me.

This was all a giant mistake.

And now I'm living in a nightmare.

"Remove their blindfolds," the king commands, and the knight beside me yanks the cloth from my eyes.

Blinking against the sudden brightness, my vision clears, and I find myself standing in the grandest room I've ever seen.

Towering walls of ice shimmer with magic. Crystal chandeliers hang from the ceiling, and massive, silver pillars frame the frozen throne where the king of the Winter Court sits.

He's more imposing than I imagined—tall and broad, with dark black hair framing his sharp, aristocratic features. His cloak of white leopard fur drapes over his shoulders, and his eyes fall on me first, then flicker to Zoey.

His eyes are silver, like Riven's. But the similarity ends there. Because the king's eyes are wild, feral, and cruel in a way that makes me feel he's an animal ready to hunt.

And the people he's ready to hunt are *us*.

SAPPHIRE

"How did you find them?" the king asks Riven.

"A Wendigo attacked. It smelled the human—her." He jerks his chin in Zoey's direction, not sparing a glance my way. "We killed it, then brought them here."

I guess that's what that terrifying monster is called—a Wendigo.

"And the other one?" The king gestures at me with a flick of his fingers, his gaze sharp and calculating. "The summer fae."

"I'm not a member of the Summer Court," I say quickly. "I didn't even know what I was until today."

Riven glares at me, his message clear.

Do *not* address the king.

The king's eyes gleam with suspicion, and I can all but see the wheels turning in his mind. "You expect me to believe that a fae—one with a strong command over water magic, from what I heard—grew up ignorant of what she is?"

"I grew up human," I insist, relying on the fact that fae can't lie to make him believe me. Even though Zoey's been making fun of me for not being able to lie, there's actually a lot of power in the limitation. "I didn't know about magic, or even about this world, until today. I didn't even know I was fae."

I hold my breath after speaking.

Hopefully that's enough.

Riven still won't look at me.

But why should I expect help from him? He's the one who

brought us here. He's not an ally of mine, no matter how much I might want him to be.

The king leans back, and I hold my gaze with his. I will not show weakness. He knows as well as I do that what I'm saying has to be true.

At the same time, something tells me not to underestimate the cruelty of the fae. Especially the ones of the Winter Court.

After what feels like an eternity, the king shifts his attention to Zoey.

"And this one?" he asks. "The human?"

"She's innocent," I say before Zoey can even open her mouth. "She's just my friend. She has nothing to do with this."

"Innocent," the king muses, adjusting the white leopard fur draped over his shoulders. "Perhaps. But I can't take risks when it comes to spies and trespassers."

"We're not spies!" I blurt, and the moisture in the air surges forward, splashing the king across the chest and soaking his fur coat.

The room goes silent.

The king's eyes widen, his hand slowly rising to touch the wet fabric.

My heart feels like it stops entirely, my blood freezing in my veins, my legs going weak.

He's going to kill me.

"You dare!" His face twists in fury, and he jumps to his feet. "Queen Lysandra thinks she can send spies to mock me in my own court? She thinks I don't know her schemes? That she's trying to kill my people near the border? Is this her latest tactic—coming here with her human child to provoke me?"

Queen Lysandra?

Her human child?

"Do you think I'm blind to the Summer Court's treachery?" he rages on, pacing back and forth in front of his throne. "She's been plotting against me for centuries. And now, coming here to mock me —to humiliate me in front of my court—"

Zoey moves closer to me, trembling.

I wish I could tell her everything's going to be okay.

Unfortunately, I can't lie. I also don't think talking is going to do either of us any good right now.

The nobles in the room shift uncomfortably, unease spreading through the crowd.

"You, Your *Highness*, have taken a step too far by coming here," the king says to me, his breaths long and heavy as he reaches for his sword. "I will take care of you myself."

"I'm not Queen Lysandra," I tell him, panic breaking through my fear. "I'm not here on her orders. I don't even know who she is."

He stops dead in his tracks, his eyes blazing. "Lies! You cannot deceive me, Lysandra. Those blue streaks in your hair are hardly a convincing disguise."

"I'm not lying," I continue, trying to calm myself, to counter the king's madness. "I don't know anything about the Summer Court, or about their queen. My name is Sapphire Hayes. I grew up human, in a small town in Maine, where I work as a bartender. I didn't even know I had magic until today. I swear it."

The king's eyes burn into mine, and I see the madness there—the deep-seated paranoia and rage, the obsession with whatever war he's waging against this queen.

Riven steps forward, his posture stiff. "Father," he says, calm and measured. "You know as well as I that she cannot lie. She's telling the truth."

The king's gaze snaps to Riven, wild and accusing. "You defend her?" he asks. "You would stand there and defend a spy of the Summer Court?"

"She is not Lysandra." Riven remains steady, despite the tension in his shoulders. "She's exactly what she claims—a summer fae who grew up ignorant of her power."

The king's eyes flicker between Riven and me, still seething, but less certain now. He clenches the arm of his throne so hard that I half-expect the ice to crack beneath his grip.

I hold my breath and take Zoey's hand, well-aware that these might be our last few moments alive.

"Take them to the tower," the king finally says, dismissing us with a wave of his hand. "We'll deal with them in due time. If, of course, the tower doesn't take them first."

The king spins around and leaves the throne room, slamming the door behind him so hard that the ice wall attached to it cracks.

Two knights move toward us, and Zoey's grip tightens around

my hand, her eyes wilder and more scared than I've ever seen them before.

But beneath the fear... determination.

I know my best friend. She's not going to give up until we're back home, or dead.

"Riven—" I start, desperate for him to hear me out.

I don't even know what I want from him—what I can reasonably expect from him. Help? Acknowledgment?

Anything but this cold indifference.

He doesn't even look at me.

"Move," one of the knights growls, grabbing my arm.

I stumble forward, Zoey beside me, and we're led across the room. The chill of the palace sinks deep into my bones, and the whispers from the gathered nobles follow us like a phantom, growing quieter as we move.

I glance over my shoulder one last time, finding Riven watching me, in what surprisingly looks like a mix of conflict and sadness.

It's gone a second later, but I know it was there.

Maybe Riven doesn't hate me as much as I think. After all, he stood up for me and Zoey in front of his father. He made sure the king didn't kill us.

But before I can contemplate it further, the massive doors swing open, and we're shoved into the hallway.

Zoey stumbles, and I squeeze her hand, giving her the only comfort I can offer.

Because I can't lie and promise we'll survive this.

SAPPHIRE

A FEW DAYS LATER, everything's a blur of cold, hunger, and exhaustion. The icy stone walls of the tower are draining the last bits of warmth from me, and my body aches in ways I didn't think possible.

Zoey's slumped against the wall beside me, her breath shallow, her lips blue. The cold has nearly consumed her, and I can feel it creeping closer to me, too.

We've barely been fed. Just small chunks of stale bread that leave our mouths dry and stomachs growling. But for me, it's worse. There's a hunger inside me, deeper than anything I've ever felt. A gnawing craving that can't be satisfied with bread.

I need meat. Rare, dripping meat. Meat's always been an important part of my diet, and given how readily available it is in the local supermarkets, I've never gone a day without it.

Now... not having it is unbearable.

Zoey lets out a soft groan, and I glance over at her. She's shivering uncontrollably, and I pull her closer, trying to share what little warmth I have left.

"We're still here," I whisper. "They haven't killed us yet. We still have a chance."

She doesn't respond.

I don't even know if she heard me.

Our cell door creaks open, and the same guard who's been

tormenting us these last few days steps inside, carrying a tray of bread and water.

I stare emptily at the bread, since as long as it's all I have to eat, that's exactly how I'll continue to feel—empty.

"What's the problem? Is our food not good enough for you?" he asks with a cruel smile as he sets it out in front of us.

I can't exactly lie and say it is.

And at this point, I'm starving and freezing.

Desperate enough that I figure it can't hurt to be truthful. Completely, one hundred percent truthful.

"Can we please have meat?" I beg, my teeth chattering from the cold. "It doesn't have to be steak. I can eat squirrel, or rabbit, or… rat. Just *something*."

"Fae don't eat meat," he says flatly. "Begging for your human friend won't get you anywhere."

I almost say that I'm not begging for Zoey, but stop myself.

Fae don't eat meat.

I want to ask more. Do they not eat meat *ever*?

If so, why can't I live without it?

I'm also not in a position to be drawing more attention to myself. Which means I have to accept the bread with a smile and pray it'll be enough to keep me going until we figure our way out of here.

The guard leaves, the heavy door slamming shut with a finality that makes me flinch.

Zoey's uneven breathing fills the otherwise silent cell, and my chest tightens with fear.

She's fading fast.

I wrap my arms around my knees, trying to keep what little body heat I have left to help warm her up. If we don't escape soon, I'll lose her—and I have a feeling I won't be far behind.

My healing magic apparently doesn't work quickly enough to save me from freezing to death in a tower made of ice. Or maybe it works *just* slowly enough to make it as torturous and drawn out as possible.

Then, as I'm contemplating the horror of a long, cold death with Zoey's frozen body next to me, something shimmers in the corner of the room near the window. A soft, ghostly glow in the shape of a woman.

The woman from the forest? The one who touched my forehead and put me through that unimaginable pain?

Then, just as quickly as she appeared, she's gone.

Great. Now I'm hallucinating.

It's probably a side effect of freezing to death.

Still, something tugs at me, drawing me toward the window. Something I can't ignore.

So, slowly, I stand, my legs trembling as I walk over to the cold stone wall. The window's high up, but I grip the edge, pulling myself up enough to peer through the bars.

Ghost is pacing near the tower's base, his massive form a shadow against the snow.

A pang of longing shoots through me. If I were down there, I could ride on Ghost's back, find Riven, and beg him to help. After all, I saw that final look in Riven's eyes as Zoey and I were sent away. He might be cruel, but he doesn't want me to die.

Why would he have made the deal to get me home if he wanted me dead? Why would he bind it with a kiss?

As I look down at Ghost, I remember what it felt like to ride on his back with Riven through the forest. I can practically feel the rush of cold air against my skin, the crunch of snow beneath Ghost's paws, the freedom of running through the trees.

I need to get down there.

Ghost looks up at me, watching me, like he's waiting for me.

Come down, his eyes seem to say. *Jump on my back again. Let me take you where you need to go.*

I wish I could. So much that I can practically feel the snow crunching beneath my feet and the fresh air outside this tower.

Then, suddenly, Ghost is standing in front of me.

I'm... not in the tower anymore.

I'm down here. On the ground, at the base of the tower. Free.

What the hell?

I blink rapidly, trying to make sense of it.

Is this a dream? Did I teleport? Am I dying again?

But there's no time to question it. I'm here, and now's the time to act—not to sit around wondering how I pulled off whatever it is I just did.

Ghost turns his massive head toward me, his icy blue eyes locking on mine.

I reach out instinctively, my fingers brushing against his fur.

He's solid. Real.

This isn't a dream.

Somehow—by some miracle—I'm free. I have no idea how to get back inside the tower to Zoey, but being up there wasn't helping either of us, anyway.

This is my chance to save us. Possibly my *only* chance.

So, I pull the hood of my sweatshirt over my head, tucking my hair inside to hide its unmistakable icy blonde color with blue high-lights on the bottom tips.

Ghost watches me, his gaze steady, as if he knows how desperate I am.

"Take me to Riven," I whisper, terrified that someone else might be lurking nearby to hear.

The giant snow leopard lowers himself to the ground, allowing me to climb onto his back. I settle in, get a firm grip on his fur, and he bolts forward with a speed that steals my breath away.

The world around me blurs as we race across the snow and weave through the trees, leaving the isolated prison tower far behind and giving me a burst of hope through the frozen fear I've been experiencing for days.

I just hope I can get back to Zoey before it's too late.

SAPPHIRE

GHOST MOVES WITH PRECISION, his paws barely making a sound on the snow, as if he knows exactly where he's going.

I don't have a plan—I barely know what I'm doing—but I trust Ghost. He's my only shot at finding Riven.

The trees thin, and finally, I see it. The palace looming ahead, its massive icy walls shimmering under the moonlight like a fortress carved from the heart of winter itself.

Ghost slows as we reach the edge of the forest and stops next to the palace's back wall, beneath an open window on the second floor.

Through the dim glow of the interior lights, I see a figure moving inside.

Riven.

Now, I need to get to him. But I can't scream up at him from down here. It's too risky that someone else will hear me. If they do, I'll be dragged back to the tower before I can plead my case to Riven in private.

I need to get up there, to what I assume is his room.

Maybe I can teleport inside. Just like how I teleported down to the base of the tower to Ghost.

I stare up at the window, focusing on my need to get up there. I imagine standing beside Riven, inside the warmth of the palace, finally alone with him again.

Nothing happens.

I curse beneath my breath and try again, pushing with every ounce of willpower I can gather.

Again, nothing.

And I don't plan on standing out here all night. So, it looks like I'll have to do this the old-fashioned way.

I glance around the area, my gaze stopping on a large tree looming nearby, its branches thick enough to hold my weight.

Without hesitation, I hurry over to it and start to climb—just like how Zoey and I used to climb trees when we were kids.

She was always a faster climber—nimbler, and more impulsive. But I could still get to the top. Slower, and with more concentration, but I never gave up.

Now, my hands are numb from the cold, but I grit my teeth and keep going, just like I did back then.

Finally, I reach the highest branch that seems remotely stable.

But Riven's window is farther away than I'd hoped. Too far to jump without breaking my neck and dying for *real* this time.

Of course, the fae wouldn't make it that easy to break into the prince's chambers. I should have known better. I was just so desperate, and so hopeful.

And catching his gaze might be even less possible than jumping through his window, because he's on his bed, reading, oblivious to anything that might be lurking outside.

I glance down at Ghost, who's still watching me from the base of the tree. His eyes are locked on mine, as if silently encouraging me to keep trying.

I attempt to teleport again.

Unsurprisingly, it doesn't work.

Zoey's face flashes through my mind, her lips blue, her body slumped in that freezing cell, so close to death. If I don't figure this out, I'll lose her.

There has to be a solution here. Ghost seems to believe in me, which means I need to have better belief in myself.

I think back through everything that's happened since the first time I entered the fae realm, stopping at the memory of running from the Wendigo. I made that impossible leap with Zoey over the fallen trees. I remember the rush of air beneath my feet, as if something unseen had carried me across.

Did I harness humidity with my water magic to propel us forward?

Maybe.

But I don't have anything long enough to gain the momentum I had then. All I have is the length of the branch.

Which means the branch will have to be enough.

Without giving myself time to second-guess the plan, I take off, sprinting along the length of the branch. Every step feels light, and I spring off the edge, pushing my magic into the air, coaxing it to propel me forward like it did when I leaped over those trees.

I'm weightless.

Everything else around me disappears—the palace, the cold night, the ground far below... all of it.

There's only me and the open window, getting closer with every heartbeat.

I'm doing it.

I'm flying.

Well, maybe not *flying*. But it sure feels close.

Everything speeds up again as I soar through the window and land hard on the floor of Riven's room, somehow staying on my feet as I do.

He grabs the sword lying on his bedside table, springs at me, and thrusts it through my chest.

I brace myself for the pain—for my final moment. I've survived a lot, but there's no way I can survive a blade through my heart.

Instead, the sword passes through me, like I'm not there at all.

Riven stumbles, thrown off balance by the lack of resistance, confusion flashing across his face.

"What the—?" His gaze snaps to the sword, back to me, then back to his sword again.

I have no answer. I just glance down at where the blade should be lodged inside my chest, finding no wound. No blood.

Impossible.

"Sapphire?" he asks, his silver eyes wide in disbelief. "I almost—" He cuts himself off, his hand shaking as he lowers his sword. "I could've killed you. You should be dead right now."

"Do you *want* me to be dead right now?" I ask, since he did, after all, try to run his sword through my chest.

"No," he growls, which is all the answer I need. "I heard someone break in through my window, and I struck. I didn't see it was you. Your hair was covered. I thought you were a thief, or worse. I wouldn't have done that if I knew it was you."

His confession sends an undeniable rush of warmth streaming through me.

And while I have no idea how I survived his attack, I need to get down to business about why I'm here. Zoey isn't going to survive that tower if I don't do something to help her.

"I'm fine," I tell him, stepping cautiously forward. "I don't understand what just happened, either. But I'm here, and I'm okay."

"How *are* you here?" he asks. "You were locked in the tower. No one's ever escaped the tower. *No one.*"

"I think I teleported," I say, continuing before he can react. "One minute I was in that cell, freezing to death with Zoey, and the next, I was outside with Ghost. I don't know how I did it, but we can figure that out later. Because right now, I need your help. Zoey's going to die if we don't get out of there. I probably will, too. I don't know if fae can freeze to death, but—"

"They can," he interrupts, his eyes cold.

I flinch, startled by his change of demeanor.

But I'm not going to let it stop me.

"So, I'm right. I might die up there," I reply, panic filling me as I realize the inevitability of it if I can't get us out. "I need your help. *We* need your help. You're our only hope."

"You escaped the most secure prison in the Winter Court," he says, even though we've gone over this already. "Then you broke into my quarters."

"Yes." I shrug. "But it wasn't just me. Ghost helped."

"He does seem quite taken by you," he mutters, still not letting go of his sword—and still staring at me like I'm a puzzle he's trying to solve. "But you shouldn't be here."

"Well, I *am* here. And you can put that down." I motion to his sword. "You clearly can't hurt me with it."

"Apparently not," he says. "But blade-proof or not, you're freezing. I'll grab you a jacket so you can try warming up. Then, we'll talk."

SAPPHIRE

RIVEN'S JACKET is heavy and lined with fur, warming me up quicker than I imagined possible.

"Better?" he asks, as on-guard with his sword as ever, assessing me like I'm an unsolved mystery.

I nod, pulling the jacket tighter around myself. "Much."

He exhales, pacing the room as he runs a hand through his dark hair. "You wouldn't even be in that damn tower if you hadn't come back," he says, sharp and condescending. "What were you thinking? We made the deal to leave. But you got around the deal."

"Zoey figured out the loophole," I tell him. "Not me."

"How?"

"She realized that you only said I had to stay in Presque Isle for a year. You didn't say whether that year had to be in consecutive months, or all at one time. Which meant it was open to interpretation."

"Your human friend thinks like a fae," he says, sounding decently impressed by it.

"Zoey's smart." I shrug. "It didn't take her long to figure it out. Plus, aren't you supposed to be experienced at wording these deals? Shouldn't you have made sure it didn't have any loopholes?"

"There are *always* loopholes," he says. "Some are more obvious than others, but they're always there."

"Then it sounds like you underestimated me," I say.

"I figured you'd be smart enough to stay out of a realm where anyone or anything you came across would want to kill you." He scoffs.

"It was only supposed to be for a bit. I didn't expect to be attacked so *quickly* like that," I shoot back. "That thing—the Wendigo—sneaked up on us out of nowhere."

"Wendigos are stealthy," he says. "It's next to impossible to hear them coming. They eat humans, and they like to play with their food. The beast was toying with you. Otherwise, your human friend would likely be dead right now."

"She has a name," I remind him. "Zoey."

"I don't care about your human's name," he snaps. "I have far more important things to worry about."

"Like summer fae teleporting into your bedroom?" I ask.

He narrows his eyes, and I prepare for him to raise his sword again.

"You shouldn't have come back to this realm for me," he says instead. "I assume you think that kiss between us meant something? That I secretly wanted to see you again?"

"You really think I came back here for *you?*" I ask, enraged by how insanely cocky his is.

"I was the highlight of your visit," he says simply.

"I came back for my bracelet," I snap. "I had it on me when I came to this realm, and it was gone when I woke up the next morning."

He blinks a few times, taking a few seconds to process what I told him.

"Let me get this straight," he finally says. "You last saw this bracelet when you came to my realm. You didn't realize it was gone until waking up the next morning in *your* realm. Which means it was gone for hours. And you believed you could track it down and *find* it?"

"I took a pretty good tumble in those bushes." I shrug. "I thought it was pretty likely that it could be there."

"And was it?" he asks. "There?"

"I don't know," I tell him, glaring at him. "We got attacked by that Wendigo before we finished looking."

He watches me as if I've lost my mind.

And honestly, maybe I have.

"Look," I say, desperate now. "I'll do anything you want. Just let Zoey go free and get her back to the human realm. Please."

"Anything?" He raises an eyebrow.

"Yes. Anything."

He's silent for a moment, contemplating it.

Say yes, I think. *Please, say yes.*

"Why's this human girl so important to you, anyway?" he eventually asks, and while it's not the yes I hoped for, at least it's not a no.

"Zoey isn't just my best friend," I say quietly, my heart hurting at the thought of her freezing to death in that tower. "She's practically my sister. We've been through everything together."

He raises an eyebrow, clearly skeptical, and waits for me to continue.

"We were kids." I pull his jacket tighter around myself, as if it can protect me from the cold memory. "It was a camping trip for a classmate's birthday. Zoey and I didn't really know each other back then, since she's a year younger than me, but everyone at school liked her. After sunset, she wandered over to a nearby lake that had frozen over. I followed, since I'd always been curious about her. She was so fearless, and outgoing, and adventurous. Everything I'm not. But she went out too far. The ice broke under her."

Riven doesn't say anything, but his eyes narrow slightly, like he's trying to imagine it as I tell him what happened.

"She fell through," I continue, the memory of that night as vivid as ever. "I called for help, but we were so far that I had no way of knowing if they heard or not. And there was no time to go back. So, I crawled on the ice to her and saved her."

"How did you save her?" he asks, more interested now.

"I don't know," I admit. "It just sort of… happened. One moment she was drowning, and the next, I'd pulled her up onto the surface."

"You used magic," he decides.

"Probably," I say, since the more I think about it, the more I believe that's what happened that night. "But magic or not, we've been inseparable since then. She's my family. I'll do anything if you let her go free and make sure she gets safely back to the human realm, as soon as you possibly can."

As I make my request, I'm careful about my wording. After all, asking him to set her free won't be enough. Freeing her from that tower won't guarantee safe passage home.

She needs to get back there safely, and *soon*.

Riven watches me for a long moment, his silver eyes piercing in that cold, assessing way of his.

Again, I pray to the universe that he'll say yes. That he'll care.

"I've never had anyone like that," he eventually says. "No best friend. No one to pull me out of the ice if I fall through. The only person who ever loved me is dead."

I blink, caught off guard by his sudden shift in tone.

Is he being vulnerable?

Is the ice prince warming up to me?

"She's the only person who's ever truly cared about me. Everyone else…" He glances out the window, as if the moonlight holds answers, then returns his focus to me. "They care about power. Control. They care about what I can give them, or what I can take away from them."

Throughout what he's saying, one word rings through my mind.

She.

A girlfriend? A wife? A soulmate?

Whoever it was, he's speaking about her in the past tense. Which means they either broke up, or she died.

"No need to look so sullen," he says, back to being as callous as ever. "The woman I'm talking about was my mother."

"I'm sorry," I say. "My mom isn't in my life, either."

"It's because your mother knew you were different," he says. "She left you. She chose to not be in your life."

His words sting.

Mainly because they're probably true.

"It happens a lot with changelings," he continues. "The mother can tell there's something off about their baby. That it's not truly theirs. So, they drop them off with someone else and leave."

My chest tightens at the hard truth behind his words.

"Who did she drop you off with?" he asks.

"My aunt," I admit, since there's no point in lying. Especially because I *can't* lie. "Her sister."

"Your aunt must be tough, to be able to raise a fae child," he says.

"Yes," I say without hesitation. "She is."

Suddenly, I'm prouder of Aunt Martha than ever.

Riven steps closer, his eyes fixed on me in that intense way that makes my heart race.

It's the same way he looked at me last night in the forest, before he kissed me.

"Would you really do anything to save Zoey?" His voice is a soft, dangerous whisper now, his eyes locking onto mine as if he's trying to size me up.

"Yes." I don't hesitate. "Anything."

The world narrows to just the two of us, standing so close that I can smell the frost and pine clinging to his body.

There's a challenge in his eyes. Something dark and alluring.

Something that intrigues me and scares me at the same time.

Before I can comprehend what's happening, he leans in, his breath brushing against my skin.

"Then let's see how far you'll go," he says, and then his lips are on mine, and he's taking my breath away just like he did last night.

His kiss is slow and deliberate, his lips firm but coaxing. Heat rushes through me, burning away the cold that settled in my bones in that tower, and all I'm aware of is him as he pulls me closer, his hand sliding to the small of my back.

Every nerve in my body is electrified, and I respond to him with a hunger I didn't know I possessed. This kiss is everything I wanted when he dropped me off at my house last night.

His lips are demanding. Teasing. Drowning out any type of rational thought. The world fades around us, and all I want is *more*.

I'm only half aware of my fingers clutching his shirt, and then he's slowly pushing me back, toward the bed.

But then, as he presses me down onto it, the truth slams into me with brutal clarity.

This isn't some passionate connection. He made that clear last night.

This is him pushing me. Testing how far I'll go.

"Wait." I pull back, trying to get some air to help me think straight.

"You said you'd do anything to save your friend," he murmurs, his breath cool in my ear, his nose brushing my cheek. "Are you going to prove it?"

My stomach drops.

Out of everything he could have asked for in exchange for helping Zoey, *this* is what he wants?

Of course it is. After last night, I shouldn't be surprised.

Recently, a *lot* of men have been asking me for more than I'm willing to give.

"No," I tell him, as firmly as I did when I rejected Matt's proposal. "This isn't what I want."

"Sapphire..." He leans in again, but I press my hands against his chest, stopping him.

I don't want him touching me.

I don't want him near me.

And then, suddenly... he's gone.

SAPPHIRE

HARD STONE PRESSES against my back, through Riven's jacket, and my eyes snap open.

I'm staring up at Zoey. She's hovering over me, her face tear-streaked, her eyes wide with fear.

"Sapphire?" She looks me over, her face scrunched in confusion. "You're okay?"

"I think so?" I push myself up, still warm from my time in Riven's quarters.

His jacket helps, too.

Zoey's more of a mess than when I left. Her skin's pale, her teeth are chattering, and there are little flecks of ice in her thick, dark hair.

"You're freezing," I tell her, and I take off Riven's jacket, wrapping it around her. "Take this. It should help."

She snuggles up inside the jacket, and as she does, she looks at me like I'm a ghost.

"You were dead," she says softly. "And then this jacket... it just *appeared* on you. Right when you woke up."

"I was here?" I ask, the cold hitting me all at once now that I'm no longer wearing Riven's jacket. "The whole time?"

"You were dead," she repeats, and she's wary as she looks me over, as if she thinks I'm going to disappear at any second.

"I wasn't dead," I tell her. "I teleported down to the base of the tower. I rode on Ghost's back to find us help."

She shakes her head, pulling the jacket tighter around her. "You were here," she insists. "You collapsed, and you were so still. I couldn't even tell if you were breathing."

I stare at her, the weight of her words sinking in, and a cold knot forms in my stomach.

If I didn't teleport, then what on Earth *did* happen?

"I touched things. I brought back this jacket." I gesture to the fur-lined coat wrapped around her. "How could that happen if I wasn't really there?"

"The jacket just *appeared* on you when you woke up," she says again. "But you were here the entire time. I'm not making it up any more than you made up everything about being fae and coming here through the portal."

Her words strike a chord with me, and I don't push back. Because Zoey believed me when I told her every crazy detail about last night. She came here with me.

This realm—and my magic—is unknown. Unpredictable.

I need to give her the same respect she gave me, and take what she's saying as truth.

Which means...

"How could I be here and there at the same time?" I ask.

Zoey frowns, still shivering. "It's just like what you said happened when you died in that fall the first time you came to this realm," she says. "You were in those trees, looking down at yourself when Riven found you. In some sort of in between state. And then, you snapped back."

"But I wasn't in an 'in between' state," I tell her. "I was there. In Riven's room. I talked with him. I *brought back his jacket.*"

"You were in Riven's room?" she asks.

"Well, I teleported down to the base of the tower first. Then I rode Ghost's back to the palace, climbed a tree, and jumped into Riven's room."

"You didn't teleport," she corrects me. "You left your body, and some other part of you—maybe your spirit or something—went on this whole adventure to Riven's room." She pauses, then adds, "You were really in his room?"

"Yes." Memories of that kiss flash through my mind—the desire I felt when he touched me, and the horror I felt about what he was asking from me.

I wanted to get away from him.

And then I *was* away from him. Back here, where my *body* had apparently been this entire time.

"So, if I didn't teleport, then I duplicated myself?" I ask.

"That's what it sounds like." She bites her lip, like she does when she's working through a tough math problem. "Did your... duplicate feel different from your real self?"

"When I landed in his room, Riven attacked me," I tell her, putting the pieces slowly into place. "He ran his sword through me. Except it went *literally* through me. As if I was a ghost."

"He tried to kill you?" she asks, anger swirling in her eyes.

"He didn't realize it was me," I instantly go to his defense, even though I'm supposed to be mad at him. "It was an accident."

"People don't 'accidentally' run their swords through other people," she says. "You could have died."

"But I didn't die," I remind her. "I'm here. I'm fine."

"But you would have been dead if your real self was there instead of this half-there, projected self."

"You think my duplicate was some sort of projected version of myself?" I ask, my head spinning as I try to get this straight.

"That's what it sounds like," she says, as if this is a normal conversation we're having over coffee. "Anyway, what happened with Riven when you—well, your projected self—was in his room? Other than him trying to kill you?"

"I told you—he wasn't trying to kill me." I glare at her, exasperated, but also relieved that the frost in her hair is melting, thanks to Riven's jacket. There's a bit of pink creeping into her cheeks, too.

"I guess I have to believe you." She sighs. "Since you're magically bound to not be able to lie."

"Apparently being unable to lie comes with some perks." I smile, trying to find something positive during all this craziness. "Everyone's forced to believe me."

"Having magical control over water comes with perks, too," she points out. "As does projecting your spirit—or whatever—to another place."

"It *was* pretty cool." My teeth chatter a bit as I talk, the cold in the tower catching back up with me.

"You're freezing." She takes off half the jacket and motions for me to come over to her. "Get in. But only if you tell me everything else that happened when you were in *Prince* Riven's room."

SAPPHIRE

"TRY AGAIN," Zoey says, and I close my eyes, picturing Riven's room for the fifth time in the past hour.

As per Zoey's instructions, I'm sitting with my back against the wall, so my body won't have an unfortunate collision with the ground if this works.

I'd probably heal relatively quickly, but still, it's better to be safe.

Project, I think, as if thinking the word can ignite my magic.

Nothing happens.

I open my eyes again, frustrated to find Zoey frowning in disappointment.

"I can't do it," I tell her.

Even if I could, what am I going to do? Tell Riven I changed my mind, and hook up with him to get what I want?

That's what Zoey said I should do. It's what *she* would do. It would also be better than staying in here and freezing to death, but I'd rather figure out a solution that *doesn't* involve sleeping with the enemy.

"Maybe you should try covering less of a distance," she says, and then she stands up, glancing out the window. "There's a guard down there now, and there's no sign of Ghost. It's not safe. But what if you try projecting yourself right outside our cell? Just to see if it works?"

"It's worth a shot," I say, since we're not doing much of anything else in here, other than freezing and starving to death.

I close my eyes again.

"Wait," she says, and I open my eyes to look at her. "You said that when you did it before, you were *looking* at the place next to Ghost at the bottom of the tower."

"Yes."

"You have to repeat exactly what you did. So, don't close your eyes. Look at the hall outside of the bars instead."

"Okay," I say, since even though Zoey's the one without magic, she seems to have a better basic understanding of it than I do.

So, I shift my position and focus on the narrow hallway just outside the cell.

Project, I think again, picturing myself standing out there, beyond the bars.

Suddenly, I'm no longer in the cell.

I'm standing exactly where I was looking.

My body lies limp on the floor next to Zoey, who's staring through the bars at me with disbelief shining in her wide eyes.

"It worked," I say, although I can't stop looking at my body.

It's lifeless. It doesn't even look like I'm breathing.

No wonder Zoey thought I was dead.

She scrambles to her feet, moving closer to the bars. "Holy crap," she says. "You're really out there. It worked."

"I'm here," I say slowly, still focused on my body inside the cell. "But I'm also there."

She hurries over to check on it, her hands hovering over it as if she's afraid to touch it—or me, or whatever this is.

I can't blame her. The sight of my own limp form, pale and still as the stone beneath it, is the strangest thing I've ever seen.

She reaches out and places two fingers on my wrist, checking for a pulse. "You're not dead, but you're definitely not awake," she says. "It's like you're in some sort of coma."

A shudder runs through me. "This is so weird."

"Definitely weird." She turns her attention from the unconscious version of me to the current version of me, watching me carefully. "You said you felt everything when you were in Riven's room, right? Like, you were solid? Minus the part where Riven ran at you with his sword?"

"Right." I reach for the bars to test it out, and while there's a slight shimmer to my skin that you'd have to be looking for to notice, the bars are as real as ever. "Totally solid."

I reach for the padlock to the cell, trying—and failing—to open it.

"We need a key," I state the obvious.

"Maybe you can steal it," she says.

"Maybe. But pulling off a prison break is going to be a lot more complicated than stealing a key. There are guards. Not a ton of them, but if one of them catches us, we'll be toast. As for my body, we can't leave it here—or anywhere. So, once we're out of the cell, I'll have to *stay* in my body. Projecting again is out of the question. I'll be too vulnerable otherwise. At least, my real self will be too vulnerable. Whatever we want to call that version of me." I glance at my unconscious form, unease prickling through me at the sight of it.

"There are definitely a lot of things we're going to have to learn and plan," she says, and she stands up, starting to pace around the cell. "But we know that if you steal the key, you can bring it back with you, since you were able to bring Riven's jacket back with you. We know that Ghost was willing to help you. If we can get far enough to find Ghost, then maybe—"

She's cut off by the sound of a door closing at the end of the hall.

Without even having to think, my projected body snaps back to the one on the floor.

My heart pounds as I sit up, the world rushing back into focus around me.

Zoey hurries over to me, making sure I'm okay as the guard approaches. It's the smaller guard—the one who takes the night shifts. He normally doesn't talk much, if at all.

But now, he stands just in front of the bars, studying us, as if we're animals in a zoo.

"I'm guessing you're not here to deliver a filet mignon?" Zoey asks him, and my stomach growls at the thought.

His eyebrows knit together, as if she's speaking in another language.

They probably don't even *have* filet mignon in this realm, given that the fae don't eat meat. I don't even know if they have cows.

Maybe they could flay a Wendigo for me. It didn't have much meat on its bones, but I'm so desperate that I'd try it.

"I just received word from Prince Riven, and was told to report to you immediately," he says, not bothering to answer Zoey's question. "Because the two of you will be taken to court again tomorrow evening, for another trial in front of the king."

SAPPHIRE

THE THRONE ROOM is as grand as I remember. Its towering ice walls shimmer with magic, and massive chandeliers hang from the ceiling, their jagged edges dripping with frozen crystals, reflecting light in a way that makes everything seem both beautiful and dangerous.

Sort of like Riven—and all the other winter fae gathered in the room. Beautiful, cold, and dangerous.

Zoey's quiet next to me, but I can feel the tension radiating from her. The tremble in her hands, and the sharp breaths she's trying to keep steady. I'm sure I look the same.

Before us, the throne looms, carved entirely from ice. Its edges are sharp and cruel, mirroring the wild, feral look in the king's silver eyes, and I know that one wrong move could mean death.

Riven's next to him. He's different than his father—stiff and controlled, any trace of emotions wiped from his face.

At least when I was in his room last night, he looked devious. Demanding. Teasing. Maybe even passionate.

This robotic version of him somehow makes me more uncomfortable than I felt after our kiss.

He's wearing the jacket he gave me. He took it back when he fetched Zoey and me from the tower a bit ago. And, of course, Ghost is by his side.

Out of everyone in the room, the snow leopard is the only one looking at me kindly.

The king's gaze flicks between me and Zoey, and I fight the urge to shrink back. But I don't. I will not let this man scare me.

At least, I won't let him *think* he's scaring me. Because anyone in their right mind would be scared of him.

He rises from his throne, his white fur cloak brushing the floor as he paces like a mad scientist coming up with a wild scheme. It's like he's completely unaware of anything other than his thoughts.

A few of the fae nobles shift uncomfortably. They won't look at Zoey or me, but they won't look at the king, either.

"I think I'll make a spectacle of your death," the king starts, continuing his pacing. "A public execution. A show for the court."

Zoey sucks in a breath beside me, but she doesn't speak. We both know better than to provoke the king right now.

Riven also remains silent. As does everyone else in the room.

The king's pacing quickens, his fingers twitching, as if already imagining the ways he'll carry out our execution.

"A show..." His voice trails off, distant, like he's not even talking to us anymore. "I can see it now. But you know what would be even more fun? For both of you to see it, too. A demonstration. So you'll know what's coming."

Slowly, he draws the long, curved blade from his weapons belt.

I'm frozen, my blood like ice through my veins.

"First," he begins, soft and menacing. "I'll sever your tendons. Slowly. One by one. Starting with the legs, of course."

He lunges at one of the knights standing in the row next to his throne, his sword moving with lethal precision as he slices the blade cleanly through the fae's knee.

A woman's scream echoes through the chamber as the man's blood spills across the icy floor, a stark red against the glistening white. He looks to her, and from the pain splattered across his face, I can tell she's someone he loves.

Two of the other knights flinch, but they make no moves against their king.

Riven's face is a mask of calm.

I'm shaking almost as much as the man on the floor. My breaths come quickly, and a breeze stirs around us, as though someone turned the air conditioner onto full blast. And on top of it all, my stomach growls, as if now's the best time to remind me about how famished I am after all those days in the tower. How every bone in my body feels hollow.

Murmurs echo amongst the fae, and I try to steady my breathing, along with the pounding of my heart and the cries of my empty stomach.

I don't want the king to sense my fear.

The room becomes still once again—minus the woman's quiet sobs as she cries in the arms of the person next to her.

The king simply smiles at her, excitement dancing in his cruel eyes. "Before you can heal, I'll move on to your arms," he continues. "I'll make sure you feel each snap as your body betrays you."

His sword flashes again, striking the fallen fae's arm with brutal precision.

The crack of breaking bone echoes through the throne room. And even though the man's arm hangs limply at his side, blood pooling beneath him, he suppresses any cries of pain.

Zoey's breath catches. Her face is pale, her eyes wide, and I know she's struggling to hold herself together just like I am.

The woman who's crying turns her head away.

I want to scream, to run, to do anything but stand here and watch this madness unfold. As it is, I can't tear my eyes away. All I can do is grab Zoey's hand to stop my body from going completely numb with fear, and from collapsing because of all the exhaustion and hunger from the past few days.

The man writhes on the ground, clutching his arm, his face twisted in agony.

"Do you see now?" The king circles the fallen fae like a predator, his sword dripping with blood, his eyes gleaming with twisted satisfaction. "This is what awaits you, Summer Fae and human companion. This is what I do to trespassers who threaten my land."

I glance to Riven, as if he'll do something to help us.

He's as frozen as the icy walls.

"We didn't threaten anything," I say, even though anything I say might cause the king to attack.

It seems like he's going to attack anyway, so I'm not sure I have much to lose.

"Quiet." He glares at me over his raised sword, frost crawling over the blade. "Or you might miss your show."

I swallow.

This man is crazy. Totally, batshit crazy.

Unsure what to do, I glance at Riven again.

He's looking at me.

And, is it just me, or does he seem... concerned?

His eyes move from mine before I have time to properly analyze. Still, hope flutters through my chest at the possibility that he might help. Because despite everything, he made sure the king didn't kill us the first time we were presented to him in this room. He got us out of the tower. He brought me home that first night.

Maybe he has a plan.

One that *won't* involve Zoey and I bleeding out onto the floor for the entire Winter Court to see.

As it is now, the room's so quiet that all I can hear are the crystals in the chandelier clinking against each other, and the movements of the fae knight as his body mends itself back together.

The king's focus returns to his man on the ground, who's starting to push himself up.

"Stay down," he snaps, and he slices the man's other knee, stopping him from standing. "Now, where were we?"

The knight's blood spreads out like a dark halo around him, and the king's smile deepens, relishing in the torment.

"Ah, yes." The king runs a finger along the sharp end of his blade, cutting it and watching hungrily as his blood drips down his hand, down to his wrist. "The final touch."

With a final, brutal motion, the king plunges the sword into the knight's chest.

His body jerks as blood spills from the wound, pooling around him.

After a few painfully long seconds, his body slumps lifeless to the floor.

I do my best to breathe through the weakness hollowing my bones. Air into my lungs, air out of my lungs.

Miraculously, it does help a bit.

The king stares down at the man's body, seemingly satisfied, then looks back up. But he's not looking at me. He's looking at the fae woman who screamed earlier, whose quiet sobs are still sounding through the room.

"We are fae of the Winter Court," the king says. "Succumbing to weak emotions is not tolerated."

With that, he throws his sword at the woman like a javelin, piercing her heart and killing her on the spot.

She collapses to the floor.

The crowd falls silent.

The air is still, as if the entire room is holding its breath. I certainly am. Zoey is, too.

If I breathe in the scent of any more blood, I think I'm going to lose it. And, as I'm learning today, blood does have a scent. Sweet, spicy, and a bit metallic, all at the same time.

Slowly, the king walks forward, reaching the woman's fallen body and pulling his sword free with a sickening suction sound. He examines the blade and runs his fingers across it, as if pleased by the mixture of his peoples' blood coating its surface.

"Your turn," he says, zeroing in on me and Zoey. "Do either of you volunteer to go first?"

As I level my gaze with his, something stirs inside me.

The unmistakable pull of magic.

I will not let this man break me. And I certainly won't let him hurt my best friend.

I'm focusing on gathering my magic—on feeling it swirling deep inside of me—when Riven's voice cuts through the silence.

"Father," he says, as cold and detached as ever.

The king pauses and turns to his son, although his blade remains pointed in our direction. "What is it, Riven?" he asks, impatience dripping from his tone.

"A public execution would be over too quickly," Riven says, as if such an idea is juvenile and inconvenient. "Their deaths should be more than a passing spectacle. Especially if you want the Summer Court to tremble when they hear what you've done."

The king raises an eyebrow, intrigued, but clearly displeased, at being interrupted. "And what, exactly, are you suggesting?" he asks.

"A series of trials," Riven says, the cruelty in his eyes almost matching his father's. "Three trials, to be exact. Ones that will draw out the agony in a slow unraveling of their will, designed to break them piece by piece. This way, when they die, it won't be over in a flash of blood and steel. Instead, it will be an annihilation of their entire souls."

SAPPHIRE

MY STOMACH TURNS at Riven's proposal, an icy knot of fear tightening in my chest.

These are not the words of someone who cares about me.

They're the words of someone who's just as sadistic as his crazy father.

The king is silent for a long moment, his eyes gleaming with dark satisfaction. Then, finally, he sheaths his sword.

"Interesting," he muses, studying his son as if he's proud of him. "What types of trials, exactly, do you have in mind?"

"They will be taken to the wild, outer parts of our land," Riven begins, not missing a beat. "And they'll start with the Trial of the Frozen Lake."

My heart skips a beat, and I freeze, my breath catching in my throat.

I told Riven about the lake. I told him how Zoey and I nearly died when we were kids—how the ice cracked beneath her, how the freezing water swallowed her whole.

This isn't a coincidence.

Riven's using one of our worst memories against us.

He truly wants to break us.

Perhaps he's even crueler than his father.

"Deep beneath the ice, there will be a key." Riven's expression is cold, detached, as though he's discussing something as mundane as a change in the weather. "They'll need to retrieve it if they want to continue to the second trial."

The king's eyes spark with interest.

"Continue," he says, and Zoey's grip tightens on my hand.

"If they don't find the key, they will drown," Riven says calmly. "Frozen in the lake's depths forever. A fitting challenge for summer spies who think they can infiltrate our court."

The king smiles, the wicked gleam in his eyes growing brighter. "Yes, a frozen death beneath the lake," he says with a chuckle. "What a spectacle."

But I can't focus on the king.

All I see is Riven.

I thought... I don't know what I thought. That there was more to him? That he might care, after everything?

But this—this is the true Riven. The cold prince of ice. His father's son through and through. And I never should have entertained anything else.

"And the second trial?" the king asks.

Riven's cold gaze flickers, lingering on me for the briefest moment before he answers. "The second trial—if they make it that far—will test their resolve to continue," he says. "They'll cross the old bridge that spans across the ravine. Well—they'll *try* to cross. After all, those born from summer don't particularly thrive on icy surfaces, and the human won't stand much of a chance. I wonder if Sapphire will jump after her friend falls? Or if she'll have the heart and strength to continue? We could place bets on it—and on other parts of the trials—to make the stakes more personal."

"An excellent challenge, and a brilliant idea." The king laughs, the sound echoing through the throne room like shattering glass. "They'll see their deaths coming with each step."

"Precisely," Riven says. "Fear unlike any they've ever experienced."

I grit my teeth, a growing sense of dread swirling in my chest.

This isn't just a series of trials. It's a drawn-out execution designed to slowly break us—to watch us fall apart before this realm finishes us off.

"I'm intrigued." The king walks over to the dead knight's body and pokes it with his sword. He twists the blade, drawing more blood, then pulls it back out and refocuses on his son. "And the final trial?"

"A hunt through the forest." Riven steps forward, his cold expression unchanging. "With them, obviously, as the prey. They'll search for the silver tree that will take them back to the mortal realm, and I'll lead my knights as we track them through the forest. When we find them, they'll die. And—make no mistake—if by some slim chance they pass the first two trials and make it that far, we *will* find them. And we will give them a death worthy of your demonstration here today."

The room silences, the words hanging in the air like a noose tightening around my neck.

Zoey's nails dig into my skin.

She's the only thing grounding me to reality. Without her, I'm sure I would have broken long ago. Likely back in that tower.

Malice shines in Riven's eyes, as if he can't wait to kill me himself.

Then, he returns his focus to his father.

"I'll oversee the trials personally," he says. "You, of course, should remain in the palace. It's too dangerous for you to expose yourself to the wilds—especially with the monsters lurking at the borders."

"You're proposing I miss out on the fun of seeing the trespassers die?" The king's voice trembles, on the verge of rage, and he reaches for his sword.

This is it.

He's going to kill us.

We won't even have a chance to fight for our lives in these brutal trials.

"I understand your disappointment," Riven replies smoothly, which seems to placate the king a little bit. "But I must remind you that you don't have an animal familiar to guide you through the forests and the chaos beyond. Without one, it will be far too risky."

The king stiffens, and he reaches for the white fur cloak draped over his shoulders. His face darkens, but not with anger. No, this is something deeper. Something fragile and broken.

Something that gives him serious pause.

"And what will happen if the girls escape during these trials?" he finally says, and I release a slow breath of relief that he didn't say no.

"They won't escape." Riven offers a small, calculating smile, his cold eyes glinting with a dangerous confidence. "My knights will be with me at all times. And, most importantly, I'll have Ghost by my side."

Ghost purrs at the mention of his name, his tail curling behind Riven's legs.

"If you think a human and a summer fae could possibly escape me, my knights, and Ghost, then perhaps you doubt the strength of the Winter Court," Riven continues smoothly.

The nobles shift uncomfortably, stealing glances at the king, Riven, Ghost, me, and Zoey.

"I will ensure these trials unfold exactly as planned," Riven presses on. "And they will serve as a warning to anyone who dares cross us again."

The king's grip tightens on his cloak draped over his shoulders.

It isn't going to work. He's going to lash out again—unleash the fury he's barely keeping in check.

But then, slowly, his lips twist into a cold smile. "Very well," he says. "Let's not waste any more time. The trials will begin now."

Riven steps forward, cold calculation gleaming in his eyes. "Before we proceed, Father, we should make an official agreement," he says. "An oath that if they make it to the silver tree, they will not be hunted once they cross into their realm. We do want them to have the motivation to try, after all. It would be quite boring otherwise."

"Motivation?" The king's laughter echoes through the room, harsh and sharp. "They don't need motivation."

He scans the gathered fae, zooms toward one of the men, and drives his blade through his throat.

Blood spurts everywhere.

Zoey gasps, and I bite back a scream.

He hits the ground, and his gurgled cries silence, blood pooling beneath him.

The men and women of court silence, too, all of us watching as the king steps over the man's body.

"Here's the only deal I'm making," he snarls, and he's talking to me and Zoey now—not to Riven. "You either enter these trials, or you die right now."

I can't move, can't breathe. But despite feeling like the world is closing in around me, I force myself to stay calm.

There's no negotiating with this man.

He's too far gone. Too twisted by his own madness.

All we can do is play his game and hope to win.

"Sapphire," Zoey says my name, her eyes burning with fierce determination. She looks more alive than she has since we were locked in that tower. "We can do this."

"We can try," I reply, since unlike her, I can't lie.

The king sheaths his sword with a flourish, as if killing one of his own men was nothing more than a casual inconvenience. "So, you both agree," he says, although he doesn't wait for a response—he simply turns to the knights lining the walls instead. "Escort them to the lake, where they'll face their first trial."

"Father," Riven cuts in again, and all eyes return to him. "Look at them. They're weak. Pathetic. The trials are meant to be slow and painful. They're supposed to unravel the cores of who they are. If they're too weak to survive even ten minutes into the first trial, their suffering will be over too soon. Where's the satisfaction in that?"

The king freezes, his cruel smile faltering as he regards his son.

Riven only smirks back, as if they're engaging in a silent battle—one that will determine which one of them is crueler and more twisted.

Horror washes over me at the reminder that I've kissed those lips.

Twice.

And that I enjoyed it.

Finally, the king leans back and sheaths his sword. "You always did have a flair for strategy," he muses, almost to himself. "Escort them to the lake, where you and your men will set up camp for the night. Let them have a few hours there to rest and gather their strength. And then... remember every detail of their prolonged deaths so you can recount every moment of it to me upon your return."

SAPPHIRE

THE ICY WIND bites at my cheeks as Riven and his knights lead Zoey and me through the frozen woods.

It's almost peaceful out here—if you ignore the fact that we're being led to our deaths.

Riven won't look at me. He won't even acknowledge that I'm here.

As we trudge deeper into the forest, I spot a group of what I can only call fae-deer, their bodies sparkling with a soft glow that pulses like light through crystal. This place, for all its cruelty, is beautiful in a way that makes my heart ache for the life I was denied. The life I would have had if my true mother hadn't traded me for a human child after I was born.

Finally, after what feels like an eternity of walking through the cold, we reach the lake.

The vast expanse of ice glistens under the moonlight—a shimmering, deadly mirror—and memories claw to the surface of the day when Zoey nearly died. And, from the way her face pales as she also looks on at the lake, I know it's probably far worse for her.

Riven and his knights begin setting up camp at the edge of the lake, their movements quick and efficient. Ghost circles the camp, as if he's on the lookout for predators.

As if there are predators in these woods more dangerous than the fae.

Once the fire is lit, Riven strides toward where Zoey and I are sitting next to it to warm up, with two plates of food in his hands.

"Eat," he says, thrusting the plates into our laps.

Compared to the stale bread given to us in the tower, the bread, fruit, and cheese should be a luxurious feast.

Zoey immediately digs in.

My stomach growls, but I stare down at the food on the plate, not tempted in the slightest.

"Is this not good enough for your final meal?" Riven sneers at me.

I study him, the flames dancing in front of us somehow making the lines on his face even more deadly and beautiful, searching for a trace of warmth in this man made of ice.

I find none.

He leans forward, his voice low and tempting, his eyes trained only on me. "Do you want me to kiss you again, Sapphire?" he murmurs, soft enough so only I can hear. "Do you regret running from me the other night?"

I glance down at his lips, my heart racing faster.

But while my body still—annoyingly—wants him, there's something it *needs* even more.

"I need meat," I tell him. "The guards told me that fae don't eat it, but I need it. I won't be at my *full strength* if I don't have it."

Venom drips from my tone at those two words, and I pray that the reminder of his desire to strengthen me up so he can torture me as much as possible will make him want to help me.

His brow furrows, clearly caught off-guard by my request.

"What game are you playing, Summer Fae?" he asks. "What sort of sacrificial human ritual do you intend to perform?"

"No game, and no ritual," I tell him. "I'm just hungry."

"Then stop acting like a princess of nothing and eat." He motions to the unappetizing selection on my plate, watching me in challenge.

He's not going to help me.

I was an idiot for thinking he would.

All because he got close enough to tempt me with those stupidly perfect lips again.

I hate him. Completely and totally hate him.

"Fine." I stand up, taking my plate with me, enjoying the feeling of looking down on him. "Perhaps it'll look more appetizing when I'm not in the presence of such unappealing company."

With that, I storm into my tent and settle down on its hard, bumpy floor.

This stupid cheese and bread will never satisfy the gnawing *need* in my stomach for meat. If I were in a grocery store, I'd march to the refrigerator section, rip open a pre-packaged steak, and inhale it on the spot.

I've barely taken a bite of the cheese when Riven steps inside, his tall frame filling the small space.

"Leave me alone so I can enjoy my 'charcuterie board' in peace," I snap, glaring at him as the flap of the tent falls shut behind him.

"I thought you didn't like cheese?" he asks, surprisingly and strangely *playful.*

So much that it takes me off guard.

"What kind of psycho doesn't like cheese?" I reply.

"Likely a fae who asks for meat." He raises a hand, and the air shimmers and crystallizes, encircling the tent like a frozen wall.

We might as well be in an igloo.

My eyes dart around, my chest tightening, needing to escape.

"I'd ask if you came in here to kill me, but that would make your torture trial game a lot less fun for you." I cast my plate to the side and back away, wanting to put as much space between us as possible.

"I created the barrier to stop my men from overhearing," he says simply.

"From overhearing what?" I shoot back. "The sound of me rejecting your advances again?"

He doesn't flinch, but there's something behind his eyes—a pain that flashes for the briefest moment, then vanishes.

"I didn't come in here for that, although if you're offering, I won't say no." His eyes travel up and down my body in a way that I wish would make me shudder in disgust instead of desire. "I followed you in here because I have something for you."

My heart pounds, my breath quickening despite my resolve to stay in control. "I don't want anything from you."

"Not even this?" He reaches into his coat pocket and pulls something out, dangling it in front of me like a treat for a trained dog.

My bracelet.

I claw at it to take it back, but he's faster than me, pulling it away before I can snatch it back.

"You stole it from me," I say, and rage courses through me, the bracelet swinging in the wind that somehow made its way through the iced over tent.

"I didn't steal your bracelet from you," he says, so directly that it must be true. "I went back for it. To the silver tree, in the bushes where you said you lost it."

I startle, frozen, and not from the ice surrounding us.

"You want something from me in exchange for it," I say slowly, since after last night, I have a good idea what that *something* might be.

"I want you to trust me," he says simply. "To know I'm not as heartless as you believe."

"I don't *believe* you're heartless," I tell him. "I know it."

"You're an infant in this world," he reminds me. "You know nothing."

I flinch back, fuming at his arrogance.

"I might not know much about this magical, wintry world of yours," I tell him, holding his gaze, unwilling to back down. "But I work at a bar. People act like bartenders are invisible—like we're part of the furniture. They say things they think we won't catch, and they do things when they assume no one's watching. But I see everything, Riven. I hear every word, notice every glance. I know more about the way people move through the world than they'd ever know or guess."

"You think listening to drunkards confess their sins at a bar makes you some kind of expert on the fae?" He smirks, apparently unmoved by my little speech.

"I think I deserve more credit than you think."

"And I think that if I was heartless, I would have let my father kill you on the spot," he says. "I wouldn't have fetched your treasured little bracelet for you. And I certainly wouldn't have kept your secret about that trick you pulled to break into my quarters."

"What are you trying to say?" I ask, on guard for any word trickery he might be trying to use on me. "That you created these twisted trials to keep me alive?"

"Yes." He nods, as if I'm finally getting somewhere. "I created these trials to keep you alive."

"Oh," I say, since given that he can't lie, he's telling the truth.

Which means it's time to switch gears. "So, tell me, Winter Prince. Why *are* you trying to keep me alive?"

SAPPHIRE

RIVEN'S EYES DARKEN, the playful smirk fading into something far more serious.

"I need you alive because you're useful to me," he says simply.

"You mean my *magic* is useful to you," I tell him. "Not me."

"You and your magic are one and the same. I want your magic, so therefore, I want you."

His eyes burn in a way that reminds me he wants far more from me than that, and my pulse quickens, betraying the anger I'm trying to hold onto.

"You're blackmailing me," I realize.

"You say it like it's a bad thing." He steps closer, his breath chilling the air between us. "There's power in being useful, Sapphire. Power you've barely begun to understand. And I think you're smart enough to know when survival means playing along."

He dangles the bracelet between us, and it moves back and forth like a pendulum, as if he's trying to hypnotize me with it to make me believe he's on my side.

"How far along are you asking me to play?" I ask, memories of last night flashing through my mind. Of the way he kissed me and backed me up to the bed as he offered his help, and how much a part of me wanted to give in.

The same part of me that wants to give in right now.

"I suppose that depends on how far you're willing to go." His eyes flare with that dangerous heat, studying me as if he can read every wicked thought running through my mind.

Every nerve in my body is alive. The air in the tent buzzes with tension, the magnetic pull that's existed between us since the moment we locked eyes at that bar as strong as ever.

I hate how my body responds to him. How his proximity sends fire racing through my veins.

Mostly, I hate that I want him, despite knowing I shouldn't.

"You're sick." I take another step back, the cold wall of the tent pressing into me, trapping me.

"Maybe." He plays with my bracelet, toying with it, just like he's trying to toy with me. "But you enjoy it. You wouldn't still be in here with me if you didn't. You'd use your little teleporting trick and disappear, like you did in my quarters."

"Don't flatter yourself. I'm still here because I'd never leave Zoey alone with you and your knights," I say, leaving out the fact that if I projected myself outside this tent, my body would remain in here, helpless to whatever this cold, heartless prince wanted to do to it.

The thought makes me shudder all the way to my bones.

If he doesn't know about that little vulnerability of mine, then I'm keeping it from him. At least for now, given that it's not *useful* to me for him to know.

"I rather enjoy flattering myself," he says proudly. "And I'd like to take this moment to remind you that your human friend is also still alive because of me."

"Because you want to use her to blackmail me into doing what you want, too," I say, having no doubt that it's true.

"Now you're getting the hang of how things work around here." He smiles in satisfaction, and I clench my fists, wanting to claw his stupidly seductive silver eyes out. "Now—let's move on to the important stuff. Because if you go into this thinking you'll die, you won't give yourself a fair shot at living. I've seen it too many times. It's not your lack of training that will kill you—it's your mind. And from what I've seen of your mind during our... stimulating moments together, it's very, very easy to distract."

I narrow my eyes, fighting the heat rushing through my body at his words. "I'm not letting this *stimulating* moment distract me now, am I?" I challenge.

"You absolutely are." He takes another step forward, closing the distance between us with a predator's grace. "You're trying so hard to resist, but we both know you can't deny what's simmering beneath the surface. Neither of us can."

Rage burns inside me so much that I swear the ice wall around us is starting to melt.

His arrogance is *unbearable.*

"What's fun is watching you think you've got me all figured out," I tell him, trying to ignore the way my heart flutters at his implication that he can't deny the insane pull between us, either. "But you don't. And that's going to cost you later. I swear it."

I'm barely finished speaking when his hand snakes around my waist, pulling me flush against him. "One kiss," he murmurs, as if he didn't even hear my threat. "To remind me why I'm working so hard to keep you alive."

His scent—winter and something darker, more intoxicating—clouds my senses. Temptation crashes over me, overwhelming me with the need to lean in and let the pull between us ignite into flames so hot that they'll melt down the entire tent.

But I spent the last few years of my life being controlled by Matt. And I'm sure as hell not going to let this seductive winter prince control me now.

"No," I say, and I shove against his chest with more force than I thought possible, making him stumble back.

The surprise in his eyes is quickly replaced by that smoldering arrogance I've come to hate, but there's something else there now. Something darker. Sharper. More threatening.

"You play a dangerous game," he warns.

"I'm not playing at anything." My pulse hammers in my throat, but I stand firm, my feet planted, my gaze hard. "You want me alive because I'm useful. Fine. But I *won't* let you control me in the interim."

Before he can blink, I snatch the bracelet from his hand and clench my fist around it, holding onto the last piece of who I was before the start of the new year, as if it has the power to keep me alive.

The approval in his eyes makes my anger flare even more.

"This isn't about control. It's about survival," he says. "And like it or not, I'm the only one who can ensure yours. So, it might benefit you to show some gratitude."

"I'm not giving you the sort of *gratitude* you've made it clear you want. And I'm definitely not thanking you," I tell him.

That would imply that I owe him a favor. *Any* favor, of his choosing.

And that's *so* not going to happen.

"Smart girl." His smirk returns, this time softer, almost amused. "But you're forgetting that you're one of us, Summer Fae. If you plan to survive around here, you need to stop resisting the game. And if you want to win it, then you have to wrap that fascinating mind of yours around who's on your side and who's not."

Does everything he says have to be laced with so much *seduction?* As if every single word out of his mouth is crafted to make me his?

As if he's casting some sort of spell over my heart?

"We both know it's not my mind you're fascinated with." I straighten my shoulders, refusing to let him see how much he's affecting me.

"Yes—we do both know that," he says, his eyes traveling up and down my body in a way that makes my head spin. "But your mind is what will keep you alive. Your magic is what will keep me on your side. The rest... that's just an enjoyable distraction."

I glare up at him, the wind rushing across the outside of the tent so strongly that I can hear it whistling through its icy interior barrier.

"It's a distraction you'll only enjoy in your fantasies," I tell him. "Because you apparently need me for far more than you're telling me. Like you said—you'd have let your father kill me back there if you didn't. Which means you're not the one in control here. *I* am. And I owe you nothing."

He watches me for a beat. Then with a sharp flick of his hand, the ice around us melts into nothing.

"You have no idea what it takes to survive here," he says. "But remember—the only reason you and your human companion are still breathing right now is because I allowed it. Convince yourself otherwise, and it *will* get you killed."

He hesitates for a moment, as if he wants to say more.

But he doesn't.

Instead, he steps out into the night, letting the tent's flap fall shut behind him and leaving me alone with the measly plate of food that's going to do absolutely nothing to give me the energy I'll need to survive the trials tomorrow.

SAPPHIRE

"Come on," Zoey says. "You're practically radiating hunger. Just... project yourself, hunt, and eat. I'll be fine here."

She's been repeating the same thing for the past two hours we've been huddling close for warmth in this freezing cold tent. It's apparently designed to keep us somewhat warm, but there's no such thing as *warm* in the Winter Court. And this time, we don't have Riven's coat to share as a blanket.

I close my eyes and press my hands to my stomach, which growls like a feral beast.

"I'm not leaving you here," I tell her, keeping my voice quiet so the knights outside won't overhear. "Plus, the animals in that forest aren't normal. Who knows what'll happen if I eat one? I could end up worse than I am now."

"If you don't get some meat in you, you won't make it through tomorrow's trial," she says. "I'm not about to lose you to an empty stomach when there's a forest full of food out there."

"Thanks for the vote of confidence," I mutter.

"I absolutely have confidence." She smiles, somehow managing to warm the tent with her positivity. "Confidence that I'll be fine if you project yourself out of here for a bit. The knights haven't checked on us since we came in here. No one's going to see you leave, since you won't have to technically leave the tent at all. And if the knights *do* decide to check on us, your body will still be in here. It'll just look like you're sleeping."

"And if they try waking me up?"

"You're a heavy sleeper?" She shrugs, smiling again. "They're more likely to believe that than that you projected a magical ghostly version of yourself into the forest to hunt down a deer."

"But *he* knows about my magic," I say, not needing to elaborate for her to know who I'm talking about.

"Riven's obsessed with you," she waves it off. "And he doesn't want you to die. I wouldn't be surprised if he's not in that forest hunting down some meat for you as we speak."

She glances at the bracelet, which will now forever remind me about how Riven went out of his way to find it and bring it back to me.

"But we can't count on him doing that," she continues. "Which is why you need to do it yourself."

She's right. I might not survive tomorrow if I'm this weak, Riven's help or not.

"It'll just be an hour. Maybe less." She props herself up, determination etched across her face. "You hunt, eat, and come back. I'll protect your body while you're gone."

I shudder, since I hate thinking about how vulnerable my body is when I project myself. I can't even feel if something happens to it. Zoey and I tested it back in the tower.

"How am I supposed to hunt?" I ask her, pushing the thought of how dead my body looks while I'm projecting myself aside. "The most hunting I've ever done is through the frozen section in the grocery store."

Zoey chuckles at that, and I can't help but join her.

"You can find something in the woods to use as a weapon," she suggests. "A tree branch, or a sharp rock. Or—and this is probably the best idea—an icicle. Just latch onto it with your magic and shoot it at your target."

"You make it sound so easy," I say, which doesn't surprise me, since basically everything Zoey does comes naturally to her. She'd already be the best magic user in the fae realm if she was the changeling and not me.

"You *have* to try," she insists again, and then she frowns, a troubled look crossing her eyes. "I won't be able to get through these trials without you. I need you to be at your best."

"You're smart, determined, and resilient," I tell her, not liking to hear this side of her with so much doubt in herself.

Zoey's never doubted herself in her life.

"I am," she agrees. "But I don't have magic. No amount of brains or strength will ever make up for the weakness of only being human around here."

I wish I could say she's wrong.

But I can't.

"Hunting isn't as complicated as you think," she continues, apparently done with discussing her humanity. "You just need to take your shot. Don't overthink it."

"The last time I held anything remotely like a weapon was a kitchen knife to slice limes for a margarita," I say, pressing my hands to my stomach as another wave of hunger gnaws at me.

She huffs, waving me off. "Look, I'm not asking you to do anything fancy. When my dad takes me hunting, we use guns, and the principle's the same. You spot your target, you keep steady, and you aim for the kill. It's about control. You can do that with your magic just as easily as I can with a rifle. Just don't put so much pressure on yourself."

"You're seriously comparing fae magic to hunting with your dad?" I ask.

"Totally," she says, and then she rattles off a bunch more hunting advice, as unwilling to give up on this as she's been with any hobby she's ever pursued.

"Fine," I give in. "But if anything happens—anything at all—you scream, okay?"

"I'll scream bloody murder if I have to." Her eyes light up, and she nods enthusiastically. "Now go, before you pass out and I have to carry your hangry ass through the trials tomorrow. And bring some sharp rocks back with you. It can't hurt to have a stash of mini projectile weapons in our pockets."

"Deal," I say, and I quietly move in the tent to peek through a small gap, barely daring to breathe as I scan the area.

Riven sits beneath a nearby tree, his eyes closed, his head tilted back as he rests. Somehow, he manages to look alert even when he's sleeping.

Ghost is curled beside him, breathing in slow, steady rhythms.

The four knights are stationed in various places around the perimeter. Two of them are resting, and the other two are alert.

Now's the tricky part. Because I can only project to a place I can see. And the place I choose obviously can't be one that will catch the knights' attention.

It'll have to be as far away as possible. But there's only so much I can see through the slit in the tent.

Then, I see it. A shimmer of golden light, beaming from the sky like a message from the stars, illuminating a tree far in the distance.

The tree has a thick branch sticking out of it—one I can surely balance myself on.

That's my target. A sign. It has to be.

So, I focus on the branch, call on my magic, and materialize on it.

From up here, the forest spreads out before me like a sea of trees and ice. The camp is barely there in the distance, and I'm far enough away that the knights probably assumed the noise was from an animal.

I have to hurry out of their line of sight.

Quickly, I eye the branches spanning before me. There are lots of other thick ones. Definitely thick enough to hold my weight. And none of them have leaves, so there's not much for me to get stuck on.

Worst comes to worse, I'll snap back into my body and no one will have any reason to think I came out here at all.

But sitting around up here isn't doing me any favors. I have to move.

So, I take a deep breath and look up at the stars.

As if they're answering my call, my skin tingles, buzzing with magic, filling me with what feels like the soft glow of night.

Time to go.

Just like when I ran along the branch at Riven's window, I hurry across it now, pushing myself off the end and landing on the nearest branch with a surprising amount of precision. My body feels so incredibly light. It's like gravity doesn't exist—as if the air is guiding my movements—and I barely feel the cold thanks to the thrill of it all.

Keeping momentum, I jump to another branch, and another, and another.

Eventually, I spot my target.

A deer-like creature up ahead, like the one I saw while we were walking with the knights earlier. Its silvery fur glistens under the starlight, and its antlers are sharp enough to serve as weapons.

Perfect.

I don't move. A single wrong step could alert it that I'm here, and there's no way of knowing when I'll find another deer.

Remembering Zoey's advice, I spot a large icicle hanging from the branch of the tree I'm in, just thick enough to make a good weapon.

With as much focus as possible on being as quiet as I can, I crawl toward the icicle. And, by some miracle, I can't even hear myself moving. It's like there's a thin cushion of air around me, protecting me from hitting anything on the tree that might cause any noise.

Before long, I'm at the icicle, reaching for it and closing my hand around its base.

Thanks to my body heat, the ice starts to melt where my skin is touching it. Which means it's now liquid water—the type of water I can control with my summer fae magic.

But it's going to take too long to wait for my body heat to melt the entire top off this thing.

Heat up, I think to the water touching my skin, focusing as hard as possible on the warmth building in my palm.

It does.

The moment the icicle's free, I inch back into a crouch and grip it tightly, feeling the solid weight of it in my hand.

The deer remains unaware of me, grazing on the frost-covered ground.

But the icicle will only remain a weapon for as long as it's frozen. Which means I have no time to waste.

Zoey's advice flashes through my mind.

Steady hands, quick aim. It's not about strength—it's about control.

I slow my breathing, imagining the air around me guiding the icicle's path with precision, just like it helped me jump through the treetops.

I raise my arm, take aim just behind its shoulder where its heart should be, and release.

The icicle flies from my hand, slicing through the air with a silent, deadly grace.

It hits.

The deer staggers, its silvery fur stained red as it crumples into the snow.

And, thanks to a magical miracle that I somehow pulled from the stars—along with Zoey's advice—dinner is now served.

SAPPHIRE

THE NEXT MORNING comes too quickly.

I wake up to the rustling of fabric, sitting up as the flap of the tent opens.

Riven.

There's no smirk this time. No trace of the predator he usually is. Instead, there's a deadly calmness to him as he steps inside, closes the flap behind him, and uses his magic to create an ice barrier along its fabric that will stop his knights from listening in on whatever he came in here to tell us.

Zoey stirs beside me, sees Riven, and shoots upright.

"What do you want?" I ask him, not in the mood for games.

"You look well," he says to me in approval. "The meal I provided for you last night seems to have satiated you more than you claimed it would."

"I was definitely satiated last night." I keep my gaze locked on his, unwilling to let him get to me. "But it wasn't from anything provided by you."

"I'm sure that whatever satisfied you last night was a poor substitute for what I could have provided." His eyes flash with amusement, that conceited smirk appearing on his face once again.

"Doubtful," I shoot right back. "I prefer my men without a side of arrogance and blackmail."

This only succeeds in making him take another step toward me, challenging me, trying to back me into a corner.

I don't let him—even though it means there's less than a foot between us now.

"You wound me, Summer Fae," he says smoothly, his voice dripping with that practiced charm of his. But there's also a darkness behind it—a dangerous edge warning me not to go too far. "But let's not pretend you're not enjoying our little games."

"Games imply there's a chance you can win," I reply, even though the tension buzzing between us is so hot that it could melt the wall of ice he created around the tent.

"I'll win when I choose to win," he says confidently. "For now, I'm enjoying watching you squirm."

Then, Zoey huffs, drawing our attention to her.

"Can we skip the foreplay and get to the part where you tell us why you're here?" she snaps at Riven, surprising him so much that he steps away from me.

He must not have been expecting a human to be so outspoken.

Which means he has a *lot* to learn about Zoey.

Keeping his focus on her, he pulls something from his coat's inner pocket and holds it out. "The trials begin within the next hour, and you need to be prepared," he says. "This is for you."

A small, light gold amulet with glowing runes etched into its surface.

"It's an amulet of warmth," he explains. "It won't make you invincible to the cold, but it will help. You'll be able to endure the conditions of the far ends of the Winter Court for longer than a human could survive otherwise."

Zoey stares at it, although she doesn't take it. "So, you meant it when you said you wanted to help us?" she asks him, shooting me a clear *I told you so* look before refocusing on him.

She frustratingly doesn't hate him as much as I do.

But it's only because he hasn't tried to trick her, seduce her, and use her.

At least, not yet.

"I want you to survive," he tells her. "Simply because as long as you're alive, I can use you to get Sapphire to do what I want."

Now it's my turn to shoot Zoey an *I told you so* look.

"Take it," I tell her, since as much as I hate it, the amulet could end up being the only thing that'll stop her from freezing to death. She's already too pale, and we haven't even started the trials yet.

She gives me a small nod, then reaches for the amulet and slips the chain over her head.

"Hide it under your shirt," Riven tells her. "If my knights see it, all bets will be off. But as a warning, it won't last forever. Think of it like a charged phone battery. Eventually, it'll run out of juice."

In this magical kingdom of his, it's strange to hear him talk about something as human as a phone. But it's also a reminder that he's been to my world. He knows where I'm trying to get back to. It's like he's the string tying his world and mine together, and as much as I hate it, he does feel a bit like a lifeline.

Zoey tucks the stone under her shirt, and Riven turns to me, pulling something else from his pocket. A small, smooth, silver stone, with lines running through it like cracks in ice.

"For you," he says simply. "It's called a whisper stone. It allows you to communicate with me during the trials. Just speak into it—preferably at a whisper, so no one else can hear—and you'll be able to reach me."

"So, this is the fae version of giving me your number?" I can't help but joke, despite the seriousness of the situation.

"Think of it more as a lifeline," he says, twirling the whisper stone between his fingers. "Though, knowing you, you'll probably only use it when you're desperate."

I don't want to take the stone. It feels too much like another way for him to control me. But the practical side of me—the part that wants to survive—knows I'll need every advantage I can get. Even if it comes from him.

With a sigh, I snatch the stone from his hand, the cool surface oddly soothing in my palm. "Fine," I say, shoving it into my pocket. "But don't hold your breath waiting for a call."

"I never wait." He chuckles softly, stepping back with that infuriating confidence of his. "I just prepare for when you come to your senses."

"I suppose being fae means you have an eternity to waste," I tell him, even though the whisper stone does have the potential to be useful.

Assuming he'll use it to guide us instead of to trick us into a painful death.

"Assuming you survive the trials, you have an eternity now, too," he says—a sharp reminder of the fact that I haven't thought much about what my life will look like after getting out of the Winter Court. "Plenty of time for you to stop fighting the inevitable."

Zoey crosses her arms, frowning as she watches us.

Unfortunately, before I can think of something snarky to throw back at Riven, he steps aside and gestures for us to follow. "Now, if you're done stalling, it's time for your first trial," he says, and the icy wall around the tent melts, allowing the three of us to exit.

Zoey and I exchange a look, then step out of the tent.

The lake shimmers under the early morning light, its surface reflecting the sky like a perfect, deadly mirror.

It reminds me so much of the lake Zoey fell into when we were kids that I can practically see the two of us as children in the center of it, me reaching for her beneath the surface to save her from a frozen, watery death.

As I'm staring out at it, one of the knights approaches us.

"All is well, Your Highness?" he asks Riven.

"Better than expected," he says with a low chuckle. "Breaking their spirits before the trials is half the fun. Now, let's see how much more they can bend before they snap."

He and his knights make their way to the edge of the lake, and we follow, knowing we don't have much else of a choice.

Zoey walks unnervingly slowly—timidly—beside me.

She hasn't stepped foot in a body of water since falling through the ice that day. Not even to go into a pool. Or a hot tub. Or even a bath.

I reach for her hand, squeezing it, trying to give her strength.

She doesn't acknowledge me. The only thing she's focused on is the lake, its icy surface unnaturally smooth. Like it's something out of a dream—or a nightmare.

Once we're at the edge of the lake, Riven turns to one of his knights—the tallest one with blond hair, who seems to be higher ranked than the rest of them.

"Time to give them their weapons," he says.

"Really?" Zoey asks. "You're going through all this trouble to put us through these death trials, and you're giving us weapons?"

"Your deaths will come too quickly otherwise," he says simply. "Given that we came all the way out here, we should at least be able to watch you suffer."

I want to ask if that's why he gave us the amulet and whisper stone—to get more of a kick out of what we're about to go through. But I know better than to reveal that information to the knights.

Riven nods to the blond-haired knight, who reaches into his weapons belt and pulls out two daggers. There's nothing ornate or magical about them. They're weapons, but I have a gut feeling they're not enchanted ones. Just cold, hard steel.

He hands one to Zoey first.

She takes it, testing the weight in her hand, turning it over as if she's handled one before.

"You're looking at that thing like you know how to use it," I tell her.

"Dad taught me a little when I helped him whittle wood." She grips the handle tighter, her eyes focusing with just as much seriousness as they did on the day in gym class when she was preparing to attempt a complicated back handspring twist dismount off the balance beam.

She succeeded, of course. She always does.

Zoey's still studying her dagger when the knight steps forward and offers me mine.

I've never held a weapon before—minus the icicle I used to kill that deer—so its weight is unfamiliar. Heavy in a way that makes my arm feel awkward. And I'm not a natural at gripping it like Zoey apparently is.

Standing there, staring down at the blade, the reality of what we're about to face sinks in. I have no idea what kind of trial we'll be up against, but one thing's clear—I'm out of my depth.

And I haven't even jumped into the lake.

SAPPHIRE

RIVEN, with Ghost by his side, leads the way to the center of the lake.

As we approach, something beneath the ice starts to glow. It's a pale blue, eerie glow—like a warning from another world.

"That glow is the key buried beneath the ice," he tells us. "Your task is to retrieve it."

"This is insane." Zoey's eyes are wild, and she's shaking with fear. "We can't—"

"You will," he interrupts her, turning back to his knights. "Surround the lake. Be ready in case they try to leave prematurely. And be aware of potential threats. We never know what might be lurking in these parts."

The knights obey, fanning out in a tight circle around the lake's perimeter, their swords drawn and gleaming in the morning light. Riven and Ghost fill in the final empty spot, their eyes trained on us.

Go, their expressions seem to say. *Before you freeze to death.*

Zoey's staring hollowly at the ice.

"We need to think this through," I tell her, knowing I'm going to have to be the voice of reason through this task, given her water aversion.

"Think it through?" Her eyes snap to mine, wild with panic. "I can't go in there. I haven't been in water since... you know when. I don't even think I can swim anymore. I'll drown."

"You won't have to." I squeeze her arm gently, trying to reassure her. "I'll be the one to go in."

"No." She shakes her head, her lips pressed into a thin line. "It's too dangerous. How am I supposed to help if you're drowning?"

"I have water magic," I remind her with a small smile. "I'll be fine."

"You've known about your magic for a *week*," she says. "You were so bad at using it that you almost drowned us in my bathroom."

I smile at the memory of us in her bathroom, soaked because the shower water sprayed everywhere.

That moment—and our entire lives in the mortal realm in general —feels like a lifetime ago.

"I think my magic's getting stronger," I tell her, and a buzz of energy rushes through me, as if it's supporting my thought. "Ever since I got here, it's like the magic of this world is sinking into my bones, helping me harness the power that's always lived inside me."

She frowns, apparently unconvinced, then looks back down at the glowing spot beneath the ice.

"Maybe you can project yourself beneath the surface," she says. "Since Riven's sword didn't touch you when he tried to kill you, it's possible that you can't die in your projected form at all. So, even if something happens to you down there, you'll be okay."

"And then we'll have to answer to the knights when they ask how we got the key while I was unconscious and you stayed up here with me," I say softly, not wanting them to overhear. "I can't give my secret away. Not yet."

She glances down at the glowing ice again, studying it, as if she can figure out a solution that doesn't involve me jumping in there.

As she does, Riven calls over from the shore, calm and mocking. "If you're going to take a swim, I suggest you do it soon," he says, leaning against Ghost, as if this is an entertaining show. "The water's not getting any warmer."

"If I freeze, I swear I'll haunt you for the rest of your immortal life," I call back, which seems to quiet him down—for now.

Satisfied, I turn back to Zoey.

"So, where were we?" I ask.

She examines her dagger, studying the blade. "I highly doubt these are sharp enough to cut through the ice. Unless they're enchanted."

"They're definitely not enchanted," I reply.

"How do you know?"

"I can sense it," I try to explain. "There's no magic in them. It's like they're dead or something."

She raises an eyebrow, no longer focused on her dagger. "So, you have a sixth sense now for magic now?"

"Apparently so," I say, and even though I doubt it'll work, I raise my dagger and ram the tip of it into the ice.

It barely leaves a mark.

Zoey does the same, with the same result.

"I don't care if that worked or not," she says with a smirk that rivals Riven's. "That felt good."

Despite the situation, it feels good to see Zoey smile.

"It definitely felt good," I agree. "But I melted that icicle in the trees. I can probably do something similar now."

"It's either that or chipping away at this ice until we freeze to death," she says. "And I'd rather not turn into a popsicle today."

"That makes two of us." I take a deep breath and focus on the ice beneath us, where the key's glow is pulsing like a heartbeat under the frozen surface. "Stand back. *Way* back. If I end up melting too much of the ice, well… I don't want you to be anywhere near it."

Fear dances in her eyes, and she puts almost fifteen feet between herself and where I'm standing.

Satisfied that she's far enough away, I kneel and place my hand on the ice—on the place where it's glowing the most. Eventually, it starts to melt under the warmth of my skin, creating a layer of water.

Now I need it to heat up faster. Otherwise, this will take forever.

With the icicle I used to hunt the deer, I heated up the water with my palm to speed up the process. I don't exactly know how I did it, but it involved tapping into the warmth I feel while using my magic and expanding it out to the water.

Heat up, I think, pulling on the magic buzzing inside me and pushing it out through my palm.

Slowly, the frozen barrier melts, turning into a small hole with glowing water splashing inside of it.

As it expands outward, I keep my hand on the ice and back away, continuing to heat it up until the hole is large enough for me to jump through it.

Some of the water splashes up at me.

It's freezing. So freezing that it makes me lose hold of my magic.

I glance over my shoulder at Riven. His smirk is gone, replaced by something that looks more like intrigue. Ghost sits calmly next to him, his tail circling Riven's legs, as if he's trying to stop him from doing something stupid.

Although, despite all the highly descriptive words I could use to describe Riven, *stupid* isn't one of them.

But it *would* be stupid to sit here staring at the winter prince instead of jumping into this icy hellhole before it has a chance to freeze over again.

I take a moment to glance back at Zoey. *She's* the last person I want to see before I do this—not Riven.

She's fidgeting with her dagger's hilt, as if readying herself to fight all the knights at once if it comes down to it.

"Saph, please—be careful," she says, and I don't like the way she's looking at me—as if she thinks these might be my final minutes alive.

"I will," I promise, even though being careful won't guarantee I'll survive this.

Heart racing, I stare back down at the hole, hoping and failing to see the key now that the water isn't covered by a layer of ice.

I see the glow, but all around it, it's dark. Really, really dark.

But I can't afford to hesitate. If I do, I'll freeze—literally and figuratively.

So, I take a deep breath, clench my fists, and *jump.*

The cold slams into me like a steel wall.

It's worse than I expected. So much worse.

Every muscle seizes up. My skin is burning, my nerves screaming as the cold sinks into my bones.

I sink fast, panic clawing at my chest as I struggle to swim. I've always been a good swimmer, but as I kick, it's like swimming through quicksand. I'm being dragged deeper and deeper into the lake's icy depths, far faster than I can handle.

The rocks, I realize.

I still have the rocks in my pocket. The sharp ones I stole from the forest last night to use as weapons in the trials.

I have to get rid of them.

Still sinking, I fumble around for them, my fingers numb and uncooperative from the cold. It takes everything I have to pull them out and let them sink to the bottom of the lake—wherever that is.

My lungs scream for air. Every instinct urges me to suck in a deep breath, even though there's nothing for me to breathe in other than freezing cold water that will cause sudden death.

How ironic would that be? Someone with water magic dying by *drowning*.

I can't do it. I can't reach the key. I still can't even *see* the key. And even if I could, I doubt I'd be able to swim back up in time.

No—I *know* I wouldn't be able to swim back up in time.

Which means I have to turn around.

The water presses in on me, suffocating and relentless, as I claw my way up.

Finally, just when I think I'm not going to make it, my head breaks through the surface, and I gasp, choking on the freezing air as my arms flail for the edge to escape this watery hellhole and figure out what to do next.

SAPPHIRE

"Sapphire!" Zoey is beside me in an instant, grabbing my arm and pulling back onto the ice. "Are you okay? Do you have the key?"

I can't stop shaking, the cold burrowed so deep that it feels like it's part of my bones now.

"No," I choke out. "To both questions."

"It's okay." She pulls me close to stop my shivering, although I can tell by the way her voice wavers that she doesn't actually believe it's going to be okay. "We'll figure this out."

"The lake's too deep," I explain, pulling away to look at her. "I can't hold my breath long enough to get to the key. I couldn't even *see* the key."

Riven's voice floats across the lake, calm and mocking. "Having trouble, Summer Fae?" he asks. "I figured you'd be a natural-born fish."

"Go to Hell, Riven," I snap, glaring at him. "You wouldn't last a second in the heat."

"I'd survive better in the flames than you are in the water," he replies without missing a beat. "Even though I don't have a lick of fire magic."

"Ignore him," Zoey says, and I swear she's shivering more than I am, even though I was just swimming in freezing water. "Maybe there's another way. Like... maybe you can put your hand into the water and try calling the key toward you?"

"Maybe."

Unable to think of a better option, I reach into the watery hole, put my hand in it, and "call" for the key.

It doesn't work.

"Why don't you just drown already?" Riven calls out again. "It'd be quicker. And easier."

I reach into my pocket for the one stone I didn't empty from it while swimming—the whisper stone—ready to hurl it at his face.

Shut up and let me help you, his voice whispers in my mind.

I freeze, startled, and look over to him.

Ready? he says again in my head.

His lips barely move, but they move *enough* that I can tell he's speaking—well, whispering—what he's saying through the stone.

Then, with one hand in his pocket, he walks over to one of his knights, Ghost staying by his side.

"What?" Zoey asks me.

I put the stone back in my pocket and keep my fingers wrapped around it, like I'm pretty sure Riven's are right now.

I lean closer to Zoey to make it look like we're brainstorming what to do next in the trial.

"When I touched the whisper stone, Riven talked to me through it," I tell her, lowering my voice to make sure the knights can't hear. "He said, 'shut up and let me help you.'"

"So, let him help you," she says, sitting back and waiting.

"How's he supposed to help me?" I ask her. "He's right next to that knight."

"Maybe he has some type of plan," she insists. "Give him a chance. He's all we've got right now."

I huff, knowing she's right, and look back to Riven.

He's watching me so closely that it's like he's trying to burn a hole through my forehead with his eyes.

"I'm ready," I say through the stone, looking to Zoey as I do, who gives me a single nod of approval.

This is so pathetically entertaining, Riven says to his knight, in a conversational enough tone that if he wasn't holding onto the stone, I wouldn't be able to hear him from this far out in the lake. *She's so new to her magic that she has no idea she can just inhale the water and breathe like a fish.*

There's a pause.

From what I can see, the knight is saying something back. But I can only hear Riven—not the knight.

You never mastered filtering oxygen out of water? Riven says, and there's another pause as the knight replies, before Riven continues. *I suppose that makes sense. It's an advanced skill for winter fae, since ice is our specialty. But since summer fae are most naturally in tune with water magic, I figured breathing underwater would be far easier for her than it is for us.*

Zoey's watching me eagerly. I can tell she wants to ask what's going on, but she also knows not to distract me from what I'm hearing.

"He's saying I can inhale water and breathe like a fish," I share with her—quietly, of course. "That there's oxygen in the water and I can filter it out."

"So, there's your answer," she says. "You don't have to hold your breath down there. You can just... breathe. In the water."

I glance back down at the hole, which is slowly getting smaller as the water re-freezes.

My chest tightens at the thought of going back in there again.

Riven and the knight are now talking about how terrible the frost wine was from last year's harvest, which I have a feeling means the help he was giving me is over.

Which means I either go back in there, or I admit defeat even though we've barely gotten started.

"Okay," I decide. "I'll try again."

"You'll be okay," Zoey says, and I'm not sure if she's trying to make me believe it, or herself. "I'm sorry I can't help. Even if I was good at swimming, I'm just a human. I don't have water magic. I don't..." She pauses, looking around at the glistening forest with a strange sort of longing in her eyes. "I don't belong in this realm."

"Which is why you're not staying here," I say, more determined than ever at the reminder of how vulnerable Zoey is in this place. "Neither am I. We're going to get home. And if that means jumping into that lake again... then I guess I'll be jumping into that lake again."

With that, I pull away from her, kneel by the hole, and put my hand on the ice.

Heat up, I think, and I push my magic through my hands, heating the ice and widening the opening once more. It's easier this time than last. I suppose I'm getting the hang of it.

Then, I jump.

The freezing water slams into me again, stealing the breath from my lungs. My body locks up.

I should fight. Get back up to the surface before I drown.

What Riven told me to do is crazy. Breathing in water isn't natural. It'll kill me.

Except… I'm not natural. I'm not human. I'm *super*natural. And I have water magic.

Water can't kill me. I won't let it.

So, I don't kick for the surface.

Instead, I open my mouth and let the lake rush in.

It hits my throat, my chest, and my lungs, filling them with freezing, suffocating water. It's colder than anything I've ever felt in my life. Every nerve is on fire, my muscles locking as I thrash around, trying to fight it as the water crushes me from the inside out.

Black spots dance in my vision. I try to scream, but all that comes out is bubbles, rising in slow motion toward the surface.

Riven tricked me. I'm going to die at the bottom of this lake.

I doubt the fae will keep Zoey alive for long after I'm gone.

And it's all *his* fault.

I reach for the whisper stone, wanting to curse him with my final dying breaths, even though I can't speak underwater.

His voice comes through again, low and conversational, clearly still having a casual chat with his knight.

My mother's the one who taught me how to do this, he says. *I was barely old enough to use my magic properly. She brought me to the edge of the Glacial River. You know the place? The water there runs so cold it's said to freeze even the heart of a winter fae if they stay in it for too long.*

My lungs scream, my body fighting the water as I try clawing my way back to the surface.

When I first breathed in the water, I panicked. I thought I was going to die, Riven's voice continues in my mind.

Something about the way he's talking—so calm, so unguarded— makes me pause.

He's holding onto the whisper stone as he speaks.

Which means he wants me to hear this story.

Technically, he's talking to his knight, but because of the stone, he's also talking to *me*.

She told me I wasn't breathing right. That the water doesn't move like air, he continues to recount the memory.

Another pause as the knight assumedly replies.

That was the big thing that made it click for me, Riven says. *She told me it wasn't about pulling the water into my lungs. You can't treat it like air. It's heavier, more resistant. You can't force it. You have to let it flow.*

He's not just telling a story.

He's coaching me.

I try to focus, even as the pain in my chest sharpens, threatening to make my lungs explode from the pressure.

The hardest part wasn't learning to breathe, he continues. *It was trusting that the water wouldn't kill me. My mother said, "You're fae. Ice and water are your allies. The more you resist, the more they'll fight back. But if you let them in, they'll help you."*

I want to scream.

Instead, I stop fighting and let the water fill me. Not as an enemy, but as something that can help. And, as I do, I allow my mind to relax into Riven's words.

There's something so melodic about his voice—almost hypnotic.

I'm positive you can learn how to do it if you try. It's all about diffusion. You don't inhale like you're breathing air. You let the water bring the oxygen to you, like how a fish uses its gills. Stop resisting, and you'll catch on in no time.

Slowly, the pressure in my lungs begins to ease.

The water isn't crushing me anymore. It's flowing through me, giving me what I need.

Air.

I can breathe.

My mother was smart, patient, and she loved fiercely, Riven says, with undeniable vulnerability in his tone. *She was the best queen this realm has ever had. She was taken from us too soon.*

Now that I can focus again, I remember what he told me in his room about his mother.

He said she's the only person in this world who ever loved him.

And, judging by how he's talking about her, she didn't abandon him like my mom did to me.

She's dead. Gone.

Forever.

And, in all the time I've known Riven—which, admittedly, hasn't been long—I've never heard him sound so genuine. It's like there's actual warmth inside that heart of ice.

But now isn't the time to contemplate this newfound depth of Riven's personality.

Now's the time to keep going with this trial.

So, with renewed strength, I kick downward, letting the water give me strength as I swim toward the glow of the key.

SAPPHIRE

THE DEEPER I GO, the colder it gets.

But Riven's words continue to echo in my mind.

Let your magic bring the oxygen to you. Don't resist.

So, I focus on the water—on the way it fills my lungs without suffocating me.

Now that I can breathe, I'm more in control than I've felt since this trial started.

I need to do this as quickly as possible. Zoey's up there, and who knows what's happening to her? She could be freezing to death, waiting for me, terrified that I've already died.

But she has the amulet of warmth. She won't freeze to death. It should be enough to keep her going for now.

So, I kick harder, reaching for my magic, begging it to help. And just like that, power rushes through me, creating a surge that propels me faster through the water.

That's when I see it.

The key.

I swim harder, the current propelling me with each kick.

The glow gets brighter, and the key's shape becomes clearer. It's a simple silver key, the blue light beaming up from it like a spotlight.

I reach out and grab it.

It's colder than the water around me, as if made of ice. The chill bites into my skin.

But I don't let go. I grip it tight, turning to swim back up, and the propulsion boosts kick in again, the surface of the lake approaching faster than I thought possible. The hole is smaller now, but there's still enough space for me to break through.

The moment I'm free, Zoey's right there, pulling me onto the ice.

"Saph!" she cries. "Did you get it?"

I open my mouth to answer, but instead of words, all that comes out is a rough, choking cough.

Water—freezing and thick—spills from my lips.

She pulls me closer, her arms trembling as she helps me sit up. "Get it out," she says softly, gently. "You're okay. You're going to be okay."

I hope so. Because right now, my lungs are trying to claw their way out of my body, rejecting the water that's still trapped inside. Each cough tears through me like shards of ice.

Finally, with one last agonizing heave, I get out the last of the water.

The pain lingers—sharp and deep—but I can breathe again.

I'm alive.

I slump back onto the ice, exhausted, the key clutched in my fist. "I'm okay," I rasp between shallow breaths. "And I did it. I got the key."

I open my hand and show it to her.

"It's beautiful," she says.

Now that it's no longer glowing, I can see that it's not simple, like I first thought. Up close, it's intricate—delicate patterns etched along the length of it, shimmering in the dim winter light.

"We can admire it later," I tell her. "Right now, let's get off this lake."

"There's nothing in this world I want more than to get off the lake," she says, and together we half-stumble, half-run to the shore where Riven's waiting with his knights.

My lungs are still adjusting to breathing air instead of water, but the weight of the key in my hand feels like victory.

As soon as I'm off the ice, Ghost prowls toward me and sniffs, as if checking to see if I'm okay.

I reach out to pet his head.

"Watch out," Riven warns. "He bites. Although, perhaps it could be more fun to watch your next trial if you're missing a hand..."

I pull my arm back to my side, although if there's one thing I know for sure—Ghost would never harm me.

He knows it, too. But the knights don't. And we need to keep up appearances.

"Start a fire. They'll freeze to death before the next trial if we don't warm them up," Riven tells the knights, and they spring into action, gathering wood and igniting it with practiced efficiency.

"How do they know how to do that so well?" I ask Riven, since I assume ice fae don't ever need to warm up.

"You're not the only summer fae we've ever kept hostage," he says coldly, and within moments, the crackling of flames fills the air, the warmth licking at my frozen skin as I edge closer.

Zoey does the same, the fire bringing color back to her cheeks.

As I warm up, I steal another glance at Riven.

He's sitting on the other side of the fire, watching me with that unreadable look of his.

His words from earlier echo in my mind—his story about his mother, and the way he guided me through the trial without making it obvious, like a secret between just the two of us. He helped me stay alive.

And the way he talked about his mom... it was with such unexpected vulnerability. A warmth beneath all that ice.

"Don't look too proud of yourself, Summer Fae," he says, snapping me back into reality. "The lake was a warm up. It'll look like a leisurely swim compared to the next trial."

The flicker of warmth I'd felt toward him vanishes, replaced by the familiar surge of anger I feel every time he says something harsh and arrogant.

Which is admittedly most of the time.

"If you think I'll give you the pleasure of watching me suffer, you'll be waiting a long time," I tell him.

"Survive if you can," he replies. "But the trials are designed to leave you broken. Mentally, and physically, as you'll discover if your body snaps at the bottom of that ravine."

"Then you'll be disappointed when I don't break." I lean forward, trying to see the man who recounted the story about his mother while saving my life.

There's nothing.

He's still the same smug, manipulative prick.

One who would apparently prefer me to die where he can see it instead of in the depths of a frozen lake.

SAPPHIRE

WE SIT around the fire for about an hour to warm up.

The knights stand in a circle around us, ensuring we don't make a run for it. Riven doesn't say another word to me.

Zoey doesn't talk, either. I think she's in shock after everything we've been through. Especially after thinking I drowned in a lake and left her alone in this crazy realm where she's weak and vulnerable simply for being human.

"Let's go," Riven eventually commands his knights. "The ravine awaits."

They lead us through the forest, the air thick with the chill of ice magic, and the trees around us shimmering with frost. The path twists and turns, leading us deeper into the woods, until we reach a cliff that drops into a deep, jagged ravine.

A long wooden bridge, slick with an icy layer of snow, stretches what must be at least one hundred feet across to the other side.

Riven, who now has the key, uses it to open the bridge's gate.

"You three," Riven commands, looking to three of his knights. "Go. We'll stay here to make sure they don't run back."

The knights stride onto the bridge, their boots gliding over the surface with practiced ease. The one ordered to stay behind is the one Riven was telling the story about his mother to back at the lake.

Riven remains by the gate. He's leaning against the post, with Ghost beside him, his silver eyes locked on mine as if daring me to show fear.

I don't give him the satisfaction.

The three knights easily reach the other side, and Riven gestures for Zoey and me to follow.

"Your turn," he says, cold and mocking, stepping to the side to allow us space to begin. "Try not to fall. It'd be a shame to end this so soon—when we still have the hunt ahead of us."

I grit my teeth, a breeze blowing through my hair.

I won't die here.

Neither will Zoey.

"It's icy," she says, already examining the start of the bridge. *Really* icy. We're not going to be able to walk across it without slipping."

"Yes—that's what it seems like," I agree, my heart rising into my throat as I gaze across the rickety bridge to the other side of the ravine.

"I've walked across ice before," she says, talking quickly as she gathers her thoughts. "I was skiing with my family, and one of the days was so icy, it was impossible to walk through town without slipping everywhere. We had to attach external cleat things to our boots. They gave us extra grip on the ice."

"And how's that supposed to help us now?" I ask. "We weren't exactly given survival bags with cleat attachments in them as a parting gift."

"Which is why we need to improvise," she says. "I can carve notches into the bottom of our boots, like treads. Then you can use your magic to freeze water into those grooves—something that's not smooth, but sharp. Like icicles."

"Except I'm not a winter fae," I remind her. "I'm a summer fae. My control is over *liquid* water—not ice."

"But you were able to warm up the ice to melt it," she says. "Maybe you can shape the water into icicles, then make it colder, so it turns to ice."

"I don't know if it'll work the other way around," I tell her, since I have no idea how the technicalities behind my magic work. "But I can try."

So, we sit down, and Zoey carves deep grooves into the soles of our boots with her dagger, cutting in precise, crisscross patterns.

I glance at Riven as she does, to try seeing what he thinks about our makeshift plan.

His expression, unsurprisingly, reveals nothing. I don't know why I bothered in the first place.

"Okay," Zoey says when she's done, sitting in a way that allows me to access one of her boots. "Your turn. Pick up some of the snow and… do your thing."

Staring at the soles, I call on my magic to melt the snow, shaping droplets between my hands. Then, focusing as hard as I can, I send the droplets into the grooves she carved, trying to make the ends as pointy as possible.

Miraculously, they bend to my will and take on the correct shapes.

From there, I will them to freeze.

Nothing happens. They just sit there, rippling slightly as I try and fail to push the magic through them.

"It's not working," I tell her, letting the droplets fall back onto the snow in a huff.

"Try again," she pushes. "Try to freeze the air around them. It'll be like how you heated it up to melt the ice covering the lake—just opposite."

"Easy for you to say," I snap. "You're not the one trying to do fancy things with magic you just got *a week ago*."

She flinches, darkness crossing over her eyes, then gets ahold of herself.

"You just turned yourself into a mermaid to swim to the bottom of a lake," she says steadily. "That had to have been harder than creating a few icicles."

I'm not too sure about that. Especially given how tired I feel after that stunt I pulled with breathing in the water.

But it's either try harder to do this right, or give up and likely fall into the ravine.

"Fine." I re-center myself, focusing on the magic I *still* have in me instead of on the magic I've already expended. "I'll try again."

"Good," she says. "Because I'm *not* dying at the bottom of that ravine simply because you gave up after one try."

"I'll do my best," I tell her, since it's the most I can promise without lying. "Now, be quiet and let me work."

Like before, I shape the water like liquid icicles sticking out of the boots.

So far, so good.

Next step—turn them into *actual* ice.

Per Zoey's advice, I focus on making the air around them colder —not warmer.

The droplets tremble, resisting, and frustration rushes through me. But I don't give up.

As I continue to push, the air around the water feels different. Colder. As if something in the atmosphere is changing in response to my magic.

The droplets harden, becoming tiny icicles sticking out of the notches Zoey carved into the soles, like little spikes ready to grip into the slippery snow.

"Yes!" Zoey grins, brightening in that contagious way of hers. "You did it! Go, Sapphire! Now—do it three more times."

"You're not going to let me relish in my victory for a few seconds?" I tease.

"You can relish at the other side of the bridge," she says. "Or, better yet, when we're home."

"Fair," I say, and I continue working my magic, until all four boots are transformed into cleats.

The temperature outside is so cold that the little ice spikes *stay* frozen.

At least the winter weather is good for something other than trying to give us hypothermia.

Now armed with our makeshift trekking boots, Zoey and I head to the start of the bridge, staring down the slick, snowy path ahead. It's not wide enough for us to cross side by side, so one of us will have to go behind the other. And its handrails look far from reliable.

I glance over my shoulder to look at Riven.

His eyes are narrowed with something unreadable. Maybe curiosity, maybe impatience, or maybe even boredom.

I *hate* how impossible he is to read. I like to think I'm decent at reading most people—it comes with the territory of working at a bar —but Riven's a constant mystery.

The blond knight next to him stares straight ahead, refusing to look at me or Zoey.

The only other one around here who seems slightly interested in our survival is Ghost.

Zoey nudges my arm, snapping me back to the treacherous path ahead. "You ready?" she asks.

No.

"Let's see what these boots can do," I say instead, not wanting Riven and the guards to think I'm weak.

She nods—she totally knows I phrased it that way because I didn't want to lie and say I was ready—then studies the bridge again.

"Want me to go first?" she asks.

Do I?

The person who goes first will be responsible for testing each plank to make sure it'll hold. It'll require bravery—a quality Zoey's always had.

The person who goes second will be watching out for the one ahead. Making sure they don't fall.

If I'm in front of Zoey, I'll spend more time focusing on looking back to make sure she's okay than on staying aware of what's happening ahead. And I need to be ready to use my magic at a moment's notice—to protect both of us.

It'll be harder to protect her if I can't see her.

"That seems like the smartest move," I decide.

"Just keep close," she says. "If anything feels off, tell me. Okay?"

"Will do." I nod, trying to match her courage, even though my stomach is twisting in knots.

She steps onto the bridge, and I hold my breath, spotting her, ready to pull her back onto solid land if she starts to slip.

The bridge creaks under her weight.

She doesn't slip.

Instead, I hear a crunch as the ice spikes on her boots dig into the packed snow.

"See?" She manages a small smile back at me, then takes another step.

Again, the spikes grip the snow.

"It's working," I say softly, as if speaking too loudly will somehow make the magic disappear.

"Told you so." She takes a cautious step, then another, keeping a solid grip on the frozen rope handrails.

I hurry behind her, since there's no way I'm letting her get too far.

But I move too fast, not giving the spikes on my boot enough time to dig into the snow.

My boot skids sideways, and I curse, somehow managing to grab the rope quickly enough to regain my balance.

"You okay?" Zoey asks, not moving.

"All good. Just… testing the sturdiness."

"Well, test slower," she says. "Because there's no way I can make it across this thing without you."

"I'm not too sure about that," I say, although from the sad look in her eyes, I can tell she *is* sure about it.

Still, she presses forward, her steps slow and deliberate.

I follow right behind, making sure the spikes dig firmly into the snow.

At our pace, the bridge feels like it goes on for miles. My fingers are so frozen that I'm surprised they're still able to grip the ropes.

"Halfway there," Zoey says after what must be an hour. "We've got this."

"Slow and steady," I repeat what we've been saying this entire time.

Then, out of nowhere, the wind picks up, making the entire bridge swing like a pendulum. It tears at my clothes, cutting through my skin like knives as I try desperately with everything I have to keep my grip firm and my feet steady.

"Zoey!" I shout, but the wind swallows my voice.

Another gust of wind slams into us.

The bridge jerks violently to the side, and Zoey loses her footing, her eyes wide in panic and her arms flailing around as she searches desperately for something to hold onto.

SAPPHIRE

"No!" I reach for Zoey, my pulse pounding in my ears, magic swelling my veins as I try with everything I have to keep my feet steady and not plummet to the bottom of the ravine.

And then—somehow—the bridge steadies.

I'm not being battered by the cold anymore. The trees are still blowing wildly on the other side of the ravine, but it's like the wind is moving *around* us, protecting us and keeping the bridge from trying to throw us off.

I manage a glance over my shoulder at Riven.

He's standing at the start of the bridge, as if he's ready to run onto it at a moment's notice. And from the way he's staring at me, I'd almost bet he'd jump into that ravine to save me if it came down to it.

"What's happening?" Zoey asks, and I snap my attention back to her, where she's gazing out at the wind whipping through the branches of the trees at the opposite side of the ravine.

The knights that Riven sent over there are waiting at the end, although they're stealing glances around themselves as well, seemingly just as confused as Zoey.

"I don't know," I say, and while the bridge sways again, it's so gentle that I barely have to try holding on. "Let's just keep moving."

"Good plan," she says, and we press forward, each crunch of the ice spikes in our boots louder than ever in the now quieted wind.

Eventually, Zoey lets out a shaky laugh, breaking the silence. "So," she says. "Do you think Riven will be impressed that we made it this far?"

"Really?" I ask. "We're navigating a deadly bridge and you're thinking about *Riven?*"

"Only because *you're* thinking about Riven," she says. "I saw the way you were staring at each other across the bridge just then."

"Just making sure he wasn't about to come after us to finish off what the wind started," I say.

"He'd never," she replies, and even though her back is to me, I can practically see the smile that I know is on her face. "Not with the twisted, icy version of a crush he has on you."

"Riven does *not* have a crush on me," I say, exasperated and still focusing on crossing the bridge, despite the wind calming down and sort of getting the hang of it. "He's using me. And he's using you. Because that's what he does. *Uses* people. He already told us this. And he's fae, which means he wasn't lying."

Zoey's laugh is shaky, but persistent. "So, you don't think he's a little bit into you?"

I grit my teeth, crunching the ice spikes on my boots harder into the snow. "I think he's exactly what he appears to be," I say. "Cold, ruthless, and very willing to watch us suffer."

"Keep telling yourself that if you want to," she says with an annoyingly entertained giggle. "But I see the way he looks at you. If that's cold-hearted, I bet it'll get *hot* when he warms up."

I huff, seriously *not* having the energy to deal with her chatting on top of trying to stay alive.

"Could you maybe think about surviving for two minutes instead of matchmaking?" I snap, a little sharper than I intended.

"If I think about what we're doing too much, I'll fall," she says simply.

"That literally makes no sense." I roll my eyes, even though she's not looking back at me.

"It makes perfect sense," she says. "Isn't that how you make your drinks at the bar? Chat with the customers while letting your hands do their thing?"

"That's different," I say.

"Why? Because it's magic?"

There's challenge in her voice—something that sets me even more on edge than I already am.

"What do you mean?" I ask.

"You're good at making those drinks because you're a natural with your water magic," she explains. "But just because I'm good at things that *aren't* magic doesn't make what I can do less important than what you can do."

"I never said you weren't important?" I ask, confused about how we got here.

This isn't like Zoey.

She's never been... well, I suppose she's acting *jealous?* Of the fact that I have magic, and she doesn't?

"You implied it," she says.

"I absolutely did *not* imply it."

"Yes, you—"

Crack.

Wood splits, the plank in front of Zoey gives way, plummeting into the ravine.

One a few feet ahead follows in its wake.

My chest tightens, fear rising in my throat.

We have to get off this bridge. *Now.*

"Run!" I grab Zoey's hand and leap in front of her, pulling her with me across the weakening planks.

Every inch of me is wired with magic, every nerve in my body sparking as I hurry us forward. I push with all I have, ignoring everything except the need to reach the other side.

Finally, with one giant leap, we land on solid ground, crashing into it so hard that it knocks the air out of my lungs.

Zoey rolls forward, although her tumble is perfectly graceful— the type you'd expect from a trained gymnast.

I can't say the same about my own.

A powerful whoosh sounds from behind us, and Ghost lands with a heavy thud on the ground beside me, with Riven steady and calm on his back.

Riven dismounts with practiced ease, so focused on me that you'd never guess the entire bridge was crashing to the bottom of the ravine behind him.

Ghost, however, leans his massive head down toward me and

sniffs my hair, as if double-checking that I'm in one piece. His presence is comforting—even more so when I see the hardness in Riven's eyes soften as he watches the two of us.

"You're remarkably good at not dying, Summer Fae," he says, glancing back at the splintered remains of the wooden planks dangling over the ravine.

"Or maybe I have a good teacher." I raise an eyebrow, suddenly finding it impossible to not goad him, despite the three knights who are watching us and taking in every word.

The other knight is still at the other side of the ravine, stranded.

Riven's hand goes to the hilt of his sword. "Are you willing to reveal his name?" he challenges.

"No." I keep my gaze locked on his, since we both know *exactly* which teacher I'm referring to.

The same one who coached me through breathing underwater.

The same one whose silver eyes are staring down at me over the gleaming tip of his sword.

And I'm keeping our secret. As much as I hate it, having him on my side is the best chance I have at getting out of this realm alive.

Zoey stands up and brushes some snow from her pants, bringing our attention to her.

"Well, that was fun," she says, her hands on her hips as she gazes over the ravine like it's the setting of a grand adventure.

"Fun?" Riven's voice drops to a dangerously low rumble, and I reach inside myself for my magic, ready to do *something* with it in case he decides to attack her. "Let's see how much 'fun' you have when you're being hunted through the forest for the final trial."

"Then we'll have to bring our A-game, won't we?" I ask, trying to sound a *lot* more confident than I feel after nearly drowning in the lake and plummeting into a ravine.

His frosty gaze locks onto mine, seemingly unimpressed by my attempt at a joke. "I'd suggest more than just your 'A-game,' Summer Fae," he says. "We're not holding back in this hunt. There will be nowhere to hide, and if you think taking a long ice bath and crossing an old bridge was difficult..." His voice trails off, leaving the threat hanging in the air like a blade ready to drop.

"Then what?" I ask. "Because we passed your first two trials, even though they weren't fair from the start. We can pass the next one, too."

"This is the Winter Court," he says—as if I needed reminding. "Fairness doesn't exist here. Only strength, survival, and sacrifice. You might have demonstrated the first two so far, but as for the third..."

His gaze drifts to Zoey in a way I don't like.

The third.

Sacrifice.

Zoey and I would never sacrifice each other or leave the other behind.

Not now, and not ever.

And if that's what the final trial requires of us, then I guess we'll be stuck figuring out how to turn this insane, deadly realm into our new home.

SAPPHIRE

RIVEN, Ghost, and his three remaining knights lead the way to the final trial. The fourth knight—the one he told the story to—had to head back to the palace after getting stranded on the other side of the ravine.

We arrive at the start of the forest just in time for sunset. The bare trees loom ahead, sharp icicles hanging like fangs, each branch twisted and glistening in the cold winter air.

"This is your final trial," Riven says. "Make it to the silver tree, and you'll find your way home."

I take a steadying breath, my eyes scanning the darkening forest. The icicles hanging from the branches make the trees feel like a vast, glittering maze designed to trap any fool daring enough to enter it.

That's what I was when I got lost on the night of the meteor shower. A fool, ignorant of what I am, and of the truth of the world around me.

But I'm not ignorant anymore. I know I have magic. And while I'm not exactly practiced at using it, at least I'm prepared to call on it whenever the time comes.

"We'll give you a fifteen-minute head start," Riven continues. "Then, we follow."

"Like some sick game of hide and seek?" I ask.

"Hiding will make this boringly easy for us," he says, and the knights fan out behind him, weapons ready, their expressions as cold and unforgiving as the harsh winter air. "And I don't have the patience to stand around watching you stare out into the woods. So, the trial begins now."

Zoey grabs my arm and *tugs*, nearly pulling my shoulder out of its socket.

"Let's go," she hisses, and without a second to spare, we sprint into the forest, ducking under low branches and weaving around icy trunks.

The world blurs around me, every sound amplified in the tense silence, overloading my every thought.

"Where are we going?" I ask, barely managing to avoid getting smacked in the head by a branch.

She glances over her shoulder, as if she thinks the knights might already be able to hear us. "The silver tree," she says. "But not straight there. The knights will assume we're going straight there, which will make us too easy to find."

"We also won't be going straight there because I have no idea where we are, let alone where the silver tree is," I say, taking an occasional glance over my shoulder as we continue to run.

There's no sign of Riven and the knights.

Yet.

We continue to run, and I hold onto my magic, using it to push us forward like I've done a few times before. Our feet are touching the ground so lightly that I'm unsure we're leaving a trail.

"Then we'll go in random directions," Zoey says, and my magic pulls under my skin as we dart through the forest, changing direction every few minutes, doubling back and zigzagging when we can.

Zoey's breathing is heavy, but she doesn't complain. She just tightens her grip on my arm and matches my pace, helped by my magic propelling us forward.

"Left," she manages between breaths, and we veer left, dodging a twisted tree.

Has it been fifteen minutes yet?

I have no idea. All I know is that we have to keep going—get as far away as possible before we can't go any further. Then, once we're somewhere they hopefully won't be able to find us, we can take a break to strategize the best way to the silver tree.

We're still going strong when the air shifts, colder and thicker, pressing in around us in a way that makes us slow to a stop.

Something's wrong.

"Do you feel that?" Zoey's eyes dart around, searching for whatever's out there.

I nod, my heart pounding with a new kind of fear.

Is it the hunt? Have they closed in on us already?

I don't know. Because it's quiet.

Too quiet.

Then, a scream tears through the night.

It's shrill and piercing, like a blade scraping against my bones. Quickly, it spirals into a wail. I clutch my head, staggering and falling to my knees as the scream burrows its gnarled fingers deep into the recesses of my mind.

Zoey also collapses, clutching her head, her face twisted in agony.

"Sapphire," she chokes out, and I can barely hear her over the scream. "What is that?"

"I don't know." I shake, closing my eyes as the pain seeps into every cell, every nerve, freezing me from the inside out.

I can't move, let alone run. All I can do is curl into a ball on the ground, barely able to see through the haze clouding my vision.

We're going to be sitting ducks for the hunt. Not just because we stopped moving, but also because Riven and his knights will surely hear the screaming as well. It'll lead them straight to us.

Focus, I think, searching for any idea for how to get out of this agony. How have I used my magic so far? The ice boots, making Zoey's shower explode, splashing Riven and Ghost at the stream, swimming in the lake—

There.

That's it.

In the lake, with the water in my ears, everything was muted. Dulled.

Maybe I can somehow use water to plug my ears?

Desperate for anything that might help, I reach for my magic and take a deep breath, prying my hand from one of my ears.

It's so agonizing that I nearly cover it again.

But I grit my teeth and force my way through it. The faster I do this, the faster I can find relief, and then the faster I can get us out of here.

So, I scoop up a handful of snow, using my magic to melt it.

147

The screaming's tearing my mind apart. But I cling to the image of water filling my ears, drowning out the sound, pushing through the pain as I press the snow to one ear and will the water to move inside it.

It follows my command, and quickly, I do the same thing to my other ear.

The piercing scream dulls to a muffled, distant echo.

Relief rushes through me.

It worked. I can think again.

With no time to waste, I crawl over to Zoey.

She's curled up with her hands pressed to her ears, crying, her cheeks streaked with tears.

"Zoey," I say, even though there's no chance she can hear me. "Hold still. I'm going to block it out."

She doesn't respond. She just whimpers, her eyes squeezed shut, her nails digging into her scalp.

I gather another handful of snow, melt it, and pry one of her hands away from her ears, guiding it inside with my magic like I did with mine.

Her breathing slows, the lines of pain on her face softening.

I do the same with her other ear.

She stills, then opens her eyes, blinking up at me in disbelief.

But she's not looking at me.

She's gazing out over my shoulder in total fear.

I turn slowly, heart hammering as I watch an eerie, spectral woman glide through the trees toward us.

She looks like something pulled from the depths of a nightmare. Her face is ghastly, her eyes hollow, her mouth stretched wide in a scream. The sound isn't debilitating like before, but it's still clawing at the edges of my mind, getting louder as she moves closer.

Zoey reaches into one of her pockets, pulls out one of the sharp rocks I gathered last night, and throws it at the woman's throat hard enough to crush her windpipe.

The screaming comes to an abrupt stop.

The woman's hands go to her throat, and she lets out a strangled, gasping sound. Like she's trying to breathe, but failing.

Then, like a candle snuffed out, she vanishes.

For a few seconds, we just sit there, frozen, the silence so heavy it's suffocating. I'm breathing hard, my heart racing from both the relief and the adrenaline. I hadn't even realized how tightly I'd been clutching Zoey's arm until she pulls it free.

"What was that?" She stares at the space where the screaming woman was, using her palm like a suction to try getting the water out of her ears.

"I have no idea." I glance around, relieved when nothing else emerges from behind the trees. "But we can't stay here. We have to go. Now."

Not leaving room for argument, I grab her hand, pull her up, and we continue our sprint through the forest.

We have to get as far as we can.

And then... well, we'll deal with whatever happens next when it comes to it.

SAPPHIRE

THE COLD BITES harder the longer we run, each breath searing my lungs.

Exhaustion settles into me as I use more and more of my magic to keep up our pace. I'm not sure how long I can keep going like this.

Eventually, our sprint slows.

Zoey lets out a low, gasping breath, clutching her side as she leans against a tree. "I just... need a second," she says, and I nod, taking the opportunity to glance around the forest.

It's well past sunset now, and animals scurry through the trees, the branches seeming ready to grab us and attack.

Hoping we're safe from nightmarish screaming women now, I remove the water from my and Zoey's ears. The *pop* as the water seeps out is extremely satisfying, and Zoey shakes her head, smiling with relief as the last drops of it run out of her ears.

"We can't outrun them forever. We need to get to the silver tree." She looks around, as if it might appear out of nowhere.

Of course, it doesn't.

"I'm going to go to the top of that tree," I say, pointing to the tallest one I can find. "Hopefully I'll be able to see the silver tree from there."

"Okay." A flicker of a hesitation crosses Zoey's eyes, but it's gone in an instant. "I'll watch your body."

My *body*.

I shudder, not thinking I'll ever like the sound of that.

"I'll be back in a second," I tell her. "I promise."

She nods, and then I zero in on the tree, appearing at the top of it in seconds.

The world is different from up here. The forest stretches like a sea of jagged shadows, glistening with frost under the pale moonlight.

One tree glistens more than the others. With leaves—not with ice.

The silver tree.

And, according to the location of the North Star, the tree is a straight shot southeast from here.

But just as I'm about to rush back to my body, movement catches in the corner of my eye.

Riven and his knights, far out in the distance. They're near the place where the screaming woman attacked.

They must have tracked us there.

How long will it be until they're able to track us here? Or until they simply give up on trying to hunt us down like prey and go to the tree, so they can attack us when we arrive?

A scream pierces through my thoughts.

Zoey.

I snap back into my body and see a little, ice dragon creature—about the size of a large bird—zooming at my head, its claws curled and poised to dig into my eyes.

I roll out of its way a second before it has a chance to blind me.

It crashes into the ground instead.

Grabbing my dagger in a flash, I reach over and stab the blade through the creature's heart.

It screeches, collapses, and melts, disappearing into the snow. But before I can catch my breath, another ice dragon swoops down from the trees, as if it was already poised to strike.

Zoey scrambles back, grabs one of the rocks in her pocket, and hurls it at the creature. The rock hits its mark, and the little dragon crashes into a tree and shatters, the pieces falling to the ground.

She grins at her success.

I push myself up, and a series of sharp, high-pitched screeches sounds from above.

More of them.

An entire *flock* of them, their crystal eyes gleaming with predatory focus, zeroed in on us.

"Behind you!" I shout, and Zoey spins, ducking as another ice dragon swoops past her, narrowly missing her head.

She counters with a swift throw of another rock, which grazes the dragon's wing and sends it into an awkward spin.

It screeches and tries to regain balance. But I lunge forward, sending a whip of water toward it from some snow I'd gathered in my hand.

The water yanks it out of the air and slams it to the ground, shattering it on impact.

Together, we continue fighting like that against the dragons. Zoey with her rocks, and me with my magic.

We're almost done. Just a few more to go.

I'm finishing off a particularly feisty one when Zoey screams. A piercing, pained scream that's definitely not one of victory.

She's clutching her arm, blood seeping through her fingers.

The final, biggest ice dragon is hovering just out of her reach, its claws dripping dark red, a victorious gleam in its frozen eyes as it prepares for another attack.

"No!" I raise my dagger, and the world narrows to the weapon in my hand, the cruel gleam in the ice dragon's eyes, and Zoey's gasping breaths, sharp with pain as she clutches her injured arm.

Without a second to spare, I hurl the blade, a flash of silver slicing through the air with an amount of precision I didn't know I had in me.

It strikes the dragon square in the center of its icy chest, and the dragon falls to the ground, shattering on impact.

Zoey's wide eyes flick from the remains, to me, then back again. "Nice shot," she says as she cradles her injured arm, her teeth gritted against the pain.

I rush to her to check on her injuries.

"Let me see," I say, prying her hand away from the wound.

Blood pulses slowly from a deep gash, the dark red stark against her pale skin.

My stomach twists at the sight, growling, taking *this* out of all moments to remind me that I'm getting hungry again.

"It's not great," she says, wincing as she tries to adjust her arm.

"Maybe there's something I can do." I hold my hand over the wound and glance down at the snow. "I wonder if I can put snow onto your arm and use it to somehow heal the cut?" I ask. "Freeze it, sort of like the opposite of what people do when they cauterize a wound?"

"This isn't like using magic on a pair of *boots*," she snaps. "It's my arm. If you mess up and freeze my blood, I could die."

Whatever I was about to say dies in my throat.

"Sorry," I say instead. "I didn't mean... well, I was just trying to help."

"We need to slow the bleeding," she says, sounding calmer now, already moved on to her next thought. "Use your shirt. Tear off a strip of it and make a tourniquet."

"Sure. Okay."

My hands tremble as I grab the bottom of my shirt and tear off a strip of fabric. The cold stings against my exposed skin, but it's nothing compared to the sight of Zoey's blood soaking through her ripped sleeve. It's getting all over my hands, and it smells just like the perfume she always wears. Spicy, with a hint of chocolate.

"Wrap it above the wound," she instructs. "Pull it tight."

I loop the fabric around her arm just above the gash and twist it hard.

She sucks in a sharp breath, eyes squeezing shut as her knuckles whiten. "Good, just like that," she says, more to herself than to me, continuing to give instructions about what to do.

I follow as best as I can, focusing on the practical—the tangible—instead of on the panic racing through my mind and the hunger rolling through my stomach.

"How do you know how to do this?" I ask her.

"I watched a lot of medical dramas when I was younger," she says. "You're doing great. Almost done."

"It's holding," I say, exhaling as the blood slows beneath the makeshift bandage.

"Nice work, field medic." Zoey tries for a grin, but winces instead.

I offer a shaky smile in return, the tension in my chest refusing to ease. "I might be the medic, but you're clearly the doctor," I say, which is enough to earn a chuckle from her.

My eyes drop to her arm again, reassessing. It's stable, but not for long. Eventually the fabric will soak through.

She looks me over as well.

"You didn't get hit once, did you?" she asks.

"I did." I touch where claws and crystal beaks grazed me, but of course, there's nothing. Only smooth skin beneath ripped fabric. "It just already healed."

Zoey's jaw tenses, and she stares at my unscathed skin as I wipe her blood off my hands, deep in thought. "That was fast," she says, and then she snaps back to it, as if nothing even happened. "Now, let's get to that tree before I start bleeding too badly again. Were you able to see it from above?"

"I did." I squeeze her uninjured shoulder lightly. "We're close."

"Good," she says, and she pushes herself up with her good arm to stand, brushing off my help as she does. "Lead the way."

I do another sweep of the area, relieved when nothing else attacks, then use the stars as guides to point us southeast toward the tree.

Zoey leans on me more and more as we walk, her steps slower, heavier. Each labored breath of hers cuts through me, a reminder that every second counts.

"You good?" I ask, glancing sideways at her.

She musters a thin smile. "Been better," she says, trying for lightness, but sounding winded instead. "Keep going."

My stomach continues to growl every so often as we trudge on, but much to my relief, there are no more screaming women or violent ice dragons. Just me, Zoey, and the cold, making our way toward the silver tree at a much slower pace than I'd like.

But as we walk, I remain alert, gazing around in preparation for attackers.

Where are Riven and his knights now?

Surely, they're closing in on us. I think Zoey knows it, too, even though she's not saying anything.

All we can do is our best and pray that it's enough. And Zoey's too vulnerable now for me to risk leaving my body for another treetop scouting mission. So, we're going to have to let the stars guide our way.

Zoey's uncomfortably not chatty as we continue, and eventually, my hand drifts to the whisper stone in my pocket.

Sapphire. Riven's voice echoes in my mind, low and urgent. *Are you there?*

SAPPHIRE

I FREEZE, and Zoey groans at the sudden stop.

"What?" She scans the area, her good hand already gripping her dagger.

I release the whisper stone, not wanting Riven to hear. "It's Riven," I tell her. "I touched the stone, and he talked to me through it."

"Well? What did he say?"

"He said my name. And asked if I was here."

"And what did you say back?"

"I haven't said anything back," I tell her. "I'm talking to you."

"Then talk to him," she snaps. "We need his help."

I hesitate, still not one hundred percent sure I can trust him. Far from it.

But things are looking desperate here. And it won't hurt to hear him out. It's not like he can track our location through the stone.

Or... *can* he track our location through the stone?

At the thought, part of me wants to throw it as far away from us as possible and run. But another part—probably the more logical part—knows that if he could use it to track us and that if he wanted to track us, he would have found us already.

So, I reach back into my pocket, wrap my fingers around the stone, and bring it out.

"I'm here," I say to him, and Zoey nods in approval.

Listen carefully. His voice sharpens, straight to business. *You can't go to the tree. The king's men are already there, waiting. You need to head northwest instead—toward the ravine that marks the end of the Winter Court's territory. It's narrower than ravine you crossed for the bridge trial, so while there's no bridge, you'll be able to jump to the other side.*

"Jump?" I echo, and Zoey's brows knit together in silent question. "Riven, that's—"

You can do it, he cuts me off, speaking quickly, apparently having no time to waste. *I've seen you do it before. Lots of times. You can jump farther than any fae I've ever seen.*

Memories flash by: jumping with Zoey over fallen trees to outrun that Wendigo, flying through the treetops and from that branch into Riven's window, and then the impossible leap to the end of the collapsing bridge.

Each of those times were fueled by adrenaline. Desperation.

If I do this crazy thing Riven's talking about, it will be different. Planned.

Which means I'll have time to overthink it. To overanalyze it.

To get scared about it.

"What's he saying?" Zoey's voice breaks through my hesitation.

Quickly, I catch her up.

She glances up at the night sky, then back to me. "Then it sounds like you need to lead us northwest, Star Navigator," she says, as if she has no idea why I'm questioning the plan at all.

"Really?" I ask. "You want to try *jumping a ravine?* In your state?"

In what state? Riven's voice echoes through my mind at the same time as Zoey tells me that I'll be the one jumping us across the ravine —not her.

Crap. I forgot to release the stone while I was talking to Zoey. Which means Riven could hear what I said to her.

"I'm fine," I say to Riven, ignoring Zoey's comment for now.

And Zoey?

"We had an incident with ice dragons. But she's alive and walking."

That's more than either of you will be if you go to the silver tree, he says. *But I can convince my knights that you wouldn't be stupid enough to cross into the Wandering Wilds. I'll divert them, while you get out of here.*

Great.

I stare at the whisper stone in annoyance. Because he's asking me to do something apparently so idiotic that he can easily convince his knights not to follow.

This isn't promising.

But he's made it clear he wants me alive.

Unless he's wanted me off his territory this entire time? Could this have all been a scheme to convince us to trust him enough to make what would apparently be the dumbest decision we could make in the trials?

I'm the only person in this entire court who cares about keeping the two of you alive, Riven says, as if he can read my hesitation through the stone. *And if you want to stay alive, you'll head west after crossing the ravine until you see a grove of frost-tipped pines. Look for a cluster of stark white birch trees with twisted trunks and follow them until you reach a fallen tree shaped like an arch. Continue through the Snow Blossom Glade, and beyond that, the entrance to the cave is hidden by a wall of frost ivy. My mother and I used to go there when I was young so she could find... well, it's not important now. Just go. I'll see you soon.*

Knowing I'll never remember all of those instructions, I rattle them off to Zoey. Riven has to correct me once or twice, but eventually, we get it.

I have to go, Riven says abruptly. *I'll see you soon. And Sapphire?*

"Yes?"

Good luck.

I stare at the whisper stone, the sound of Riven's last words echoing through my mind like a drumbeat.

Good luck.

It feels like a farewell, a promise, and a warning all at once.

Doubt coils in my stomach like a living thing as I think through our options.

If we go to the silver tree, we'll face the king's men. If they're anything like the king—or simply follow his orders, as I expect— then they'll kill us. Violently.

I shove the stone back into my pocket and turn to Zoey. She's pale and shivering, her breaths shallow and sharp, her blood staining the makeshift bandage that I'm not sure will hold for much longer.

There's no saying how far we are from the border of these Wandering Wilds.

But what other option do we have?

"Looks like we're going northwest," I finally say.

Zoey's lips twist into the shadow of a smile. "Lead the way, Navigator," she says. "When did you learn how to navigate by the stars, by the way?"

"I don't know." I shrug and look up at the night sky, comforted by the blanket of sparkling little lights overhead. "I just *know*."

"Must be a fae thing." She winces again, reminding me time is of the essence. And there's no way she can run like that...

"Hop on my back," I tell her.

"What?" She balks. "No way. I'm light, but not *that* light. I can walk."

"We don't have time to walk. We need to *run*," I insist. "And ever since getting here, I've been feeling stronger. At least let me try."

"Fine," she gives in, and then, after a few awkward tries, she's situated on my back in a way that's not totally uncomfortable for her arm.

"Hold tight," I say, and I burst into a sprint, recalling Zoey's advice from the bridge earlier.

If I think about what we're doing too much, I'll fall.

So, I force myself to *feel* instead of *think*.

The forest blurs around us, the snowy ground dipping and rising, roots tugging at my feet as if trying to hold us back. But I move with surprising speed, with strength that carries us over obstacles as if they're nothing.

Zoey's grip tightens with each leap and lunge, but she doesn't complain.

Occasionally, I glance at the sky for guidance, letting the stars lead the way. They paint a picture of the forest in my mind, like a compass engraved into my soul. I don't know how they're doing it, and I don't know how to control it, but I'm happy to let it happen.

Zoey's blood continues to soak my clothes. It smells sweet, as blood always does. And it's making me hungry. I'd stop to feast on some deer again if I wasn't running for our lives.

Finally, the wind shifts, and the trees break open into a dark expanse.

The ravine ahead stretches like a gaping wound in the earth, and I skid to a stop at the edge, sending snow scattering into the deep, dark abyss that will surely mean our deaths.

SAPPHIRE

Nausea rises into my throat as I stare down the ravine.

It's so deep that I wouldn't be surprised if someone told me it was a portal to the Underworld.

I can't cross that. There's no way I can cross it. Especially considering Zoey's condition.

"You're going to need a running start for momentum," Zoey says, clutching my neck, her skin frighteningly cold. "About one hundred feet of it, give or take. More is better than less."

I glance back at the forest we just burst out of, where animals scurry through branches and shadows flicker across the sparkling trees. I don't hear the hunt yet. But if we hide, they'll find us. Riven won't be able to keep his knights from searching in the right places forever.

Our only known way back to the human realm is blocked.

Leaving Winter Court territory is our best chance at safety.

Assuming we don't end up broken and dead at the bottom of that ravine.

Which means somehow, I have to get us to the other side.

I have to jump.

I turn and walk away from the ravine, counting my steps as I go. One hundred feet feels like an eternity, but when I turn back around, it doesn't seem like nearly enough.

I zero in on the ground on the opposite side of the ravine—the place where I'll be landing. It's dark out, but with the light of the stars, I'm able to see. My supernatural vision is probably helping, too.

"You've got this," Zoey says, and I wish she was also fae, so I could know whether she believes it, or if she's lying. "Go. Now."

Don't think, I remind myself, since it worked while running through the forest. *Just feel.*

I take a deep breath, reaching for my magic to ground myself.

"Hold tight," I say, and Zoey adjusts her grip, her fingers curling around my shoulders.

Then, I sprint.

The wind rushes past me, biting cold and sharp against my skin. But at the same time, it guides me. Propels me. Drives me forward.

One hundred feet feels like a lifetime and a heartbeat all at once.

The edge looms, and holding tightly onto Zoey, I push off with everything in me, legs coiling and releasing in a single fluid motion.

The world tips.

Then we're airborne, weightless, suspended over nothing. It's like the air itself is lifting us, pushing against my back with a subtle, unseen force, guiding us to the other side of the ravine.

I don't look down.

The impact comes faster than expected. But I bend my knees to absorb it, refusing to make a mistake like I did when first landed in the fae realm. Not just for myself, but also for Zoey. She can't afford another injury.

I fall forward, my shoulder smacking hard against the frozen ground, the side of my head quickly following. Pain shoots through me in a blinding light. But somehow, Zoey remains safely on my back.

I roll onto my side, shaking the dizziness from my vision as Zoey shifts and slides onto the ground.

Her eyes are wide, pupils blown, and skin pale.

There's also a glimmer of relief that makes me wonder just how confident she really was back there when she told me I could definitely jump that ravine.

"Wow." She props herself up on her good arm, releasing a breathless laugh. "You did it."

I push myself up, my injuries from the landing already dimming, and gaze out at the ravine. "Yeah," I say. "I guess I did."

"That was amazing," she says, and despite the pain I know she's feeling, she keeps going. "You flew. Like, I know that fae don't actually have wings—well, I obviously didn't know that until a week ago —but I swear you were flying."

"It did sort of feel like that," I agree, and then I get down to business and look her over, inspecting her injury.

The bandage is soaked through. And her blood... my stomach growls again, reminding me about how much magic I've been using, and how I'm apparently expending so much energy when I use my magic that I get hungrier faster.

Her blood should *not* be reminding me of a juicy steak right now. And yet—

"It must be bad," she interrupts my thought. "It feels bad. I think you're going to have to carry me the rest of the way to the cave. I'm sorry. I just feel..." She shakes her head, and I notice how glassy her eyes look. "I need help."

I swallow, nodding. The only time Zoey's ever needed my help— before we got to the fae realm, of course—was when I saved her from drowning in that lake when we were kids.

"You need a fresh bandage." I rip off another piece of my shirt, not leaving room for argument.

I move quickly, fingers stiff with cold as I work through the knot.

She flinches, a soft hiss escaping her lips, but holds still.

"Almost there." I keep my hands steady as I untie it, even as the spicy scent of her blood curls at the edge of my senses.

I'm about to put the fresh bandage on her when a chill sweeps through the air. It's different from the cold in the Winter Court— sharper and deeper. A reminder that we've crossed into unfamiliar territory.

The Wandering Wilds, Riven's voice echoes through my mind. Not from the whisper stone, but from the memory of when he said it to me earlier.

I tense, scanning the tree line on this side of the ravine.

As I do, a figure steps forward. Tall and lean, with skin that glistens like stars, and eyes that are as dark as night. Black wings unfurl behind him, slow and lethal, stretching and folding like the sweep of a predator who's just located its prey.

And apparently, that prey is us.

SAPPHIRE

THE TALL, winged man flicks a wrist, and wind slams into Zoey, flinging her at a tree like a rag doll.

She crumples against it, her body going limp.

"Zoey!" I scream, hurrying to her, clutching the clean strip of fabric I was about to use to bandage her arm.

I skid to a stop halfway there, the winged man blocking my path.

He smirks, sharp and predatory, and strides forward. Every step is graceful and deliberate, as if he's ready to spring like a cobra and bite.

I freeze.

Whatever this man is, he's not a mindless monster like the Wendigo or the ice dragons. He's not fae, since fae don't have wings.

He's more like a dark, seductive, calculating angel from the Underworld.

"That was one long jump." He looks me over, studying me in a way that makes my blood run cold. "Your command over air is remarkable."

"What are you talking about?" I ask, since I'm not sure what I expected him to say, but that certainly wasn't it.

"Air magic," he repeats, his eyes so intense that it's like he's trying to see my soul. "You're skilled at wielding it. The question is—why is a vampire sneaking around in fae territory?"

"I'm not a vampire." I keep my hands out, palms facing him, to show I mean no harm. The last thing I need is to be accused of being a spy on dangerous territory—again.

"Vampires have air magic," he says simply, slowly, as if I'm not doing a very good job keeping up with him. Which, admittedly, I'm not. "You just used air magic."

"I don't have air magic," I say simply. "I'm fae."

"Fae?" He raises an eyebrow, amused, and I nod. "Then prove it. Use your water magic."

"All right," I say slowly, not wanting to make any sudden moves. "I'm going to pick up some snow from the ground, so I can show you. Okay?"

"Go ahead." He nods for me to continue, and I kneel, scraping a handful of snow from the thin layer of it on the ground. Technically, I could try pulling water from the humidity in the air again, but that trick uses a lot more energy than simply using my magic on water that isn't evaporated. And right now, I need to conserve as much energy as possible.

Plus, as I grab the snow, I steal a glance at Zoey.

She's still. Too still.

Don't be dead, I pray. *Please, don't be dead.*

"Stop stalling," the man commands, and the intense way he's staring at me pulls at me, bringing me back into focus.

I need to demonstrate my water magic. Now.

Then he'll know I'm not lying, since fae can't lie. Then he can... well, there's no saying that he'll leave us alone and let us go on our way—assuming Zoey will be able to go anywhere anytime soon—but at least he's hearing me out and not attacking. It's more than the Wendigo, that woman in the woods, or those ice dragons did.

So, focusing hard, I warm the air enough to melt the snow into a pool of water that gleams under the starlight.

But after that, nothing happens.

My body feels heavy, my head fuzzy. I've used so much energy today. And after that flying leap off the cliff, I'm depleted in a way I never imagined possible.

Then, of course, there's the hunger gnawing at my bones. It's deep and brutal in a way I've never experienced before.

The man steps toward me, his wings lifting behind him, the wind whistling through their dark feathers. "No water magic," he says, as if he's chiding a misbehaving kid. "Just like I thought."

"No." I glance at Zoey—who's still frighteningly still—take a deep breath, and ground myself.

I can do this.

Reaching for my magic again, I connect with the water and coax it to glide up my skin.

My heart leaps as I watch it obey.

It's working.

Feeling confident again, I guide the water to coil in my hand, lifting and twisting it like a living ribbon crawling up my arm. Finally, somehow staying focused through the man's stare, I pool it into a floating sphere that pulses in sync with my heartbeat and sparkles as if it contains stars.

"See?" I meet his eyes and keep my voice steady, even as my breaths quicken. "I'm fae."

"Impressive," he drawls, but there's no admiration in his tone.

Only calculation.

Then, without warning, he blasts wind straight at my chest.

I lose control over my magic and stumble back, miraculously catching myself instead of falling to the ground.

In seconds, I have my dagger in my hand, even though apart from shattering little ice dragons, I have no idea how to use it. Projection isn't an option, since it'll leave my real body vulnerable to his attacks. Which means I'm going to have to fight back with every bit of instinct and remaining magic I have inside myself.

He smirks and blasts wind at my dagger, knocking it out of my hand and sending it clattering to the ground. He's holding water in his other hand, and it shapes into a spear that he shoots toward me, glistening and lethal as it flies toward me.

I drop at the last second, the spear slicing past so close I feel the cold burn on my cheek.

"What are you?" I ask between panicked breaths, barely dodging out of the way of another spear.

He doesn't answer. Instead, he summons another spear from the air and launches it at me.

He must really love those spears.

My muscles scream as I throw myself to the side, and the spear embeds into the earth where I stood, cracking through the frozen ground and turning back to water.

That was close.

Too close.

I gather more snow in my hand and reach for the spark of magic still inside of me, fingers twitching as I pull at the water, forcing it into a swirling shield in front of me.

He strides forward, his wings flexing as he closes the gap between us.

I brace myself for another attack.

But instead of attacking with another spear, he pauses, studying me with those hypnotizing dark eyes of his that send a strange wave of calm through my body. "What I am doesn't matter," he says, low and coaxing. "What matters is that you show me your truth. The one you've yet to discover."

"I don't know what you're talking about."

My arms shake, and the shield quivers. It's flimsy—a hollow barrier that won't last.

Seeing my weakness, he flicks his wrist, and more wind surges toward me, bursting my shield apart and driving me back.

This time, I fall to the ground with so much force that pain shoots through every bone in my body.

He raises his hand to blast me again.

No.

I can't take another hit.

So, I raise mine right back and scream, forcing as much magic as possible out at him to stop him from pushing me down.

A shockwave of air bursts from my palm and collides with his magic between us, the force splitting the night with a sharp, crackling roar that startles me nearly as much as him.

His smirk returns, this time sharper, almost triumphant. "There is it," he says. "Air magic."

"I'm not..." I trail off, relieved when he doesn't attack again. "I don't understand."

He moves in a dark blur straight at me, crashing into me and slamming my back to the ground.

My breath escapes in a choked gasp, eyes wide as he pins me down, anchoring me in place.

"Stay still," he commands, his face hovering inches from mine, shadowing both of us with the fierce spread of his wings. "Relax."

His eyes lock onto mine, dark and probing, and a strange calm floods my senses.

The world softens, and my fear blurs around the edges.

It's him.

Somehow, he's doing this. Manipulating my emotions. Making me want to relax when I should be wanting to fight.

"Get off me." I try to push up, but his wings wrap around us, the world narrowing to a prison of feathers and shadows.

"Not until I know what you are," he says, and I can barely see now that his wings are blocking the stars.

I'm trapped.

Not knowing what else to do, I slowly reach into my pocket as I continue to squirm beneath him, my fingers wrapping around the whisper stone.

"I'm fae," I say, but as I speak, I know it's not a complete truth.

"Not just fae." His face is so close now, eyes dark and unrelenting, insisting on more.

"I came here to escape the Winter Court. Then you attacked the moment we crossed that ravine, and now you're trying to kill me," I say. "I don't know what I am, but I do know that attacking me and torturing me won't get me to tell you something that's a mystery, even to me."

Through all of this, I don't release the stone.

"You used air magic and water magic," he continues to push. "Yet, you're not of my kind. Your blue eyes—and your lack of wings—are enough to tell me that."

His breath is sweet, like a drug he's infusing into my soul. It makes me stop squirming and relax.

But as I do, I still remember to hold onto the stone.

"I thought I was human until a week ago," I say, barely able to focus as I float in this warm, winged cocoon he's creating around us. "I swear it."

The tension between us crackles, sharp and charged, his face so close I can see the flecks of red in his dark eyes.

He takes a deep breath as he studies me, as if he's unsure whether to believe me or not.

Believe me, I think. *Please.*

"If you don't know what you are, then perhaps I'll be able to taste what you are," he decides, and his head dips down, his lips brushing the skin of my neck with an almost cruel softness.

Then two pricks cut through my skin—fangs—and I cry out, the pain mingling with a warmth that spreads like wildfire through my veins, wrapping me in a mix of agony and unwelcome bliss that numbs my bones and drowns my senses until I can barely form a single thought.

SAPPHIRE

THE DARK ANGEL continues to drink, and I'm trapped beneath him, body frozen, heart pounding.

It's like he's pulling the very essence of me out with my blood, sifting through it, searching for answers. It's intoxicating. A pull that tugs at the last shreds of my will to fight. And as he continues, my breaths slow, every muscle in my body loosening as my mind threatens to submit to darkness.

But no.

I won't give in.

Not like this.

Especially when I still have one more weapon at my disposal.

My magic flickers weakly inside me, buried under the suffocating weight of his power. And even though my vision swims, the edges of my world blurring into darkness, I don't let go. I can't. If I do, all will be lost.

And so, I push past the heaviness in my limbs and strain to see above him—at the small piece of ground I can make out behind him, between where his wing ends, and the sky begins.

I need to be there. Not here.

Project, I think, but nothing happens.

I'm still underneath him as he draws more blood from me, pinning me beneath his weight, my body sinking into the frozen ground.

Focus, I tell myself, and an image of Zoey floats through my mind, unconscious and bleeding at the base of that tree. If I don't make it through this, she won't either. My aunt and her parents will never know what happened to us, and it will all have been because of me. Because I couldn't get my act together and use my magic when I needed it the most.

I refuse to let that happen.

So, I draw a breath, gaze out at the slit of the ground I can see above his wings, and *push.*

In an instant, I'm there, standing behind him in my projected form.

He's hunched over me, his back facing me, his wings spread wide. They touch the ground on both sides, barely allowing me to see above them.

But I take one step forward, then another. As I do, I get a better look at myself pinned under him, unconscious as he continues his feast.

I've seen myself like this before—that first time when Riven found me in the forest, and then when Zoey and I were testing out my magic in the tower. But this...

This is different.

If I don't do something—now—I might never wake up.

Quickly, I scan the area around me. Zoey's still unconscious and bleeding by the tree. But I can't go to her now. All it will do it delay what needs to be done. And much to my relief, her chest is still rising and falling, so at least I know she's still alive.

Finally, I see it.

My dagger, barely visible in the snow, glistening in the starlight.

I move, grasping it, holding it in front of me.

Gripping the hilt, I return my focus to the dark angel.

He's consumed with drinking from me. But still, I need to be quiet. If he hears me and sees me, the upper hand I currently have will be lost.

Don't think, I remind myself. *Feel.*

I break into a sprint, my vision narrowing to the single point of his back—the vulnerable space between his wings. And then, with a soundless scream, I drive the dagger forward with every ounce of strength I can muster.

The blade sinks deep, cutting through fabric, muscle, and bone until it lodges in the center of his heart.

His body stiffens. Then, a shudder ripples through him, his wings flare, and a chilling gasp escapes his lips.

Slowly, I pull out the dagger.

The moment it's out, he collapses forward, heavy and lifeless, trapping my unconscious body beneath him.

I snap back into my body in an instant.

The hazy numbness is gone. Instead, pain throbs at my neck where his fangs bit deep, and where his weight crushes my chest. I try to suck in a breath, but I can barely get any air. My arms are pinned, weak, and trembling, my head is spinning from blood loss.

I squirm, trying to free myself from his weight, but all it does is send another jolt of pain through my body. I push at him, but he's so heavy that he might as well be a boulder pinning me to the ground.

But, as I continue struggling beneath him, my healing kicks in, and the pain ebbs.

Feeling better by the second, I suck in a shallow breath, grit my teeth, and push again.

His weight shifts just enough for me to roll out from under him.

I'm free. I can breathe again. My body's healed. The place where he *bit* me...

I reach for the spot on my neck where his fangs pierced my skin, and even though my fingers come back bloodied, the holes where he broke through skin are gone.

Now, his lifeless form slumps into the snow, his wings splayed around him like a fallen storm cloud.

My dagger glints underneath one of his wings. It came with me when I snapped back into my body, but I must have dropped it when I came back into consciousness.

Knowing better than to leave weapons lying around, I stumble to my feet, pick up the dagger, and hurry to Zoey. Her face is pale, almost translucent, and a dark smear of blood trails down her temple. The wound on her arm is raw and angry, exposed because I hadn't gotten a chance to rewrap it, and possibly infected already.

My chest tightens as I kneel beside her, panic rising within me. She's still breathing, but for how long?

I need to finish bandaging her arm.

So, I rip another piece of cloth from my shirt—which is slowly turning into a midriff instead of a tunic—and wrap her arm. My hands are cold and clumsy, but I keep going, tightening the knot even though my fingers feel frozen.

Finished, I sit back and examine my work. It seems okay for now. And she's still breathing. The gash on her head looks nasty—an angry bruise already forming around it—but when I touch it, it's relatively shallow.

"Zoey," I say through the hopelessness gnawing inside me, a dark, heavy weight pressing down on my chest. "Open your eyes. Please."

She remains unresponsive.

"We have to get to the cave," I say, praying she'll somehow hear me. "Riven will find us there. It's our only chance of safety."

Still, nothing.

I'm too weak to carry her. Even though my body is healing itself, my magic needs time to replenish.

If more of the dark vampire angels come...

A sob claws at my throat, and I reach for Zoey's hand, finding a strange sense of comfort in it. "I don't know what to do," I tell her. "I'm sorry."

If she was awake, she'd know what to do.

But now, it's just me.

And not only do I not know what to do—I don't know what I *am*.

SAPPHIRE

IN ONE WEEK, I've gone from thinking I'm human, to thinking I'm fae, and now to thinking I have a mix of both fae magic *and* vampire magic.

It's likely why I've always loved my meat rare—bloody—even though fae are natural vegetarians. Because I need blood to survive. Not straight blood like vampires require, but enough to satisfy whatever vampire magic runs inside me.

At the thought of blood, a sudden, fierce hunger sears through me, sharp and all-consuming. It's different from the quiet, gnawing hunger I've felt in the past. This is primal—a need that coils in my chest and twists down to my core, demanding to be satisfied.

My eyes drop to Zoey's bandaged arm, her blood already seeping through the torn cloth. Its spicy, chocolatey scent fills my senses, and my mouth waters, desperate for a taste.

It's quickly replaced by bile creeping up my throat, and I back away, putting space between us, horrified at myself. The thought of taking from Zoey, of drinking from her to sate this need—it's monstrous.

I tear my gaze away from her, squeezing my eyes shut and focusing on the icy air biting at my cheeks, trying to cool down my appetite.

The hunger doesn't wane. It's a steady thrum in my veins, making my vision pulse with it and my bones ache.

My tears are freezing on my cheeks when a breeze sweeps past, and with it, a scent that makes me freeze.

Metallic and rich, tinged with the coldness of death.

The dark angel's blood.

My eyes fly open, and I look over at his body, his wings sprawled across him like remnants of a storm. The wound on his back is seeping blood, the bright red pooling in the snow around him, tempting me in a way I never would have believed possible even a day ago.

His body is dead, but his blood is fresh. It calls to me, singing with a promise of strength and satisfaction, despite the revulsion at myself surging beneath the craving.

It's this or nothing, a pragmatic, cold voice whispers at the edge of my mind.

Zoey won't make it without help. Neither will I.

And here this man is—a man who violated me in the worst way in my life—lying there like freshly caught prey.

He's *my* prey.

I push myself to my feet, my legs trembling and my heart thundering with a mix of fear and anticipation as I stumble toward his body. As I get closer, the scent grows stronger. It drowns out everything else—the freezing wind, the burn in my muscles, even the steady thud of my heart.

All I can think about is how close I am to regaining the strength I need. The strength Zoey needs me to have.

Finally, I reach him and kneel beside him. The wound is deep, his blood staining the snow. I take a deep breath, and the hunger claws again, urgent and insistent.

"I'm sorry," I say, and I dip my fingers into the wound, bringing them to my lips.

An electric current snaps through me, my vision sharpening in seconds. But I'm only able to enjoy it for a moment. Because a pang of sharp pain cuts through my gums—sudden and fierce, like an injection at the site of a wound.

I wince, my hand flying to my mouth as the unmistakable points of *fangs* push through.

Hunger twists at my stomach, stronger than before.

I need *more.* And I'm going to have it.

I roll him over, although his wings break as I do, and study him for a few moments.

He's just as beautiful in death as in life. Sharp features, and inky black eyes that are darker than a moonless night. It's haunting, and mesmerizing, and horrifying all at once.

But I'm not here to admire the beauty of whatever species he is.

I'm here to satiate the hunger roaring inside me like a hurricane.

My gaze shifts to his neck. To the same spot where his fangs broke my skin— where he drank from me to taste my blood and my fear.

He's going to pay for what he did to me. Not only that, but he's going to strengthen me in the process.

And so, with a growl that sounds more animal than human, I lean down and bite, my new fangs piercing his cold, tender skin.

The taste of his blood floods my senses, warm and powerful, rushing through me like wildfire. I've never experienced something this satisfying in my life, and as I continue to drink, my exhaustion vanishes, replaced by a fierce, revitalizing heat that seeps into my muscles and sharpens my mind.

It's dark. Potent. And with each fresh pump of his blood through my body, I regain strength, clarity, and control.

I'm not the prey anymore.

I'm the predator.

And I'm absolutely relishing in my latest kill.

Eventually, the rush of blood slows to a trickle, and I bite down harder, desperate for every last drop inside him. But there's nothing left. As hard as I try, I come back empty.

Enough, I tell myself, and I pull back, my face flushed, newfound power pulsing through my veins.

His beauty's still there, despite his deathly pale skin, his neck marred by my bite.

You did this to him, a small voice sounds in my mind. *You killed him. You fed from him. You're a murderer. A monster.*

The world narrows around us—just me and this dark angel, one of us alive, and one of us very, very dead. But as I look down on him, all I see are his eyes, predatory and merciless as he fought me, pinned me down, and took the very source of what keeps me alive.

He did this to himself. He didn't have to fight me. He didn't have to fling Zoey aside like a piece of trash.

But he did.

It was either going to be him or me, and I'm glad it was him.

Not wanting to look at him a second more, I stand and rush back over to Zoey.

The bruise on her head is worse, and her blood is already dotting the fabric of the recent makeshift bandage.

I kneel beside her, slide my arms beneath her, and stand. The weight that felt insurmountable moments ago is nothing now. She's light—strangely light—and her breath, while still shallow, is there.

"We're going to make it," I tell her, holding her close as I turn to the forest, stride toward it, and step into the trees, setting off along the path to Riven's cave.

I still don't know if I can trust him.

I still don't know what he'll want from me when—if—he comes for us.

And I don't know if he purposefully sent us across that ravine so the dark angel would find us and attack.

But I do know this: I'm stronger than ever. And if he tries anything against me, he's going to discover just how dangerous I can be.

FALLEN STAR

PART TWO

SAPPHIRE

Zoey's blood seeps through my shirt as I carry her through the forest, leaving a trail that anyone—or anything—can follow. Her breathing is shallow, her skin burning with fever despite the freezing air around us as I use the wind behind me to run through the forest in the Wandering Wilds.

A place that's apparently more dangerous than the Winter Court.

A place where a dark angel with black wings and mesmerizing eyes, with both air magic and water magic, tried to kill me and Zoey the moment we left Winter Court territory.

And then... I killed him.

I ran my dagger through his heart, killed him, and satiated my growing hunger by draining his corpse of blood.

Who's more of a monster? Me, or him?

I don't know.

Right now, all that matters is getting to safety and saving Zoey's life.

"Just hold on," I whisper to her, keeping momentum, refusing to slow down. "We're going to make it."

She doesn't respond. She's as unconscious as she's been since the dark angel flung her aside like trash, slamming her into a tree.

But she's not going to die. I refuse to let her die.

Head west after crossing the ravine, until you see a grove of frost-tipped pines, I repeat Riven's instructions in my mind as I run.

A rabbit darts out from beneath a bush, stopping when it sees me.

Its eyes go wide, and it bolts away so quickly that snow sprays up behind it.

I keep going.

As the small animal knows, it's the prey. I'm the predator. Best to get as far away from me as possible.

Eventually, the grove of frost-tipped pines appears ahead, their crystalline needles sparkling under the starlight.

It's beautiful. But I'm not here to sightsee.

What's next?

Look for a cluster of stark white birch trees with twisted trunks, I remember Riven saying to me.

Zoey and I repeated his instructions dozens of times so neither of us would forget them.

As I continue running through the pine grove, the memory of drinking the dark angel's blood flashes through my mind. The way his life force strengthened me. The way my new fangs pierced his skin.

But I can't think about that now. I have to follow Riven's directions. I have to bring Zoey to safety. Every minute that passes is a minute she's closer to death.

Suddenly, a shadow moves through the trees to my left.

I spin toward it, clutching Zoey closer.

Nothing's there.

But that doesn't mean nothing *was* there.

"Riven?" I call out softly.

Hopefully it's him. Hopefully he heard me through the whisper stone when I reached out to him while the dark angel was trying to kill me. Hopefully he's coming to help me as I navigate these mysterious, magical woods that hum with a dark sort of power that's impossible to ignore.

Silence answers.

More shadows flicker through the trees, and my chest tightens.

Did his knights follow us? Or are there other creatures in these Wandering Wilds, waiting to attack?

But I can't just stand here.

I have to keep going.

Zoey's life—and my life—depends on it.

Eventually, panic sets in, squeezing my lungs so tightly that it slows my running.

Did I make a wrong turn somewhere? Am I lost? Am I going to run in circles until another dark angel—or maybe a group of them—finds us and *actually* kills us?

I don't know.

But then, finally, I burst out of the pine grove.

Ahead, stark white birch trees with twisted trunks reach toward the night sky like gnarled fingers ready to grab anyone who passes their way.

I'm about to take off running again, and a deer steps into my path.

It rears back, terror flashing in its eyes, and bolts back into the forest.

Power rushes through me as I stare at the opening where it disappeared.

Apparently, I ooze predatory darkness now. Which is somehow unnerving and comforting at the same time.

Putting it out of my mind, I reach for my magic, calling on the wind to propel me forward as I run, holding Zoey's unconscious body closer to my chest as I do.

Follow the birch trees until you reach a fallen tree shaped like an arch, the next part of Riven's instructions plays through my mind.

The forest hums, alive with energy, every step through the snow echoing louder than it should.

Be quiet, I think to myself. *I am* air. *I can walk on it—create a thin padding between myself and the ground. It'll take more magic—and thus, more energy—but I can do it. Silently, leaving no tracks.*

My steps immediately feel lighter, like I'm floating just above the ground as I run. Almost like I'm flying.

The shadows shift again, darting behind a nearby birch. My heart races as I scan the area, pounding so hard that it makes me dizzy.

Something's out there.

Not a rabbit. Not a deer.

Something far more dangerous.

I don't know how I know.

I just *do.*

But Zoey doesn't have time for me to entertain my paranoia. So, I clutch her tighter and push forward, calling on the air to make me light as a feather, and as fast as the wind.

Something scrapes against bark overhead.

I freeze, scanning the twisted branches above me.

The shadows between them are darker than they should be. They're moving in ways that shadows shouldn't move.

Or maybe it's just this realm in general? Maybe the Wandering Wilds are playing tricks on my mind?

Anything's possible.

But the one thing I know for sure is that I need to keep going.

I have to find the fallen tree shaped like an arch.

Scrape, I hear again, closer this time. Like skeletal fingers dragging across wood. I cringe as a chill runs through my brain, like when hearing nails against a chalkboard, or like when I hear *anything* against styrofoam.

I've always hated styrofoam.

I glance upward, searching the canopy of twisted branches for the source of the noise.

There it is.

A creature clings to the tree trunk, impossibly thin and skeletal. Its limbs are elongated and jointed at unnatural angles, and its body is wrapped in bark-like armor that blends seamlessly into the birch.

If it wasn't moving, I'd think it was another branch. But as it shifts, moonlight catches on what looks like ribs protruding from its chest. My eyes travel down its arms—to its razor-sharp claws that dig into the bark.

Its hollow eyes lock onto mine.

For a heartbeat, neither of us moves.

Then, its jaw unhinges, revealing rows of terrifyingly jagged teeth.

It's hunting us.

I'm going to have to fight it—while also protecting Zoey's unconscious body. If I don't, it's going to follow us, like it's been following us for who knows how long already.

Unless...

It'll be risky. I'll be leaving both Zoey—and myself—vulnerable.

But to fight this thing, I'm going to have to separate from Zoey no matter what.

Best to keep this tree monster as far away from Zoey as possible. And right now, there's only one way I can think of to do that. A way that's worked for me in the past—and will hopefully work for me now.

Decision made, I place Zoey down as gently as I can, situate myself beside her, and project.

One second, I'm on the ground.

The next, I'm balancing on the branch, right next to this creature that looks like a deformed, monstrous, supernatural child of a person and a tree.

Then, I drive my dagger—the one still stained with the dark angel's blood—straight at the creature's chest.

SAPPHIRE

I MISS.

I don't know how, but I *miss.*

Instead of piercing the tree monster's chest, my dagger slashes through its side. Black sap sprays out of its wound, like poison.

It howls, its cry echoing through the silent forest.

Loudly enough that anything within a mile radius would likely be able to hear.

So much for a silent kill.

I need to finish this—quickly.

I yank the blade free, bringing more of its black, sap-like blood out with it.

It smells like syrup. A scent I know well after serving drinks at the Maple Pig.

My heart hollows with longing as I think about my time as a bartender in Maine. It feels like a lifetime ago.

Now—in *this* lifetime—a tree monster flails wildly in front of me, its claws slashing through the air.

I barely twist away in time to avoid being impaled.

I can't be impaled in projected form, I tell myself, remembering when Riven tried and failed to run his sword through me when I broke into his quarters.

It's a *major* benefit for fighting in projected form instead of in my regular body.

My regular body—which is unconscious and vulnerable next to Zoey's. And which, unlike my projected form, isn't immune to injury.

I need to finish off this tree monster quickly. Because the longer I stay in my projected form, the longer I put my real self and Zoey in danger.

So, I grab the trunk to steady myself, using the wind to stay balanced.

The creature pulls itself higher into the tree, dragging itself out of reach of my dagger. Its glowing, hollow eyes narrow as it studies me, and its mouth gapes open, unhinging farther than before.

Its sharp teeth are dripping with sap.

I glance down at the ground.

As I already knew, Zoey's unconscious body is lying next to my real one. If our clothes and skin weren't stained with blood, I'd think we were peacefully sleeping. Two sisters, side by side, resting in a magical forest. Well, not *actually* sisters—her thick black hair is so different from my white-blonde hair with blue streaks at the ends that we're clearly not related—but we're sisters at heart.

We have been ever since I saved her from drowning in that icy lake when we were kids.

Sap drips onto me, yanking me out of my thoughts. The creature's a few branches overhead, and I grip my dagger tighter, repositioning myself.

I can't project from a projection.

Which means it's time to climb.

Using the branches like a distorted ladder, I hurry up the tree—faster than I thought possible—and level myself with the creature again. The wound on its chest is only halfway healed, which is much slower progress than any supernatural I've seen so far.

Maybe its healing magic moves slower because its blood is made of sap, and sap moves slower than blood?

I don't have time to contemplate the technicalities. Instead, I slash again, catching it across what passes for its throat.

More blood. More shrieks.

Its skeletal form trembles, and it backs away from me, its hollow eyes dimming with fear.

Of *me*.

Thrill rushes through me.

I have it cornered.

Now, it's time to finish it off.

As I size up where to aim my dagger for the final blow, movement flashes below.

My heart stops at the sight of a shadowy form creeping toward Zoey and me—well, the *real* me. Long, sleek, and impossibly silent, it's like a living shadow, its edges rippling as it moves. Its steps are measured, with a predator's precision, ready to pounce.

It's ten feet from our bodies, and it's closing in fast.

No time to think.

I snap back into my body, the world spinning as my consciousness slams home.

I open my eyes and force myself to sit up.

The shadow creature is a few feet away. It's like black smoke given physical shape, with red eyes and dozens of sharp teeth.

Not good.

I jump to my feet, grabbing my dagger and positioning myself between the shadow creature and Zoey.

The edges of its body ripple and pulse like a heartbeat.

Then, it lunges.

I dive to the side, slashing with my blade.

But the shadow monster is faster. It moves around my strike, those red eyes fixed on me with terrifying intelligence. And since I'm no longer in my projected form, I *can* get injured now.

The shadow monster comes at me again, faster this time.

I dodge out of the way, but it gets close enough that its cold aura brushes over my skin as it passes me and heads to Zoey.

No.

I reach for my magic, gather the humidity in the air, and blast the monster with water as hard as I can.

The shadow monster is unphased.

More, I think, and I throw my air magic behind the water, turning the droplets into pellets that make the shadow monster flinch and twitch with each shot fired. More, and more, and more, until it's seizing up like a person being attacked by an assault rifle.

One final blast, and it's down.

With no time to waste, I launch myself at it with so much power that it's like I'm flying, and drive my dagger through its heart.

The monster's otherworldly screech makes my ears ring.

I'm staring straight into its eyes as its form wavers, the shadows disappearing like mist in the wind, leaving nothing behind but a dark blackish stain in the snow.

Something thuds behind me, and I spin around, unable to take even a second to relish in my victory.

The branch monster is climbing down the tree's trunk, ungracefully thunking into branches, thanks to the multiple wounds I inflicted on it.

It's slower than before, but its eyes are fixed on me with murderous intent.

I could keep fighting it. Finish it off while it's wounded.

But Zoey's just as vulnerable as ever.

What if there's another shadow monster close by? Or another branch monster?

I can't risk it. Not again.

So, I scoop up Zoey and run, calling on the wind to make us lighter, faster.

Snow sprays up behind us as I sprint through the trees, searching desperately for the landmarks Riven described.

What's next?

A fallen tree shaped like an arch.

There.

It's curved over the path like a gateway, with the Snow Blossom Glade spread out beyond it. I've never heard of a snow blossom before, but it's safe to assume they're the thick beds of flowers shaped like snowflakes.

I race through, my feet barely touching the ground as I push myself to go faster, faster, faster.

A furious screech echoes through the trees.

It's followed by another, and another.

Closer than I'd like.

But I can't look behind. I have to keep moving.

The entrance to the cave is hidden by a wall of frost ivy, Riven's final instruction echoes through my mind.

I scan the area frantically, Zoey's body growing heavier, thanks to how much magic I've used.

Finally, I spot it.

The ivy's frosty leaves sparkle like a beacon in the moonlight. It's similar to what I imagined, but at the same time, a hundred times more magical.

I run the final stretch in a blink, and then I'm clawing my way through the ivy strands. The leaves chime softly, sending a magical buzz over my skin where they touch it, eventually revealing the cave beyond.

The moment I'm through, the screeches silence.

I stumble the last few steps, my legs trembling as I lay Zoey down on the cold, hard floor. Her skin is burning with fever, but her cheeks are flushed. Her heart's beating. Her chest is rising and falling with slow, shallow breaths.

She's alive.

We're both alive.

For now.

Now that things have calmed, I examine her bandage. Her blood's already dampening the fresh cloth, all I can see in my mind is that image of us unconscious at the bottom of the tree.

I'm so vulnerable when I project—when I leave my body behind like a hollow shell, waiting to be destroyed. My ability is valuable, but it's dangerous, too.

I need to figure out how to use it better. Because next time, I might not be fast enough to snap back in time.

And next time, we might not be so lucky.

SAPPHIRE

The cave is cold.

Not the biting kind of cold that brushes your skin. Instead, it's a deep, still cold that seeps into every crack and crevice, all the way down to your bones.

Frost coats the walls, its soft glow making it possible to see. Otherwise, we'd be in total darkness.

Zoey doesn't stir.

I want to shake her. Force her awake.

But that would probably make things worse.

As for her wound—I can smell her blood. Sweet and spicy.

For now, my feast on that dark angel is still satiating me. But what's going to happen when I'm hungry again? When I need fresh meat—or worse, fresh blood?

I don't want to think about it.

I can't.

As it is now, I need help.

And there's only one person who knows where to find me.

My hands shake as I pull the whisper stone from my pocket. It doesn't hum like it does when Riven's holding the stone connected to mine, but I have to try.

"Riven?" My voice echoes through the cave, making me feel more alone than I already did. "I'm in the cave. I followed your directions. Zoey's hurt. She's burning up, and I don't know what to do."

Silence answers.

The stone remains flat and lifeless.

I tighten my grip around it, desperation clawing at my chest.

"Riven, please," I beg. "We were being chased—there was a dark angel, and a branch monster, and a shadow monster. They would have killed us if I hadn't…"

The memory of the dark angel flashes through my mind, and my throat tightens. His seductive eyes, and the way his blood tasted, rich and intoxicating.

"If I hadn't stopped him," I say instead.

Nothing.

I bring the stone closer to my lips, as if it can somehow amplify my voice. Make him hear me, even though he's clearly not holding onto his stone.

"Zoey's dying," I tell him, hot tears welling in my eyes. "I don't know what I'm doing. I don't know how to save her."

The stone stays cold and silent.

Anger bubbles inside me, hot and suffocating.

"Did you send us here to die?" I snap, resisting the urge to throw the stupid stone at the wall. "Was this a trap? Get me out of Winter Court territory and let the Wandering Wilds finish the job?"

As expected, there's no answer.

I sink down to the ground beside Zoey, cradling the stone in both hands.

This isn't working. And it's not like a phone that I can reboot and try again.

Nothing I do will *make* it work.

I'm powerless. I have more magic than is supposed to be possible, and yet, I'm trapped, scared, and powerless.

"I trusted you," I say, even though Riven's obviously not listening. "I came here because you said it was the only way."

The tears threaten to emerge, and I press my palm against my eyes, willing them away.

Crying won't help.

Meanwhile, Zoey's blood is creeping farther across the bandage with every passing minute.

Suddenly, as I gaze down at her, I remember—the amulet of warmth. The one Riven gave her in the tent before our first trial.

She was cold then. But she's burning up now. Her fever needs to break.

Could the amulet be doing more harm than good?

I don't know. But I'm desperate enough to try anything.

The clasp is cold, but the warmth of the charm radiates through my fingertips as I undo it and slip it off Zoey's neck. The glow dims as I set it aside, and the air around her feels colder, sharper.

Hopefully it's enough to break her fever without freezing her completely.

Please be enough.

Unable to do anything else—and desperate to escape the scent of Zoey's blood—I stand and walk around the cave, keeping her in sight as I do.

Shelves have been carved into the walls, and they're lined with bottles and vials of all shapes and sizes. Some are empty, and others are filled with liquids that glisten with an otherworldly glow. There are also dried plants, smooth stones, and something that looks disturbingly like old blood.

Riven said he and his mother used to come here when he was young.

Is this what they were doing? Making potions?

I pick up one of the vials, holding it up to catch the wall's light.

The liquid inside swirls with an electric orange energy that makes my skin tingle. A blue one emits waves of calming energy, and a red one makes my heart race simply from looking at it.

What were Riven and his mom trying to do here?

I don't bother asking the whisper stone. Clearly, I won't get an answer.

So, setting the vial down, I sink onto a nearby stool, my head spinning. Not just from exhaustion, but from everything that's happened. Everything I've learned about myself.

I thought discovering I was fae was overwhelming enough.

Now, I'm apparently part vampire.

A laugh bubbles up in my throat. One week ago, I thought I was human. Now I'm some sort of fae-vampire hybrid that can astrally project.

My hands shake as I rest my head against the workbench. I'm so tired. Apparently not even the blood of a dark angel can reduce my need for sleep.

Maybe if I rest—just a little bit—I'll be able to think clearer. Figure out what to do next. After all, I'm no good to Zoey if I'm delirious.

Decision made, I walk back to her and sit against the wall, with my dagger resting on the ground beside me.

A few minutes of sleep. That's all I need.

"Just for a little while," I tell her, closing my eyes as the cold seeps into my bones. "Just enough to stay strong. For you."

With that, my eyes drift closed, and darkness claims me before I can change my mind.

SAPPHIRE

SOMETHING RUSTLES at the cave entrance.

My eyes snap open, and I grab my dagger, positioning myself between Zoey and whatever's coming.

The frost ivy's leaves chime as they part, and my heart rises to my throat, my fingers tightening around the dagger's hilt.

Did the branch monster find us? The shadow monster? A dark angel? Or something worse?

As I stand there, bracing myself for anything, a massive white leopard emerges from the shadows.

Ghost.

Which means...

Riven steps through behind him, his silver eyes gleaming in the frost-light as they lock onto mine.

Relief floods through me, and all at once, I can breathe again.

"You're alive." His voice is neutral, betraying nothing of what he's thinking as he places the large pack he's carrying on the ground.

Ghost has a pack on his back, too.

"Barely," I say, but despite my relief, I don't lower my dagger. "What took you so long?"

His brow lifts slightly, but he doesn't rise to my bait.

Instead, his eyes shift to Zoey.

"What happened?" he asks.

"You tell me." I lower my weapon. Obviously, I'm not going to attack him, given that a few hours ago, I was begging a rock for him to come help me. "We were attacked when we crossed that ravine. Dark angels, branch monsters, shadow creatures. Take your pick."

"I heard you through the stone while you were being attacked. I came as fast as I could," he says. "I had some… obstacles on my way here."

"I had some 'obstacles,' too." I huff, glaring at him.

"You told the dark angel something before you killed it." He steps closer, a hum of electricity filling the space between us. "That you didn't know what you were."

Crap.

I did say that. I was trying to communicate with Riven through the whisper stone while answering the dark angel's questions, which means he heard everything I said during the exchange.

More than I wanted him to hear.

"The dark angel tried to kill you," he continues. "Torture you. Make you reveal something that you claim is a mystery, even to you."

"My projection magic," I say quickly, scrambling for a way around the fact that the dark angel was talking about my air magic. "I used it near the dark angel. But I don't know how I can do it. It's not a fae ability. He didn't know, either."

"No," he agrees. "It's not."

Panic rushes through me. I can only skirt around the truth for so long.

I have to change the subject. Quickly. Before he pushes for more.

"Zoey's dying," I repeat, tears welling up in my throat as I motion to her unconscious body. "Those ice dragons slashed her arm in the forest, and the dark angel flung her into a tree. The wound on her arm is bad. So is the bump on her head. She needs help, and I made that bandage for her, but I don't know what else to do."

His expression shifts, concern crossing his face as he walks to Zoey, kneels beside her, and presses his palm to her forehead.

"The fever's bad," he says. "So is the wound."

I kneel on Zoey's other side, looking Riven straight in the eyes.

Is it just me, or does it look like he actually cares?

"Can you help her?" I ask. "Make a healing potion or something?"

He's quiet for a long moment, still examining her.

"Basic healing potions are simple to brew," he finally says. "But those are for cuts before infection sets in, or a single fractured bone. This…" He gestures to the blood-soaked bandage on Zoey's arm, and the angry bruise on her head. "Her skull is cracked, she has several shattered bones, she's lost a lot of blood, and her wound has progressed to a whole-body infection. Given her state, the potion would have to be brewed by someone with extreme magical talent."

My stomach drops. "But you can do it. Right?"

He has to be able to do it. He's a fae prince. If anyone has extreme magical talent, it's a prince. Especially one who came out here to brew potions that couldn't be made in Winter Court territory.

Illegal potions, if I had to guess.

"It'll take some time, but I know where to find the ingredients," he says slowly. "However, one of them that might prove to be problematic."

"Problematic how?" I ask, not liking the sound of that.

"It requires extreme magical talent to properly extract," he says. "Talent that I don't have."

"No," I say, since I won't accept that. "Maybe we can improvise. I did it all the time at the Maple Pig. If we ran out of an ingredient and I needed to make someone a drink, I'd feel it out. I'd make it work anyway. And I've never had a dissatisfied customer. You even admitted the drink I made you was good, even though you don't like pink drinks."

"I never said I didn't think it would be good," he reminds me. "I asked if I seemed like the type of guy who orders pink drinks."

"Right now, you seem like an arrogant winter prince who's finally admitting a fault—at the worst time ever," I say, motioning to Zoey again. "There has to be something you can do to help her."

Pain flashes across his face, catching me off guard.

"It's not that simple," he says, quieter now, as if the weight of what he's about to say stole some of his insufferable confidence.

"What do you mean?" I ask.

He doesn't meet my gaze right away. Instead, his hand trails along the frost-coated floor, tracing absent patterns in the ice.

Finally, he exhales, a breath that sounds more like surrender than frustration.

"My mother was a potion-maker. She claimed to be the best in the Winter Court," he says. "There was one potion she refused to give up on trying to make. She was missing an ingredient, but she thought she was talented enough to create it anyway."

He pauses, and I give him space to continue, having a feeling where he's going with this.

"She died because of it," he says, and the words hang in the air, heavy and brittle.

"I'm sorry," I tell him, not knowing what else to say.

Because that pain in his eyes—it's grief. Deep, agonizing, soul crushing grief.

"She brought me to this cave so many times when I was young," he continues, his silver eyes clouded as he thinks back on it. "She made me memorize recipes, ingredients, and techniques. She wanted me to be just like her. But I was never as skilled as she was. I could follow the instructions, but I didn't have her instincts. I didn't feel the magic like she did. But you..." He pauses, his eyes sharper now, staring at me in a way that makes it seem like he's seeing straight into my soul.

"What about me?" My heart races faster, and I glance down at Zoey, unable to push down my anxiety at the thought of Riven putting her life in *my* hands.

"Those drinks you made at the Maple Pig weren't just drinks," he says. "They affected people. Changed their moods. Made them feel exactly what they needed to feel in that moment."

I swallow, knowing he's right.

I didn't know it at the time, but at that bar, when I made those drinks, I was using magic.

Water magic.

Potion magic.

"I think that's why Ghost led me there," he continues. "He sensed your talent. Your magic. He wanted me to meet you, so he brought me to you."

His gaze lingers on me, and something shifts in the air between us. It's subtle, but undeniable. The weight of his grief and the situation's tension fades away, leaving us alone in the cave.

His eyes flicker to my lips, and my breath catches in my throat.

"Maybe Ghost was right," he murmurs. "Maybe you're exactly who I needed to find."

"Riven..." His name leaves my lips in a whisper, and he moves his hand to brush his fingers against mine, gazing down at me with a hunger in his eyes that I'd recognize anywhere.

I yank my arm back, glaring at him.

"Seriously?" I snap. "You're trying to seduce me *over my best friend's dying body?*"

"I can't help it that you're irresistible when you're on your knees begging for my help." He smirks, back to his aggravatingly cocky self, as if he hadn't been pouring his soul out to me a minute earlier.

I glare at him again, heat rushing to my cheeks. "You're unbelievable."

"I've been told that before." He shrugs, his smirk firmly in place. "Although, normally after certain... activities."

"Yeah, well, this isn't the time for your little games," I snap again, gesturing to Zoey. "In case you forgot, she's dying."

His smirk fades, and his gaze softens. "I haven't forgotten."

"Good." I cross my arms, unwilling to back down. "Because apparently, you're terrible at making potions. And now you're asking me—someone who's never brewed anything more complicated than a hangover cure disguised as a margarita—to save her life."

"You said you've never had a dissatisfied customer," he points out. "I'm betting you won't start now."

I open my mouth to fire back, but the weight of what he's asking crashes over me like a tsunami.

This isn't about making a drink that will get someone through a bad day or help them forget about their ex for a night.

This is life or death.

Zoey's life or death.

I glance down at my best friend. Her pale face is slick with sweat, her breaths shallow and uneven. Worse, her bandage is soaked through.

My chest tightens—possibly from the scent of her blood as much as the fear of what will happen to her if I can't pull through—and I press my palms against my thighs, trying to ground myself.

"What if I can't do it?" I ask, hating how vulnerable I sound. "What if I mess up, and she—" My throat closes around the rest of the sentence, refusing to let it out.

"You won't." Riven's voice is firm, cutting through my spiraling thoughts like a blade.

"You don't know that," I say. "You said yourself that your mother thought she could do it, and she couldn't. She was the best, and it *still* went wrong."

Riven moves closer, his eyes locking onto mine in a way that makes my breath hitch. "You're not my mother."

I blink, caught off guard by the conviction in his tone.

"You don't have her fear clouding your judgment," he continues. "You don't have her doubts or her baggage. You have instincts—you know how to feel your way through the unknown, and that's what makes you different. That's what makes you capable. That's why fate—well, Ghost—led me to you."

I swallow hard, his words sinking in despite the storm raging in my chest.

He believes this. He believes in *me*.

But can I believe in myself?

The silence stretches between us, heavy and charged. I'm hyper-aware of how close he is, the way his presence fills the space between us.

"Did you come alone?" I ask swiftly, breaking the spell. "Did your knights follow you?"

Is this a trap?

His jaw tightens, and he moves away from me, running a hand through his midnight black hair.

"No," he finally says. "My knights won't be following us."

The way he says it makes my blood run cold.

"What do you mean?" I ask.

"When I heard you through the stone, I ran to find you." His voice is flat, emotionless. "But they followed me. Tracked me through the forest."

"And?" I press, even though I'm not sure I want to hear the answer.

"There was only one way to stop them." He clenches his jaw, pressing his lips together, not saying more.

Which tells me everything I need to know.

"You killed them," I say the words he apparently can't.

"I did what I had to do," he says, stone cold. "I slew my own men for you. Which means the three of us—me, you, and Zoey—are fugitives from the Winter Court."

SAPPHIRE

"Fugitives," I repeat, the word tasting bitter on my tongue.

"Yes." He holds my gaze. "So, if you're having second thoughts about trusting me, now would be the time to voice them. Because there's no going back. Not for any of us."

I glance between him and Zoey.

Riven killed his own knights—men who served him and were loyal to him—to come help us.

Either he's completely insane, or...

Or he really does want to help.

And right now, looking at Zoey's pale face and blood-soaked bandages, I don't have the luxury of questioning which it is.

"I'll do it," I say, my voice steady despite the storm raging inside me. "I'll brew the potion."

Riven doesn't look surprised. If anything, he looks like he expected this.

Every muscle in my body tightens, immediately on edge.

"Good," he says, nodding slightly. "But if we're going to do this, we need to make a deal first."

"You want to negotiate *now?*" My voice sharpens. "When Zoey's right here *dying?*"

"You forget that she means nothing to me," he says coldly. "I'm invested in *you*. You're the one I need alive. Not her. She's simply a means for me to have you."

A breeze blows through the cave—one that could easily be

blamed on coming through the frost ivy hanging over the entrance—but I know where it's really from.

Me.

It's my air magic. The type of magic only vampires should have.

I have to control it.

Riven can't find out what I am.

So, I take a deep breath and pull my magic back inside me, refusing to let it come out.

Zoey's life is on the line.

I won't let her die because I lost control of my magic and let Riven discover I'm a monster.

"Tell me what you want," I say once I'm confident I've gotten control of myself.

He stands and moves away from Zoey, clearly having forgotten about her already.

I stand as well, not wanting him to have the upper hand. He towers over me anyway, but it's better than remaining on the ground.

"My father," he says, strictly business now. "He's not just cruel. He's losing his mind. Day by day, he becomes more paranoid—more erratic. The court whispers about it, but no one dares speak against him."

I think back to the wild look in the Winter King's eyes when he wanted to execute Zoey and me. How quickly his mood shifted from calculated to murderous.

How he murdered his own people as an example of what he planned on doing to us, in front of everyone in that throne room, without blinking an eye.

"You want to be the one who stops him?" I ask, since it seems like a daunting task—especially when it's his own father he's talking about. "To kill him? To become king in his place?"

"No. Not like that. I'd never do that." He runs his fingers through his dark hair, the tension in his shoulders making him seem almost vulnerable. "I've been working on a potion to make him sane again."

"To heal his mind," I realize. "Just like how we're going to heal Zoey's body."

"It's more complicated than that," he says. "But I need it to work. The alternative is chaos. If my father continues down this path, he'll destroy the Winter Court. And I'll do anything to stop that from happening."

"Including blackmailing me?"

"Especially including blackmailing you." He steps closer to me, challenging me. "You're the most gifted potion maker I've ever seen. More so than my mother. You don't just follow instructions—you *feel* the magic. Now, you need the training and skill to harness that talent. To do things with it that are useful."

"But you left the bar," I remind him. "And when I fell into your realm and found you again, you brought me home and told me to never come back."

"Only because I knew you wouldn't listen. That you were smart enough—and determined enough—to find a loophole. Because I wanted you to prove that you have what it takes to survive around here."

"I wasn't the one who found the loophole." I glance at Zoey, swallowing down the lump of tears in my throat. "She was."

"She's not useless," he agrees. "But she's not the one I need. *You* are. So, what do you say, Summer Fae? Do you want to hear my offer, or not?"

I glare at him again, since as much as I hate it, I need him as much as he needs me.

No—I need him *more* than he needs me. Which gives him an advantage when it comes to negotiating.

I hate him. I don't care how tempting he can be sometimes—well, a lot of the times. I will *always* hate him.

"Fine. What's your offer?" I ask, since if I want Zoey to have a chance, what choice do I have other than to hear him out?

His smirk flickers, but it's gone almost instantly, replaced by a cold, calculating expression that makes me want to punch him in the face.

"You help me create the potion for my father—to the best of your ability," he says, smooth and sharp as glass. "In return, I'll help you create the potion to heal Zoey—to the best of *my* ability."

I narrow my eyes at him, waiting for the catch.

With fae bargains, there's *always* a catch.

"What about afterward?" I ask. "Because we need to get Zoey back to Presque Isle as soon as she's healed."

"To get her back to Presque Isle, we'd have to return to the silver tree, which is in Winter Court territory" he says. "But until I have the potion to help my father, it's too dangerous to go back there. We're fugitives—remember?"

"As if I could forget," I mutter. "But she can't stay in this realm. She's not going to survive here. She's..."

I gesture to her unconscious form on the ground, since it speaks for itself.

"She's capable," he stands firm. "She proved that during the trials. She's stronger than you give her credit for."

"I know she's strong," I say, exasperated now. "She's good at anything she tries. And she tries *everything*. But she's human. She'll always be weak here, no matter how many random skills she has. She doesn't belong in this world."

"It sounds like I believe in her more than you do." He shakes his head, as if disappointed in me.

"I believe in her," I snap. "Just... let me think for a minute."

"Think away." He steps back, infuriating me as he does. "But remember—every minute you take is another minute your friend's life hangs in the balance."

His words hit me like a punch to the gut.

He's right. Of course, he's right.

But it doesn't make it any easier to accept.

However, I can't just agree on the spot. Fae are tricky. I have to make sure there are no loopholes in his offer.

I square my shoulders, my mind racing. "I need specifics—every detail," I tell him. "No vague promises or open-ended terms. I might be new to this realm, but fae deals are like razor blades. I'm not slicing my throat open on a technicality."

Riven's smirk returns, infuriatingly smug. "Smart," he says. "You're learning."

"I might be 'just a bartender,' but I've always been smart," I snap, although my anger isn't totally directed at him.

Matt used the fact that I worked at a bar while deciding my college major—if I could even figure out how to *afford* college—against me. Because of him, I hate when someone assumes that what I do as a job means I'm not smart.

But I'm not talking to Matt right now.

I'm talking to Riven.

And I need to focus.

"First, you said you'd help me heal Zoey to the best of your ability," I say. "What exactly does that mean? Because I don't want you bailing halfway through because you think you've 'done enough.'"

"It means I'll guide you through the entire process," he says without missing a beat. "I'll provide the ingredients, explain the steps, and give you all the guidance I can to help you brew the potion correctly."

"And what if something goes wrong?" I ask. "What if you're wrong about the ingredients or the process?"

"I don't make mistakes," he says coolly. "Any mistakes made will be yours, as a result of not following my directions well enough. Which means that while we work together, you can't afford to get distracted."

His eyes linger over every inch of my body, and I can't help it—I turn the humidity in the air into water and splash him in his beautifully arrogant face.

SAPPHIRE

RIVEN BLINKS, water clinging to his lashes as he wipes his face with the back of his hand.

"Really?" he says, his voice laced with dry amusement. "Is that your idea of negotiating?"

"It's my idea of keeping you focused," I say, refusing to admit that I lost control from his testing my patience. "And proving a point."

"Point noted." He nods approvingly, already dry thanks to using his own water magic.

"Good." I steady myself, refusing to let him throw me off balance again. "Now, back to the deal. Promise me that Zoey will be safe. That this—" I pause, motioning to her. "Won't happen to her again."

His approval vanishes. "I can't do that," he says. "This realm is dangerous, and so is the journey we'll be taking. All I can promise is to do everything in my power to protect her. The rest will depend on her—and on you."

"Fine." I bite the inside of my cheek, hating that every moment I spend interrogating him is another moment closer to Zoey's death. "Any other catches I should know about?"

"Just one." He steps closer, his gaze locked on mine.

The air between us crackles with tension, and I know I should step back. But I don't.

"What now?" I ask, my magic buzzing at the tips of my fingers.

He leans in, his eyes glinting with something dark and wicked. "This deal needs to be sealed."

My heart flutters at the memory of the last time he and I sealed a deal.

"A handshake," I say firmly. "You said deals can be sealed with a handshake."

"A handshake isn't what I'm offering," he murmurs. "If you want to make this deal—which I know you do—then we're sealing it with a kiss."

My breath catches as his eyes drop to my lips. "You can't be serious."

"I'm always serious about sealing deals." His voice drops lower, and it's like my feet are anchored to the ground, refusing to move. "Unless you're scared?"

"Of kissing you?" I scoff, even as my heart races. "Please. I've already done that twice."

"Then what's once more?" He brushes his fingers across my cheek, sending fire running across my skin. "Other than something that will save Zoey's life?"

My breaths grow shallow, and my body warms.

I hate how much I want this. How much I want *him*.

Even more—I hate how much he knows it.

"Fine," I tell him, since every moment spent arguing is a moment Zoey doesn't have. "But make it quick."

"That's something I won't agree to," he says, closing the distance between us in one swift moment.

It's like the collision of two powerful forces, creating a surge of electricity that courses through my entire being, the world around us fading away as I melt into his touch.

The taste of him is intoxicating. It's like a forbidden fruit I can't resist. And as our mouths move in a desperate dance, his ice magic awakens, tingling against my skin, leaving a trail of frost in its wake.

Suddenly, he's pushing me back, pinning me against the cave wall, making me lose all capabilities of rational thought.

A breeze stirs around us, but I don't care. All I can think of is him. All I want is *him*.

He pulls me closer, his body flush against mine, making it clear that he wants me, too.

But instead of pushing for more, he breaks the kiss, resting his forehead against mine. "Careful," he warns. "Or you might end up giving me more than a kiss."

"Not in your wildest dreams," I say, and I'd back away, if it weren't for the wall behind me.

"Do you want me to tell you my wildest dreams?" he asks, amused now. "Because I promise they're wilder than your sweet summer mind could ever imagine."

I want to say no, but I can't.

"Do you ever stop?" I say instead, hating how my heart keeps racing, giving away how much he's affecting my body.

"I'd prefer not to," he says. "However, the deal is now sealed. Which means we have to get started on saving your friend's life. And indulging in a *distraction* wouldn't be the best I can do to help. Far from it given that the distraction I intend on giving you would last a long, long time."

I stare at him for a long second as I take in what he said.

"Did you just try to compliment yourself and threaten me at the same time?" I finally say.

"I didn't just *try*," he says with a smug smile. "I *did*. And you're shivering. I have an amulet of warmth for you in my pack. It should help."

He doesn't wait for me to accept. He just steps back, his movements calculated and smooth as he rummages through the huge pack of supplies he brought with him.

Ghost—who's resting next to it—looks at me with eyes that might as well say, *Riven's always going to be Riven. There's nothing either of us can do to change him.*

I just shake my head at the huge snow leopard and press my fingers to my lips, willing the sensation of Riven's magic and kiss to fade. But the tingling lingers, like a phantom touch I can't shake.

Eventually, he pulls out an amulet like the one he gave Zoey, and turns back to me. "It won't last forever," he says. "But it should help you warm up."

Cautiously, I walk toward him and take it, my fingers brushing his as I do.

The gem's warmth seeps into my skin immediately, spreading through my body like a soft, soothing flame.

"Better?" he asks, watching me closely.

I nod begrudgingly, refusing to meet his eyes as I slip the chain over my head.

"Yes," I say, hating that I need his help.

At the same time, it would be stupid to not take it. Freezing to death isn't going to do anyone any favors. Assuming fae vampire hybrids can freeze to death... but that's not a science experiment I want to attempt.

Seemingly satisfied with my decision, Riven leans casually against the wall, studying me with that calculating gaze of his.

"What?" I ask, since he clearly wants to say something.

"Two nights ago, before the trials," he says slowly. "When you asked for meat instead of bread and cheese. Were you serious, or were you trying to get under my skin?"

My stomach drops.

He knows. He has to know.

No. If he knew he wouldn't be here. He'd dismiss me as a monster and leave.

Or would he? Does he need my potion making skills enough to make a deal with a monster? To *kiss* a monster?

I don't know.

And I don't want to find out.

So, I force a casual shrug, keeping my voice steady as I contemplate a way to dance around the truth. "I was serious," I say. "Aunt Martha cooked us meat every day. It's what I grew up on. I know it's not a fae thing, but it's what I'm used to. A little taste of home, I guess."

It's not a lie. Aunt Martha *did* cook meat every day. And it *does* remind me of home.

I just leave out the part about how I need it to function. How my body craves blood now more than ever.

"Sentimental attachment to human food." Riven's voice is neutral, but something in his eyes makes me wonder if he believes me. "Interesting."

"Not everything has to have some deeper meaning," I say, desperate to change the subject, to stop his probing. "Now, if you're done psychoanalyzing my eating habits, it's time for us to start following through on our deal and make that potion for Zoey."

I hold my breath, praying he'll drop it with the meat.

"First, we'll need soulberries," he says, all business now, and I can finally breathe again. "Small, deep purple berries with a silvery shimmer. We'll mix their juice with water for the base."

"Because water is the element controlled by fae?" I ask.

"Of course." He nods approvingly. "But the berries are just the start. We also need starlight moss, which has to be gathered at night."

"And let me guess: under the stars?"

"Smart girl." He smiles in that annoying way that makes my heart race. "Then there's the moonlit fern. It's best gathered on the night of a full moon, but..." He glances at the cave entrance. "Tonight's a waxing crescent."

"Will that work?"

"It can. Better than if it was a new moon. But it means the potion will be harder to brew correctly." His eyes lock onto mine. "Think you can handle it?"

I think of Zoey—of how pale she looks, and of how shallow her breathing is. "I have to," I say simply.

"Good. We also need twilight thistle—"

"Let me guess," I interrupt. "Gathered at twilight?"

"You're catching on. But the last ingredient..." He trails off, his expression darkening. "That's where it gets complicated."

"How so?"

"We need the blood of a dove. But not just any dove's blood. You'll have to kill it yourself and perform a spell as you do. If done correctly, the dove will come back to life."

My stomach turns. "And if I fail?"

"Then the dove stays dead, and we start over."

"Which will take time that Zoey can't afford."

"Get the spell right the first time, and you won't have to worry about that," he says. "Doves only come out during the day, and the blood needs to be fresh when added to the potion. Which means we'll gather it tomorrow, after I collected everything else tonight."

"We?"

"You'll need my guidance for the spell. And I won't let you go alone." His tone leaves no room for argument. "Ghost can guard Zoey here in the cave."

I glance at Zoey's unconscious form. "I don't want to leave her."

"Ghost will protect her with his life. Like he's always done for me." Riven's voice softens, just slightly. "But if you don't have my guidance for the spell, you're less likely to do it correctly. Then all our work will have been for nothing."

I groan, since he's right. Of course he's right.

"Fine," I give in. "When do we start?"

"Tonight. I know where to find the first four ingredients. My mother and I gathered them—plus many others—around here often." He moves to a corner of the cave, where Ghost is waiting for him, curled up like he's been waiting to go to bed for a while now. "But I've been up all night getting here. I need rest to be at my best tonight."

"I'll keep watch," I say, and he's already settling down, using Ghost as a pillow.

"Wake me in six hours. That'll give you a few hours to sleep with Ghost and I keeping watch, so you can stay awake when I'm gone," he says, and within moments, his breathing evens out.

I sit against the wall, keeping my eyes on Zoey.

The dark angel's blood still courses through me, but I can feel its effects waning. I'll need to feed again soon.

But Riven can't know. I won't risk him discovering what I am— not when I need his help so desperately.

Which means I have to be careful. Hide my air magic. And feed without him knowing.

I press my fingers to my temples, trying to push away the anxiety brewing from how overwhelmed I feel.

One problem at a time.

For now, I just need to keep watch for the next six hours, to make sure the three of them—Zoey, Riven, and Ghost—remain safe.

Because without them, I have nothing.

SAPPHIRE

THE CAVE FEELS HEAVIER at night, like the darkness is pressing in closer now that Riven and Ghost have left to gather the ingredients.

I sit near the entrance, clutching my dagger, trying to stay focused on keeping watch. But my mind keeps spinning in circles.

The blood-soaked bandage on Zoey's arm. The sweat clinging to her skin. The potion that Riven and I have to make. The dove I'll have to kill. The spell I'll have to cast on it.

I wrap my arms around myself, the warmth of Riven's amulet a small comfort against the chill.

Finally, the frost ivy parts, and Ghost strides in.

Riven follows close behind, the small pouches attached to his weapons belt hopefully carrying all the ingredients he went out to gather.

"Did you miss me?" he asks lightly, but his eyes are sharp, scanning the cave and zeroing in on Zoey.

Is it just me, or does he look relieved she's still alive?

Of course he does.

Without her, he loses some of the leverage he has on me.

"Not even a little." I stand, forcing a calmness into my voice that I definitely don't feel. "Did you get everything?"

"As promised." He spreads the materials across the table. "Soulberries, starlight moss, moonlit fern, and twilight thistle. All accounted for."

The soulberries glisten like glass, the moonlit fern pulses with a gentle glow, and the twilight thistle shimmers like the last moments of sunset. As for the starlight moss, it looks like there are real stars twinkling inside it.

I stare at them in amazement, wanting to touch them, but unwilling to risk doing anything that might mess up the spell.

"Now comes the real test," he says, motioning for me to join him. "Ready?"

"Tell me what to do."

"Crush the soulberries into juice, then mix them with water," he says, picking up a bowl and placing a handful of berries inside.

"How do I crush them?" I ask.

"With passion." His eyes glimmer with mischief. "Channeling the same amount of passion you had while kissing me should be enough."

"You're insufferable." I glare at him, pick up the pestle, and get to it.

"Not bad," he says, his gaze locked on my hands as I work the pestle over the berries. "You have good rhythm."

I narrow my eyes at him, stopping my crushing. "Are you complimenting me, or insinuating something else?"

"Maybe both." He grins, a glint of silver mischief in his eyes. "Though if you're this good with berries, I can only imagine how—"

"Don't finish that sentence," I cut him off, my cheeks burning. "I swear, Riven. Do you ever just... not?"

"Not what?" he asks, leaning closer. "Fluster you? Annoy you? Make you smile when you're trying so hard not to?"

"I'm not smiling." I grip the pestle tighter, trying to ignore the way his words curl around me, stirring something I don't have the time to deal with.

"You're definitely smiling." His voice lowers, teasing but edged with something darker. "And blushing. Though that could be from all the pounding."

I glance up sharply, glaring. "Do you actually want this potion to turn out right, or is this just an excuse for you to flirt?"

"I'm supervising," he corrects me, clearly getting a rise out of this. "Making sure you're thorough."

"Then supervise from over there," I motion to a few feet away from me. "After all, you're not *helping* me by *distracting* me."

He frowns, but does as asked, although his eyes remain fixed on me as I continue to work.

Once the berries are crushed, he has me add a precise amount of water and swirl the mixture until it hums with magic.

"Now, the moss," he says, handing me a few soft, glowing strands. "Tear it into small pieces and add it slowly."

I do as he says, my hands trembling slightly.

"Easy there," he says. "Don't rush. It's all about taking your time—feeling the texture, knowing when to press, and knowing when to let go."

"Do you have to make everything sound so suggestive?" I snap.

"I'm just teaching you proper technique." His smirk returns, and he leans casually against the table.

"Proper technique?" I raise an eyebrow. "That's what we're calling it?"

"You have to admit," he says, stepping closer again, his voice dropping into that infuriatingly intimate range, "I'm very good at technique."

It takes all my self-control to not rip the moss in half to show him exactly how I feel about his *technique.*

But I don't. For Zoey.

As we continue, the fact that her life is in my hands right now is the only thing stopping me from losing control.

"You have good instincts," he says as I stir. "You can feel how the ingredients want to come together."

I glare at him for that one.

At the same time, he's right. It's like the ingredients are singing to each other, and I'm simply helping them find harmony.

"There." I hold up the finished potion, now a deep violet liquid that catches and holds the light. "Is this right?"

He examines it closely. "Perfect," he says softly, all traces of teasing gone as he pours it into a satchel. "Better than I could have done. Now, all that's left is the dove blood."

He holds it out to me, and the satchel's weight feels like more than just a potion—it's the weight of Zoey's life in my hands.

"Ready to hunt a dove?" he asks calmly, as though we're heading out on a stroll and not preparing for what feels like the most important moment of my life.

I glance at Zoey, her shallow breaths rattling in the quiet of the cave.

Ghost is curled up beside her, his massive form a comforting barrier against anything that might try to get through.

I don't want to leave her.

But I want to save her life. I can't do that if I don't trust that Ghost will keep her safe.

Plus, I can't project, so one version of myself stays here, and the other goes with Riven. My real body would be a sitting duck if anything entered the cave. And I suspect that if my real self dies, my projected self will die, too.

As I remind myself all this, Ghost's intelligent eyes remain fixed on me, like he's promising he'll keep Zoey safe.

"Watch out for her," I tell him, and then I turn back to Riven, trying to stop myself from shaking. "Let's do this."

He nods, and together, we step through the frost ivy and into the night.

Stars scatter the sky, illuminating the forest in a way that feels both serene and ominous. And while the cold air bites my skin, the amulet of warmth wards off the worst of it.

I have control over air, I realize. *Shouldn't I be able to control the temperature of it around me?*

Maybe. It's worth a try.

Later.

When Riven's not around to possibly see.

"Doves like edges," he says as we walk. "Forests, water sources, shrubs. There's a stream not far from here. We should be able to find one there."

"For a prince, you sure know a lot about tracking birds," I say, not seeing even a single sign of one of them nearby.

"Let's just say I'm well-versed in handling delicate creatures," he counters, and I can't help feeling comforted by his teasing.

"I wouldn't call myself delicate," I reply. "Unless we're counting your ego—because I'm handling that just fine."

"Oh, you're handling something all right," he says. "But I wouldn't call it my ego."

We continue like that for the next few minutes, following what seems like an endless stretch of trees. But no matter how hard I try focusing on Riven's banter, my mind circles back to Zoey. Every second feels like another step closer to losing her.

That's when I hear it.

A crunch in the snow.

Heavy. Deliberate.

Riven tenses beside me. "Don't move," he whispers.

Another snap, closer now.

"What is it?" I ask, my magic stirring beneath my skin.

"Be quiet, and stay close," he says, and a shadow emerges from the trees—a hulking, humanoid figure that's almost nine feet tall, with frost-covered skin and eyes that glow like embers.

"A Stalo," Riven says, drawing his sword. "They die if you stab them in the heart. The trick is getting close enough to do it. And whatever happens—don't run."

Before I can reply, the Stalo looks at us, charges, and the forest explodes into chaos.

SAPPHIRE

THE STALO'S roar shakes the forest.

Riven's sword flashes like silver lightning, and he charges, fluid and precise.

The monster swings a claw toward him. But Riven slashes his blade in a wide arc, and a sheet of ice races across the ground, spreading toward the Stalo's legs.

From there, everything happens in what feels like a blink as Riven goes in for what should be blow after crippling blow.

Each time he gets in a hit, the Stalo's skin hardens. The wound sparkles with frost, and in less than a second, it's sealed. Faster than any supernatural healing I've ever seen.

Although I'm hardly the most experienced in all things supernatural, given that I didn't know supernaturals existed until a little over a week ago.

Still, I clutch my dagger, looking for an in so I can help.

"Its skin is like armor!" Riven calls out, ice forming beneath his feet as he slides gracefully away from a devastating blow.

Where the Stalo's fist hits, the ground fractures.

It swipes again, but Riven pivots, his sword meeting the Stalo's arm in a clash of steel and frozen flesh. Frost creeps from his blade, spreading up the creature's arm and slowing its movements.

Finally spotting an opening, I gather water from the snow and hurl it at the monster's eyes.

"Riven!" I call out as the Stalo rears back, one massive claw raised to strike.

With a flick of his wrist, an ice spear forms in his free hand, and he hurls it at the Stalo's chest.

The monster staggers, but it doesn't fall. Instead, it snarls and pulls out the ice spear, the wound healing in a second.

Riven continues his assault, and my magic stirs within me as I remember the way I attacked the shadow monster. A deadly combination of water and air, pelting it with makeshift bullets until it collapsed in the snow.

My nerves crackle with the need to do it again. To use my air magic combined with my water magic.

I can't hold it back any longer.

And Riven's too focused to notice.

So, summoning the moisture from the air, I coax it into tiny droplets and fling them toward the Stalo with as much wind power as possible.

But unlike the shadow monster, the Stalo's skin is so hard that while the droplets pierce its shoulder and back, they don't do much damage.

They are, however, enough to turn its attention to me.

Riven curses and slams his hand against the ground.

A wave of frost surges upward, encasing the creature's legs once more, this time with ice so thick it cracks and groans under the strain of the Stalo's thrashing.

From there, Riven alternates between sword strikes and ice magic, while I assault the monster with water pulled from the snow. When I'm sure Riven's attention is elsewhere, I use subtle bursts of air to throw off the monster's aim.

But it's not enough. The Stalo is too tuned in—too aware of our movements, making it impossible to catch it by surprise.

Riven curses as another ice spear shatters against the Stalo's thick hide.

Suddenly, he grabs my arm and drags me to an old, hallowed tree with space inside it for both of us—barely. "Get inside," he says, and we dive through the opening just in time to miss getting pancaked by the Stalo's clenched fist.

He presses his hands against the bark, and ice spreads from his fingers, reinforcing our shelter.

"Any bright ideas?" I ask, trying to ignore how close we are in this space—how his magic chills the air around us.

"Yes," he says sharply. "You."

"What about me?"

"You need to project. Take my sword. It's enchanted, so it'll be more effective than your dagger." He hands it to me, the hilt cold and heavy in my hand. "Flash right behind the Stalo, take it by surprise, and drive the blade through its heart."

My stomach drops, and I tighten my grip on the hilt. "Riven," I say, scrambling for the right words. "When I project, I—"

"I ran my sword through you, and it was like slicing through air," he interrupts. "That thing can't kill you when you're in your projected form. So, flash yourself out there and kill it. *Now.*"

The Riven I'm looking up at right now isn't the one who made teasing innuendos back in the cave.

This is the ice prince. The soldier who killed his knights so he could leave the Winter Court and save my life.

The monster's fists crash into the tree again, and some of the ice around it cracks.

"Go." Riven glares at me with so much rage that I swear he'd push me out there if it wouldn't mean risking my *actual* body.

The ice cracks further.

Without a second to spare, I look at the space behind the Stalo and project.

One second I'm inside the tree, my body pressed against Riven's. The next, I'm standing behind the Stalo, watching it methodically hit the tree—where I just left Riven alone with my now unconscious body.

The monster doesn't notice me standing behind it. Not yet.

Riven's frost-covered sword hums with magic in my hands.

I rush forward, the air behind my heels, and I jump, driving the blade into the Stalo's back, deeper and deeper, until it pierces its heart.

The Stalo roars, its body freezing mid-punch.

Frost spreads from the wound, turning the monster into an ice sculpture.

Cracks splinter through the ice.

It explodes into shards, and the shattered pieces fall to the ground, leaving the forest eerily silent.

It's done.

I killed it.

Just like how I killed that dark angel.

But I can't dwell on that right now. So, I snap back into my body with a gasp, open my eyes... and find myself cradled in Riven's arms.

His face is tight with barely controlled rage.

"This was how I found you that first night," he says, sounding far calmer than he looks. "By the silver tree. I thought you hit your head and passed out. But you weren't unconscious—you were projecting."

"Yes," I tell him, and as I look at him, I'm not sure why I didn't tell him yet.

Although, we haven't exactly had much time to go over the finer details of my ability. We've either been fighting, making bargains, trying not to kill each other, or saving each other's lives.

Not to mention the kissing.

I could never forget the kissing.

"I thought you hit your head," he says, and beneath the anger, I hear something else. Fear? "I didn't realize you just... die every time you project."

"I don't die." I squirm out of his arms, which he doesn't look happy about. "I go unconscious. And yes, it makes using the ability risky. I'm aware of that."

"You should have told me." His voice is tight and controlled, like he's holding back an explosion. "We're going on a dangerous journey, and you left out an important detail about how your magic works. Do you have any idea how insanely *careless* that is?"

My heart jumps into my throat.

If he's this angry about not knowing that my body becomes defenseless while projecting myself, I don't want to know what'll happen if he finds out about my air magic.

I have to divert him from this conversation.

Now.

"I don't know much more about my projection magic then you do," I quickly tell him. "But now you know what happens when I project. And I did what you asked. I killed that thing. It's done. We can move on now."

"That's your defense?" His voice rises again. "You think you don't owe it to the people you're working with to mention that an important ability of yours leaves you—the *real* you—helpless?"

"Oh, I'm sorry," I snap. "Were we going to discuss the pros and cons of my magic while the Stalo was punching its way through the tree?"

"Don't try twisting this around." He moves closer, reminding me just how little space we have inside of here. "You had plenty of chances to tell me. But instead, I had to figure it out by watching you collapse like you were—"

"Like I was dead," I finish for him. "That's what this is really about, isn't it? You thought I wasn't coming back. You were scared."

His jaw tenses, and for a moment, I think he's going to deny it.

"I thought you were gone," he says flatly. "And that there was nothing I could do to save you."

The vulnerability in his tone catches me by surprise, and I shift the satchel on my shoulder, buying myself a second to think.

"I'm sorry," I finally say. "Really. I am. And maybe it wasn't the ideal way for you to learn what happens to me when I project, but it's done now, and I can't change how you found out."

"Well, I'm glad you're alive," he says, gathering himself back together. "You wouldn't be any use to me—or to my father's sanity— if you were dead."

There he is.

The cold winter prince that I know and definitely *don't* love

"You'll never forget to remind me where I stand with you," I say, and a breeze blows through the tree's opening, as if it's testing me— or reminding me what else I'm keeping from him. "But we need to find that dove. And I doubt you're helping me to the *best of your ability* by hanging out brooding in this tree."

"I'm not brooding," he snaps, although from the way his silver eyes twist with irritation as he makes his way out of the tree, he definitely *was* brooding.

At least now I know how to get to him—make him think I'm gone.

"Yes, you were." I make my way out as well, brushing some dirt off my pants and taking a deep breath of fresh air. "Now, are you going to help me find this bird, or are we going to stand here until another Stalo shows up?"

"Let's go," he says, and he brushes past me, not checking to see if I'm following before he continues to lead the way through the forest.

SAPPHIRE

THE FOREST STRETCHES around us in an endless maze of frost-covered trees and snowy paths glistening in the morning light.

As we walk, Riven coaches me through how to cast the spell on the bird. He quizzes me relentlessly, not resting until I know every detail of what I'm supposed to say, feel, and think.

Eventually, the forest thins, and Riven stops at its edge, scanning the area.

There are shrubs, a stream, and grass poking out of the snow.

"There," he whispers, pointing at a dove perched on a low-hanging branch near the water.

It's beautiful. Innocent.

The thought of what we're about to do twists my stomach.

"How am I supposed to catch that?" I ask, glancing at Riven.

"You project," he says simply. "Appear next to it. Catch it by surprise. Literally, and figuratively."

I frown, since the memory of our argument about my vulnerability when I project is fresh in my mind.

"Sit down first," he continues. "I'll hold you, so you don't collapse and scare it off. Unless you have a better idea that doesn't involve me scooping your unconscious body off the ground for the second time tonight?"

"Fine," I say, dropping to the ground near the stream. "But don't you dare try anything. If you do, I'll make sure you'll regret it."

"Is that a threat, Summer Fae?" he asks. "Or an invitation?"

I glare at him, heat rising to my cheeks. "It's a promise."

"Promise accepted." He chuckles softly, lowering himself behind me. "Now, lean back."

Not sure what other choices I have—and secretly liking this one —I sit down and let my back press against his chest. His arms wrap around me, firm and steady, and his breath is cool against my ear, the chill of the forest fading against the heat radiating between us.

My heart races, and I have to fight to keep my breathing even.

"Comfortable?" he asks, and from the slow way he says it, I have a feeling he's as affected by this closeness as I am.

"Just don't get any ideas," I say, trying to focus on the dove rather than how close he is—or how his hands linger a second too long as he adjusts his grip.

"You're the one whose heartbeat is giving us away, Summer Fae," he says. "Are you sure I'm the one getting *ideas?*"

I don't dignify that with a response. Instead, I steady my breath and focus on the dove. It's still there, preening its feathers, unaware of what's coming.

Here goes nothing.

One moment I'm wrapped in Riven's embrace, and then I'm standing next to the dove.

It startles, but I'm faster, my hands closing around it before it can take flight.

Its heart hammers against my palms, wings fluttering frantically as I keep my hold on it.

That was easier than I thought it would be.

"Do you plan on coming back, or are you too busy making new friends?" Riven asks, and I look over at where he's cradling my unconscious body in his arms.

As always, it's unnerving to see myself lying there limply, looking dead.

No wonder he was so freaked out the first time he saw it happen.

"I'm bringing it over." I walk slowly toward him, and he shifts his grip on my body, placing it gently on the ground as I approach.

When I'm close enough, I hand him the dove. His fingers brush mine as he takes it, and his gaze flickers, like he's searching for some-thing in my eyes—well, in my *projected* eyes.

"I have it," he says, slow and steady. "You can let go now."

Let go, I repeat in my mind, and I snap back into my body, my heart pounding as I regain my senses.

"Nice catch," Riven says, watching me intensely as I sit up and adjust myself.

As if he's making sure I'm *actually* alive.

"Now what?" I ask, even though I know exactly what comes next.

It's the part I've been dreading.

The part I've been desperately trying to not think about.

"Now," he says, glancing at his hands, where the dove is miraculously starting to relax. "You do the hard part."

I'm frozen, unable to tear my gaze away from the bird.

I don't want to do this.

But I *have* to do this.

For Zoey.

"Your dagger, Sapphire," Riven reminds me, gentler than ever. "You need to use your dagger."

I take it out, the blade feeling heavier than it should.

The dove coos softly, unaware of its fate.

"How do I..." I force myself to look away from the dove, meeting Riven's gaze instead.

"Quick and clean," he says. "Don't hesitate, and it won't feel a thing."

I nod, gripping the blade tighter, and position myself beside the bird.

"Ready?" he asks, his voice steady.

I swallow hard. "Ready."

And then, with one swift motion, I do it.

The scent of blood hits me like a storm.

Rich, sweet, and inviting.

I freeze, dagger still in hand as the aroma curls around me like smoke, weaving through my thoughts, drawing something dark and hungry out from inside me. My hands tremble, and I press my lips together, clenching my jaw so tightly it feels like my teeth might crack.

Not here. Not now. Not like this.

"Focus, Sapphire." Riven's voice cuts through the haze, cool and commanding as he collects the dove's blood in the satchel. "Start the spell. Now."

Right. The spell.

Forcing myself to concentrate, I cradle the bird and start chanting the spell he drilled into me earlier. The words feel strange on my tongue, but there's power in them—power so strong that the air hums with energy.

"Feel the magic," he coaches me through it. "Like you did with the potion."

Focusing as hard as I can, I will my magic into the dove's tiny body, praying to every god in the universe that this will work.

The blood glows, the spell taking hold, shimmering like liquid sunlight.

"Good." Riven watches me intently, ready to intervene at the first sign of failure. It's infuriating and comforting at the same time. "You're doing great."

The dove's body grows cooler in my hands, the last of its blood dripping into the satchel.

I feel like a monster the entire time I watch. Because I did this. This delicate, beautiful creature is dead because of me.

Eventually—finally—there's nothing left to come out.

Now, we wait.

I stare at the dove's broken body, holding my breath, continuing to pray.

Nothing happens.

Panic flares in my chest.

Did I do it wrong? Did I—

A soft coo breaks the silence.

The dove's chest rises and falls, its wings fluttering as it looks up, as alive as when we first spotted it in the clearing.

Relief crashes over me like a tidal wave, and I lower my dagger, wiping the rest of the dove's blood off on my pants.

"You did it," Riven says, the intensity in his gaze making my stomach flip. "Do you have any idea how rare it is for someone to succeed with that spell on their first try?"

As he studies me, the space between us feels charged again—like a live wire humming with tension.

But we don't have time for... whatever always happens between us when he looks at me like this.

There are far more important things for us to do right now.

"We need to get back to Zoey," I say, pushing to my feet and breaking our connection.

Riven nods, back to looking as detached and as unimpressed as ever. "Right. Let's go."

He transfers the glowing satchel back into his pack, the dove watching him with curious, trusting eyes.

Then, as if wishing us luck, the dove spreads its wings and flies away.

SAPPHIRE

THE MOMENT RIVEN and I step back into the cave, my heart drops.

Zoey's as pale as the snow outside, her breaths shallow and uneven. It looks like the only thing keeping her from completely slipping away is Ghost, who's curled around her, his fur pressed close, as if reminding her she's not alone.

I rush to her side and drop to my knees, reaching for her, but stop myself.

I don't want to touch her and hurt her.

Not when I'm so close to saving her.

Riven crouches beside me, assessing her with sharp eyes. "We're not too late," he says. "But we don't have a second to waste."

He hands me the satchel, and my fingers tremble as I uncork it.

The purple potion glows brighter now—possibly from the dove's blood, or maybe from the way the ingredients have had time to properly merge. Either way, it pulses with magic, like it knows exactly what it needs to do.

Riven kneels beside me as I lift Zoey's head, bringing the satchel to her lips. "Careful," he says. "Too fast and she might choke."

I shoot him a glare. "I know how to help someone drink something."

He gives me an amused smile and sits back.

I don't look at him. Instead, I tip the satchel, coaxing Zoey to drink.

The change is immediate.

Color rushes into her cheeks, her breathing steadies, and the bruise on her head fades.

I peel back the blood-soaked bandage on her arm, relieved to see that the gash there is healing just as quickly.

It's working.

The potion is *working*.

Finally, just when I don't think I can take it anymore, her eyes flutter open.

"Sapphire?" she asks, and while her voice is weak, it's there.

Tears spring to my eyes, and I throw my arms around her, as if I'm afraid she's going to dissolve into the shadows if I don't. "You're alive," I say in amazement. "You're okay."

"More than okay." She hugs me back, then pulls away, examining her newly healed arm. "What happened?"

"We made a healing potion," I tell her quickly. "Riven helped me gather the ingredients. There was a dove, and some moss, and a few berries, and—"

"And your best friend is the most gifted potion maker I've ever encountered," Riven interrupts, studying me with an intensity that takes my breath away. "Given how bad your wounds and infection were, it should have taken you hours to heal. Maybe days. But this took less than a minute."

I shift under his scrutiny, feeling uncomfortably exposed. "I just followed the instructions." I shrug, even though we both know it was far more complicated than that.

"No," he says, quieting me. "That was more than just skill. It was the kind of talent that comes from a strong magical lineage. No exceptions."

My heart leaps into my throat—panic about whether this "strong lineage" of mine has to do with the side of me that's part vampire—but I force myself to meet his gaze.

"Or maybe I was just really determined to make sure Zoey didn't die," I finally say.

He doesn't reply, but the way he looks at me—intense, searching—makes my skin prickle.

"Well, whatever you did, it worked," Zoey interrupts, breaking the tension between me and Riven. "What happened while I was out? How long was I unconscious?"

"Almost two days," I tell her. "That dark angel threw you into a tree and knocked you out. Then I fought him, and I…" I trail off, not wanting to get into the details. "I killed him and brought us here. Then Riven found us, and he helped me make the potion that healed you."

Ghost lets out a low rumble, as if reminding us that he helped, too.

Zoey smiles at him and pets his head. "Don't worry," she says. "I'd never forget you."

He purrs in contentment and snuggles into her.

Has he *really* decided he likes her better than me already?

She leans against the cave wall, using her fingers to brush Ghost's thick fur. "Speaking of going places," she says. "When can we head home?"

My stomach clenches.

I knew this question was coming, but that doesn't make it easier to answer.

"We can't go home," I say simply. "At least, not yet."

Her smile fades. "But we survived the final trial," she says. "Riven's here. He saved our lives. Which means he can take us home. Right?"

As she speaks, I can tell she realizes it isn't going to be that simple.

We are, after all, dealing with the fae.

"About that…" I start, glancing at Riven for help.

He simply raises an eyebrow, leaving this to me.

Thanks for nothing, Winter Prince.

So, given that he's apparently not going to help, I turn my attention back to Zoey.

"I made a deal with Riven," I tell her.

Her eyes narrow. "What kind of deal?"

"The kind where he helped me save your life, and now I have to help him save his father's sanity." The words tumble out in a rush. "We can't go home until I help him make a potion he needs for his father. And we couldn't go back to the silver tree anyway, since we're sort of fugitives from the Winter Court, since Riven killed his own knights to come here and help us."

"His own knights?" She gapes at Riven, who shrugs, as if murdering his men is nothing worth discussing.

"The point is," I continue, "going back isn't an option. Not until we have what we need to cure his father."

"So, we're trapped here." Zoey slumps against Ghost, who nuzzles her shoulder.

"Not trapped," I say. "Just... taking a detour."

She lets out a hollow laugh. "A detour through a realm that wants to kill me just for being human."

"I won't let anything happen to you," I promise. "Neither will Riven or Ghost."

"Like how you stopped that ice dragon from slashing my arm? Or how you stopped that dark angel from throwing me into a tree?"

I suck in a sharp breath, and she winces, immediately looking guilty.

"I'm sorry. I know you did everything you could. I just..." She runs a hand through her tangled hair, which has long fallen out of the thick bun she had on the top of her head when we set out on the first trial. "I hate feeling so weak."

"You're not weak," I tell her, although while it's generally true, there's far more to it than that.

"I'm human. In this realm, that means I'm weak," she says, although she gets herself together before I can reply, looking me dead on and straightening her shoulders. "Anyway—where do we need to go to get these potion ingredients?"

"Really?" I blink, caught off guard by her sudden attitude shift. "You're cool with coming with us?"

"It doesn't seem like I have much of a choice," she says, still stroking Ghost's fur. "Unless you want to keep fighting about it?"

"No," I say. "I just—"

"There's a woman hidden in the Wandering Wilds," Riven interrupts, speaking for the first time since this conversation started. "She's older than both courts—Summer and Winter—combined. She knows the most ancient potions ever created. If anyone knows how to cure my father's madness, it's her."

"And how do we find her?" Zoey asks, at the same time as I wonder why he hadn't mentioned this entire part of the plan to me.

Maybe because I didn't ask?

"We follow the stars," he says. "There's a map in the sky that will guide our way."

Zoey furrows her brow, staring at Riven as if he said the stars will drop from the sky and lead us there by hand.

"A map in the sky?" she repeats. "Seriously?"

"My mother said that every star has a purpose," he continues, sounding dreamy now, his voice softening at the mention of her. "She insisted there was a pattern—a way to find anything if you knew how to read it."

"Do you know how to read it?" I ask him, praying he's better at reading maps than he is at brewing potions.

His jaw tightens, and I have a sinking feeling that I'm not going to like where this is heading.

"I've tried. But I always end up going in circles." He runs his fingers through his dark hair, frustrated. "I was figuring it out, but then the disappearances near the border started happening, and I got sidetracked."

SAPPHIRE

"DISAPPEARANCES?" Zoey's voice sharpens. "What kind of disappearances?"

"The kind where fae never came back," Riven says darkly.

"The dark angels. They could be the ones taking the fae," I say, even though I know that's not what they *really* are.

They're more like vampire fae with black wings.

However, dark angel is a fair enough abbreviation.

"I've never seen one before," Riven says. "None of us have. Only the two of you, and assumedly every fae they've killed."

"Or taken," Zoey points out. "If you never found any bodies, they could have been taken."

"Did you work as some sort of detective back in the human realm?" Riven asks, although he's so sarcastic that I have a feeling he wants her to sit back, be human, and let him be the prince who knows all the answers.

"I binged every CSI episode in like, two weeks straight when I had the flu." She shrugs.

He scrunches his brow, looking clueless about what that means.

"Crime Scene Investigation," Zoey clarifies. "It's a television series."

"I don't think they get Netflix in the Winter Court," I say with a chuckle.

"It was on Hulu, not Netflix," she corrects me, smiling.

"If both of you can put your DVRs on pause for a minute, we can discuss things that actually matter," Riven breaks in, reminding me that while the Winter Court is his home, he's been to the mortal realm before. "Because now that we're fugitives, we have all the time in the world to figure out how to follow the stars."

"Actually," Zoey says. "Sapphire's weirdly good with stars."

Riven's intense gaze shifts to me, and heat rises to my cheeks. "Is that so?" he asks.

"It's how she was leading us through the forest during the hunt," she tells him.

"I got lost in the woods on New Year's Eve," I break in, since apparently, they both need a reminder about that. "That's how I ended up in this realm in the first place. I'm hardly an expert navigator."

"That was in the human realm." Zoey waves off my concern. "We're in the fae realm now. And you were doing great during the hunt."

"Look—following the North Star is one thing. Following some magical map in the sky is completely different," I tell her, then turn to Riven. "Your mother must have told you more than just 'follow the stars.'"

He's quiet for a moment, his eyes distant. "She said the stars sing to each other," he finally tells me. "If you listen closely enough, you can hear their whispers guiding you forward."

A chill rushes over me as I remember the way the stars pulsed during the hunt. How they drew me forward, like they were trying to tell me something—to point me to safety.

Riven's gaze sharpens. "You hear them," he says simply.

"Maybe." I shrug. "A bit."

"Sounds better than Riven's bit," Zoey says, and I can't help but laugh.

He glares at her, then looks back to me. "My mother said the brightest stars are like beacons," he continues. "But they're not the ones that matter. It's the dimmer ones that create the true paths."

"Like threads of silver," I murmur, the words coming from some-where deep inside me. "Connecting the spaces between."

His eyes lock onto mine. "You can see them?"

"Sometimes." I look away quickly, since I'm not sure exactly *what* I see. But I also know I can hear it, and smell it, and *feel* it.

And I have no idea how to fully explain to them how it happens. Especially since it only just started happening to me.

"If you give me a better idea about where we're trying to go, maybe it'll work," I say, although not wanting to make empty promises, I add extra emphasis on the final word. *"Maybe."*

"All right." He looks at the glowing wall, as if he can see the sky laid out on it. "She used to say, 'Follow the brightest star to find your way north, but to find your true path, look for the four crossed stars."

"Like the Southern Cross?" Zoey asks, excitement dancing across her eyes.

I'm not surprised. Even though I can *feel* the stars, she likely knows more facts about them, thanks to the "space phase" she went through sometime in seventh grade.

"She didn't have a name for them," he says. "But she said they would always point to where the old paths converge, where the universe knows no beginning, and no end."

"Interesting," Zoey says, though her tone makes it clear she doesn't entirely understand. "Do you know what she meant by the 'old paths?'"

"Ancient trails," he explains. "Invisible to most, but still there if you know what to look for. They're said to lead to places of power—places where the land remembers what came before. Where the moon, the sun, and the stars touch to create a perfect storm."

The moon. The sun. The stars. A storm.

Something about those four things together feels strangely *right.*

I pinch the bridge of my nose, thinking. "I think I might be able to make sense of it," I tell them. "I can't promise anything, but when I'm actually out there looking at the stars, it might be possible."

Riven nods. "That's the plan. We'll rest until nightfall, and then we'll begin."

"I'm not tired. I've literally been unconscious for two days," Zoey protests, but a yawn betrays her.

He reaches into his pack and pulls out a small vial filled with dark blue liquid. "This will help you get proper rest," he says.

She eyes it suspiciously. "What is it this time? Truth tranquilizer? Fae Ambien?"

"Relaxation potion," he says with an exasperated sigh. "It won't knock you out, but it'll help you rest properly. Think of it as more like… fae Xanax."

"Or fae gummies," I add, which only gets a glare from her. "It won't hurt you. And he's right—you need real sleep. We all do."

"Fine." She takes the vial with an exaggerated sigh. "But if this turns me into a toad, I'm holding both of you personally responsible."

She downs the potion like it's a shot of cheap vodka, and almost immediately, her eyelids start to droop.

Ghost shifts, making himself more comfortable for her to lean against.

She curls into his fur, as if she's done it a thousand times before, and falls asleep.

I glance at Riven.

The determination in his expression is impossible to ignore, and I realize that for the first time in a while, I'm actually feeling *hope*.

"Get some rest, too," he says. "You'll need it. We all will."

I nod, even though I know sleep won't come easy. Too much is riding on what happens next.

But for Zoey—for all of us—I have to try.

We might not survive if I don't.

SAPPHIRE

Sleep proves impossible.

My stomach twists with a familiar hunger—one that's been growing stronger since the dark angel's blood started wearing off.

I'm going to have to feed before our journey. If not, I'll be too weak to help anyone, and Riven and Zoey will be wandering lost under the stars until the end of time.

But there are no animals in the cave. None. Other than Ghost, but obviously he doesn't count, since I'm looking for animals I can *eat*.

Right now, the giant snow leopard is curled beside Zoey, sleeping.

Riven's sleeping with his back against the wall, one hand resting on the hilt of his sword. Even in sleep, he looks ready for battle. I'm sure he'll be at his feet, prepared to kill, if anything barges in here.

Which means I'll have to be careful.

Very careful.

And since I can only project to places I can see, this won't be as easy as closing my eyes and appearing outside the cave.

I'll have to be sneaky about it.

So, I focus on the space directly in front of where I'm lying.

In a heartbeat, I'm there, looking down at my unconscious body.

There's no way to tell that the body at my feet is a hollow shell. Because I still look like I'm sleeping, curled up beneath my cloak.

However, if either of them wakes up and tries to talk to me, they'll know I'm projecting, since I'll be completely unresponsive.

Which means I have to go, and I have to get done what needs to get done quickly.

I'm weightless. Silent, I tell myself as I use my air magic to cushion my steps, moving toward the cave entrance. My feet don't even feel like they're touching the ground.

Suddenly, a flicker of movement catches my eye.

Ghost.

His ice-blue eyes are open, watching me.

My heart stops.

But he doesn't growl. He doesn't move.

It's almost like he's giving me permission to leave, with a promise to keep my secret.

Thank you, I think, even though I know he can't hear me.

Able to breathe again, I move as carefully as a shadow toward the exit, focusing hard on my magic as I slip through the frost-draped ivy.

The ivy doesn't clang against itself, thanks to the air barrier between the leaves I'm creating, which forms protective cushions around each one of them to stop them from hitting each other.

Finally, I'm out.

Free.

The snow glitters under the pale sunlight, like the ground has been scattered with shards of crystal. Small blue and white blossoms peek out from it in clusters, their petals untouched by the cold. Everything here feels untouched and pristine. As if no creature has dared to disturb the peace in ages.

But anything that looks remotely peaceful in this realm is a lie.

I, more than anyone, know it.

I grip the hilt of my dagger and move carefully across the clearing, scanning for signs of movement.

Tracks dot the snow—some small, and others large. Something passed through here recently. A rabbit, maybe. Or a deer.

I follow the tracks into the trees, and there it is.

An elk, separated from its herd, pawing at the snow to find grass beneath.

My stomach twists violently at the sight of it, hunger gnawing at me with an intensity I can't ignore.

It doesn't even know I'm here until it's too late.

The kill is quick and clean.

Blood seeps into the snow as I tear into the meat, desperate to rid myself of the hunger. But while the meat is fine, it isn't satisfying. Not like it used to be.

Not when I know what I really need.

And so, with shaking hands, I lower my mouth to the elk's throat.

My new fangs extend, and I bite down.

The blood floods me with strength. The hollow ache in my bones disappears.

It's incredible. Intoxicating.

I drink until there's nothing left.

When I finish, I stare at the elk's body, guilt churning in my stomach despite the satisfaction humming through my veins.

"I'm sorry," I whisper, and I get to work quickly, gathering leaves and snow with my magic to hide what I've done.

To bury the evidence of the monster I've become.

All that remains when I'm finished is a giant lump in the snow, like a car left outside during a blizzard.

Not wanting to look at it for a second longer, I snap back into my body, where it's been this entire time in the cave.

Riven is still against the wall, his hand on his sword, his breathing steady. Zoey lies curled against Ghost, her face peaceful in sleep.

Ghost's eyes don't open.

Did he actually see me earlier at all? Or was it in my imagination?

I don't know. But, since I seem to have returned from my little field trip without getting caught, I close my eyes and pull my cloak tighter around me, letting exhaustion take hold.

I don't know how long I can keep this secret. How long I can stretch out my time between meals.

But I hope that for the next few days, what I had just now will be enough.

ZOEY

We've been walking for hours.

Well, Riven and Sapphire have. I've been riding Ghost because, let's face it, there's no way I'd keep up otherwise.

Not without slowing them down even more than I already do.

I hate this feeling. Helplessness. One I barely experienced back home, if I'm being honest.

Everyone in Presque Isle knows me as the girl who can do anything she tries. The one who excels at every hobby she picks up.

Now look at me. Being carried through a magical forest like an invalid.

A breeze swirls around us, and I glance at Sapphire, her white-blonde hair shimmering with streaks of silver and blue in the dim light as she gazes up at the stars. She's like a celestial goddess, walking beside Riven as if she belongs in this magical, deadly wilderness.

Because she *does* belong here. She has magic—actual, real magic.

And what do I have?

Guilt about how I'm a burden weighing them down.

"My parents probably think I ran away and dragged you with me," I say to Sapphire, since talking is the best way to get myself out of my head. "They must be calling everyone we know, putting up missing person posters..."

"The police are probably involved by now," she agrees. "Aunt Martha's probably made a home for herself at that station."

"Patrick's probably helping, too," I say before I can stop myself. "He always said he'd be there if I needed him."

"Patrick's an idiot who didn't deserve you the first time around." She scoffs. "You can do so much better."

Easy for you to say when you have an actual prince who can't take his eyes off you, I think, although I stop myself from saying it.

No need to cause conflict. Not when I'm causing so much trouble for them already.

"Maybe." I try to shrug it off, but the memory of Patrick's smile—the way his eyes would crinkle at the corners when he laughed at my random stories—makes my chest ache. "But he was starting to come around again. The week before winter break, he asked about the pottery class I was taking."

"Is this the same Patrick who dumped you because you ditched soccer for tennis?" Her voice hardens. "Who said he didn't think you'd have enough in common if you didn't play the same sport?"

"He wasn't that bad," I say, although it's not totally true.

Good thing that unlike Sapphire, I can lie.

Bonus points for the human.

"There's a waterfall up ahead," Riven says, uninterested in my human relationship drama. "We should rest there for a moment. Hydrate. Get our bearings."

The sound of rushing water grows louder as we approach, and soon we break through the trees into a clearing.

We're at the top of gigantic falls—the water as black as ink in the night, glittering in the starlight as it crashes into a pool below. And something about the way the water moves... it's soothing. Calming. Like a symphony played just for us, to help us unwind after a long day of trudging through a frozen forest.

Sapphire and Riven must hear it, too, because they relax, and quietly, we make our way to the riverbank.

Ghost lowers himself so I can slide off his back, and I try not to wince at how stiff my muscles feel.

Sapphire steadies me, her hand on my elbow.

"I'm fine. Just need to stretch my legs a bit. And refill my waterskin," I say, shaking her off and taking out the leather pouch that passes as a water bottle around here. "Drinking from this river won't bring me to another realm, right?"

Given how Sapphire and I got to this realm in the first place, I'm only half kidding.

"There's no marker," Riven says, which I assume is a reference to the silver tree. "But let me check it out first to make sure it's safe."

He walks over to a break in the rapids and kneels to take a closer look.

The water churns.

In seconds, waterlogged, humanoid, skeletal creatures rise from its depths, their bodies covered in slimy, moss-like tendrils.

There are so *many* of them.

And they're coming at us from all directions.

"Nixies!" Riven shouts, which I figure is either a fae curse, or the name of these water creatures.

I'm guessing the second.

They're surrounding us so quickly that I suddenly forget how to breathe.

"Get back on Ghost!" Riven tells me as he moves to the closest creature—well, nixie—easily managing to continue to talk as he kills it with his sword. "And whatever happens, don't let them grab you."

Heart pounding, I scramble onto Ghost's back and reach for my dagger, which I'm only mildly capable of using, thanks to those years of wood whittling with my dad.

A nixie lunges at us, but Ghost pivots, letting me slash at it with my dagger.

The blade catches its shoulder, and muddy water sprays from the wound.

Another point for the human.

"Good hit!" Sapphire calls out, hurling her water magic like deadly spears at two more of them.

Her spears go right through them, not affecting them in the slightest.

Apparently, water zombies can't be killed by their own element.

Riven swoops in, taking them down with his sword before they can get to her.

But I can't celebrate. Because more of them are emerging from the falls, their bodies twisting unnaturally as they climb over the rocks, groaning like zombies.

"Stay close," Riven says, and he, Sapphire, Ghost, and I keep our backs to each other, our formation tight, guarding ourselves against the nixies as they close in.

"What happens if they grab you?" I ask Riven, my dagger ready to strike.

"They'll drag you into the river and drown you," he says casually, killing two more of them with his sword.

My heart drops, and I scan the area, looking for a break in circle of them surrounding us.

Other than the space where the waterfall starts, there's nothing.

And I'm *not* letting one of these nixies get me. They can grab me and drag me into the water over my dead body.

Ghost apparently feels the same way. Because he lets out a rumbling snarl, his massive paws striking out at an attacking nixie and tearing it to watery shreds.

Riven's spinning, his sword flashing, sending three of their heads flying at once. Muddy water spurts out from their open necks, and they disintegrate into puddles on the ground.

Sapphire screams as one of them claws at her, but she stabs it in the head with her dagger before it can grab her.

Ghost and I work in sync, like we've been fighting together for years instead of hours. When he lunges, I strike. When he dodges, I duck.

I'm not useless.

I can do this.

Sapphire's now pelting four of them with small rocks, muddy water spraying from the holes in their bodies as they drain out.

"They keep coming!" she shouts, not letting up.

"We need to—" Riven's warning cuts off as a particularly large nixie bursts from the pool, sending a wave crashing over us that floods my mouth and my nose, making it impossible to breathe.

Terror squeezes my chest, and I sheathe my dagger, grabbing Ghost's fur.

I have to hold on.

His growl rumbles through his body, fierce and protective.

But the water strikes again, harder this time, a wall of ice and fury that steals the air from my lungs.

My fingers slip.

"No!" I cry out as a slimy, skeletal hand wraps around my wrist, yanking me off Ghost's back with so much force that my shoulder pops.

I kick and scream as it pulls me close, leveling its slimy, rotted, algae-covered face with mine.

Bile rises in my throat.

If vomit is able to kill this thing, then I'm about to slay it better than I ever could with my dagger.

I don't get a chance. Because it snarls and hurls me over the edge of the waterfall—as if I'm a rotten apple it picked from a tree—and I'm soaring, screaming, my stomach lurching as the world twists around me in a blur of stars, water, and jagged cliffs.

Then, I'm plunging downward.

I need to grab something. Anything.

But there's only open air and the endless, violent roar of the rushing water.

Time stills and speeds up all at once.

"Zoey!" Sapphire screams, but her voice is drowned out as I crash into the pool at the bottom of the falls.

Cold seeps into my bones as the current pulls me under, spinning me in every direction as I kick and thrash, my chest burning as my lungs beg for air.

Move! I scream at myself. *Do something!*

But I don't know how to move.

I don't know how to *swim*.

Every muscle locks up, memories of that icy lake when I was a kid flooding back. The way the cold shocked my system, how the darkness swallowed me whole, the absolute certainty that I was going to die.

Back then, Sapphire had pulled me out, her arms shaking as she saved my life.

But she's not here now.

I'm alone, and I'm going to die. For real this time.

In the occasional moments when I break the surface, I hear Sapphire screaming my name and see flashes of Riven's blade.

But I can never stay up for long.

Then, something tugs at me. Not the water, but arms wrapping around my waist and yanking me upward.

Air bursts across my face, and I gasp, choking as I'm pulled out of the water.

Not by a nixie.

By a dark angel.

His face is sharp and beautiful in a way that feels wrong—like it was carved from shadow—and his black wings look somehow darker in the night.

Terror floods back, just as paralyzing as my fear of drowning.

"Sapphire!" I try to scream, but my voice is too weak from all the water I inhaled.

She sees us anyway. Even from this distance, I can make out the horror on her face as the dark angel carries me higher, away from the battle still raging by the waterfall.

The world tilts as he ascends, the trees shrinking below us.

Sapphire's screams are lost in the wind rushing around her, and Riven's sword gleams, a blur of silver as he cuts through the nixies with brutal efficiency.

But they're getting smaller, farther away.

"No!" I thrash against the dark angel, but his grip is iron strong. "Let me go!"

"Be still," he commands, and I do.

Not because I want to stay with him. But because if I fall from here, it'll be surer death than if I was still trying—and failing—to swim at the bottom of those falls.

Plus, there's something about his voice that calms me. That helps me relax.

Now, all I can do is watch helplessly as we glide above the tree-tops, break through the canopy, and descend into a small clearing, where a massive black jaguar waits with eyes gleaming like golden coins in the darkness.

The dark angel lands smoothly, his wings folding behind him as his boots touch the ground. But he doesn't release me. Instead, he carries me to the jaguar and sets me down, grabbing a length of rope from a satchel at the animal's side.

I start to make a run for it—the burst of energy exploding inside me like a firework—but he easily yanks me back.

"Don't struggle." He shifts me onto the jaguar's back and ties the rope around me with practiced efficiency, studying me with intense, midnight eyes. "It will only make this worse for you."

"Make *what* worse for me?" I ask, desperation rising in my voice, knowing there's nothing I can physically do to stop him. "Why did you save me? What do you want with me?"

He doesn't answer my questions. He just adjusts the rope, tightening it, ensuring there's no way I can fall—or escape.

Once he's done, he jumps on in front of me, his wings retracting into his back so they don't smack into my face.

"Hold tight," he says, and the jaguar surges forward, faster than any horse I've ever ridden. Even faster than Ghost.

The forest blurs around us, and my mind races, panic clawing at my chest as I glance back over my shoulder.

No sign of Sapphire. No sign of Riven.

Only darkness and the pounding of the jaguar's paws against the frozen earth.

I'm sorry, I think, tears freezing on my cheeks as I remember the devastation in Sapphire's eyes as I was carried away, knowing she couldn't reach me in time. *I was too weak to protect myself. Again.*

And unlike last time, saving me is going to be far more complicated than a single vial of healing potion.

SAPPHIRE

"No!" I scream as the dark angel soars away with Zoey, her dark hair streaming behind her as he carries her farther and farther from us.

He doesn't stop. He doesn't even falter.

"Focus!" Riven's voice slices through my haze of terror as he beheads another nixie.

He's right. I can't go after Zoey. Not yet. Not with these monsters still coming at us, their bodies dripping with rotting algae as they drag themselves out of the river.

I'm going to kill every one of them.

Rage burns through me, and I grip my dagger tighter. The nixies are immune to my water magic—they're literally made of it—but that won't stop me from tearing them apart.

When the first one lunges at me, I duck and drive my blade up through its jaw. It explodes into a shower of muddy water, soaking me to the bone, but I don't care. I just move on to the next one, and the next, letting my anger fuel every strike.

And using the wind at my heels to help me move faster.

"Behind you!" Riven shouts, and I spin just as another nixie reaches for me with its dripping claws.

I slash through its arm, then its throat, my movements faster than I thought possible. Probably because I'm using tiny bursts of air magic to increase my speed, to make my strikes hit harder.

"Nicely done," Riven says, cutting down another nixie with a swift, precise strike of his sword.

"No time for compliments!" I yell back, already spinning to face the next one.

There are three left, their hollow eyes locked onto us.

One lunges at me, faster than I expect.

I pivot and slam the heel of my boot into its side, throwing it off balance just long enough to drive my blade into its core.

The force of the impact sends me stumbling backward, but I keep my footing.

Thank you, air magic.

Riven finishes the second one with a brutal slash to its chest.

But I'm already zeroing in on the final one—the largest of the group. Maybe the leader? I don't know.

All I know is that if it wasn't for these *things*, Zoey would still be here with us.

The nixie lunges.

Fueled by anger, I hurl the dagger with all my strength.

The wind guides it like an invisible hand, and the blade flies true, slicing through the air and striking the nixie square in its chest.

There's a moment of stillness.

Then the nixie bursts into a spray of filthy water, its remains splattering onto the ground.

I stare at the spot where it was standing in shock.

It's over.

They're gone. All of them. At least, it seems like it.

Breathing hard, I retrieve my dagger from the rocks and sheathe it by my side. My hands are shaking—not from exertion, but from the crushing weight of what just happened.

I can barely process it. I'd think it was a nightmare if it wasn't for Zoey no longer being here with us.

Riven steps beside me, his eyes sweeping the clearing for any remaining threats. "I think that was the last of them," he says, although from the way he refuses to look at me, I have a feeling he's bracing himself for my reaction about Zoey and the dark angel.

Ghost is next to him, and the sadness in the snow leopard's eyes shows me that he's devastated about what happened to Zoey, too.

"I have to find her," I say, projecting before Riven can fight me on it.

One second I'm on the ground. The next I'm balanced on the highest branch of the tree I saw Zoey disappear behind, scanning the sky for any sign of those black wings.

The stars pulse overhead, but they're no help now. There's nothing but darkness stretching in every direction.

I leap to the next tree, moving with impossible grace. Then the next. And the next. My desperation grows with each jump, the forest remaining silent and empty below me.

She's gone.

My best friend is gone.

I got her that potion. She was supposed to be okay. And now...

I have no idea how to find her.

With a cry of frustration, I snap back into my body—where I'm currently cradled in Riven's arms. He's moved us behind a large boulder near the falls, sheltered by a cluster of frost-covered pines.

His silver eyes are blazing with fury.

"Are you completely out of your mind?" he snarls, his grip on me tightening. "You can't just project yourself without warning when we're in hostile territory. What if another wave of those things had emerged while you were—" He cuts himself off, his jaw clenching. "While you were *dead* to the world?"

"I had to try." I push against his chest, trying to break free. "Zoey's gone. That dark angel took her, and I—"

"And you almost got yourself killed in the process." His voice is sharp as ice. "What good would you be to her then?"

"I don't care!" The words tear from my throat. "She's my best friend. My *sister*. And now she's in the hands of those monsters, and it's all my fault. I should have protected her better. I should have—"

"Stop." His grip gentles, but he doesn't let me go. "This isn't your fault. But getting yourself killed won't help her."

I slump against him, the fight draining out of me as the reality of the situation crashes over me.

"I lost her. I promised I'd keep her safe, and I lost her." I finally manage to break free of his grip, stumbling to my feet. "We're going after her," I tell him. "Now. I don't care how angry you are at me for projecting. I don't care about anything except finding her."

"Sapphire—"

"I promised her she'd be safe!" My voice cracks. "Less than a day ago, I promised her. And now she's gone. She's human, Riven. She can't survive in this realm without us. And if she dies, it's going to be my fault for bringing her here in the first place."

"Listen to me." He stands, reaching for my arm, but I jerk away.

"No, you listen." Wind stirs around us, and I take a deep breath, not needing the drama of him realizing I have air magic on top of what just happened to Zoey. "She's going to die. She's going to die because I was too weak to—"

"She's not dead."

The certainty in his voice stops me. "You don't know that."

"Think about it." He moves closer, and this time when he reaches for me, I let him. "You projected yourself through those trees, searching for her. What did you find?"

"Nothing," I say, the word bitter on my tongue. "I couldn't find anything."

"Exactly." His fingers tighten around my wrist. "You found nothing. No body. No sign of violence. Which means there's a higher chance she's alive than if you'd found her broken at the bottom of those trees."

I hadn't thought of it that way.

And my hearts breaks at just the *thought* of her "broken at the bottom of those trees," like he just said.

But that's *not* what I found.

There's still hope.

I have to hold on to that hope. If I don't...

He's telling the truth, I tell myself to calm myself. *He can't lie. He wouldn't have said it if he didn't think it was the truth.*

It helps.

A bit.

"But we still have to find her," I insist, although some of the panic ebbs from my voice.

"And how do you suggest we do that?" He raises an eyebrow. "We have no idea how fast those dark angels can fly, or what direction the one who took her is heading. For all we know, they could have changed course the moment they were out of sight."

I want to argue. I want to scream that he doesn't understand how much it hurts that I failed Zoey. But the calm determination in his voice, the unshakable logic—it's like a lifeline, dragging me back from the edge.

"So what?" I finally say. "We just give up? Leave her to die?"

No chance.

I'll never give up on her.

Never.

"No." The gentleness in his voice surprises me. "We keep going. We find the ancient woman. She knows secrets older than both courts combined—she might be able to help us locate Zoey. At the very least, she can tell us more about these dark angels. About where they might have taken her."

"But that could take days," I say. "Weeks, even."

"I know." He moves his hand from my wrist to my cheek, and the tenderness in his touch makes my breath catch. "I know how much she means to you. I've seen it in the way you look at her and protect her. The way you fight for her."

A tear slips down my cheek. "She's all I have."

"That's not true anymore." His thumb brushes the tear away. "And I promise you—we'll find her. But we have to be smart about this. Strategic."

I study his face—the determination in his silver eyes, the way his jaw is set with resolve. This isn't the cold winter prince who sealed our deal with a kiss. This is someone who understands what I'm going through.

Someone who might care.

Someone who's lost someone he's loved before, and who doesn't want me to suffer that same fate.

Or someone who's doing everything he can to get me to focus on getting the ingredients for that potion for his father, instead of trying to help me save my best friend.

Unfortunately, no matter what his motives are, he's right. We have no idea where to go to find Zoey.

The ancient woman might be our only hope.

"Okay," I finally say, taking a shaky breath. "We'll do it your way."

He nods, dropping his hand from my face. "The stars are still clear. We should keep moving while we can."

I look up at the sky, searching for the pattern that will lead us forward. Lead us to answers.

Lead us to Zoey.

Some of them glow more than the others. They sing to me. Point to each other. Whisper in my mind in a language I don't know how I understand.

"This way," I say, and I turn away from Riven, keeping an eye on the sky as I lead our way through the night.

ZOEY

THE DARK ANGEL refuses to speak to me as we run on the jaguar's back through the forest.

It should be freezing. But, somehow, the air around us remains charged with warmth. A small miracle I'm grateful for, given how much my body aches after so many hours on Ghost's back.

We stop in front of a snowbank.

He raises his hand, and the snow *moves*, revealing stone steps leading down into darkness. Then, he dismounts and unties the rope holding me to the jaguar, although he keeps some of it around me, holding onto it like a leash.

"Inside," he commands, gesturing toward the steps.

I plant my feet firmly in the snow. "Not a chance."

There's no way I'm following this guy into a dark, underground death trap.

His grip on the rope tightens. "That wasn't a request."

"I don't care." I pull against the rope, trying to put as much space as possible between us, which isn't much, given his strength. "You kidnapped me, dragged me who knows how far, and now you think I'm just going to stroll into your creepy lair? No thanks."

He sighs, both exasperated and oddly indulgent, as if he's dealing with a tantrum-prone child. "You can walk," he says, "or I can carry you. Your choice."

I spin around, ready to run, but he's too fast. His arms lock around my waist, and suddenly my feet aren't touching the ground anymore.

"Put me down!" I twist and kick, but his grip is unyielding, and before I know it, he's carrying me down the steps into the bunker.

"I will," he says coolly. "Once we're inside."

The darkness swallows us as we descend, the morning light disappearing behind us. I expect the air to grow colder, but it doesn't. Instead, there's a strange warmth, like the space itself is alive.

The stairs give way to a polished floor, and I stop struggling, my breath catching as I take in the room around me.

This... isn't what I expected.

It's a room that looks like it was ripped straight from a palace.

The walls are black, reflecting the glow of silver sconces. Rich purple drapes hang from the ceiling, and a dark wood table and chairs sit off to the side, near a small kitchen.

But what steals my attention is the bed.

It's massive, draped in velvet blankets so soft they look like they'd melt under your touch. Pillows are piled high, the kind that seem like they'd swallow you whole if you sank into them. My entire body aches with longing as I stare at it.

The dark angel sets me down and releases the rope, and I don't even think—I stumble toward the bed, collapsing onto the plush surface.

It's like falling onto a cloud in heaven.

After days in that ice tower, a night in a tent, and sleeping in a cave, I think I've forgotten what it feels like to sleep on a bed.

"Are you going to kill me?" I ask, sinking onto the mattress, too tired to care about the answer.

Instead of replying, he moves toward an armchair near the corner of the room, unfastening his cloak and draping it over the back.

His movements are slow, deliberate, like he has all the time in the world. And he keeps his wings retracted, as if he's finished intimidating me with them—for now.

"If I wanted you dead, you'd already be dead," he says, alarmingly casual. "I'm Aerix. And this is Nyx."

The jaguar settles onto a plush rug near the bed, watching me with those intelligent golden eyes.

I give her a small smile.

I might hate the dark angel—Aerix—but I could never hate an animal.

He approaches the bed slowly, his midnight eyes catching the light from the sconces. There's something maddeningly calm about the way he moves—like he thinks he controls the room, the situation, and most of all, *me.*

"What do you think you're doing?" I snap, my exhaustion forgotten as anger surges through me.

He leans down and brushes a piece of lint off the velvet blanket, like he's preparing the bed for himself. "Getting comfortable," he says. "It's been a long night."

"Oh, no." I sit up fully now, gripping the edge of the blanket like it's a shield. "You are *not* sharing this bed with me."

"It's large enough for both of us." He tilts his head, amusement flickering in his eyes.

"Over my dead body."

My dagger's in my hand before I can think it through, and I launch myself at him, aiming for his throat.

He catches my wrist like I'm moving in slow motion, twisting until the dagger clatters to the floor.

His fingers are like steel bands around my arm, but while his grip is firm, it's not painful.

"That," he says, surprise flickering across his face, "was unexpected."

"Let. Me. Go." I struggle against his grip, but it's like fighting a mountain.

"You tried to kill me," he says slowly, as if it hasn't actually set in. "Most humans are more... receptive to my kind."

"Sorry to disappoint," I growl at him. "Maybe try kidnapping someone with lower standards next time."

To my shock, he laughs.

Then he releases me, and the weight of his gaze is suffocating, like he's peeling back layers to see parts of me I don't understand.

I hate it.

I hate *him.*

But before I can lunge for the dagger again, he waves a hand, and the weapon flies across the room.

It lands on the table with a soft thunk.

Crazily enough, I've faced so much insanity over the past week that I'm not sure I'm even scared anymore.

I just want this all to stop.

I just want to sleep for an entire day on this plush bed. Maybe I'll wake up and this will have all been one crazy nightmare.

"I didn't bring you here to hurt you," he repeats. "Or to kill you."

"You're lying."

"I'm not."

He holds out his hand, and water materializes above his palm, swirling into intricate patterns and dissolving into mist.

"I'm part fae," he says simply. "Which, as you may or may not know by now, means I can't lie."

"Or maybe you can *partly* lie," I shoot back. "Since you're only *part* fae. And also part vampire, judging by that air magic you've been using."

A breeze passes through the room, as if he's saying yes without actually *saying* it. "You're exhausting," he says instead.

"You're the one who kidnapped me. And who's looking at me like I'm the best piece of bacon at a breakfast buffet."

My stomach growls at the thought of bacon.

"Look," he shoots back, his tone sharp. "If I wanted to feed on you, I would have. If I wanted you dead, you'd already be buried. Is that clear enough?"

"Crystal." I glare at him, my mind racing. "But that doesn't answer the question. Why not just leave me to drown in that waterfall? Why did you take me? And why did you bring me *here?*"

I motion around the room, as if what I'm referring to isn't obvious already.

He crosses his arms, leaning casually against the bedframe. "You're not ready for that answer."

I narrow my eyes. "Try me."

"I'd rather not waste my breath trying to explain things you'll only understand later."

"Well, lucky for you, I'm a quick learner," I snap. "So, go ahead. Enlighten me."

ZOEY

Aᴇʀɪx sɪɢʜs, pinching the bridge of his nose. "You ask too many questions."

"And you give too few answers."

"You say that as if you're entitled to answers."

I glare at him, since he's right—I'm *definitely* entitled to answers.

"You made me stop struggling earlier with just your voice," I continue. "That's not fae or vampire magic."

At least not that I'm aware of, given what I've picked up so far from Sapphire and Riven's conversations.

"Very observant." He settles onto the edge of the bed, and I scoot back, maintaining as much distance as I can. "Humans aren't usually aware of my kind's influence."

"Then sorry to break it to you, but your 'influence' must be a little rusty," I reply, not backing down. "Maybe you should workshop it? Because so far, the thing I've been the most *influenced* to do is to stab you. Well—*try* to stab you."

He lifts a hand, silencing me with a flick of his fingers. "I'm night fae," he finally says. "An ancient hybrid of fae and vampire."

"So, you drink blood." A pit of fear forms in my stomach that probably should have been there since being dragged into this palatial bunker. "Human blood?"

"Human blood is preferred, yes," he says, so casually that it's like he's discussing his coffee preference.

My stomach twists. "Great. So, you're saying you could've drained me dry if you felt like it."

"I could have," he says, watching me with those infuriatingly calm midnight eyes of his. "But I didn't."

"What incredible restraint." I roll my eyes, since refusing to back down is probably the only thing that's emotionally getting me through all this insanity right now. "Really appreciate not being someone's midnight snack."

"I also could have let you drown at that waterfall," he continues. "But I didn't. Because that's what would have happened, you know. Your friends weren't going to get to you in time. The *only* reason you're alive right now is because of me."

I glare at him in response.

Aerix smirks. "You're welcome."

I clench the blanket tighter, forcing myself to stay composed. "So, why did you save me?" I try again.

"You ask too many questions."

"And you give too few answers," I shoot back. "So, come on, Mr. Can't-Lie. Spill."

"That's all you're getting." He stands, his towering frame looming over me, and I feel the full weight of his presence—dark, magnetic, and unnervingly calm. "Now, given that I rescued you from drowning and dragged you halfway across the forest, I'd like to rest, too."

I scowl as he lowers himself onto the other side of the bed, making no effort to ask or even pretend he needs permission.

"Absolutely not." I grab one of the pillows and shove it down the middle of the mattress, so tired that I don't think I'm fully comprehending that a dark fae-vampire hybrid is casually jumping into bed with me.

But he clearly doesn't want to kill me right now. And if I somehow manage to escape the bunker, I'll definitely die in that forest.

So, what reasonable choice do I have?

"This is the line," I tell him. "Cross it, and I'll stab you again."

"A pillow fortress." He glances at it in amusement. "How formidable."

"I'm serious," I hiss, scooting as close to the edge of the bed as I can without falling off. "Stay on your side."

"Relax, Zoey." He stretches out with infuriating indifference. "I'm not going to dismantle your monumental barrier. You're safe with me."

"How do you even know my name?" I ask, since I definitely didn't take the time to introduce myself to him.

"Your friend screamed it back at that waterfall," he says simply. "Where I saved you."

I'm seconds away from sarcastically thanking him for specifying which waterfall he meant, when I remind myself about one of the rules of the fae—never thank one of them, unless you want to owe them a favor. And sure, maybe since he's part fae, I'd only owe him *part* of a favor. But I have no interest in finding that out.

Plus, his mention of Sapphire's scream is a blow to my heart.

She must be going out of her mind with worry. I can still see her face as I was carried away—the devastation in her eyes when she realized she failed me.

Then another thought strikes me, making my stomach sink even further.

The deal she made with Riven.

She swore to help him find the potion for his father's sanity to the best of her ability. And "the best of her ability" probably doesn't include a detour to rescue her human best friend who got kidnapped by a fae-vampire to an underground bunker magically hidden under a snowbank. She wouldn't know where to start looking for me, either.

She might have no choice but to leave me behind.

My fists clench around the blanket, my chest tightening. It's not Sapphire's fault, but it doesn't stop the hurt or the betrayal that edges into my thoughts. All I can see is her face as I was dragged away—her fear, her helplessness.

Now all I have is Aerix and his smug expression as he watches me to see if he's making any progress on breaking down my metaphorical—and physical—walls.

"You're upset," he observes, interrupting my spiraling thoughts.

"I'm going to sleep." I don't bother looking at him, instead rolling onto my side—facing *away* from him—and closing my eyes.

Even with the pillow barrier, the space between us feels suffocatingly small.

And then there's his scent—dark and intoxicating, like rain on burnt wood. No matter how much I try to block it out, it seeps into my senses, making it impossible to ignore him.

I hate it.

I hate him.

I hate this place.

And most of all, I hate being powerless.

I'm finally starting to drift to sleep when the mattress shifts.

Jolting awake, I look over to see Aerix's arm brushing against my pillow barrier.

"Do you mind?" I hiss, throwing as much venom into the words as I can muster.

"Relax." He raises an eyebrow, looking far too comfortable for someone who kidnapped me and forced me to share his bed. "Your precious barricade is still intact. Although, I have to say, if you're trying to ward off evil, you might want to try something sturdier than finely woven silk."

"Just... stay on your side," I say, more defeated than angry by this point.

I'm too tired for this. Too tired to think about Sapphire, about almost drowning, about being kidnapped, or about *any* of it.

"Sweet dreams, little human," he murmurs, and I hate how his voice seems to wrap around me, softer than the silk sheets I'm relying on for protection. "And you have no idea how grateful you should be that you remind me so much of her."

Not having the energy to continue this back and forth with him, I don't reply.

Instead, I close my eyes and let exhaustion pull me under, praying that when I wake up, it won't be to Aerix sinking his fangs into my neck for a cup of the vampiric version of morning coffee.

SAPPHIRE

Just before sunrise, the stars that have been guiding me all night fade. Exhaustion drags at my limbs, and even though I'm pressed against Riven's back as we ride Ghost through the forest, I can barely keep my eyes open.

"There." Riven points to a dense group of frost-tipped pines ahead. "The branches will give us cover, and the roots create a natural barrier. It's as defensible as we'll find out here."

As much as I hate stopping, I can't keep guiding us through the day, when the stars are no longer out. Well, minus the sun, but clearly that doesn't count in this circumstance. Plus, Ghost's pace has slowed considerably. He's as exhausted as we are.

Riven dismounts first, then reaches up to help me down.

My legs shake as they hit the ground, and I have to grip his arm to stay steady.

We barely spoke while riding Ghost's back, minus my instructions about which way the stars were pointing us. I couldn't. Because all I feel is guilt, and all I see is Zoey's terrified face as she was flung over that waterfall, and all I hear is her scream as that dark angel carried her away into the forest.

I'm only halfway present as I follow Riven to the space between the trees, which forms a sort of hollow, the ground carpeted with soft needles. He clears away some snow and fallen branches, creating a small shelter while Ghost sniffs around the area, as if making sure it's safe.

Riven settles into the space he's cleared, reaching into his pack and pulling out a bundle wrapped in cloth.

"We need to eat," he says, unwrapping the package to reveal a chunk of dark bread and a handful of berries. "It's not much, but it'll keep us going."

I drop onto the makeshift bed of pine needles, hugging my knees to my chest. I'm still fairly satiated from the elk, so I'll be fine eating the bread and berries for now.

But I'll eventually need blood again. I assume in two more days, judging by how long I lasted between the dark angel and the elk.

"The stars were clear tonight," Riven says, settling beside me and breaking off a piece of bread. "You read them well."

Something about his voice calms me. I don't know why, but it just *does.*

"They sang to me." I take a small bite of the bread, remembering the way the constellations pulsed with their own rhythm, harmonizing with each other, connecting to each other—and to me. "Like they were trying to show me the way forward."

He studies me with an intensity that makes my skin prickle.

"My mother used to say the same thing," he finally says.

The sadness in his voice makes my heart hurt.

"I'm sorry," I say softly. "About what happened to her."

"Don't," he says sharply, but then he sighs, as if giving in. "Just eat. Rest. We have a long journey ahead."

I pick at a berry, tears welling in my eyes as I eat it.

He watches me, clearly aware of the fact that I'm seconds away from bursting into tears. But he doesn't push me to talk about it. Instead, he's quiet, giving me space to decide what I want to say, and what I don't.

"I can't stop thinking about her," I eventually tell him, finishing off another berry.

He sets his food aside and leans forward, resting his elbows on his knees. "You're carrying the weight of this like it's your fault," he says. "But it's not."

"I brought her here. Because of a stupid *bracelet.*" I motion to the delicate sapphire bracelet around my wrist—the one thing my mother's ever given me—suddenly hating the piece of jewelry that I've always loved. "If I'd just left her back in Presque Isle, she'd be safe right now. Not—" My chest tightens, and I force myself to take a shaky breath. "Not wherever that dark angel took her."

"We have every reason to believe she's still alive," he repeats what he told me earlier, as if he's trying to will the truth into the world. "After our deal is completed—when I've given my father the potion, and the Winter Court is stable again—we'll do what we can to find her."

I want to believe him.

But all I can see as we finish off the food is Zoey's terrified face as that dark angel carried her away.

"Try to sleep," he says once we're done eating. "Ghost and I will keep the first watch."

I laugh bitterly. "Sleep. Sure. Like that's going to happen."

He gives me a pointed look. "You need rest. You're no good to Zoey—or to yourself—if you don't take care of your body."

"I can't just turn my brain off," I say, pulling my knees tight to my chest. "Every time I close my eyes, I see her. I hear her scream. I can't just *forget*."

"Here." Riven reaches into his pack and pulls out a familiar vial of dark blue liquid. "This won't make you forget. But it will help ease your mind."

I bolt upright, my exhaustion forgotten as fury surges through me. "You want to drug me?"

"It's the same relaxation potion I gave Zoey," he says. "You saw how it helped her—"

"No." I glare at him. "I will *not* take something to 'relax' me when I'm alone with you. Not after how pushy you've been with me ever since I got here."

His expression darkens. "You think I'd—" He cuts himself off, jaw clenching. "Is that really what you think of me?"

"For as long as we've known each other, you've made your intentions quite clear."

"Unbelievable," he mutters, shaking his head. "You think I'd drug you? That I'd—" He cuts himself off, exhaling sharply, his voice dropping dangerously low. "Trust me, Summer Fae. If I wanted you in my bed that badly, I wouldn't need to resort to a potion. It ruins the fun if they're not willing."

The crude words hit like a slap.

"Wow. You're a shining example of chivalry." I glare at him again, shivering as the wind picks up around us.

"And you're being ridiculous." He runs his hand through his dark hair, frost crystallizing at his fingertips. "You've been awake for over a day. You're exhausted, you're emotional, and you're no good to anyone—especially Zoey—if you can't even think straight."

"I'm fine."

"You nearly fell off Ghost three times in the last hour."

"I said I'm fine."

"For the love of—" He takes a deep breath, the frost retreating from his hands as he tries to calm himself.

When he speaks again, his voice is steadier. "You don't want the potion? Fine. But at least let me help you another way."

I eye him suspiciously. "What way?"

"Breathing exercises. Meditation techniques. Things I've learned over the years from my training." His lips quirk slightly. "Unless you think I can somehow seduce you through breathing exercises?"

Despite everything, I laugh. "I wouldn't put it past you to try."

"There she is." His expression softens. "Come on. Sit down before you fall down."

Too tired to argue anymore, I sink back onto the pine needles. Ghost curls up beside me, radiating warmth, and I hate how safe it makes me feel.

"Close your eyes," he says. "Focus on my voice."

"If this is some sort of trick—"

"Sapphire." The way he says my name—soft but firm—makes something flutter in my chest. "Just trust me. Please."

I want to snap back that I don't trust him at all. That I can't trust him. Not when I'm hiding what I am, and he might turn on me if he discovers the truth.

But apparently not all of that is true, because I can't bring myself to say it.

And, as frustrating as it is, I can only speak the truth.

"Fine," I give in, sinking back onto the pine needles. "Show me."

He crouches in front of me, his movements sharp and controlled, like he's holding himself back.

"Close your eyes," he says again, his voice softening slightly.

"Focus on your breathing. In through your nose for four counts. Hold it for four. Out through your mouth for four."

I do as he says, although my breaths are shallow and unsteady at first.

"Now, picture a box in your mind, going from one ear to the other," he continues. "Inhale, imagining that you can breathe in through your right ear. Hold it inside the box. Exhale from the left ear. Then from the left to the right. Over and over."

I try to follow his instructions, but my thoughts keep tugging back to Zoey—to her scream, and the terror on her face as the dark angel carried her away.

"It's not working," I eventually say.

"It will," he insists. "You're fighting it. Stop. Let your mind follow the rhythm."

I bite back a retort and try again, focusing on the imaginary box and pretending like I can breathe in through my ears.

Slowly, the edges of my thoughts blur, the rhythm of my breathing pulling me into a surprising sense of calm.

His voice washes over me like waves on a shore, and despite everything, my body tingles as I feel myself drifting.

The last thing I register is Ghost's rumbling purr beside me, and Riven's quiet voice.

"Sleep well, Summer Fae."

ZOEY

I CAN'T PINPOINT the exact moment I fell asleep. But awareness creeps back slowly, and the first thing I register is warmth—a solid presence beneath my arm that's definitely not my pillow barrier.

My eyes flutter open, and my heart stops.

My arm is draped across Aerix's chest, the pillow fort demolished between us. His shirt has ridden up. And, to make it worse, my fingers are grazing the bare skin of his stomach.

My stupid, traitorous body must have shifted in the night.

I risk a glance at his face, praying he's still asleep.

Instead, I find him very much awake, those midnight eyes glinting with barely concealed amusement.

He quirks a brow, smiling smugly. "Comfortable?"

Heat floods my cheeks, and I yank my arm back so quickly that I nearly tumble off the bed.

"Don't flatter yourself." I sit up, trying to ignore my racing heart. "I must have been... sleepwalking."

"Fascinating." His smile widens. "I wasn't aware humans possessed the ability to walk while horizontal. Tell me—is that a new evolutionary development?"

"Maybe I'm just an overachiever," I shoot back, crossing my arms over my chest.

"Clearly." He stretches lazily, like a cat basking in the sun, and props himself up on one elbow. "Though next time, maybe keep your achievements on your side of the bed. Or don't. I certainly didn't mind."

I grit my teeth and push down the flush creeping up my neck. "Trust me, I will. And if you touch me, I'll—"

"Stab me?" he interrupts, raising an eyebrow. "I think we've established how that misguided attempt would end."

My glare could probably shoot a laser beam through his forehead. "Don't tempt me."

Aerix chuckles again, clearly enjoying himself far too much.

But before I can come up with a retort, my stomach betrays me, letting out a loud, grumbling protest.

He rises in one fluid motion, moving to the cabinets near the small kitchen area. There, he begins pulling out various items—dried herbs, preserved vegetables, something that might have once been bread, and a few others.

"Really?" I eye the sad collection of ingredients. "That's what passes for breakfast in a five-star bunker?"

"My apologies." His voice drips with sarcasm. "I'd order room service, but I imagine it would take a while."

Shrugging off his comment, I move to inspect what he's found, my mind cataloging possibilities of what I can do with it. The herbs are decent—thyme, rosemary, and garlic. The vegetables, while preserved, still have life in them. And that bread... well, it's seen better days, but I worked with worse during the summer I volunteered at the soup kitchen at church.

"Move," I say, nudging him aside to dig through the cabinets. "Do you have a way to start a fire?"

He pulls a flint and steel from a drawer, holding it up between two fingers. "I can manage that much. The question is whether you can do anything with this sorry lot."

"Challenge accepted."

While he sets to work building the fire, I keep my focus on assembling ingredients.

Once the fire is going, I set a dented iron skillet on the heat and add a splash of oil I found in a dusty bottle. Next, I chop the vegetables and toss them into the pan, and they hiss and pop, smelling somewhat decent.

"What exactly are you making?" Aerix leans against the counter, watching me as if I'm casting a spell.

"Improvising." I slice the bread into thin cubes, rub it with the garlic herb mixture I've thrown together, and arrange it on a flat piece of stone to toast near the fire.

Within minutes, I've turned the meager ingredients into a rustic open-faced sandwich. Toasted bread topped with sautéed vegetables, shredded meat, and a drizzle of herb-infused oil that adds just enough flavor to make it feel intentional.

"Where did you learn to do this?" he asks.

"I volunteered at a soup kitchen for a bit." I shrug, adding the final touches. "We didn't have much to work with, but I had a knack for improvising."

"Very interesting," he says, studying me in a way that makes me look away and refocus on arranging the food. "Shall we eat in bed?"

"Absolutely not." I grab a plate and move to the table, putting as much space between us as possible. "I've already spent enough time in that bed with you."

"Yet you seemed so comfortable there earlier..."

"One more word about that," I warn, pointing my fork at him, "and I'll show you exactly how creative I can get with those cooking knives."

He doesn't bother to respond. Instead, he settles into the chair opposite me, leaning back with infuriating ease and studying the plate I've set before him.

Finally, he picks up a fork and takes a bite, surprise flickering across his face. "I have to admit," he says, "you're more talented in the kitchen than most of the fae I know."

I arch my brow, unable to resist a little teasing. "Maybe I added a little something extra into it."

"Trying to poison me?" He smirks, clearly amused. "I hate to disappoint, but fae aren't affected by human toxins."

"You're safe—for now," I tell him. "Poisoning someone is way too much effort before breakfast. Plus, I'm going to need some help with the dishes."

He laughs, which sends a strange thrill down my spine.

"I think you misunderstood me as someone who takes orders," he says. "However, I'd say this meal is only the start of what you owe me for saving your life."

"I owe you nothing." I glare at him, snapped back to the reality of *why* I'm stuck in this place with him to begin with.

We eat in silence for a moment.

Finally, I break it with the question that's been tugging at the edge of my mind since right before I fell asleep. "That person I remind you of," I begin carefully. "Did she cook?"

"You heard that?" he asks.

"Yes. I heard it."

"She didn't cook," he says after a few tense seconds, setting his fork down with deliberate precision. "At least, not well. And don't speak of her in past tense. She's alive."

Just like that, his walls are back up.

I internally curse myself for bringing it up. Because apparently, he's a minefield. One wrong step, and he completely shuts down.

Eventually, Nyx pads over and nudges my arm, her golden eyes fixed on my plate with obvious interest.

"Really?" I can't help but smile. "The fierce jaguar wants table scraps?"

She makes a rumbling sound that's almost a purr, butting her head against my shoulder.

"Here." I tear off a piece of the herbed bread. "But don't tell your master I'm spoiling you."

She takes it delicately from my fingers, and my heart melts a little. She might be a massive, beautiful predator, but she's still just a cat at heart.

Aerix watches the exchange with a raised brow. "She doesn't usually take to strangers."

"I volunteered at an animal shelter for a few weekends this past fall." I scratch behind Nyx's ears, and she leans into my touch. "Spent most of my time working with the cats."

"Let me guess," he says. "Your favorites were the difficult ones?"

"Always," I admit, smiling slightly. "There was this one cat—Milo. Total terror. Hissed at everyone, wouldn't let anyone near him. But I spent hours sitting outside his cage, talking to him, letting him come to me on his own terms."

"And?" His voice is deceptively casual, but there's an edge to it, like he's waiting for something.

"Eventually, he let me pet him," I say, meeting his gaze. "He's mine now. I adopted him."

I hope Milo's doing okay without me. That my parents are treating him okay.

Well, more like that he's treating *them* okay.

"You're not the only one around here who likes a challenge." Aerix leans forward, holding me down with those midnight eyes of his. "And I must admit—you're far more capable than I thought you'd be, given how much you were struggling in that water. It's intriguing, to say the least."

I should be angry at him for assuming I could be anything less than capable, simply for not knowing how to swim.

Instead, the air between us charges again, like the moment before lightning strikes, and I forget how to breathe.

Then, thunder crashes overhead, making us both jump.

"We need to leave." He stands abruptly, all business now. "The storms in this area can turn deadly. But if we move quickly, we can reach the court before the worst hits."

"The court?" My stomach drops as I flash back to the terror that was the Winter Court. "A fae court?"

"The Night Court," he says, and I swallow, not liking the sound of that. "Unless you'd prefer to stay here and get trapped by the storm? Even after having used our final ingredients for our gourmet meal, and knowing the *other* ingredient I need to consume to remain satiated?"

He glances at my neck, and another crack of thunder emphasizes his point.

"Fine." I push away from the table, hating that he's probably right. "But don't think this means I'm going quietly."

"I wouldn't dream of it." His smirk returns. "Nor would I want it, given that you've proven far too entertaining when you're being difficult. Just like that cat of yours—begging to be tamed."

"Begging to be tamed?" I scoff, hating him all over again. "You'd have better luck with that storm."

"We'll see," he says, and the way his gaze lingers leaves me wondering if he means the storm outside—or the one brewing between us.

SAPPHIRE

Hours pass as Riven and I ride on Ghost's back through the valley.

Every shift of his muscles reminds me of our fight earlier. Of the anger in his voice when I accused him of wanting to drug me, and of the way that anger melted into something gentler as he taught me those breathing exercises that lulled me to sleep.

"The stars still singing to you?" he asks, startling me at the sound of his voice after such a long time of silence.

"Still north." I try my hardest to stay calm—to not let him know how much he's affecting me. "A few miles or so, and we'll turn right."

He nods without looking back. "Got it."

We lapse into silence again, and flurries begin to fall, catching in Ghost's fur and swirling around us like glittering specks.

It's beautiful. The kind of moment that feels pulled from another life—one far simpler than the one I'm living now.

But then the wind picks up, and the snow starts coming faster. Heavier.

A low rumble echoes across the valley.

"Was that—?" I start to ask, but Riven answers before I can finish.

"Thundersnow." Tension threads through his voice. "We need to find shelter. These storms—"

Lightning splits the sky, painfully bright.

In seconds, the wind howls louder, and the stars vanish, swallowed by the storm clouds churning overhead. The snow's whipping in every direction, and I tighten my grip on Ghost's fur to keep from slipping.

Another flash of lightning brightens the valley, followed by an earsplitting crack of thunder.

Ghost rears back.

It happens too quickly. So quickly that I lose my grip, the wind tearing me off him, even as I search for something to hold onto.

"Riven!" I scream as I hit the ground hard, the breath knocked out of me.

I try to scramble to my feet, but the storm is ruthless, the wind pushing me back down as snow blinds my vision. The world's turned into a wall of white, the wind screaming so loudly I can barely hear myself think.

I can't see Ghost. I can't see Riven.

Panic claws at my chest, my breathing shallow and frantic.

I'm lost. Alone.

I'm going to die out here.

Focus, I tell myself, closing my eyes and thinking. *Air is one of my elements. Feel the wind currents. Just like how I harness it when I run.*

Taking a deep breath, I reach for my magic and release it through my palms, letting it fan out like invisible threads.

It's like opening my eyes underwater, and suddenly, the roaring wind isn't just noise anymore. It's a symphony of currents that carries everything—sounds, movement, and presence. A song like the one sung by the stars.

Finally, I feel it.

A disruption in the flow. A solid body in the raging storm.

I stumble in the direction the wind tells me, the storm fighting me every step of the way.

Lightning flashes again.

With it, I catch a glimpse of Riven, his dark form moving against the blinding white snow.

"Riven!" I shout again, pushing toward him.

He turns just as I reach him and locks his arms around me, as if he's terrified of losing me again.

"Where's Ghost?" I have to scream to be heard over the wind.

Another crack of thunder shakes the air around us, and the snow swirls harder, reducing visibility to nothing.

"We got separated," he replies, holding me tighter. "We have to find him."

"We will," I say, and as we search, he releases me with one arm, keeping the other locked around my waist. His ice magic creates a partial shield against the worst of the storm, and I do my best to lower the strength of the wind howling around us, making it a bit easier to fight against the gusts.

There's only so far Ghost could have gotten. He has to be here somewhere.

But he's nowhere to be found.

Eventually, we stop in front of a pine tree that offers us a slight break from the chaos.

"Nothing," I say, shaking from a mix of the cold, frustration, and fear.

Riven's jaw tightens. "We can't stay out here. The storm's only getting worse."

"What about Ghost?" I ask.

"Ghost is smart," he says, although from the way his body tenses up, I can feel his anxiety. "He knows how to survive. But we need to get out of this storm. No amount of magic will save us if we stay out here."

He's right. The wind is getting stronger, the snow so thick I can barely breathe.

"There's a cave." I point toward the outline of the mountain ahead—one that I felt earlier with my air magic. "We can go there."

"All right," he says, and together, we push forward, the storm battering us as we make our way to the mouth of the cave.

The moment we're inside, he spins toward the entrance, using his magic to create a thick barrier of ice that seals us in. It's like when he turned that tent into an igloo back at the lake, but on a far larger scale.

The sudden silence is jarring. Especially since we can see through the ice, at the storm raging outside.

"Ghost is smart," Riven says again, but his voice is tight with worry. "He'll find shelter. He has to."

"How long do these storms normally last?" I wrap my arms around myself, since even with the entrance sealed and the warmth amulet hanging from my neck, the cold is continuing to seep into my bones.

It doesn't help that my clothes are drenched.

Riven reaches forward, touches my shoulder, and within seconds, I'm dry.

"Better?" He watches me closely, not moving his hand away.

"Yes," I manage to say, my heart pounding, my entire body feeling trapped under his intense, silver gaze.

After a few long seconds, he brings his arm back to his side.

My heart drops.

But what was I expecting? For him to kiss me again?

It's hardly the time for that. Which is saying a lot, given that this is *Riven* we're talking about here.

"These storms can last for a day," he says, glancing around our small shelter. "Maybe two."

"Two *days?*"

He places his pack on the ground, which thankfully stayed on his shoulder through our fall, and starts going through it. "We have some food," he says. "Not much, but if we ration it, we'll be fine."

I watch as he sorts through what's left of the berries and bread, mentally calculating how long it will last.

For him, it might be enough.

For me...

Soon, the hunger will start gnawing at me again. That deep, primal need for blood that no amount of foraged food will satisfy.

Being trapped in this cave with Riven while that happens...

"Here." He hands me a small portion of bread. "We should eat something now. Keep our strength up."

I take it without argument, but my stomach twists.

Up to two days in this cave. Two days of hiding what I am, and what I need to survive.

Would his blood taste as sweet as his lips?

No. I step back, fear rising inside of me at the fact that my thoughts even went there. *I can use the least amount of magic and energy as I can. I can control myself.*

I won't do *that* to him. No matter how much I hate him.

"He has to be okay," Riven interrupts my dark thoughts, staring at the ice barrier, clearly referring to Ghost. "He's always okay. From the moment he found me in that forest when I was a boy, he's always..." His voice catches. "He's never left me."

The pain in his voice makes my chest ache. I've never seen him like this—vulnerable, worried, his walls stripped away by fear for his familiar.

"We'll find him," I say, reaching out and touching his arm before I can stop myself. "As soon as the storm breaks."

He looks down at my hand, then up at me, and something shifts in the air between us. The cave suddenly feels smaller. More intimate. And I'm achingly aware of how alone we are—of how much I want to comfort him, even though I know I shouldn't.

"You should rest." He pulls away from me, and my heart drops in disappointment. "I'll take first watch."

"No." I shake my head. "You've been using your magic more than I have. You need sleep."

"I won't be able to sleep." He settles against the wall, his sword already out and across his lap. "Not until..."

He doesn't finish, but he doesn't have to.

Not until the storm's over, and we know Ghost is safe.

ZOEY

Nyx carries Aerix and me through the forest like a shadow, swift and silent.

The ropes tying me to them dig into my arms. Not enough to hurt, but enough to remind me how powerless I am right now. And the wind snatches away any possibility of conversation.

The landscape shifts from forest to hills, the thunder growing softer behind us until it's gone completely.

Somehow—miraculously—we outran the storm.

Eventually, we crest over a hill, and a black archway looms ahead. It's like a giant version of Stonehenge, but with only one of the rock formations instead of many.

"What's this?" I ask, unable to ignore the ball of fear in my throat. As if this single arch is trying to warn me away.

He doesn't bother replying. Instead, he digs his heels into Nyx's sides, coaxing her to continue forward, under the arch.

As we pass through, a ripple of magic washes over me, like a buzzing along my skin. It's subtle, but undeniable. Like the air itself is taking note of my presence.

Then, it's there.

The Night Court.

It rises from the earth like a dark crown, jagged and angular, yet impossibly graceful. Fog floats through the narrow cobblestone streets, which have short, sharp buildings lining the paths. And then, in the center of the town—nearly piercing the clouds—stands a palace that reminds me of a giant, dark version of Cinderella's castle at Disney World. The moat surrounding the palace contains water as dark as night, and it's like the stars themselves are twinkling from its depths.

It's beautiful. Dangerous. And it buzzes with undeniable magic.

Powerful magic that chills me to the core.

"We need to walk through the town to get to the palace," Aerix says the first full sentence he's spoken in hours. "Don't squirm. Don't look at anyone. And most importantly—be quiet."

His tone is laced with so much warning that I bite back a snarky comment about how being quiet isn't one of my many charming personality traits.

"Understand?" he pushes.

"Yes," I reply, unable to tear my gaze away from the looming palace.

"Good."

Slowly, Nyx leads us down the hill and starts down the winding streets. The fog curls around her paws, and the buildings lean inward, like guards trying to trap us. It's beautiful in a cruel, fore-boding way. A place that seems alive with secrets waiting to devour the unprepared.

"It's sort of like one giant Diagon Alley, isn't it?" I say quietly, gazing around with growing unease.

"Diagon what?" Aerix asks.

"Diagon Alley," I repeat. "I guess you're not a big—"

I don't get a chance to finish my sentence regarding the fact that he apparently doesn't read much.

Because *they* appear.

The night fae, emerging like shadows, their attention snapping to us like moths to a flame.

No. Not to us.

To *me*.

I try to follow Aerix's instructions—don't squirm, don't look, be quiet. But it's impossible not to notice how they shift and move as we pass, or how the air grows thick with whispers. It's like watching a train wreck—horrifying, but impossible to look away.

Some of them have their wings out, while others have them retracted. They all have the same midnight eyes as Aerix, with sharp, arresting beauty—the type of beauty that makes it impossible to look away.

"Look what the darkness dragged in," a melodic voice carries from somewhere to my left. "Fresh meat."

"She's a pretty one," says one off to the right.

"Wonder if she'll last."

My chest tightens, and I press myself closer to Aerix. The ropes binding me to him are the only reason I don't topple off Nyx entirely.

"Relax," he murmurs, cold and detached. "They won't touch you. Not when you're with me."

"Of course." I roll my eyes. "My fae-vampire knight in shining armor. With retractable wings and a black jaguar to match."

"I told you not to say anything," he snaps quietly, and I press my lips together, not wanting to provoke any more reactions from these creatures than I already have.

We continue our agonizingly slow walk through town, and a group of men lounging outside what appears to be a tavern lean forward as we pass, their eyes gleaming like cats in the darkness.

The way they watch me feels like being stripped bare. Vulnerable in a way I've never experienced.

"Do you think one of the royals will keep her?" one of them says.

"The king, no doubt," another replies. "Just *look* at her."

"Trust me—I'm looking," chimes in another, and even though I'm not supposed to, I meet his gaze with a death glare that makes him go silent.

The deeper we go into the town, the more luxurious the buildings become. Sturdier, more symmetrical, and more ornate. Even the cobblestones are darker now, polished so they're as smooth as glass. And the fae lining the streets are dressed more elegantly, in silk fabrics instead of cotton, which are intricately designed with lace and gemstones.

The whispers continue.

"I call first taste when he's done with her."

"If there's anything left to taste," someone else laughs. "You know how these things usually end."

My heart pounds so hard I'm sure they can all hear it. And some-how, the rope binding me to Aerix feels less like a restraint and more like the only thing keeping me from being torn apart by the hungry crowd of vampiric fae.

I swallow hard and force my gaze to the cobblestones beneath us, ignoring the stares, the whispers, the low chuckles that seem to follow us through the increasingly elaborate streets.

Eventually, we reach the moat.

And that's when I realize—the reason why the water is so dark is because it's red. *Dark* red.

The same color as blood.

I can smell it now, too. Sharp and metallic, so strong that I can taste it in the back of my throat.

"Is that...?" I ask Aerix, my stomach lurching at what I'm looking at.

"You are truly terrible at obeying orders," he observes. "But yes— that's the Crimson Tide, which is what we've affectionately named our moat of blood mixed with the darkest water of the night."

My stomach lurches at the confirmation, but I force myself to stay composed as Nyx crosses the black stone bridge spanning the blood-filled moat, which leads into the courtyard.

Opulent black fountains sit in the center of the gardens, with the same nauseating blood and water mixed liquid coming out of them as the moat. But the most terrifying thing is the palace looming ahead, carved from jagged black stone veined with crimson lines. Towers spiral upward, their tips glowing with moonlight, while sharp, angular arches frame enormous double doors. The building hums with energy that makes my skin prickle—an ancient, dark magic so dense it feels alive.

Two fae guards stand on each side of the doors, their sleek black armor gleaming in the moonlight, their dark wings out for us to see.

They take one look at Aerix, push the doors open, and reveal the cavernous hall, leaving me with a sinking feeling that I'm stepping into the mouth of a monster.

ZOEY

Finally, now that I'm close to being permanently fused to Nyx, Aerix dismounts and unties the ropes holding me down.

I slide down awkwardly, my legs wobbling beneath me the moment I hit the ground.

"Try not to fall on your face," he mutters, brushing past me as if I'm not even worth the effort of helping.

"Thanks for the concern," I snap under my breath, even though I don't have the energy to put much bite into it. My legs tremble from hours on Nyx's back, and every muscle in my body aches.

"Move," Aerix commands, jerking his head toward the open doors.

Given that escape from here would be futile—I have zero interest in crossing the blood-filled moat and running through the fae-infested town where everyone wants to eat me alive—I follow reluctantly, stumbling after Aerix as he leads the way inside.

The grandness of the foyer makes my jaw drop.

The ceiling soars so high it disappears into shadows. Huge crystal chandeliers float in mid-air, moving like constellations in the night. And mirrors with ornate, silver frames line the walls, reflecting the black marble floors veined with crimson, creating patterns that shift and dance like shadows.

It's such a stark difference from the gritty town surrounding it that it feels like stepping into a nightmare.

As we pass through the main hall, more fae linger in the shadows, their gazes following us. I feel their eyes on me, their whispers barely audible but sharp enough to cut.

"Another one," someone murmurs.

"Hopefully she'll last."

"It would be a shame if she didn't. She's lovely."

I press my lips together and fix my gaze on Aerix's back, refusing to give them the satisfaction of knowing how much their words get to me.

Nyx, thankfully, stays by my side.

Aerix guides us through a series of corridors, each more beautiful and unsettling than the last. What looks like servants bow as we pass, their eyes lingering on me with that same hungry curiosity as all the rest.

We turn down a narrow hallway and stop in front of a set of wooden doors. They're smaller than the grand ones we entered through—and the material doesn't fit in with anything I've seen here yet—but they're still beautifully ornate.

"This is the human wing," Aerix says curtly, pushing the doors open.

Two fae women wait in plain black dresses, each beautiful in that sharp, dangerous way that seems standard here. And they have their wings retracted, unlike Aerix, who has his out on full display now.

"See her to a room," he instructs them. "And make sure she's cleaned up. She smells worse than Nyx after hunting in the bog."

I flinch, glaring at him. "Sorry I didn't have time to freshen up between almost drowning, being kidnapped, and then paraded through this creepy town," I say, and I swear one of the women smiles slightly.

His hand shoots out, fingers wrapping around my upper arm.

The touch sends a jolt through me—part fear, part something else I refuse to name.

"A word of advice?" His voice drops low, meant for my ears alone. "I highly recommend that you behave yourself better here than you have so far around me. And if you try to leave this wing, the guards will teach you exactly why your kind fears the dark."

His midnight eyes bore into mine, and the weight of his threat settles over me like a suffocating blanket.

I want to lash out—to fight back. But the rational part of me knows it's pointless.

It's clear after that march through town that the fae here want to rip me to shreds, drain me dry, and do God knows what else.

"Understood," I say instead, strained but steady.

He smirks, clearly satisfied with my response, turns on his heel, and sets down the hall.

Nyx follows him, her sleek form disappearing down the corridor with a flick of her tail.

Something inside me feels empty as I watch them go.

Alone.

Like a speck of dust in a court of blood and nightmares.

One of the servants—at least, I assume from their plain attire that they're servants—pointedly clears her throat, bringing my attention to her. "This way," she says. "Let's see what we can do about..." she gestures vaguely at me, "...this."

I square my shoulders and follow her, unwilling to let them see me break.

I've been through far too much to fall apart now.

Gold-framed mirrors and matching sconces hang along the halls of this wing, the floors a warm wood that almost feels like home. And it doesn't just feel warmer than the rest of the palace—it also *smells* warmer. Like sitting around a campfire on a crisp, cold night.

Eventually, we stop in front of an unassuming door, and they open it into a room that's far nicer than I expected.

The bed is massive, draped in dark, luxurious fabrics, and a copper tub sits near the fireplace, already filled with steaming water. A wardrobe stands in the corner, its doors slightly open to reveal clothing that looks far too elegant for a human in the Night Court.

One of the fae gestures toward the tub. "Bathe. Change," she instructs. "You'll be summoned when you're needed."

"Summoned for what?" I ask, but they don't answer.

They simply leave, the door closing behind them. Then there's a distinct turning sound of them locking it shut.

My body goes numb.

I'm alone. Confused. Trapped in a world I don't understand, in a realm where I don't belong.

I glance around the room again, my gaze lingering on the tub.

I hate baths. I hate submerging myself in water, period. I'm a shower girl, through and through.

Plus, what if the water is mixed with blood? Or—maybe worse—poison? What if it seeps into my skin and slowly kills me?

Death by bathing in the Night Court.

It would be quite the unexpected way to go.

But screw it.

The dirt and grime caked on my skin is unbearable.

So, with a heavy sigh, I strip off my filthy clothes and make my way into the water, which is thankfully clear of blood. The heat soothes my aching muscles, and I let myself relax, sinking deeper into the tub.

Somehow—and I have no idea how that will be—I'll get out of this place. I'll do whatever it takes to survive around here. After all, some of the fae were whispering that they "hope I'll last," which means there's a chance I'm not an animal being prepared for slaughter.

I'll do whatever it takes to live.

Even if that means getting cleaned up, putting on one of their ridiculous dresses, and playing along with whatever games are coming my way in the Night Court.

ZOEY

Once I'm clean and dried off, I begin exploring my gilded cage.

The room is larger than my parents' master suite back home, with a small sitting area off to the side, a single chandelier floating in the center of the ceiling, and two windows with velvet blue drapes hanging to the floor.

Sapphire would love it here. She's always loved beautiful things.

She must be worried sick about me. Just like I am about her. Yes, she and Riven were doing a great job fighting those nixies, but what if there were too many of them? What if they got too distracted by my being flown away that they were overtaken?

What if they're dead?

No. I can't let myself go there.

I have to believe they're alive. And that somehow, they'll find me.

I just have to *stay* alive until they do.

Figuring it's best to be as aware of my surroundings as possible, I move toward one of the windows and glance out.

There's a large courtyard right outside—which is surprisingly normal-looking compared to everything else I've seen in this place so far. Probably because it's in, as Aerix referred to it as, the *human* wing. A few people are in it, doing surprisingly normal activities— playing cards, reading, and drawing. The only thing obviously "wrong" about the courtyard is the tall concrete wall surrounding it, like a rock-solid cage.

Beyond the courtyard, the blood-filled moat is as foreboding as ever, the stars reflecting on its surface. The city sprawled out on the other side is alive, pulsing with haunted energy, and the space all the way out on the hill shimmers, reminding me of the magical ward we passed to cross into the Night Court.

I trace the edges of the window frame with my fingers, assessing its width, its height, and trying to calculate how I could climb out without breaking my neck.

But even if I succeeded, then what? Learn why—as Aerix so lovingly put it—my kind "fears the dark?"

No. If I'm getting out of here, it won't be through brute force. It will be by winning whatever game they have in store for me.

From what I know so far of the fae, they *love* games.

Faerie Games, I think. Like that book I read and loved a few years back.

And right now, I need to dress the part.

So, I make my way to the wardrobe to see what I have to work with.

The gowns inside are strikingly beautiful.

Deep, shimmering blacks that catch light like the surface of a moonlit lake. Another with a sheer material that looks like mist caught in the starlight. There's one of deep crimson, fading into black as it flows down into the skirt. The one behind it has the most intricate beading that I've ever seen in my life—rubies, sapphires, jade, and amber—swirling as if they're alive. And the final one is black leather and velvet, overlaid with sharp silver embellishments that mimic the curve of crescent moons and the sweep of wings.

What kind of game am I dressing for?

Beauty, I think.

As I was walking through town, that's what the fae kept mentioning. How pretty they thought I was. And, as I look out at the people spending time in the courtyard, there's no denying that they're all attractive.

If my looks will keep me alive, then best to lean into that as much as I can.

After a bit of deliberation, I settle on the one in the back—black leather and velvet. The moon patterns will hopefully show an interest in the night, and the wing design will hopefully show a message—I might not *be* one of you, but I can still *think* like one of you.

Now, my hair.

It's always been long, thick, and hard to control, which is why I've been watching videos online for how to manage it for as long as I can possibly remember. Plus, it might be relaxing to have something to do with my hands, instead of pacing around and getting more anxious by the second. Sort of like how I sometimes do puzzles to calm my mind.

Inside the vanity, I find an array of silver-handled brushes and combs.

Then I look into the mirror and gasp.

My reflection shows someone I barely recognize. Pale and thin, with eyes that look too large in my face, and cheekbones that give me a distinctly hollow look.

This past week has left its mark on me.

I need to get to work.

So, I section off my hair and begin weaving it into an intricate pattern of braids—one of the ones I learned during that phase where I was obsessed with historical styles. It takes forever, and my arms ache by the time I'm done, but the result is worth it. It's almost crown-like—elegant and severe at once.

I am not soft. I am not weak.

And they will not break me.

A knock at the door makes me jump.

The two fae women from earlier glide inside, and I shoot up, fidgeting slightly as their eyes sweep over me.

"Not bad," one says, circling me slowly. "You clean up well."

The other fae steps forward, her expression more scrutinizing.

In a flash, she reaches for my dress and yanks at the neckline, rearranging it so it dips dangerously low.

I jerk back instinctively, pulling the dress back up so I'm not at risk of popping right out of it.

Not to mention the fact that I've buried the amulet of warmth as close to the bottom of my breasts as possible. The only thing keeping it there is the dress's tight bodice.

Any lower of a neckline, and the amulet might become visible.

The fae woman shakes her head and gives me a pointed look.

"You're here to please, human," she says, challenge in her dark, midnight eyes. "Don't forget that."

My stomach twists.

Because it's my blood. I know that's what they want. What else could they want?

Well, there are definitely some other things they might want. But I'm not going to let myself go there. At least, not yet. It's far too much to process at once.

The only thing I have to do right now is get through tonight.

"Follow us," the other woman commands, already turning toward the door.

Once we're out of the human wing, the maze of halls seems designed to disorient. Every turn reveals another identical hallway of black and crimson marble floors, floating chandeliers, and mirrored walls, until I'm totally lost.

Finally, we reach a set of doors that tower at least thirty feet high.

"The throne room," the servant who didn't touch my dress—the nicer one—tells me. "Remember—keep your eyes down. Speak only when spoken to. And when you do speak, keep it brief."

"Not exactly my strong point," I mutter.

"Then make it one." She places a hand on the door and pushes it open, revealing an enormous throne room.

It has the same black and crimson marble floors as everywhere else in the Night Court so far, but there are also thick columns lining the walls, and a ceiling is so high that it's like staring into space itself. Giant crystal chandeliers float at various heights above, although the edges of their crystals are sharp and tinged with red, as if coated with blood. Most strikingly, there's a thin crescent moon hanging above them—which is the moon phase we're in right now—its pale light casting a gentle glow over the windowless room.

And there, at the top of a raised platform at the far end of the room, are the thrones.

Six of them, arranged in a crescent.

Five of them are occupied.

The fae sitting on them wear flowing fabrics that shimmer and shift like liquid moonlight and blood, their black feathery wings spread behind them in a display of power. Their eyes, dark and predatory, sweep over me with varying degrees of curiosity and disinterest, as if I'm a piece of art up for auction.

I try not to flinch under their collective gaze, but it's impossible not to feel like prey in front of a pack of predators.

Probably because I *am* prey in front of a pack of predators.

The one in the center speaks first.

"Come forward."

My feet move before I can think, carrying me closer until I'm standing in front of them, although the steps leading up to the thrones put them at a much higher level than where I'm standing right now.

"Welcome to the Night Court," he says. "I am King Thanatos."

He's dressed in black and crimson, his shoulders draped in a shimmering, inky cloak. His dark brown hair flows over his shoulders, and his eyes are the same midnight color I've come to realize is shared by *all* night fae.

Authority radiates off him, but I keep my eyes locked on his.

First impressions are important.

And I will *not* let him see me as weak.

"My queen, Ravenna," he says, gesturing to the woman beside him.

Where the king radiates cold authority, the queen is darkness incarnate, with her jet-black hair and dark red velvet dress that trails out onto the floor around her feet.

Her gaze meets mine, and it takes every ounce of will power to not look down at my feet.

"And my children." The king motions the others. "Prince Malakai, Princess Mirena, and Princess Cierra."

Each one is beautiful in their own terrifying way. But most interestingly of all is that none of them resemble their parents, and they definitely don't look like each other. Which makes me think that while he might *call* them his children, they're likely not related by blood.

If vampire lore in this realm is anything like it is back home, I assume they were turned by their parents—not born to them.

"And I believe," the queen adds with a cruel smile, "you've already met my son. Prince Aerix."

SAPPHIRE

RIVEN STARES at the storm raging outside the wall of ice barricading the cave, lost in thought as he worries about Ghost.

I don't like seeing him like this. It's unnerving. Different from the Riven I've known since that night at the Maple Pig.

So, I walk over and settle beside him, relieved when he doesn't stand.

"Tell me about Ghost," I say, keeping a respectable amount of space between us. "How did you meet?"

He's quiet for so long that I think he won't answer.

"I was eight," he finally says—still looking at the icy barrier and not at me. "Lost in the forest at the edge of Winter Court territory after sneaking out of the palace. I was angry at my father. I thought if I ran far enough, I could leave it all behind."

His words surprise me—both the vulnerability in his tone, and the fact that he's telling me this at all.

"What happened?" I ask, curious, but also not wanting to push.

"Ghost found me. He appeared through the trees, like he was made of snow itself." His fingers trace absent patterns in the frost beneath us, as if he's back there in that forest instead of here with me. "I thought he was going to eat me."

I try to picture Riven as a child, lost and terrified, staring into the eyes of a wild snow leopard. It feels wrong somehow—to imagine him vulnerable and helpless.

"But he didn't," I say, drawing him out of the memory.

"No." He smiles, as if he's watching it all happen again. "He just… walked up to me. Sat there, staring like he was trying to figure me out. Eventually, I stopped shaking long enough to reach out, and he let me touch him. That's when the bond formed."

"The familiar bond?"

He nods. "He led me back to the court," he continues. "Saved my life. I've never doubted him since. No matter what, Ghost has always been there. *Always.*"

He says it as if he's reminding himself that wherever Ghost is out there, there's no way he'll get lost in that storm.

"He found you once," I say, wanting to be encouraging, but also not wanting to lie. "Which means he can most likely find you again."

"He'd better." Riven chuckles. "He's my only friend. The only one who doesn't care about titles or politics. Who sees me, and not my crown."

My heart aches at the loneliness in his voice. "I always wanted a pet," I admit. "Something to care for. But Aunt Martha refused. She couldn't stand the thought of an animal 'dirtying' our home."

"Ghost isn't a pet." There's no anger in his voice, just certainty. "He's my constant. The only one who's always been there—who hasn't become lost to me."

My heart aches at what I suspect is going through his head.

His mother died.

His father's losing his mind.

As far as I know, he's an only child.

If he loses Ghost… I can't help but worry something in him will break. Permanently. Just like what happened to his father when he lost his queen.

"We'll search as hard as we can," I say, and without thinking, I reach for his hand. "I promise."

His fingers intertwine with mine, sending a rush of warmth through my body. And when he looks at me, the intensity in his silver eyes steals my breath away.

"Sapphire…" he breathes my name like a prayer, his gaze flickering to my lips.

My heart pounds, a chaotic drumbeat in my chest.

I don't move away. Despite everything that's happened so far, this feels different. This isn't a deal we're making, and it isn't a bribe to blackmail me into doing what he wants.

It's just me and Riven, in a moment of vulnerability, in a bubble of calmness sheltered from the storm raging outside.

The tension finally snaps.

He closes the distance between us, his lips capturing mine in a kiss that's slow and deliberate.

Like he's giving me a chance to stop him.

But I don't. I can't. The heat of his touch, the taste of him—it's overwhelming and intoxicating, and I lean into him, gripping his shirt like he's the only solid thing in the room.

The storm rages on outside, but in here, all I can feel is him. Every touch, every movement, pulls me deeper under his spell.

I don't want to fight it.

I never wanted to fight it. Not really. I thought I *should* fight it, and I tried, but it wasn't what I wanted.

But in here with him now, everything's different.

"If you want to stop, tell me now," he says, his voice a rough whisper against my skin. "If you don't—"

"No," I interrupt before he can continue. "Don't stop. I don't want to stop."

He pulls me closer, and for the first time in what feels like forever, I let myself forget about the storm, about Zoey, about the impossible journey to come.

Right now, all that exists is the way his body fits against mine, and the storm raging between us that's far stronger than both the one howling outside, and the hunger growing steadily inside me.

ZOEY

My stomach plummets as Aerix strides into view, his midnight eyes colder than ever as they sweep over me. His shadowy wings are unfurled, framing him like a living nightmare, and his silk finery gleams in the moonlight.

Prince.

He's a *prince*.

All those hours together—the shared meal, the conversations, the journey through the forest—and he never once mentioned his true identity.

Then again, I hadn't thought to ask.

Without a word, he strides past me and takes the sixth and final throne.

"Leave us," the queen commands the servants, and they're out the door before I can blink, closing the doors behind them.

We're alone now. Just me and the royal family of the Night Court, in their terrifyingly massive throne room.

My fingers twitch at my sides, aching to grip something solid— anything to protect myself. But there's nothing. Not my dagger, since Aerix took that from me after I tried to kill him with it. Not even a rock.

Just me, without an inkling of magic, standing in front of beings who could tear me apart without breaking a sweat.

King Thanatos descends the steps, moving with that same unnatural grace they all seem to possess, and gliding toward me.

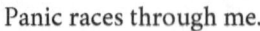

Panic races through me.

Is this it? Is he going to kill me?

I glance at Aerix, praying for *some* sort of hint from him about what to expect—but I get nothing.

All I'm aware of is the king's wings shifting behind him as he circles me, the shadowy feathers catching the light overhead. His gaze is purely predatory, like a cat deciding how it wants to play with a mouse before delivering the killing blow.

"Your hair," he finally says, stopping in front of me. "It's not a style I've seen before in my court. Who arranged it?"

"I did." My voice comes out steadier than I expect, even though my heart pounds so hard I'm sure they can all hear it.

"Did you now?" he says, and his hand rises, yanking one of the braids free.

Fear colder than what I felt in the tower prison in the Winter Court rushes through me, and I shudder at his touch.

"Tell me, human," he says, weaving his fingers through the braid, unraveling it from the bottom up. "What made you think it was appropriate to make yourself look so severe?"

I want to push him off me, but I have a feeling that won't end well.

So, I stay where I am, pulling on every thread of strength inside myself to stay steady, although I don't completely succeed.

"Probably all the pins in the vanity," I say, not breaking his gaze.

If I do, he'll have more power over me than he already does.

"You tremble, yet you dare to talk back?" He yanks another braid free. "I wonder, is that courage or stupidity?"

Aerix's eyes are on me now, and I can see the warning brewing in them.

Is this really how it's going to end? Killed because a man didn't like the way I styled my hair?

My scalp prickles as he unravels the second braid, as if he's unraveling my spirit along with it.

"You're meant to be soft," he continues, scaringly calm now. "Pleasing to look at. Decorative."

His hands move with unnerving precision, undoing braid after braid, as if peeling back the layers of a facade he doesn't approve of.

My scalp burns with every sharp tug, but that's not what hurts the most. It's the casual way he touches me, as if I'm nothing more than an object to be adjusted to his liking, that feels like the deepest violation.

I force myself to stay still, even though every instinct screams at me to swat his hands away. Because I know better. The memory of the fae in the streets—their predatory eyes, their whispered threats—is too fresh.

And apparently, I'm not even prey.

I'm a trinket.

One meant to be *decorative*.

Which might be even more demeaning.

As the king continues to methodically destroy my hour of work that I put into my hair, the others watch with varying degrees of interest.

Cierra seems bored. The queen is dark and heartless. Mirena's expression carries a flicker of what might be sympathy. Malakai leans forward in his throne, his hungry gaze making me want to crawl out of my skin.

Aerix watches carefully, as if he's undoing each braid simply by looking at them.

"You worked hard on this, didn't you?" The king's tone turns mockingly thoughtful. "All this effort, and yet, it only serves to highlight how much you'll need to be tamed."

There's that word again.

Tamed.

I'm starting to really regret bringing up the story about Milo to Aerix. It's like the entire world was listening, and is now using the fact that I tamed a cat against me.

"And here I thought that styling my hair was the same thing as taming it," I say sweetly, as if I'm not imagining how satisfying it would be to swat my hand at his face and slash at his skin with my nails like a feral cat.

He pauses, looking down at me with a slow, cruel smile. "So quaint. You *thought*."

A laugh echoes from one of the thrones behind him—Malakai. "The human's a philosopher," he says. "How charming."

"Isn't it?" The king tugs the final braid, and my hair falls loose, cascading over my shoulders in thick, dark waves. "Much better. Now you look like what you are."

"And what's that?" I ask, the words slipping out in a desperate attempt to regain some semblance of control.

His eyes gleam, sharp and dangerous. "A pet. *My* pet."

The word lands like a blow.

I step back, but his hand shoots out, wrapping around my wrist with unnerving ease. The strength of his grip is absolute—unyielding, but not crushing.

He's toying with me, like a cat with a mouse, savoring my fear.

I glance around the room, desperate for someone—anyone—to intervene.

Mirena averts her eyes. Cierra studies her nails. The queen's lips are pressed together in a harsh line. And Aerix stares straight ahead, indifferent, as if I'm no more interesting than a plain piece of furniture.

The king's wings flare, casting deeper shadows around us, and then I see them—his fangs. Long, sharp, and glinting in the moonlight.

"No." It's the only protest I can manage as he moves toward me, but it feels so small, so insignificant in the face of his overwhelming presence.

He tilts his head, considering me with mild amusement. "No?" he repeats, as though tasting the word. "Do you think you have a choice?"

Panic surges through me as he moves toward my neck.

He's going to bite me. Claim me. Drain me.

I would have preferred to have drowned in that waterfall—or even in their blood-filled moat.

"Father." Aerix's voice cuts through the tension, and the king jolts to a stop, clearly caught off guard. "A moment, if I may?"

Irritation flashes through the king's eyes, and he snaps his attention to Aerix, his fangs still bared. "What is it?"

"I apologize for interrupting, but I must point out that she's unworthy of your attention," he says, rising from his throne. "She's weak. Obstinate. And, as you pointed out after she talked back, stupid."

The king raises his brow after that last point—when Aerix said this was something he'd *already pointed out.* "Go on," he says, keeping his fingers wrapped around my wrist in a clear warning that I'm not to move.

"She can't swim," Aerix continues, sounding almost bored. "She's a creature so fundamentally senseless that she's unable to do such a basic skill, even for humans. She nearly drowned at that waterfall where I found her, flailing about like a child. Imagine the embarrassment of having a pet who can't keep herself afloat."

A ripple of laughter echoes through the room, Malakai's the loudest.

The king straightens, frowning, and turns back to me. "Is this true?"

My cheeks heat, and from the way the king glares as me, I feel like that was as much of a response as he needed.

"Not to mention," Aerix continues, descending the steps, his wings growing behind him as he approaches. "She's incapable of following simple instructions. She questions everything, argues constantly, and displays no sense of proper deference. Yesterday alone, she attempted to stab me. Twice. You'd waste more time disciplining her than enjoying her."

Malakai laughs at that, a cruel sound that echoes through the chamber.

Queen Ravenna leans forward, as if entranced by the entire confrontation.

The king's grip on my wrist loosens as he considers Aerix's words.

"Beauty alone isn't enough to justify your effort, Father." Aerix stops in front of me, his midnight eyes meeting mine, as if he's a cat sizing me up. "And yet, she's too pretty to send to the nobles. We don't want to give them unrealistic expectations for what they might get in the future. So, since I'm the one who brought her here, I'll take responsibility for her. It's only fitting that I bear the burden of her shortcomings."

I suck in a sharp breath at the cruelty of his words.

He might as well be driving my own dagger through my heart.

Queen Ravenna rises, her dress rippling like shadows as she glides down the steps to stand next to the king. "He has a point, my love," she says, trailing her fingers down his arm—the one he's not using to hold me in place. "Why waste your energy on such a dense, foolish, half-witted human? Let Aerix deal with her deficiencies. You have far better, more enjoyable, ways to spend your time."

The king says nothing, and panic squeezes my lungs so much that I start growing lightheaded.

I don't want his fangs touching my skin. I don't want *any* part of him touching me, for that matter.

In a strangely twisted way, I'm almost grateful for Aerix's insults.

"Perhaps you're right," the king finally says, and he releases me and steps back, frowning as he examines me. "However, before I make a final decision, I want to see this so-called deficiency of hers for myself."

ZOEY

"All of us." The king's smile grows predatory, and he gestures toward the palace doors. "To the Crimson Tide."

My stomach plummets with horror.

This is how they fill the moat with blood, isn't it?

They're going to take me out there, and they're going to...

"No," I say to Aerix, but if he hears me, he makes no sign of it.

The other royals rise, their movements graceful and deliberate as they follow the king's lead.

I'm frozen in place, unable to move.

The king spins around and sneers, his fangs gleaming in the moonlight. "Is the human so stupid that she's unable to walk?" he says, and a breeze stirs in the room, making the crystals in the chandelier clank together overhead.

I stare at him in shock.

When did it become "stupid" to fear a *moat filled with blood?*

"You either come with us, or you're dead," the king says, sounding bored. "Which will it be?"

I swallow, taking a second to think.

If I stay here, he'll surely kill me. If I go with them, I might have a chance.

Play along, I remind myself of what I was telling myself earlier.

It might be my only way out of this living nightmare.

So, not wanting to make this worse than it has to be, I hurry behind them, following them out of the throne room, down the mirrored halls, and out a side door that leads us through the gardens to the moat.

The scent hits me first.

It's metallic and thick, clawing its way into my throat and settling in my chest like a weight. I want to gag, but I force it down, focusing on putting one foot in front of the other as we move closer.

The others seem unfazed, their elegant strides unbroken. Even Aerix moves with his usual, infuriating calm, as if the blood-filled trench surrounding the palace is just another part of their nightly routine.

For them, maybe it is.

The moat is massive, and we stop at the edge, my boots skidding slightly on a particularly icy patch of ground.

The blood laps lazily against the banks, and I suspect the only thing maintaining its watery consistency is that it's diluted with water.

Blood mixed with water—clearly representing both the vampire and the fae sides of the Night Court.

"Fascinating, isn't it?" The king steps closer, the hem of his dark coat brushing the stone. "We call it the Crimson Tide, but it's more than just a moat. It's a guardian. A collector. Every drop of blood spilled in our territory finds its way here, drawn by the magic that binds this court."

I shudder, unable to hide my revulsion. "It's alive."

"Of course it's alive," he replies, as though I've just stated the obvious. "It feeds on fear and death. It ensures the strength of our court. It is our legacy."

My body shakes. Not just from the cold—it's from fear.

I glance around, contemplating making a run for it. But the closest bridges across the moat are far enough away that the fae will catch up with me before I reach them. And if I even do manage to cross one, I know what's waiting for me on the other side in that town.

Night fae, leering at me, wanting a taste of me.

There's no way out.

I'm trapped.

"To give you a fair chance," the king says, unsheathing his sword, which glistens under the light of the crescent moon, "you'll need to shed this beautiful garment. Which was a fine choice, if I may be honest."

"You have to be honest," I reply, venom in my tone. "You're fae."

His eyes narrow, sharper than his blade.

Then, in one fluid motion, he slices through the velvet fabric with terrifying precision.

It crumples to the ground around my feet, leaving me standing in nothing but my thin chemise, the cold air sinking into my skin.

I gasp, my arms instinctively crossing over my chest.

The chemise, despite being nearly sheer, would be a modest outfit to wear at home.

Here, I feel basically naked.

Aerix steps forward, his eyes fixated on my chest.

No—not on my chest.

At the amulet that's now visible beneath the thin chemise.

"What's this?" he asks, and with a sharp tug, he tears it away, studying it. "Humans have no rights to magical trinkets—unless they're gifted to them by their owner. And, since you belong to me, I'll be holding onto it."

"She's not yours yet," the king reminds him.

Aerix's jaw tenses, but he doesn't fight his father on it.

Then, before I can process what's happening, the king raises his hand and blasts a gust of wind at me, driving the air from my lungs.

I'm airborne.

My stomach flips, and I crash into the bloody water in the center of the moat.

Thick, metallic water floods my nose and throat, and I sputter, kicking out wildly.

No—not just water.

Blood.

I'm in a moat full of *blood.*

I can't breathe. Can't think. All I can feel is the suffocating pressure of the water closing in around me.

I kick harder now, trying to force my way back to the surface, but it's no use. Not only do I not know how to move, but the cold is so numbing that I feel more sluggish by the second. Plus, there's also the sinking horror of the fact that I'm in a moat full of *blood.*

I could just stop, a traitorous thought whispers in my mind. *Let the* water take me. Sink into its depths and escape whatever cruel fate the Night Court has planned for me. It would be better than becoming their plaything —their pet to torment, drink from, and do who knows what else to me at their will.

But no. I refuse to die like this.

So, I thrash harder, my arms and legs aching as I fight to break the surface. But it's useless. Every kick feels futile, the water dragging me down like it has a will of its own.

Fight, I tell myself. *Just keep fighting.*

But my strength is failing. My chest is about to explode.

Just as my vision starts to fade, strong arms wrap around my waist, pulling me upward with impossible speed.

My head breaks the surface.

I gasp, choking on air and water, and then I'm sprawled on the icy ground at the king's feet, coughing and shaking, drenched and freezing.

The previously white chemise is now a nearly transparent red from the water, leaving nothing to the imagination as I lay exposed before the entire royal family, drenched and coughing up watery blood.

After there's nothing possibly left in my stomach, Aerix crouches next to me, his midnight eyes locking onto mine. "You're lucky," he murmurs, low enough that only I can hear. "I don't like my toys broken before I've had a chance to play with them."

"You," I choke out, my throat burning, my eyes stinging. "You pulled me out of there. Again."

"You're no use to me dead," he says, and he rises, facing his father, who's looking down at me as if I'm vermin.

Shivering, I force myself up, trying to save what dignity I still have. "Congratulations. You win," I say to him. "You've officially proven you're stronger than a human who can't swim."

Malakai's laughter cuts through the night. "She really doesn't know when to shut up, does she?"

"No," the king says. "She doesn't."

"Do you treat all your guests this way, or am I just lucky?" I snap, both at the king and Malakai.

"Enough," the king commands, and suddenly, my tongue feels heavy in my mouth.

My racing heartbeat evens out, the anger rushing through my veins calming to practically nothing.

"That's better." He circles me, inspecting me like a broken vase. "You're much more palatable like this. Quiet. Obedient."

I want to scream, to curse him, but my mind feels like it's swimming in molasses.

Or—more appropriately—*blood*.

Aerix removes the amulet of warmth from his pocket and examines it.

Could it have been doing more than just keeping me warm? Protecting me from night fae emotional manipulation?

If so, my being able to resist Aerix's compulsion wasn't because I'm special. A part of me hoped it was, but unsurprisingly, I'm just as human as ever.

And now here I am—sopping wet, having nearly drowned in a moat full of blood, my hair a wreck, and my body on display for all of them to see.

It takes every ounce of willpower to not collapse to the frost covered ground and cry.

"You're just as stupid and helpless as my son claimed." The king waves his hand dismissively, backs away from me, and looks at Aerix. "Take her. Perhaps you can mold her into something marginally useful."

The queen glides to her husband's side and places a hand on his arm, although her focus is also on Aerix. "If she proves too difficult to train, I'm certain the nobles would be delighted to have such a... spirited pet," she says.

"No one will touch her." Something sharp flashes in Aerix's eyes, and his wings flare, their shadowy edges cutting through the mist like blades. "She's mine. If anyone so much as looks at her the wrong way, they'll answer to me."

Malakai snickers. "Oh, look at him, getting all territorial over his little toy."

"Laugh all you want. But you are no exception to my claim."

"Relax, brother," Malakai replies. "I have no interest in your scraps."

Apparently bored with his brother's antics, Aerix crouches beside me again, a breeze surrounding me as he does.

Then, without warning, he reaches forward and places his palm on my chest, right below my throat.

"Don't touch me," I snap at him, flinching back from his touch.

"We're far past that stage of our relationship." He grabs my wrist, and then he's pulling away the icy wetness clinging to my skin, my clothes, and even my hair, leaving me dry but no less humiliated. "There. Better, isn't it?"

My fingers clench into fists at my sides, the nails digging into my palms.

"You should be grateful," he says. "After all, I've saved your life. Twice now. Technically four times, since I allowed you to live after both times you tried to stab me with that dagger."

"Grateful?" I repeat, trembling. Not from the cold this time, but from fury. "To the man who dragged me to this nightmare and decided I'm his *pet?*"

"Yes. Because from now on, I'm the one taking care of you. Feeding you. Protecting you." He leans in closer, his face inches from mine, and the air between us crackles with tension. "And I'll be the one who determines your fate."

He forces me up, and as he drags me away, I keep my head high, refusing to let him or anyone else in his monstrous family see the fear twisting in my gut.

But deep down, I know the truth.

I'm more powerless in this place than anywhere else I've been so far in this awful realm.

No one's on my side. Not Sapphire, not Ghost, not even Riven.

Which leaves me at the complete mercy of whatever twisted plans this dark fae prince has in store.

ZOEY

Now that the royals are finished with me—including my new "owner," Prince Aerix—one of the fae women from earlier leads me down the halls, back to the human wing. The nicer one with the brown hair, which is at least a bit of a relief.

As we walk, she tells me a bit about what to expect around here. Specifically, that I'll be able to go anywhere I want in the human wing, but I'll require a fae escort to go anywhere else.

I don't remember if she told me her name. If she did, I was probably too spaced out to notice. I've only really been half aware of what she's saying, due to the shock of being in a chemise dyed with blood, walking to a gilded prison in a nightmarish palace ruled by vampiric fae in a different *realm*.

How is this real?

I'm still half expecting to wake up at any moment, in my bed, with this being a long, intense, crazy dream.

Instead, we eventually arrive at the same wooden double doors Aerix led me through a few hours ago.

The human wing.

Two girls hurry past us as we make our way down the hall, whispering so quietly that I can't hear. Judging from their normal, non-inky black eye colors and lack of wings—and from knowing we're in the human quarters—I can immediately tell that they're not fae.

"This will be your room," my fae escort says, stopping in front of an intricately carved wooden door and pushing it open.

Decorated in golds and creams, with an elegant chandelier floating overhead, and plush furniture arranged in the common area, it's even nicer than where they put me in when I first got here. But I don't think it's all mine. Because three doors branch off from the main space. Each one is identical, except for the small plaques engraved with names: Sophia and Victoria.

The third plaque is blank.

"Dinner is in thirty minutes," the fae woman says, giving me a quick once-over. "You're expected to join the others and present yourself appropriately. There are a few dresses in your room that are suitable for dinner. They'll be slightly big, but they'll work. You'll be fitted for your own dresses soon."

With that, she spins on her heel and leaves, the door clicking shut behind her.

I barely have a moment to process it all before one of the other doors flies open, and a girl steps out. She's petite, with dark hair cascading in loose waves down her back. Her dress is elegant but simple—green silk that swishes around her ankles—and she looks slightly younger than I am. Fifteen, or maybe sixteen.

"Hi," she says with a surprisingly bright smile, given our circumstances. "I'm Sophia. Welcome to... well, you know. Prince Aerix's guest suite."

Guest suite?

"Is that a fancy way of saying 'luxury prison?'" I ask, and while her smile wobbles, it doesn't disappear.

"You'll adapt," she says, but there's something in her eyes—a hint of weariness that makes me think she hasn't quite "adapted" herself.

"Does this include spa days and gourmet food?" I ask, motioning around the luxury suite. "Perhaps even the free—"

I'm interrupted by another door opening—the one labeled *Victoria.*

The woman who steps out is older—mid-thirties, maybe—and in her red velvet dress, her entire demeanor screams *do not mess with me.* She's slightly taller than I am, with brown eyes, and dark, perfectly styled hair.

I can't help seeing the similarities between the three of us.

Apparently, Prince Aerix has a type.

"Well, isn't this cozy," she says with disdain, looking me up and down. "Another stray for our prince's collection."

"Victoria," Sophia says softly. "She's new. She's probably scared."

"She doesn't look scared." Victoria steps closer, her sharp gaze making me feel like a bug under a magnifying glass. "She looks... bedraggled. Disheveled. Unkempt."

"Studying for your SATs?" I raise an eyebrow.

"What?" She scrunches her face in confusion.

"Don't mind Victoria," Sophia jumps in. "She's Canadian."

Victoria huffs and crosses her arms, turning her attention back to me. "Keep it coming," she says. "The prince might like his toys to have some spirit, but test him too much, and you won't last long here."

She glances at the door with a blank plaque, and I have a feeling she's referring to whoever occupied that room before my apparent assignment to it.

"Good to know." I raise an eyebrow, unwilling to let this girl think she can walk all over me. First impressions matter, especially in places like this. "Anything else, or are we done with the veiled threats?"

"There is no *veil* here," she replies, forcing an obviously fake smile. "Would you like some help choosing what to wear to dinner? I know exactly what Aerix likes. And what he doesn't."

"I know how to dress myself," I say, although judging by the fact that I'm standing here in the equivalent of Night Court underwear, I suppose I can see how that might be unapparent. "But I need a minute. Alone."

Victoria snorts. "Take all the minutes you want. Just don't be late for dinner, or we'll all pay for it."

"Don't scare her," Sophia protests, but Victoria's already retreating to her room, the door shutting with a decisive click.

"Let me guess," I say when it's clear she's not coming back out. "She was going to recommend something she knows Aerix will hate?"

"Victoria's..." Sophia shrugs, taking a moment to think. "It's not easy being here. Especially at her age."

"What do you mean?"

"The royals—the king, queen, princesses, and princes—only want the young and beautiful. Once we age out..." She swallows hard. "There's another place. Not like this. We call them the barns, although I've heard they're more like bunkhouses. That's where the older humans go. They keep them there for the nobles."

Horror rises in my throat. "You're talking about them like they're livestock."

"The nobles don't *kill* them," she clarifies. "They just... share them."

With that, Aerix's warning rings through my mind.

If anyone so much as looks at her the wrong way, they'll answer to me.

The royals clearly don't like to share.

Although that apparently no longer applies when we get older and "washed up."

"And you're just okay with this?" I ask. "You've... adapted?"

"What's the alternative?" Her smile is faint and brittle.

"Escape," I whisper, softly enough that Victoria won't be able to hear through the door.

I shouldn't trust this girl so easily. But I have no one here, and this is a lot to process, and I need someone on my side. Desperately.

I've always thought of myself as an independent person, but I also never thought I'd have to face something like *this*.

"Trying is a surefire way to get sent to the barns." Sophia's expression darkens. "Or killed."

I frown, since neither of those things are on my list of things to do after being abducted to the Night Court and claimed by the dark prince who took me here.

"Maybe I can help you get ready?" she offers, in an obvious attempt to change the subject. "I know it's a lot, but the better you look, the better chance you have of staying here. Of staying *safe*."

"Until my expiration date." I glance at Victoria's door, feeling bad for her, despite her less than welcoming introduction.

But I made a resolution when I got here.

Play the game. Be smart. Be strategic.

Stay alive.

If that means putting on a pretty dress, then so be it.

"Fine," I say before Sophia can reply to my little expiration comment. "I suppose I can use the help."

Judging by the king's reaction to my hairstyle, it's true.

"Great." Sophia smiles, relieved. "Let's go in and see what we can do."

ZOEY

Sophia chooses a deep green gown with gold embroidery along the neckline. It complements my eyes—which are hazel, unlike her and Victoria's brown—and she swears Aerix will love it.

It's slightly too big, but with a few pins, we're able to make it work.

Obviously, I wear my hair down.

Sophia won't tell me anything about the girl who owned the dress before me, who lived in this room. And, taking the hint, I don't push.

In actuality, I'm not sure I want to know. Not yet.

The walk to the dining hall is silent, although every few steps, Victoria shoots me a glare that could freeze hellfire.

"Here we are," Sophia says as we approach a set of ornate double doors.

She pushes them open, revealing a dining hall with soaring ceilings, floating gold chandeliers, and six ornate round tables spread throughout the room, each one with three seats around it.

But it's not the room that makes me stop dead in my tracks.

It's who's sitting at one of the tables.

"Matt?" The name tears from my throat as I stare at him, shocked.

Matt Larkin. Sapphire's ex-boyfriend who tried to make her give up bartending to live with him. The one who proposed to her on New Year's Eve—ten days ago—and then left her alone in the woods when she said no.

"Zoey?" He jumps up so fast his chair nearly topples over.

I race over to him, ignoring Sophia's surprised gasp. "What are you—how did you—" The questions tumble out as I grab his arms, needing to confirm he's real.

Needing to confirm that I'm not alone here anymore.

"I could ask you the same thing," he says. "When you and Sapphire disappeared..." Pain flashes across his face. "They tried to find you. But they couldn't. They kept questioning me. I think they thought..."

"They?" I ask.

"The police."

Right. Of course the police were involved. I assumed as much.

"But how did you get *here?*" I motion around the dining hall, in the Night Court, in an entirely *different realm.* "What happened?"

"No one could find you two," he says, and his eyes go distant, as if he's experiencing the pain all over again. "They were trying to pin it on me. I *know* they were. They were trying to find evidence to make it look like I dragged both of you into the woods and killed you or something. So, I got in my car and kept driving, as north as I could get. But the roads were icy. I thought I saw something in the woods —a light, or... I don't know. Lost control of the car. Went right off into a ravine."

My heart pounds. "How did you survive?"

"I don't know." He shrugs. "There was the impact, and then I woke up, and *she* was there."

"One of the night fae?" I ask, since it would track with how I got here.

"Not just *one* of them," His entire demeanor changes, his eyes taking on a dreamy, unfocused quality. "Ravenna. *Queen* Ravenna. She saved me, Zoey. She gave me the potion herself—the one that healed me. I'm alive because of her."

The way he says her name—as if he worships her—makes my skin crawl.

"You're on first name basis with the queen," I say, having a sinking feeling where he's going with this.

"You should see her," he continues. "The way she moves... it's like she's an angel. And when she speaks, it's like nothing else matters. Nothing but her."

I watch him carefully, more on guard than ever. Because this isn't the Matt I know. The ex-quarterback who's been worn down by endless hours toiling away in the garage, who's been desperate—and way too pushy—to keep his relationship with Sapphire going, even though we all knew it was falling apart.

"Matt," I say slowly. "Are you okay?"

He blinks, focusing on me again. "Better than okay. After Sapphire said no to my proposal, I thought something broke in me. Forever. Then the police blamed me. And after the crash... I should have died. But Ravenna saved me. She *loves* me. I'm alive because of her."

One of the other guys at his table snorts. "She said she loved me, too," he says, looking at Matt like he wants to drive a fork into his eyeballs. "But then she forgot about me. Just like she'll eventually forget about you."

Matt's expression darkens. "It's not like that with us."

"Sure, it's not," he says, quickly switching his focus to me. "Welcome to the Night Court. I'm Elijah."

"Zoey," I introduce myself, although I can barely focus on the exchange.

Because Matt's here.

In the Night Court.

With me.

Out of all the things I was expecting, it certainly wasn't *this*.

"Go to your table." One of the fae women materializes beside us, her voice like ice. "Now."

Matt sits back down and nods at me to comply as well.

Reluctantly, I let Sophia guide me back to the table where Victoria's waiting for us.

I barely have a chance to get comfortable before the fae servants glide into the room with silver platters. The food looks incredible—roasted meats, fresh vegetables, fresh bread that makes my mouth water, and more. We're even given wine.

After the past few days of barely eating, it's like a feast from a fairy tale.

Which, I suppose, it kind of is.

Just not the kind with happy endings.

"Time for the run down on who's who around here," Sophia quietly says to me as we're served. "You already know Matt and

Elijah. The other one at the queen's table is Henry. I think he's flirted with every girl who comes through here."

Henry shoots her a smirk, as if he knows she's talking about him.

Victoria laughs, as if she and Sophia are in on some private joke.

Sophia blushes, straightens, and looks away from Henry. "The quiet ones at the end are Prince Malakai's. Lacey, Katerina, and Brenda. They don't spend time with anyone other than each other," she continues. "And the king's are the three pretty ones over there—Aurora, Genevieve, and Isla."

"How old's the little one?" I ask, referring to Isla, who looks like a tiny China doll.

"Thirteen, I think," Sophia says. "She's new. The same age I was when I was brought here."

I look back and forth between Sophia and Isla in shock.

"I'm sorry," I finally say, since I can't imagine being thrown into something like this at such a young age.

"Don't be." She shakes it off and motions to a blond, lanky guy sitting alone. "That's Nathaniel. Princess Mirena's only pet. She doesn't like to share. And those three at the far table are Princess Cierra's—Jake, Tanya, and Sebastian."

My attention catches on Jake. And it's not just because he's watching me with an intensity that makes my chest tighten.

It's because he reminds me of Patrick. My ex-boyfriend. The one I've been hoping to get back together with for weeks now.

Maybe it's the way he holds himself—that same quiet confidence Patrick had on the soccer field. Or maybe it's the slight curl to his dark hair, just like Patrick would get after practice.

Patrick liked playing soccer with me during my short stint on the girls team at school. Then I dropped soccer for tennis, and that was it for him. Suddenly we didn't have enough in *common* to be together anymore.

Jake offers me a small smile that's so much like Patrick's it makes my heart ache.

"Jake's nice," Sophia says, apparently noticing our little exchange. "One of the few here who hasn't let this place change him too much."

Victoria scoffs. "Give him time."

I scowl at her, and one of the fae women—I suppose they're sort of like our handlers, as awful as it is to think of it that way—clears her throat.

The message is clear: no more bickering

The conversation turns soft and demure—like when there's tension while you're dining with your family at a fancy restaurant, but you're trying to not make a spectacle of yourself.

Jake's gaze lingers on me throughout the meal. It's different from the way the others look at me. There's no hostility, no calculation. Just interest. Maybe even concern.

Matt refuses to look at me. Not even for a second.

When the plates are cleared, Jake makes his way over to our table, his eyes locked on mine the entire time. "Welcome to the Night Court," he says when he reaches me. "I'm Jake."

"Zoey," I introduce myself, as if he didn't already know that from that little confrontation with Matt and Elijah at the start at the meal.

"Nice to meet you, Zoey," he says with a shy smile that warms my heart. "After dinner, I like to spend time in the courtyard until curfew—which is at dawn, by the way. Come join me out there after you change. If you want."

"After I change?" I ask, confused.

"Out of your dinner dress..."

At that, I glance to Sophia. "We just put these on," I tell her, motioning to our dresses. "Now we're supposed to change?"

"Life at court." She shrugs. "We go through a few dresses a day."

"Lovely." I huff, since changing in and out of fancy dresses is hardly how I like spending my time. Not when there are far more interesting things to do. Like tennis, and pottery, and horseback riding, and wood whittling, and cooking, and figuring out how to escape a palace ruled by fae-vampire hybrids with dark wings and hypnotizing eyes that dig into my soul.

"Zoey?" Jake asks, bringing my focus back to him, where he's watching me with puppy dog eyes. "Hopefully I'll see you later?"

"I'll see if I can work you into my busy schedule," I say, trying to keep it light, which earns me another smile from him.

"Looking forward to it," he says, and as he walks away, I notice how gracefully he moves. Like an athlete.

Like Patrick.

It's not just that he reminds me of Patrick, I realize. *It's that he reminds me of home.*

But Jake's not from my home. Not really—not from Presque Isle. Matt is.

But when I look for him, he's gone, along with most of the other humans.

Another one of the girls makes her way over to me and Sophia— Aurora. One of the king's pets. She's the most beautiful of all of us, but she barely looked up during dinner.

"Don't get attached," she warns when she's next to me, barely above a whisper. "To Jake. To anyone. It only makes it harder when..." She trails off, but I know what she means.

When we're sent to the barns. When we're too old to be worth keeping. When we're nothing but food to be shared amongst the nobles.

I look back at Jake one last time—at the way he carries himself with dignity, even in captivity.

How long can we hold on to who we were before this place?

Even scarier—will we recognize ourselves when it's over?

If it's ever over?

ZOEY

"Do you want to go out to the courtyard?" Sophia asks after Aurora and Victoria leave the dining room. "To see Jake?"

"Do you know where Matt is?" I ask her instead.

"Um..." She fidgets uncomfortably, tugging at the ends of her sleeves. "You'd have to ask either Elijah or Henry. The queen's other pets."

"Can we call each other something else?" I snap, although I immediately feel bad about my tone, so I shift it back to friendly. "'Pets just sounds so..." I pause, searching for the right word. "Dehumanizing."

"That's sort of the point," she says, pity shining in her eyes. "But words won't change what this place is. What we are. At least, not to them."

As much as I hate it, I suppose she's right.

Besides, no matter how demoralizing it is to be called someone's *pet*, I have more important things to focus on than semantics.

"Where are Elijah and Henry now?" I ask, since what matters the most right now is talking to Matt. *Really* talking with him, where no one else can hear.

"Elijah's been secluding himself recently," she says. "He's probably in their suite."

"Then take me to their suite," I say, quickly adding, "please?"

Her frown deepens, but after a moment, she sighs. "Fine," she gives in. "But you saw how Matt was earlier. He's... entranced by her. By the queen."

"I understand. But entranced or not, I want to see him," I say, and she leads me through the maze of corridors, past other doors that lead to suites like ours.

Finally, we stop in front of a large wooden door carved with intricate designs of moons and stars, embossed with gold paint, with marble columns on each side. It's far fancier than the doors to our suite. As if the queen's declaring that her pets are more important than the others.

"Go on," Sophia says, motioning for me to knock.

I do, and after a moment, Elijah opens the door.

His expression clouds when he sees me.

"Matt's not here," he says before I can ask.

"Where is he?"

"With the queen." His voice is flat. "In her quarters."

I frown and glance at Sophia, who won't look at me.

There's no need to ask what Matt's doing in the queen's quarters. I've been getting a decent idea of what goes on around here, and judging by the look in Matt's eyes when he spoke about the queen, she's doing more than just drinking his blood.

"When will he be back?" I ask instead.

"Don't know." Something bitter creeps into his tone. "He's been sleeping there every day since he arrived."

"Sleeping—" I cut myself off, processing this. "Wait. What about the king? Doesn't that… bother him to have someone else in there with them?"

Elijah's laugh is hollow. "The royals don't share quarters."

"Oh." I frown again, since I've never heard of a husband and wife who don't share a room. "So, Matt will be back tomorrow night?"

This nocturnal schedule is going to take a while to get my mind around. And I hope I'm not here for long enough for it to start feeling normal.

"Sometimes she keeps them longer," he says simply.

"Them?"

"Her favorites." His eyes are distant, like he's remembering something he'd rather forget. "She always gets attached to the new ones. For a while."

"And then what happens?" I ask.

"Then they end up here." He gestures to the suite behind him.

"With the rest of us. Until she finds someone new to obsess over, and to eventually replace one of us. But look—if you want to talk to Matt, come back tomorrow night. Just don't expect him to be the person you remember. None of us are. Although, he's changed faster than most. She really did a number on him."

I remember how quickly Matt fell for Sapphire—basically at first sight. Obviously, it's happened all over again, but this time, with the queen of the Night Court.

Hopefully when I see him, I can talk some sense into him.

"Thanks for the help," I say to Elijah, since clearly, there's nothing more he can do for me. "When Matt comes back, tell him I need to talk to him."

He shrugs noncommittally and closes the door, leaving me standing there in the hall with Sophia.

"Do you still want to go to the courtyard?" she asks. "To see Jake?"

I hesitate. Because after everything with Matt, I'm not sure I'm in the mood for company.

Then again, maybe that's exactly what I need right now. Something to take my mind off all of this.

Well, more like some*one.*

"Yes," I decide. "Show me the way?"

She brightens immediately. "Come on. It's through here."

We wind through more halls until we reach a set of glass doors that lead outside.

The courtyard beyond is beautiful, but in an eerie way. It's all black and red flowers and twisted trees, with paths made of black stone, marble picnic tables scattered throughout, and blood-tinged water flowing from the multi-tiered fountains.

But, most noticeably of all is the tall, solid, concrete fence lining it on all sides. The one I saw from my original guest room.

The walls of our prison. It feels like it's buzzing with magic, which I suppose makes it more of an electric fence.

Second most noticeable is that Jake isn't here.

I recognize a few of the others, though. Nathanial—Princess Mirena's sole pet—who's writing in what looks to be a journal. All three of Prince Malakai's are playing a card game at one of the far tables. They whisper something to each other, look up at me, give me small glares, then return to their game. Lastly, there's Aurora, whose head is buried in a book.

I also can't help but notice that it's warmer out here.

Maybe from the fence?

I have no idea, but I have no complaints about it.

"I have to head back," Sophia says, giving me a knowing smile. "Don't worry. He'll be here."

"What do you have to do?" I ask.

"Oh, you know." She waves vaguely. "Things."

Then she's gone, leaving me alone with the others, who clearly don't want to be sociable.

But I don't want to leave without giving Jake a fair chance.

So, needing something to do in the meantime, I walk to the far end of the path where it meets the fence, since there are some small sparkly rocks along the side of it. When I was younger, I loved hunting for interesting stones. Their shapes, their textures... there's something grounding about them.

I also really enjoyed that moment in the third trial when I made that awful woman in the forest stop screaming by throwing a rock at her throat.

Her scream was so shrill that I swear it'll haunt me until the end of time.

I kneel and pick up one of the rocks, turning it over in my hands. It looks normal on the outside, but given that this is another realm, maybe there could be something different about it. Something hidden beneath the surface.

"What are you doing?"

I jump at Jake's voice, nearly dropping the stone.

"Sorry," he says quickly. "Didn't mean to startle you while you're..."

He trails off, waiting for me to continue.

"Looking at the crystals," I explain.

"Those are rocks."

"They *could* be crystals." I shrug. "If they were smoothed over."

Jake raises an eyebrow, his expression caught somewhere between amusement and genuine curiosity. "Interesting," he says, although given that he's looking at me instead of the rock in my hand, I don't think he's referring to the rock.

"Crystals have different energies," I explain. "Like, if this is quartz, it could help with clarity. Or if it's amethyst, it might help with peace of mind." I turn it over, examining it. "I'm trying to gather whatever positive energy I can find in this place."

"And you think these rocks are going to change anything?" he asks, crouching down next to me.

"It can't hurt," I say, gathering two more stones. "Besides, we need all the help we can get in this place."

"We?" There's a hopeful note in his voice that makes my chest tighten.

"Well, yeah. I mean, look at Victoria. She's so bitter, but I get it. I'd be scared too, if I was in her position." I examine another stone, avoiding his gaze, hoping he'll be receptive of what I'm going to say next. "If we work together instead of against each other, maybe we'll have a better chance."

"Better chance of what?"

"Getting through this." I glance up at him to clarify. "Getting out of here."

His expression falls, and he touches my hand, stopping me from picking up another stone. "There's no 'getting out of here,'" he says sadly. "But we can find ways to be happy. To make the best of what we have."

The way he says it—with the gentle emphasis on *we*—makes my heart skip. Because he's offering something. A connection. Maybe even more.

And I'm tempted. Especially because he looks so much like Patrick that it hurts.

At the same time, there's no way in Hell I'm going down without a fight.

"Did you know that penguins search for pebbles for each other?" he continues before I can reply.

I blink at the sudden change in topic. "Penguins?"

"Yes. Penguins," he repeats, picking up one of the smoother stones. "When they're courting, the male penguin searches the beach for the perfect pebble to give to the female he's interested in. If she accepts the pebble, she's accepting him as her mate."

Despite myself, I'm intrigued. I've always enjoyed learning random facts.

"How do they know which pebble is perfect?" I ask.

"They look for the smoothest, roundest ones they can find." His fingers trace the edge of the stone he's holding. "Sometimes they'll spend hours searching. And if another male finds a better pebble, they might even try to steal it."

I can't help but laugh. "Penguin pebble theft?"

"It's serious business." He picks up a smooth, pale stone and holds it out to me, his eyes meeting mine. "Here. For clarity. Or whatever else you need."

It's a sweet gesture. So, I take it, letting my fingers brush against his as I do.

"It's beautiful," I say softly.

"Yeah," he says, although he's not looking at the stone anymore. "It is."

We sit in silence for a moment, the weight of the Night Court's suffocating rules fading just enough to feel normal.

At least, as normal as we can get here.

"Zoey," he says, soft and hesitant.

I glance up, and before I can process what's happening, he leans in.

I let him.

His lips are soft and gentle. Nothing like the urgent way Patrick used to kiss me. And while it doesn't send the spark through me, it feels like a silent promise.

I'm here.

You're not alone.

And right now, that's exactly the sort of promise I need.

ZOEY

I LEAN into Jake's kiss, enjoying the comfort in the simple human connection. In the reminder of home.

When he pulls back, his eyes search mine, waiting for a reaction.

"I know this place is awful," he says quietly. "But maybe we can make it less awful? Together?"

The sincerity in his voice makes my chest ache. Because here in this twisted court of monsters and magic, he's offering me a chance to not feel so alone.

At the same time, what just happened between us means nothing. Jake might look like Patrick and remind me of Patrick—although less so after that kiss—but that doesn't mean he *is* Patrick. Plus, the only things we talked about before he made a move on me were crystals and penguins.

That's hardly a solid base for a strong relationship.

A throat clears behind us before I can answer, and Jake pulls back quickly.

I turn to find Henry—the third pet of the queen—leaning against one of the twisted trees, his predatory gaze making my skin crawl.

"Don't be greedy, Jake," he says with a smirk. "The rest of us deserve a chance with the new girl, too."

Suddenly, all three of Prince Malakai's girls are here with us— Lacey, Katerina, and Brenda.

Like Aerix, Malakai has a type. All three of them are blonde and curvy. Although, all of them have eyes so haunted it makes my heart ache.

Whatever Malakai does to them seems to have broken them.

I stand, and Lacey frowns, looking up and down at my dress, which is dirty from kneeling to hunt for rocks.

"Zoey," she says, with what sounds like genuine concern. "You have to maintain certain standards around here. The royals tire of pets who don't present themselves properly."

There's something haunting about the way she says it—like she's seen it happen too many times before.

Behind her, Katerina stares at the ground, her shoulders hunched, as if she's trying to make herself invisible.

Brenda at least meets my eyes, although her gaze holds the same hollow warning as Lacey's.

"Why does it matter right now?" I ask, although I brush some of the dirt off my dress, suddenly overly aware that it's there. "Aerix isn't here."

Brenda sighs, glancing around as if making sure no one else is listening. "It's not just about him being here or not," she says. "Presentation is important in the Night Court. If the prince starts seeing you as less than perfect, it could change how he feels about keeping you."

"Keeping me?" My voice is sharper than I intend, but her words hit a nerve.

"We're not trying to upset you," Lacey says quickly. "We're just trying to help."

Katerina shifts uncomfortably, although she still doesn't speak.

"Maybe instead of worrying about getting dirty, we could do something useful. Like looking through that garden over there," I say, motioning to the one with dark flowers that I noticed when I entered the courtyard. "Maybe there's sage or some other herbs in it. We can gather it to cleanse ourselves and our rooms. Make them feel more like our own spaces."

"Zoey," Lacey says my name again, pity filling her eyes. "There are no magical herbs in that garden. And if you keep digging around like this, you're going to get yourself sent to the barns."

The barns.

Hearing it said like that makes me shiver.

Katerina's looking at me like I'm a dead girl walking.

Brenda moves closer to Katerina and takes her hand in a small gesture of comfort.

"The barns won't be an issue," Henry cuts in, his eyes trailing down my body in a way that makes my skin crawl. "Aerix won't be casting this one aside anytime soon. She's far too... entertaining to look at."

"It's funny." I step forward, unwilling to back down. "You talk like you're in charge, but as far as I can see, you have no crown, no wings, and no magic. You're as powerless as the rest of us."

His eyes flash with anger, and I brace myself for him to lash out.

"No wings, no title, and no magic—but I'm still standing," he says, calmer than I expected. "That's more than some of us can say."

I can't help but glance at Katerina, who's still staring down at her feet, refusing to look at me.

"You're pretty." Henry moves closer, apparently not done yet. "But pretty can only get you so far. And if you keep talking like that, you'll learn how quickly things can go wrong. Because around here, it's not just the fae you need to worry about."

"You think you're a threat to me?" I say, even though from what he's saying, it sounds like he might be. "Because you lean against a tree and throw around cheap warnings? Let me guess—you're trying to feel powerful in a place that's made sure you'll never be anything but a pet, just like the rest of us."

Jake shifts beside me, his posture tense, but he stays silent.

This is my fight to win—or lose.

Henry's smirk falters, but he recovers quickly. "You've got spirit," he says, with obviously mock approval. "But spirit doesn't mean much when it gets you sent to the barns—or worse."

"Spirit's gotten me through life just fine so far." I cross my arms, meeting his gaze head-on.

Hopefully he doesn't see how rattled I am inside. Because sure, my spirit's gotten me though things like arguing my grades up, fighting for a prime spot on the tennis team, and pushing myself to learn new skills in gymnastics.

But none of that comes close to being anything like the place and situation I've been thrown into here.

"You don't get it yet, do you?" Henry chuckles, low and humorless. "The fae don't care about spirit. They care about obedience, beauty, and submission. You've got the beauty, which should keep you going for a few months. But keep playing tough, and you'll see that your looks will only get you so far."

Jake steps in, his hand brushing mine—a silent offer of solidarity. "Henry," he says, steady but firm. "Back off. She's new. She doesn't need this from you."

"Fine." Henry throws his hands up in mock surrender, although it doesn't stop him from checking me out again. "Do whatever you want. Just don't say I didn't warn you."

"Noted," I say, as flatly as I can manage.

He steps away, retreating toward the tree he'd been leaning on earlier, and the other girls follow his lead. "Good luck, Zoey," he calls over his shoulder. "You'll need it."

The space between me and Jake is silent for a few seconds.

All I can do is stare at where Henry was just standing, with a strange mix of anger and fear racing through my veins.

"Come on," Jake says, bringing me out of my frustrated haze. "Let's go to the garden. You said you wanted to see if there were any useful herbs there, right?"

I highly doubt he knows anything about herbs, but it'll be a good activity to take my mind off everything.

Keeping my brain occupied is my favorite way to push aside my worries and doubts.

So, together, we walk over to the garden.

"I'm sorry about them," he says once we're out of their earshot. "Henry especially. Being one of the queen's pets has gone to his head."

"Malakai's girls are all so broken," I say, crouching down and starting to look around. "Especially Katerina. Does she ever speak?"

Jake kneels beside me, his shoulder brushing mine, his expression darkening. "Not since whatever Malakai did to her three months ago," he says. "No one knows exactly what happened, but she hasn't said a word since."

I shudder, unable to imagine what could silence someone so completely. "And the others just accept it? They don't try to help her?"

"What can they do?" he asks. "We're all just trying to survive here.

Some cope by following every rule to the letter. Others try to gain whatever power they can by aligning themselves with the strongest players."

"And you?" I ask. "How do you cope?"

"I try to hold onto who I was before. And..." He hesitates. "I look for connections that remind me that I'm still human."

The weight of his words settles over me. Because we're all searching for something to keep us from breaking—whether it's perfectly polished appearances, borrowed power, or simple human contact.

I look away from him, focusing on the flowers instead.

They're beautiful—I've never seen black roses before—but there's no sage here.

"You're different," Jake says, plucking a flower and holding it out to me. "Most new pets either have a mental breakdown from the shock of it all, or they shut down completely. But you... you're strong. Determined. Smart. Stubborn."

"Are those good things?" I ask, tilting my head slightly.

"They're potentially dangerous things," he admits, leaning closer and studying me with a fire in his eyes that I didn't notice before. "But maybe they're exactly what this place needs right now."

SAPPHIRE

I WAKE at sunset to the storm still howling outside, battering against Riven's ice barrier like it's trying to break through.

It won't. His magic's too strong for that. But the translucent wall gives us a perfect view of the blizzard, although there's nothing to see except endless white.

Riven's already up, staring through the ice like he's willing Ghost to appear. He looks as desperate to find Ghost as I feel to find Zoey.

But despite fear for my best friend, I can still feel the imprint of Riven's lips on my skin—of how much being together felt *right*.

Heat rises to my cheeks at the memory.

Well... *memories.*

There were a lot of them.

"We should..." He clears his throat, his voice rough as he glances at the ice wall again. "We should make use of this time. Since we're stuck here, we might as well—"

He pauses, and my heart races—in a good way—at the assumption that he's about to say we should have a repeat of last night.

"We should train," he says instead, and I flinch slightly, although I'm not sure he noticed. "You're a natural with your magic, but your combat skills need work. And it wouldn't hurt for you to learn how to use a sword."

"I'm not *that* bad with weapons," I say. "I killed that dark angel with my dagger and the Stalo with your sword."

"By projecting and killing them from the back," he snaps. "By leaving yourself—your *real* self—unconscious on the ground. But you won't be able to do that all the time. You can't leave your real self that vulnerable. You need to be able to fight head on."

"I think I did a pretty decent job against the nixies..."

I trail off, since did I *really* do a good job against them?

No. Because if I'd been a better fighter, Zoey would still be here with us.

Guilt slams into me all over again for what happened to her.

But I have to hold onto hope that she's alive. That somehow, eventually, we'll find her and get her back.

"Your form is sloppy," Riven interrupts my thoughts, pulling his sword out of his weapons belt and examining the blade. "You're going to learn how to use this."

Tension crackles between us as we hold each other's gazes, sending more memories of last night flashing through my mind.

The sword he's offering isn't the one I want to be practicing with right now.

But he moves closer to me, holding it out. "Take it."

I eye the weapon warily. "I have my dagger."

"A dagger won't save you against someone with superior reach."

"Fine," I say, and when I grasp the hilt, a chill races up my arm, like the blade itself is made of winter.

"Balance your grip." He moves to stand behind me, his hands covering mine, adjusting my fingers on the hilt.

His closeness sends more electricity rushing through me than the sword, and I'm suddenly very aware of his breath against my ear.

"Keep your stance wide," he continues. "Center your weight."

I try to focus on his words and on his hand guiding mine, but it's impossible with him so close. "Like this?" I manage, and from the way he pulls me closer, I know he has similar things on his mind that I do.

"Better," he says. "Now, move with me."

He guides me through basic forms—how to strike, how to parry, and how to use my opponent's momentum against them. His touch is professional, but it's impossible to forget how those same hands felt on my skin just hours ago.

"Focus," he says sharply when I miss a block. "Your enemy won't be distracted by whatever's going through your mind right now."

"I'm focused." I hold his gaze, but from his smirk, we both know I'm lying.

Well, I'm not *really* lying. Because I *am* focused.

On him.

"Prove it." He draws my dagger—which he's been using in lieu of his sword—and comes at me with a speed that makes me stumble back.

I barely get his sword up in time to block.

The clash of metal-on-metal rings through the cave, and my arms shake from the impact.

"Better," he says. "But your footwork is sloppy. Again."

We continue like that for hours. And even though my supernatural healing is quick, I still feel every blow. Every break.

Finally, I catch him along his bicep with the edge of the blade.

The cut isn't deep—his reflexes are too good for that—but blood wells up, bright red against his skin.

The scent hits me like a storm.

Rich. Intoxicating. Everything I've known I'd need since my last feed.

He moves toward me, worried, as if *I'm* the injured one and not him.

"Don't." I stumble back, dropping his sword with a clatter. "Don't touch me."

Want pulses through me—not desire, but hunger. Pure, primal need that makes my fangs ache to descend.

I will not feed on him, I tell myself. *I will not feed on him. I will not feed on him.*

"Sapphire?" His voice sounds far away. "What's wrong?"

Everything, I want to say.

But I can't tell him. Can't let him know what I am. What I need.

So, I make my breathing as shallow as possible, to push down the hunger until it's manageable. Until I can trust myself to look at him without wanting to lick that blood off his arm.

It's better now that the cut's healed—now that the blood isn't flowing—but I'm far more aware of my hunger than I was when I woke up in his arms earlier.

"I'm fine," I say, now that I've regained some sense of control. "I think I'm just tired. And worried about Zoey."

He studies me for a long moment, and my heart races with worry that he might push for more.

Finally, he nods. "We should break for food anyway," he says.

Food.

If only he knew how right he is about the fact that I need to eat.

But he's wiping the now not-fresh blood off his arm with a cloth, and then he picks up the sword, cleaning it as well.

When he rises, we're so close that it makes my breath hitch.

I have no idea when we'll have a chance to be like this again—just the two of us—after the storm ends. This cave has somehow become our little piece of Heaven.

Apparently, he feels the same, because in a flash, he's kissing me again, this time with a fierceness that leaves no room for hesitation.

The sword clatters to the ground.

And in here, with Riven, the world narrows to just us, and we're pulled back into a storm that's purely our own.

* * *

Afterward, wrapped in Riven's arms, even the howling storm feels distant.

And for once, he looks unguarded, his eyes softened in the dim light of the cave. It's a version of him I don't think anyone else gets to see—a glimpse beneath the frost.

"You're quiet," he says. "Regrets already?"

"No," I quickly say. "I was just… thinking."

He shifts, propping himself up on one elbow to look at me. "About?"

"About you," I admit, turning to face him fully. "And Zoey, and Ghost. I'm sorry you didn't have anyone else who was there for you. Really, *truly* there for you."

"My mother was there for me," he says without pause. "Before she…"

He looks away, his eyes distant.

I stay quiet—not wanting to push, but also wanting to give him space to share.

"My mother wasn't like the others in court," he finally says, turning back to me. "She was softer. Kinder. Everything a Winter Queen wasn't supposed to be."

I stay still, barely breathing, afraid that if I move or speak, he'll retreat behind his walls again.

"The court whispered about it constantly," he says. "How she showed too much mercy. How she let her emotions guide her decisions, instead of logic. She heard every word, even when they thought she didn't."

"That must have been hard for her," I say softly. "And for you, watching her go through that."

"She wanted to change. To be what they wanted." He glances at the ice barrier—as if she could be waiting outside in the storm—then turns his attention back to me. "So, she started searching for a way to suppress her emotions. To be the Winter Queen she thought they needed."

"That's why she was so desperate to make that potion," I say, everything starting to click.

The potion that killed her.

"Yes," he says, tightening his arms around me. "She couldn't find the final ingredient, but she was gifted and intuitive with her magic —like you are. So, eventually, she decided she was confident enough to try anyway."

"It killed her," I whisper what I already know is true.

"Froze her heart completely." The words come out rough, like they're being torn from his throat. "My father and I found her in her quarters. She was just sitting there, like a statue made of ice. And when he touched her, she shattered."

I push up onto my elbow so I can see his face, and when he meets my gaze, the raw honesty there takes my breath away

"I won't lose my father like I lost her," he says. "The court needs stability. A ruler who can balance logic and emotions without being destroyed by either. So, we'll get the ingredients for the potion. All of them. And then we'll—well, *you'll*—brew it correctly. And then, hopefully, he'll be okay. Hopefully everything will be okay."

I wish I could say it'll all work out like he wants it to.

But I can't. Neither of us know how any of this will turn out.

"I'll do my best," I say instead, and I mean it.

Not just because the faster we get this potion made and give it to his father, the faster we can start searching for Zoey. But also because I want to do this for Riven. Even if we didn't make that deal to help each other, I'd want to do it for him.

It breaks my heart to see him so alone.

He shifts closer, his arm wrapping around me as he settles back against the pack we're using as a pillow. "Get some sleep," he says. "We'll need our strength when the storm ends."

I nod, but as I close my eyes, his story lingers in my mind.

The woman who tried to be something she wasn't. The man who broke when she died. And the son left to pick up the pieces.

Then there's the quiet truth I don't dare say out loud: I think Riven's stronger than both of them.

And I can't help wondering what the Winter Court would be like if *he* was the one who was king.

ZOEY

A KNOCK POUNDS on my door, startling me awake and swinging open before I can ask for a few minutes to get out of bed.

The fae servant who brought me from the throne room to my suite is there. The nice one. Her posture's perfect, her face is expressionless, and her wings are retracted, like all the servants around here seem to keep them.

"Prince Aerix requires your presence," she says, and my stomach drops.

I know what this means. Jake warned me about it during our time in the courtyard.

The *feeding.*

"You'll need to get ready." She eyes me up and down in disapproval—as if I should somehow look perfect, even after being jolted awake. "Would you like my help, or would you prefer to prepare yourself in private?"

"In private." I don't have to think twice about my answer.

"Very well." She nods and closes the door, giving me space to "prepare" myself.

There's no getting out of this. And I'd rather go to Aerix willingly —with my dignity intact—than be dragged out of here and carried to wherever he wants to see me.

I eventually settle on a cream-colored, ankle-length, silk dress with long sleeves and a corset-style top—one of the dresses Sophia explained was a "morning dress." Also known as: a dress appropriate to wear for the start of the day.

Well, start of the night, due to the Night Court's nocturnal schedule. But same idea.

Of course, I leave my hair down. After what the king did to me, I never want to wear it up ever again.

The fae woman nods in approval—apparently, I've finally done something right around here—and leads me out of the suite.

Sophia and Victoria are still asleep.

Lucky them.

"Do you have a name?" I ask her when we're out in the hallway.

"Aethelthryth," she replies. "But the humans always have difficulty with it. You can call me Ethel."

"Nice to officially meet you, Aethelthryth," I say, making it a point to show her that even though I'm a human, I'm perfectly able to call her by her true name.

She gives me a small nod, although I swear I see a bit of a smile. Then she leads me out of the human wing and through the winding halls of the Night Court.

As we walk, my mind races.

Maybe I can reason with Aerix. Make him see me as more than just food. After all, he saved me from his father—that has to mean something. And he seemed almost human back in that bunker, when he complimented my cooking and I told him about my time working at the animal shelter.

As I think, I try to memorize the path we're traveling on. But everything looks the same—black and crimson stone floors, floating chandeliers, and gilded mirrors lining the walls.

Yes, the fae are good-looking—*beautiful* is a better word—but judging by the numbers of mirrors in this place, they must be completely obsessed with their appearances.

Aethelthryth doesn't say another word to me as we walk.

Finally, we stop in front of a door larger and more ornate than the others—black inlaid with intricate crimson designs.

She knocks once, then leaves me standing there alone.

"Enter," Aerix calls from inside.

I could run. Sprint through the mirrored halls and try to find my way back.

But even if I managed to get back to my suite, what would happen then? Would I get sent to the barns? Or worse?

Play their game, I remind myself.

So, taking a deep breath, I straighten and push open the door.

Lounging in a high-backed chair near the massive fireplace, Aerix is the perfect picture of predatory elegance. His black hair is swept back, his sharp features illuminated by the flickering firelight. He's wearing a dark shirt unbuttoned at the collar, revealing just enough of his chest to be distracting. His legs are stretched out in front of him, crossed at the ankles, and his midnight eyes pin me in place the moment I step inside.

As for his chambers—they're exactly what I'd expect from a fae-vampire prince. Black stone walls, an ornate fireplace, and floor to ceiling windows overlooking the town.

Then, of course, there's the massive four-poster bed dominating one wall, with sheets the color of blood.

I shudder at the reminder of blood—at the river, and the blood that coated my skin and filled my mouth.

"You came," Aerix says after the door closes.

"I suspect that if I didn't, I'd be dragged," I reply. "And I've had enough of being tied up and dragged around after the first time we met."

"And if I haven't?" he raises an eyebrow suggestively.

I cross my arms, as if they're a shield guarding me from whatever he wants to do to me. "Why am I here?" I ask.

"Why do you think you're here?"

"I'm the one who asked you," I retort.

He smirks and gestures to the chair opposite his. "Sit."

"I'd rather stand."

His smirk falters, and his eyes flash with something darker—something dangerous. But then he sighs and leans back in his chair, waving a hand dismissively.

"Fine. Stand if it makes you feel better," he says. "We can do it either way."

It as in feeding from me?

Or *it* as in…

My cheeks flush, and his eyes continue to bore into me, as if he knows *exactly* what I'm thinking.

Of course he does. He's the one who coaxed my thoughts in that direction.

"I want my amulet back," I say, pointedly changing the subject.

"And why would I do that?" He chuckles, a low, rumbling sound that makes my stomach twist.

"Because it's mine," I say evenly. "You have no right to take it."

"I have every right," he counters smoothly. "You belong to me now. Everything you have is mine. Or have you already forgotten what I told you at the river?"

"I don't belong to you," I say through clenched teeth. "I'm not a piece of property."

"Oh, but you are." His eyes narrow, and the temperature in the room drops. "In case you've forgotten, you're alive because of me. I saved you from drowning. Twice. I brought you here. I claimed you. Now you're mine, whether you like it or not. And judging by the night we shared in that bed, I believe you're going to like it. A lot."

"I move a lot in my sleep," I say quickly, heat rising into my cheeks again. "I was *unconscious*. You can't judge the actions I made while I was unconscious."

"The unconscious mind projects what we want in our awakened state, but are too self-conscious to act on otherwise," he says simply.

"You're completely out of your—"

"Enough." He rises from his chair in one fluid motion, and suddenly he's standing in front of me, towering over me with a presence that's almost suffocating. "I could have left you to die. I could have handed you over to my father to do with as he pleased. But I didn't. I chose you. I spared you. And this is how you repay me? With defiance and disrespect?"

"I'm a person. With skills, and thoughts, and..." I trail off, an idea popping into my mind. "Maybe we can make a deal? I could be useful to you in other ways. I'm good at a lot of things. Cooking, for instance—you saw that yourself. Or I could help around here. Organize things. I'm also really good at—"

"Stop." His voice cuts through my bargaining like a blade. "You seem to be under the impression that you have something to negotiate with."

"No—*you* stop interrupting me," I snap back.

His hand shoots out, grabbing my chin and forcing me to look up at him, his cold fingers sending a chill over my skin.

"You're nothing," he says, low and venomous. "A human. A fragile, insignificant creature who doesn't know her place. And yet here you are, acting as if you have a right to bargain with a prince of the Night Court. Maybe I was right when I told my father how stupid you are. How much of a brat."

I try to pull away, but his grip is like iron. And, as we stand there in a silent staring battle, my mind's a whirlwind of fear, anger, and something else—something I don't want to acknowledge.

Something that makes my cheeks burn and my pulse quicken.

"Speechless," he murmurs, smiling cruelly. "That's more like it."

"I'm not stupid," I say. "And I'm not going to just give in to being your personal blood bag."

His eyes darken, and his grip on my chin tightens. "No. You're going to fight," he says, his fangs slowly extending. "And I'm going to enjoy every second of breaking that spirit of yours."

He's not wrong about that first part.

So, drawing on every bit of gymnastics training I have—along the bit I can remember from those few weeks of karate classes I took in fifth grade—I twist away from his grip and aim a kick at his chest.

He moves back just enough for my foot to miss, his midnight eyes lighting up with amusement. "Impressive flexibility," he says. "Show me more."

I drop into a low crouch and sweep my leg toward his knees.

He staggers slightly, his balance faltering, giving me just enough time to spring to my feet and lunge forward, aiming an elbow at his ribs.

His movements are almost lazy as he twists away.

"Your form is excellent," he says, studying me as if I'm the most fascinating thing he's ever seen in his life. "And such precise control. You must have—"

I interrupt him by spinning into a roundhouse kick, putting all my strength behind it.

He catches my ankle mid-air.

But rather than using it to throw me off balance, he holds me there.

"Let. Me. Go." I use his grip as leverage, pushing off the ground with my other foot in a move that knocks him back.

Then, in a blur of speed, he's behind me, his hands gripping my wrists and twisting my arms behind my back.

"Just as I hoped," he murmurs, his breath cold against the back of my neck. "You're going to make this fun."

"I'm not here to perform for you," I snarl, struggling against his hold.

"But you are." His grip tightens, and suddenly I realize how close we are. "Everything you do is for my entertainment now. And I must say—you've put on quite a show. I'm very much enjoying it."

Horror dawns on me as I realize—he's been toying with me this whole time. Letting me think I had a chance. Watching me spin and flip and fight like I'm some sort of performer in a circus.

He's in front of me before I can react, grabbing my wrist and twisting me around, pulling me flush against his chest. His other arm snakes around my waist, locking me in place.

"I hate you," I whisper, but my voice shakes.

"No, you don't," he says. "Not really. Your heart's racing, but not from fear." His cold fingers trace my neck, finding my pulse point. "You enjoyed it too—the thrill of the fight, the way our bodies moved together. You gave me a wonderful performance. Now, it's my turn."

"Don't—" I say, but he interrupts me again—this time with his fangs piercing my neck.

ZOEY

THE PAIN IS sharp but brief, quickly shifting to something darker and deeper. It's like being wrapped in silk and shadow, and calm blooms inside me, spreading from the point where his fangs sink into my skin through the rest of my body.

I try to fight the feeling, to hold onto my anger and fear. But it slips away like water through my fingers, replaced by a floating sensation that makes everything cloudy and dream-like.

The room spins, and I'm distantly aware of my heartbeat pounding in my ears like a drum. My breaths come shallow and quick. But most disturbingly, heat blooms inside me, centering in places I shouldn't let myself think about.

I should be terrified. Furious. Disgusted.

Instead, my skin is on fire, and I melt into him as his fangs sink deeper.

A low groan escapes him—a sound that vibrates through his chest and straight into mine.

"Stop," I whisper, but it comes out as a plea, soft and shaky, without the bite I meant it to have.

His lips curl against my neck, and he drinks slower, savoring me.

The heat in my veins sharpens into something else—something raw and consuming. Every nerve in my body comes alive. The soft brush of his lips against my skin is electric, the cool press of his fingers on my waist both grounding and maddening.

My body's betraying me in ways I can't even process.

No, a small voice inside my mind finds its way through. *Fight.*

I try to push against his chest, but my hands fall uselessly, my fingers clutching weakly at the fabric of his shirt instead of shoving him away.

"Please," I breathe, though I don't know what I'm asking for.

For him to stop? For him to keep going?

The thought makes me want to crawl out of my own skin.

He pulls back just enough to meet my gaze, his midnight eyes blazing, his lips stained crimson.

Blood.

That's my *blood.*

"You taste better than I imagined," he murmurs. "Better than anyone else I've ever tasted."

"And how many people have you *tasted?*" I say, glaring at him through the haze.

"None as delicious as you." He scoops me into his arms, cradling me as if I weigh nothing, and lays me down on his bed.

The silk sheets are cool against my overheated skin, and I lie there, my mind hazy, staring up at the dark canopy above and trying to regain control of my body.

He doesn't give me that chance.

He's on the bed with me in an instant, his hand sliding under my neck, lifting me slightly to expose the bite he's already left.

The hungry way he's staring down at me makes my lungs squeeze with panic.

It's like he's lost all sense of control. Any bit of humanity I thought I saw of him that night in the bunker is gone.

It probably never existed at all.

His fangs sink in again, and the world spins, my body growing lighter with every pull of his lips.

I clutch at the sheets beneath me, desperate for something solid—something real.

It's too much.

He's taking too much.

Just when black spots start dancing at the edges of my vision, he moves away and gets out of the bed.

I just stare at the ceiling, trying to piece myself back together. But every nerve in my body is still buzzing, and I'm so lightheaded that I can't bring myself to speak, let alone move.

"Here. This will help with the blood loss," he says, sitting back down next to me and holding out a cup of juice. "I have cookies, too, but you should have this first."

"Cookies?" I reach for my neck, expecting to find a wound, but it's completely healed. "After all of that, you're giving me *cookies?*"

"There's the fiery human I love." He holds the cup out closer to me. "Drink."

"I hate you," I say again, somehow managing to push myself up to lean against the insanely soft pillow.

"So you keep saying." He presses the glass to my lips. "Open up."

I should refuse. Knock the glass away and tell him exactly where he can shove his fake concern.

But my head is spinning, and my limbs feel like lead.

And really, after his venom, what's a little juice going to do?

So, I drink, the sweet liquid cool against my throat. It tastes like berries and moonlight, if moonlight had a taste.

"Good girl," he murmurs, and before long, I've finished it all.

Steadier now, I take the glass from him and place it down on the nightstand, next to what looks like shortbread cookies. "If that kills me," I say, "at least I won't have to deal with you anymore."

"You're resilient," he says. "I'll give you that."

"And you're insufferable."

His smirk widens. "I've been called worse."

Angrily, I take a cookie and bite.

It melts on my tongue, rich with butter, vanilla, and an herb I can't quite place.

Aerix leans back against the headboard, his long legs stretched out beside me, his arms crossed lazily over his chest. The casualness of his posture only pisses me off more, like he knows he's the one in control of this situation.

Which, to be fair, he is.

"Very impressive." He studies me as I eat, his midnight eyes glittering with amusement.

"The way I inhale cookies?" I reply, grabbing another one.

"The way you bounce back."

"Glad to know I'm meeting your high standards," I say, taking another angry bite.

"Tell me something," he says as I chew what turned out to be *way* too big of a bite. "All of these things you're good at. Cooking, gymnastics, cat taming, horseback riding, building pillow fortresses, throwing a punch—or trying to, anyway."

"How do you know I did horseback riding?" I ask, since there's no way I ever told him that.

"Your posture when you were on Nyx's back," he says simply. "And given that humans in the mortal realm don't typically ride jaguars, horseback riding was the logical guess."

I press my lips together, hating that he's right.

"Anyway," he continues. "What's the one thing you're truly passionate about? The thing you've stuck with? The thing that defines you?"

I swallow the cookie, buying time. "I have lots of passions."

"Do you?" His midnight eyes narrow. "Or do you just have lots of hobbies that you've dabbled in?"

"What's the difference?" I ask, although his words hit closer to home than I'd like.

"The difference," he says, "is commitment. Dedication. The willingness to pursue something beyond the initial excitement of learning something new."

"I stick with things," I protest, but even as I say it, I know it's not entirely true.

Gymnastics lasted until I discovered soccer. Soccer gave way to tennis. Pottery led to painting, then woodworking, then jewelry making. Each one replaced by something new once I'd gotten decent at it.

"I thought so," he says, leaning back again. "You've tried everything, haven't you? Always searching, always chasing, but never committing. Never sticking around long enough to truly master anything."

"I just like to explore," I tell him, which is the same thing I told Patrick. "To keep my options open."

"You're searching," he says, continuing to study me in that annoyingly intense way of his. "Always trying new things, never settling, never finding what truly calls to you."

"Maybe I just like variety."

"Or maybe you're afraid of committing to something and discovering you're not as naturally talented at it as you'd like to be."

Anger flares inside me.

How dare he try to psychoanalyze me? This monster who brought me here, claimed me, drank my blood, and now thinks he knows me?

I open my mouth to tell him I want to leave—to get as far away from him and his "insights" as possible—but something else entirely comes out instead.

"Since you're apparently invested enough to have taken extreme notice of my varying interests, I want some things to keep me occupied," I tell him.

His eyebrows rise slightly. "Things?"

"A wood whittling kit, for starters. And paint supplies. And a—"

"A wood whittling kit?" he interrupts, laughing. "How quaint."

"Are you going to let me finish?" I snap.

He raises his hands in mock surrender, his smirk still firmly in place. "Please, continue."

"Sketch paper and pencils," I tell him, rather enjoying his allowing me to make demands of him. "Watercolors too, with good brushes. Some clay would be nice—the kind that air dries, since I doubt you have a kiln lying around this place."

"Anything else?" he asks, amusement dancing in his eyes.

"Yes, actually." I lift my chin defiantly. "Thread and needles for embroidery. And yarn for knitting. Oh, and a garden plot."

"A garden plot?" Now he looks genuinely surprised.

"Yes. Nothing big. Just enough space to grow some herbs and flowers. I took a class on medicinal herbs last spring," I add, although I don't mention that I only attended three sessions before getting distracted by archery.

"Interesting," he says. "And what, exactly, do you plan to carve with your whittling kit?"

"Why can't you move on from the wood whittling?" I ask, irritation rising inside me.

"Since you're the one making demands, it's fair I ask questions," he says, though it's clear from his tone that my demands are another source of amusement for him.

"What I carve is none of your business," I say, because the truth is, I don't know yet. I just need something—anything—to keep my hands busy while I brainstorm possible ways to get out of this place.

"You don't know what you're going to make," he says, angering me further. "Do you?"

"I'll figure it out." I hold his gaze in challenge, putting the remainder of my cookie down. "I always do."

"All right. I'll consider it." He stands, moving toward the door with that fluid grace that makes my stomach flip. "Although I suspect by the time your supplies arrive, you'll have thought of a dozen new hobbies to pursue."

"You're making fun of me," I accuse.

"Not at all." He pauses at the door. "I find your determination fascinating. Now, finish your cookies and rest. Aethelthryth will come fetch you when you're recovered enough to return to your room."

With that, he's gone, leaving me alone in his chambers with nothing but cookies, anger, and the unsettling feeling that Aerix sees far more of me than I want him to.

ZOEY

WITH EVERY CORNER turned through the Night Court's mirrored halls, I'm half expecting Aerix to materialize out of the shadows and hit me with another smug observation about my character flaws.

I shouldn't let him get to me. Not the prince who drank my blood like it was fine wine, not the predator who delights in poking at my vulnerabilities.

But somehow, he does.

Victoria and Sophia are waiting in the common area, already dressed and ready for the day. Well, for the night. Which is day to the vampires.

"Well?" Sophia asks. "How are you? Are you okay?"

"Define what you mean by 'okay,'" I say, since even though I'm physically recovering from Aerix's drinking from me, I'll *never* be emotionally recovered.

I know that deep in my soul.

"You know…" She glances down at the floor, shrugs, then turns her focus back to me. "How much did he take?"

"I managed to stay conscious, if that's what you're asking," I say, moving to an armchair and sitting down.

I almost didn't stay conscious, but they don't need to know that. And I don't feel like sharing any more details.

What happened in there with Aerix feels too personal. Too private.

Victoria's eyes zero in on my neck. "So, he did it," she says. "He fed from you already."

There's something in her tone that makes me pause.

Hurt? Jealousy?

"He always feeds from me when he first wakes," she continues, confirming my suspicions. "He has for years. Ever since I first got here."

"It was probably just a one-time thing," Sophia reassures her. "You know how they can be with anything new."

"Aerix has never been like that." Victoria scowls.

But I'm still focused on what Sophia said.

"New things," I repeat flatly. "Like I'm a fancy dessert he's never tried before."

Victoria's laugh is hollow. "That's exactly what you are. What we all are."

The casual way they discuss this—like it's perfectly normal to be treated as food—makes my skin crawl.

I need to get out of here. Away from their knowing looks and loaded comments.

"I need some air," I say, already heading for the door.

"Zoey—" Sophia starts, but I'm already gone.

I wander the human wing until I find my way to the courtyard. The night air is surprisingly warm, the watered-down blood bubbles from the fountains, and the dark roses shimmer in the moonlight. Thankfully, the water in the fountains here doesn't smell as much like blood. Maybe there's less of it in the water? Or because it's not stagnant? No idea.

The entire courtyard would be beautiful, if it wasn't essentially a prettier version of a prison yard.

Hours pass as I sit by one of the fountains, watching the moonlight dance across the water, replaying the moments of Aerix drinking my blood.

It doesn't feel real. Especially since every time I touch my neck, the skin there is perfectly smooth, as if it hadn't been violated the way it was.

As I sit there, I steal glances at the others in the courtyard, who seem intent on ignoring me.

Malakai's humans—Lacey, Katerina, and Brenda—are playing a

card game off to the side. Apparently, cards are their favorite pastime. Aurora sits across the way, reading. Nathanial's sketching next to the garden.

When Henry comes out, he thankfully doesn't bother me. He just takes off his shirt and starts working out.

Jake's nowhere to be seen. Maybe he's with Princess Cierra.

Other humans come and go, and while they give me curious looks, they don't come over.

Finally, as midnight approaches, the handlers begin setting up tables for lunch.

The thought of food makes my stomach growl—those cookies feel like ages ago.

Sophia and Victoria are the next ones who enter the courtyard. Victoria immediately heads to one of the round tables, and Sophia hurries over to me.

"That's our table," she says, pointing to the one Victoria's now sitting at. "Come on. She's not that bad all the time. I promise."

Given the fact that Victoria's glaring at me as if she wants to murder me with her cutlery, I have trouble believing Sophia on that.

But I don't have time to figure out what to say to Victoria when I sit down, because the next person who files in is the one I've been hoping to see all day.

"Matt!" I call out, waving him over.

He's guarded when he looks at me—so unlike the Matt I knew back home—but he weaves through the tables and stops at ours.

"Zoey," he says calmly. "How have you been settling in?"

His tone startles me, and I stand up, searching for the boyishness of the Matt I remember.

There's nothing. It's like he's been replaced by someone else entirely.

"Aerix sent for me this morning," I say, miraculously keeping my voice from wobbling.

"And?" He leans in, speaking quieter now. "How was it?"

"He..." I reach for my neck, touching the place where the wound would be.

"It's incredible, isn't it?" His eyes are wide, just like they were at dinner yesterday when he spoke of the queen.

His gushing makes me suddenly not hungry for lunch.

"I came to see you last night," I tell him, needing to change the subject. "You weren't there."

"I sleep in the queen's quarters," he says proudly.

"Elijah told me." I swallow, my heart dropping with the realization that it's going to be more difficult to get through to Matt than I hoped. "Can we go to my room after lunch? We need to talk."

"Zoey," he says, almost pitifully, taking a step back. "I'm not going with you to your room. I'm with the queen now. I would never do something like that to her. I wouldn't—"

"Oh my God," I cut him off. "You think I was inviting you back to my room to *sleep with you?*"

"Why else would you have asked?"

Before I can answer, Henry strolls over to us.

"Did I hear something about an invitation to your room?" he asks me, his smirk nearly as devious as Aerix's.

"No," I snap at him. "Go away. Both of you."

Matt sheepishly runs his fingers through his hair, unable to meet my eyes, and strides over to the table where Elijah's already situated.

"Go," I repeat to Henry, and I reach for my fork, holding it like a dagger.

"Stop," Sophia says, her fingers wrapping around my wrist. "You'll get sent to the barns if you attack him."

I don't let go of the fork, instead keeping my eyes locked on Henry's, daring him to try anything.

"No witty comeback? Don't tell me Aerix already wore you out," he finally says. "Guess you don't have the stamina for this place after all."

With that, he turns around and joins Matt and Elijah at their table.

Sitting back down, I take a deep breath and scan the other tables, which have been quickly filling up.

"Where's Jake?" I ask Sophia, glancing at the table where Princess Cierra's pets are already seated. Sebastian and Tanya. They both look sweet and innocent, like Jake.

"He's with Princess Cierra," Sophia replies, just like I expected. "He always spends lunch with her. But she tends to be quick. He's usually back by dessert."

"Cierra doesn't like to linger after her meals," Victoria adds with a smirk.

"Are you upset?" Sophia asks with concern. "Because you know he doesn't have a choice. None of us do."

"I know," I say. "I'm not upset. I was just wondering."

It's the truth. Because unfortunately, it's not Jake's eyes I can't get out of my mind right now.

It's Aerix's.

Sophia thankfully doesn't push it.

She just quiets and waits for lunch to be served—which, like everything else in the Night Court, is decadent.

First comes a light salad with crisp greens, thinly sliced radishes, and a tangy vinaigrette. I prefer ranch, but after a week of stale bread in the Winter Court, I have no complaints. Next is a creamy tomato soup, with fresh bread to dip in it. Finally, the main course—roasted chicken legs with mashed potatoes and green beans.

I devour it all.

"Delicious, isn't it?" Sophia asks with a smile. "Before I came here, I'd never had anything like it."

"What was your life like?" I ask her. "Before all of this?"

Sophia sets down her fork, her smile softening. "It wasn't great," she says, quiet but steady. "I lived with my mom, brother, and sister in Portland—in one of those neighborhoods where you don't go out after dark. My mom worked three jobs, but no matter how hard she tried, it was never enough. Some nights, she'd skip dinner so the three of us could eat. I used to pretend I wasn't hungry, just to make it easier on her."

I pause mid-bite, the taste of green beans turning bitter in my mouth. "That sounds... rough," I say, because how else am I supposed to respond? I certainly can't relate. And I won't give her the indignity of pretending I can.

"It was." She shrugs, as if brushing it off. "But I had to help. I started working when I was twelve. Babysitting, cleaning houses, whatever I could find. It wasn't much, but it kept the lights on most of the time. Even then, there were nights I'd wake up to hear my mom crying in the kitchen, trying to figure out how she was going to stretch one meal to feed four of us."

I glance at Victoria, expecting some sort of snarky comment.

But she's uncharacteristically quiet, pushing a piece of chicken around her plate.

Sophia tells me a bit more about her life before all of this, and before long, our plates are being cleared.

Jake strolls into the courtyard as dessert is being served.

Sophia nudges me. "See? Like clockwork."

He takes his seat at the table with Sebastian and Tanya, but his eyes find mine across the courtyard. For a moment, he hesitates, his expression almost guilty.

It makes sense.

After all, I now know how intimate it is when they drink from us. And I have a sinking feeling that what Aerix took from me was just the beginning.

I nod, letting Jake know it's fine. Not like it matters, since the pebble he gave me wasn't a literal proposal, but I can tell that my acceptance matters to him.

He nods back, his shoulders relaxing, and turns his attention to his table.

I look down at my fruit tart, suddenly finding it impossible to eat.

I'm sitting there playing with it when Aethelthryth appears beside our table, carrying an armful of packages.

My eyes widen as she begins setting them down.

The courtyard falls silent, everyone staring as she unloads the satchels.

There's wood and carving tools, several sketchbooks with high-quality pencils, clay, yarn, knitting needles, and even a small set of watercolors. And that's just the start.

"From Prince Aerix," she explains—as if it wasn't obvious. "He says you're to have full use of these items, and that he'll have a plot in the garden cleared for you by tomorrow. He also asked if there's anything else you'll be needing—specifically regarding the tools he sent for the wood whittling."

Victoria's fork clatters against her plate. "You've got to be kidding me," she says, her eyes narrow. "You *asked* for all of this? And he *gave* it to you?"

"I didn't think he'd actually..." I trail off, staring at the items in disbelief.

"What did you do for him?" Her voice is clipped, as if she's accusing me of something. "Or rather, *to* him?"

"Nothing," I say, my fingers drifting to where his fangs broke through my skin. "At least, nothing I assume you haven't done for him."

"Then in the span of a few hours, you'll have had to have done more *activities* with him than I have in the past sixteen years," Victoria says with a smug smirk. "And I can assure you—that's far from possible."

"He's never done this for anyone before," Sophia says, her brows furrowing as she watches Aethelthryth unload the final armful of stuff. "At least, not that I know of. They sometimes give us small things to keep us occupied—cards and such—but never at our request. And certainly not all at once."

I glance at Aethelthryth, who nods in confirmation.

"He's trying to keep you entertained," Victoria says with a bitter laugh. "Like a cat with new toys. The novelty will wear off soon. In the meantime, enjoy your arts and crafts."

I ignore her, instead focusing on Aethelthryth.

"Tell Aerix—"

I'm interrupted by Sophia kicking me under the table.

I glare at her, and she shakes her head, her eyes wide with warning.

Oh.

She's worried I was about to tell Aethelthryth to tell Aerix thank you.

She highly underestimates my ability to adapt. Not just to this world, but to *every* hobby I've ever pivoted to in my life.

"Tell Aerix I'll make good use of his gifts," I say calmly, trying to hide the thrill running through me at the fact that he's done something so unique for me.

"I'll pass along the message," she says, and after one last confused, lingering glance, she turns and goes back inside.

ZOEY

AETHELTHRYTH LEAVES the satchels with me—presumably so I can transport all this *stuff* to wherever I want to take it.

After lunch, I waste no time. If Aerix wants to amuse himself by giving me everything I asked for, then fine—I'll take full advantage of it. So, I put everything back into the satchels and walk over to the largest fountain in the middle of the courtyard, sit down in the grass, and bring out the wood whittling tools.

The wood is smooth beneath my fingers—high-quality. Just like everything else in this gilded prison.

"Anyone want to join?" I call out, my voice carrying across the courtyard.

Sophia immediately bounces over, settling beside me.

To my surprise, Victoria lingers, eyeing the supplies with poorly concealed interest.

"Here." I hold out another knife. "Assuming you'd rather whittle than take a stab at me?"

"Please." She rolls her eyes, takes the knife, and sits down. "Physically harming anyone else here is a surefire way to get send to the barns."

"And if anyone tried to attack a fae?" I eye the knife, confused about *why* Aerix would so easily give me such a weapon.

"If you attack a fae, then you'll *wish* you'd been sent to the barns." A haunted look crosses her eyes—one that tells me to not push further.

I can't help thinking about those times when I launched myself at Aerix with that dagger. And his saying that he saved my life each of those times by not killing me on the spot.

Then there's that person I remind him of. The one he didn't want to talk about.

I want to know more.

So, I vow to get it. Eventually.

Meanwhile, Jake hurries to my side, and after him, others drift over. Sebastian and Tanya, then Isla, who looks at the wood with wide-eyed wonder. Even Elijah joins, although he maintains a careful distance.

Matt remains at his table, arms crossed as he talks quietly with Henry.

They both look pointedly at me, then leave the courtyard.

My heart drops in disappointment. I was so happy when I saw Matt—of all people—here with me. Well, I wasn't happy that he'd also been taken here, and that he's changed so much, but it was nice to see someone I've known all my life. Someone from Presque Isle.

But he belongs to the queen now. And I have a feeling that I best not forget that.

Aurora gets up and heads in our direction, and I think she's going to join us, but she simply walks by and situates herself at another fountain, book in hand.

"So," Jake says once she's passed. "What are we making? Maybe a group project? A tic-tac-toe board or something?"

"Or a chess board." Isla's eyes light up.

"Aren't you a bit young for chess?" I ask her.

"I'm thirteen." She straightens her shoulders, looking insulted by my comment. "I started playing when I was seven."

"Noted," I say, reminding myself to not underestimate her. Clearly, she's done something right to survive around here. "And sure. We can make a chessboard."

Kings. Queens. Knights. Bishops. Pawns.

I start running through the different pieces in my mind, since I went through a brief chess phase after watching that television series about the chess prodigy girl on Netflix.

"I'll make the king," Isla decides. "It might feel good to… take a knife to him."

She holds up the blade, and her eyes gleam with something shocking—something dangerous.

I'm definitely not going to underestimate her.

From there, we each decide which piece we're going to work on first.

I claim the knight, without hesitation.

The knight is the only piece that moves differently from the others on the board. It's not the most powerful, but it's unpredictable, weaving its way across the grid in an L-shape no one ever seems to expect. It doesn't charge forward recklessly like the pawns, or overwhelm with sheer force like the queen. It's strategic. A piece that survives by staying flexible, adaptable—by thinking outside the box.

Kind of like me.

"I'll take the bishop," Jake declares, like he's just claimed the ultimate prize.

I stifle a laugh, unsurprised by his choice.

"What does the bishop do again?" he asks.

"It moves diagonally," Isla tells him.

Jake's brow furrows. "Diagonally? That's it?"

"Yep."

He stares at the block of wood, as if it's personally offended him. "That's kind of lame."

"It can move as far as it wants diagonally," I add, not wanting to completely crush his ego. "So, it's not useless. It's just… situational."

Victoria snorts quietly, and I give her a look, but Jake doesn't seem to notice. He's too busy examining the wood again, as if reconsidering his choice.

"You know," he says after a moment, "I think I can make it work. Diagonals are underrated, right?"

"Absolutely." I smile despite myself. "You'll be the master of diagonals."

"Damn right I will." He starts carving with exaggerated confidence, his movements clumsy but determined.

Isla, meanwhile, is attacking her soon-to-be king with so much focus that I half-expect her to carve it into dust.

I run my fingers over the smooth grain of the wood that I'm holding, letting the rhythm of carving soothe me.

The others are equally as focused, and I give them pointers, so they have places to start.

"So," I say casually, glancing up from my work. "What do you all think we could make besides chess pieces? Specifically, things that are useful?"

"Useful, how?" Elijah asks.

"Tools," I say softly. "To help us. Somehow."

Sebastian pauses his carving. "What are you getting at?"

"Getting out of here." I run my blade along the wood's grain, keeping my movements smooth. "The yarn could be braided into rope. The clay could be used to make impressions of keys..."

Isla's hands pause mid-carve, Elijah shifts closer, and Tanya's shoulders tense, although she doesn't look up.

"Are you actually this stupid?" Victoria's sharp voice cuts through the quiet.

"Victoria—" Jake starts, but she cuts him off.

"No, I want to know." She sets down her half-carved piece. "Because apparently Prince Aerix was right about you. You really are too dense to understand how things work around here."

"And how do things work here, Victoria?" I ask, although I keep carving, not wanting to let her get me riled up. Or at least, not wanting her to *see* that she's getting me riled up.

"There's no escape," she says, keeping her voice to a whisper. "The wards, the fae, the guards—we're powerless here. But hey, maybe you can try swimming away through the moat." Her lips curl into a cruel smile. "But wait—you can't swim, can you?"

My knife slips, nearly cutting my finger. "How do you know that?"

"People talk." She glances around the circle, and the others avoid my eyes. "Everyone knows about your little performance for the king. How pathetic you looked flopping around in that bloody water. How you're only alive because Prince Aerix wants to use you and break you. When you're used up, he'll have broken you so much that you won't even be suitable for the barns. He'll simply drain and throw you into the moat. With a bit left in you to add to the rest of the blood in there, of course."

Ice runs through my veins, and I place what I've started of my knight onto the ground. "Has that ever happened?"

"The royals enjoy knowing that certain pets only belong to them," she says. "They'd rather them dead than have them become scraps for the nobles."

"Prince Aerix normally isn't like that," Jake adds, glancing at Lacey, Katerina, and Brenda—who are playing cards on the opposite side of the courtyard—before turning his attention back to his bishop.

The message is clear.

Prince Malakai *is* like that.

No wonder those three are so haunted. And who knows what else he does to them behind closed doors.

As for Victoria...

"I know we're all trapped here. And I know we're all scared." I set down my knife, meeting her gaze. "But we should be helping each other. Giving each other hope. Finding ways to make this bearable, at least. Because right now? The only ones benefiting from us fighting are the fae who put us here."

"I'm not scared." Victoria stands abruptly, her piece of wood falling forgotten to the grass. "But have fun playing with your toys. See how far that gets you."

She storms off, leaving the courtyard.

Tanya hesitates, then follows, leaving her unfinished pawn behind.

Elijah places his piece down, although from the curious way he's looking at me, I have a feeling he's intrigued. "You have hope," he says. "More than I've seen from any humans I've ever met here. But be careful. Okay?"

"He's right," Sophia adds. "I like you. Truly. But maybe it's best to direct your positive thinking toward appreciating what we have right now?"

"Like fruit tarts and fresh chicken?" I snap, and she flinches back, clearly hurt.

Guilt twists in my stomach. Because given what she told me at lunch, it was a low blow.

"I'm sorry," I tell her. "I didn't mean it like that."

"You're in shock," she says. "I understand. But I'm going to check on Victoria."

With that, she places her piece down—a castle—and goes back inside.

Jake, Isla, Sebastian, and Elijah stay here.

Jake looks at the place where the others left, his expression troubled. "Zoey..." he starts.

"I know what you're going to say," I tell him. "That I shouldn't talk about this stuff. That it's dangerous."

"It *is* dangerous." He sets down his bishop, turning to face me. "I don't want to see you get hurt."

I study him for a moment, seeing the genuine concern in his eyes. He's not like Victoria, lashing out from fear. He's simply accepted this life. Found ways to make it bearable.

He sees me as one of those ways.

He wants to make me happy. I can see it in the way he's looking at me.

"Are there any lakes around here?" I ask. "Ones that *aren't* full of blood?"

"There's a pond," he says, watching me, waiting for where I'm going with this.

"Are we allowed to go there?" I ask.

"Sometimes." He tilts his head, curious. "With supervision, of course. Why?"

"Because you're going to teach me how to swim."

His surprise melts into a slow grin. "Am I?"

"Yes." I focus on my carving, ignoring the way the others are watching us. "Because I'm not weak. And I'm done letting anyone— human or fae—make me feel otherwise."

SAPPHIRE

I WAKE the next day to afternoon sunlight filtering through the ice barrier.

The storm is stopping.

The silence feels strange. Almost too quiet after the howling, unforgiving winds.

Riven's already alert and watchful, studying the ice barrier more intensely now that there's better visibility.

Meanwhile, we've been in this cave for a day and a half.

It's been three days since I fed from that elk. The hollow feeling in my bones is intensifying. The fangs hidden in my gums ache, as if it wasn't enough that my entire body is begging for blood.

If the cut that made Riven bleed yesterday happened right now... I'm not sure I'd be able to control myself.

Just the thought of it makes my stomach growl, as if the hollow bones and aching fangs wasn't enough. I sit up, rubbing my temples, trying to focus on anything but my sick, monstrous craving.

"The storm's weakening," Riven says, his voice tight as he stares through the ice. "Did you sleep well?"

"Well enough," I say, and this time when my stomach twists, it isn't from hunger.

It's from fear.

Just a few more hours, I tell myself. *I can make it a few more hours. Once we're out there, I'll figure something out. Find a way to feed without him seeing.*

Or I could just tell him. Right here, right now, when we have a few hours left before having to leave this cave. He'll have to understand that this isn't my fault. That I can't control what I am. What I *need.*

After everything we've shared in this cave, maybe he won't see me as a monster.

But he thought he was here with the Summer Fae changeling who has exceptional natural talent with her magic. The one who's grown to trust him, and who he—hopefully—has also learned to trust.

He doesn't know Sapphire, the vampire-fae hybrid. The monster who drained a dark angel dry. Who almost lost control and drained *him* dry.

The thought of him looking at me with disgust makes my heart ache with pain worse than the hunger rushing through my veins. Especially after the way he's been looking at me in here—like I'm something precious. Something worth protecting.

Something possibly worth *loving.*

"We need to leave," he says abruptly, making me jump where I'm sitting.

"But the stars aren't out yet." I frown. "I won't know where to go—"

I cut myself off, feeling like an idiot for speaking without thinking it through.

"You want to search for Ghost," I realize. "Before sunset."

"We're weaker without him. More vulnerable. If something happened to him in that storm..." He swallows hard, tensing his jaw. "I need to know."

"Then we'll leave as soon as we can." I push myself to my feet, ignoring the way my hunger makes me dizzy, and something flickers in his eyes—gratitude mixed with something deeper that makes my heart race.

"We have a bit more food," he says. "Let's eat, then head out."

Food.

My stomach growls again.

If only he knew how much he was torturing me by mentioning it.

* * *

We gather our supplies, and Riven lowers the ice shield, revealing the aftermath of the storm.

The snow is piled in towering drifts, its surface smooth and unbroken. Ice clings to the trees, their branches heavy, some snapped under the weight. Strangest of all, the air is unnaturally still, as if the storm stole all the sound with it.

On top of everything, the weak afternoon sunlight makes me squint in a way that it never did back home.

Maybe because things are different in the fae realm. Or maybe because I'm partly a creature of the night.

Riven strides ahead, focused on the open expanse of white. It's he's trying to will the universe into revealing Ghost's whereabouts through sheer determination.

"Wait," I call out to him, and he spins to look at me, irritation flashing in his silver eyes.

"What?"

"We should split up," I say quickly. "Cover more area. We'll have a better chance of finding Ghost that way."

"No." His hands still on the hilt of his sword, which is hanging from his weapons belt. "Absolutely not."

"But if we split up—"

"I said no. I can't..." His voice catches, and he swallows hard. "I can't lose you, too."

The raw emotion in his voice steals my breath away. It's so different from his usually controlled attitude that for a moment, I forget about my hunger.

But it's back a few seconds later.

"I can take care of myself," I say, gentler now. "You know I can. And by splitting up, we'll cover twice the ground. Time saved might be important if Ghost is hurt."

Splitting up will also give me a chance to feed without Riven knowing.

"You saw how quickly we got separated in that storm." He moves closer and grips my shoulders, as if he's afraid I'll disappear if he lets go. "I won't risk that happening again. Not with you."

"But the storm's over now," I say gently. "I'll be okay. Plus, we have the whisper stone. If anything happens to me, you'll be the first to know. And if I find Ghost, you'll be the first to know, too."

Please let that be enough to convince him...

"No," he repeats, and the pain in his eyes is the kind I've only seen one other time—when he told me about what happened to his mom.

"Okay," I say softly, reaching up to touch his face. "We'll stay together."

The relief in his expression makes my chest ache with guilt.

If he knew what I really was, would he still look at me this way? Or would that relief turn to disgust?

His eyes search my face, as if looking for permission—despite everything that happened during our time in the cave today.

I shouldn't.

Instead, I give him a small nod, and he brushes his thumb across my cheek, leans forward, and kisses me. A soft kiss—the kind where we know it's not going to progress to more. It's just two people, taking a moment to be close to each other, letting the other know that they care about each other and are here for each other, no matter what.

When he pulls back, he rests his forehead against mine, lingering there with what might almost seem hesitation.

"I love you, Sapphire Hayes," he whispers, his breath warm against my lips. "I've loved you since the moment I saw you at that bar. You're *my* summer fae. And I can't lose you. Not like I lost my mother. Not like I might have lost Ghost."

My heart stutters.

Three simple words that make everything more complicated—and yet somehow clearer than ever.

"I love you, too," I say, and the truth of it hits me like an avalanche.

I do love him. Maybe I have since that first night at the Maple Pig, when he walked in and turned my world upside down.

But I'm not a summer fae. Which means I'll never be *his* summer fae. Not really.

He kisses me again, quick but fierce, then straightens, as if that part of business—the part where he opened his heart to me completely—is done. "Let's find Ghost."

I nod, pushing aside my fears and focusing on the task at hand.

Finding Ghost. Doing my part in helping make Riven—the man I love—whole again. Well, as whole as he can be, given everything that's happened to him.

So, we set off across the snow-covered landscape, our boots crunching through the fresh powder, leaving a path in our way. Subtly, I call on air magic behind us, using as little as possible to send a breeze over the snow to cover up our tracks.

Hours pass. The sun sets. Stars emerge, their light clear and bright—perfect for following the map in the sky to lead us to the ancient woman.

Perfect for continuing our quest to find the ancient woman who might be able to help us save Riven's father.

Instead, we're still here, growing more desperate with each passing minute.

We have to try harder. Be less cautious.

I call Ghost's name softly, not wanting to draw attention to us. But my voice carries across the snow and is swallowed by the silence.

Riven tries as well. "Ghost. Come on, boy," he says, undeniable panic flashing in his eyes.

There's nothing. No sound, no movement. Just the endless trees and snow.

Our calls grow more frantic, bouncing off the ice-covered branches. And with every step, the frustration inside me builds. Not just because of the growing hopelessness of this search, but because I can feel my hunger sharpening, the ache in my bones intensifying.

My fangs threaten to descend every time I glance at Riven—every time the memory of his fresh blood seeping out of his skin yesterday flashes through my mind.

His pulse… his warmth…

Stop, I tell myself. *I have to stop.*

"Ghost!" Riven stops, planting his hands on his hips as he stares out over the snow. "Where the hell is he?"

"He was here during the storm. He has to be somewhere," I say, but the words feel hollow, since while he's definitely here somehow, there's no way of knowing if he's alive or not.

I glance back up at the sky. The stars are fully out now, shining brighter.

Riven follows my gaze. Anger swirls in his eyes, and he raises his hands, blasting spears of ice at the nearest tree and splitting it in two.

"Ghost!" He splits another tree with his magic, the crack echoing through the clearing. "Ghost, where are you!"

A shadow shifts through the trees. A flash of black.

"Riven—" I start to warn him, but the dark angel is already there, her black wings spread wide against the starlit sky, her eyes fiercely determined as she dives toward us.

SAPPHIRE

This dark angel is different from the male who attacked me and Zoey. Smaller, but faster, her sleek form gliding through the air with practiced precision.

The sword she's carrying is long and dangerous, the wind propelling her forward like a storm unleashed.

I pull out my dagger.

Riven's sword flashes, slicing through the icy air to meet the dark angel's attack. The clash of metal rings out, and ice surges from his blade, snaking toward her and forcing her back.

She recovers with startling speed and lands in the snow, crouched low, her wings spread wide. Her midnight eyes gleam with malice, and she hisses, a sound that chills me to the bone.

"She's fast," I mutter, shifting into a defensive stance.

Wide stance. Center your weight. Use your opponent's momentum against them, I think, remembering what Riven taught me in the cave.

He nods, as if he can read my thoughts, his sword steady in his grip. "Stay close."

The dark angel lunges again, whipping her wings forward. A gust of wind howls toward us, sharp and biting, carrying shards of snow and ice.

I scream and throw up my arm, calling on my air magic to buffer the attack. The wind slows just enough for Riven to step in front of me, his sword flashing in a defensive arc that drives her back.

"Stay behind me," Riven orders, cold and steady.

"Not a chance." I reach out with my magic, pulling water from the snow at my feet. It gathers in glistening droplets, hardens into razor-sharp shards, and with a flick of my wrist, I hurl them at her like tiny bullets, putting wind behind them to propel them faster.

The dark angel's lips curl into a cruel smile as she turns to me. "What's this? A fae with both water and air magic?"

My stomach rises into my throat, and I steal a quick glance at Riven.

He's not looking at me. Instead, he runs toward the dark angel and strikes, his sword cutting through the air in a deadly arc. His blade catches her shoulder, drawing blood.

The scent hits me in a wave of mouthwatering sweetness, and my fangs ache to descend.

Not now. Please, not now, I tell myself, forcing my attention back to the fight.

The dark angel's wound heals, and my hunger ebbs. Slightly.

Recovered now, she comes at me with terrifying speed.

I duck and roll like Riven taught me, narrowly avoiding her blade. That was close. Too close.

I come up behind her, my dagger ready to strike, but she spins faster than I expect.

Her wind slams into my chest, sending me sprawling into the snow.

The impact knocks the breath from my lungs. My dagger flies from my grip, landing in the snow across the clearing, and a massive white blur explodes from the trees.

Ghost. He barrels into the dark angel with a growl that shakes the ground, colliding with her in a blur of teeth and claws.

She screams, trying to push him off with a blast of wind. But his jaws close around her neck, biting down, sending blood spurting out in a crimson arc.

It splatters across my face—rich, intoxicating, and *alive.*

A drop reaches my lips.

The taste.

The hunger erupts into an inferno, and my fangs descend, sharp and aching with desire. Before I can process what I'm doing, I'm on my feet, and a blast of air magic sends Ghost stumbling back with a startled growl.

He hits a tree, shaking snow from its branches.

With the snow leopard out of the way, I pounce on the dark angel with inhuman speed, pinning her to the ground and holding her there with strength I didn't know I had.

Her midnight eyes widen, and I lower my head to her neck, sinking my fangs into the place where Ghost's bite broke her skin.

Her blood floods my mouth, and the world explodes, every nerve in my body surging to life. It's rich and electric—the most wonderful thing I've ever consumed in my life. This is pure power, ancient and potent, singing through my veins with each desperate swallow.

She struggles beneath me, her wings beating uselessly against the snow, her hands clawing at my shoulders. But I barely feel it. Nothing matters except the blood. The feed. The primal satisfaction of taking what I need.

More. More. MORE.

I drink deeply, the world fading away until there's nothing but the rush of her life pouring into me.

Her struggles weaken, her pulse fluttering under my lips like a dying bird. She's so delicious. I want—no, I *need*—every last drop.

But then, through the haze of bloodlust, a single word breaks through my mind.

Zoey.

This dark angel might know where the other one took her. But if I drain her dry, we lose our only lead. And I will *not* let lack of control over my hunger destroy our chance of finding her.

So, with every ounce of willpower I possess, I wrench myself away from her neck. My fangs retract, leaving a raw ache in their place, and I shove her limp body away from me.

Her chest still rises and falls in shallow breaths. She's alive. Barely.

I stare down at her, heart pounding, head spinning as I process what I just did.

Shame rises inside me. I don't want to look at Riven. I can't. But I have to.

So, I wipe the blood off my face and turn to face him.

He's frozen in place, his silver eyes wide with horror. It's like he's

364

seeing a stranger. A monster. Everything we built in that cave—every tender moment, every confession, each whisper of "I love you"—crumbles in the space between us.

The world tilts under my feet. My blood turns to ice.

I've lost him. Just like I've lost Zoey.

But no—Zoey might not be lost. Not if we act quickly. That's what I need to focus on. Acting quickly.

"We need to take her back to the cave," I say, and while I hear myself speaking, it's like I'm looking down from above, watching someone who's not actually *me*. "She might know how to find Zoey."

Riven doesn't move. Doesn't speak. Just keeps staring at me with those haunted eyes that held so much warmth a few hours ago.

"Riven." I force steel into my voice, even as my heart shatters. "The cave. *Now*."

Blood stains the snow around us—a stark reminder of what I am. What I'll always be. The monster lurking beneath the summer fae Riven thought he loved.

"Please," I beg. "She might know something—not just about Zoey, but maybe about the ancient woman, or the potion for your father. We have to bring her back. Tie her up. Talk to her. *Force* the answers from her."

I'll torture her if I have to. Anything to save my best friend.

Riven studies me for a few, hard moments.

He's going to say no. He's going to tie me up and force answers from me as much as from her.

Slowly—hopefully too slow for him to notice—I move my hand toward my dagger.

Finally, he nods, his jaw tight. "We'll put her on Ghost's back, bring her to the cave, and interrogate her there," he decides, pulling the rope out of his pack and getting to work.

He doesn't say another word as we walk. He won't even look at me.

Shame rises in my chest with every step. Guilt. Fear. And so many more emotions I can't place right now, but I know will hit me like a sledgehammer when I do.

The stars are brighter now. Clearer. But they're far from beautiful. Because no matter how much I gaze up at them—no matter how many answers and paths I seek from them—they'll never guide me back to the way things were before.

Before I knew I was fae. Before I knew I was part vampire. Before I lost my best friend.

And before Riven knew that the girl he thought he loved was a monster.

FROM THE AUTHOR
TWO BONUS SCENES

Hi! I hope you enjoyed reading *Trial of Frost*.

If you enjoyed the book, I'd love if you wrote a review. (One or two sentences is fine!) Reviews are extremely important to authors, because they encourage more readers to pick up the book. Plus, I read every review I get, and they motivate me to write faster.

* * *

Now, as something special for this edition of the *Fae Bound* series: I've written two bonus chapters for you from Riven's point of view.

One is from when he met Sapphire for the first time in the bar, and the other is a spicy scene from the first time he and Sapphire had sex in the cave. He's a very complicated character (you'll learn more about him as the series continues, as you get more chapters from his point of view) and I'm excited to share these chapters with you now.

Turn the page to check them out, and I hope you enjoy them!

RIVEN

I LISTEN to the cacophony of human voices around me, fighting the urge to let my magic frost the water glass in my hands. The warmth of this place—this "Maple Pig Bar and Grill"—grates against my senses, but I force myself to remain still. Composed. Winter Court royalty does not fidget.

Ghost had led me right to this establishment. My faithful companion has never been wrong before, and his behavior tonight has been particularly strange. Insistent. As if he's found something important, something worth the annoyance of these mortals and their ceaseless chatter.

I stare into my water, contemplating my next move. The Winter King—my father—grows more unstable with each passing day. The madness that has been slowly consuming him since my mother's death has reached a breaking point. Without the potion, the court will crumble under his increasingly erratic rule.

And I still need that final ingredient.

"That man looks like he could use a drink," a young woman with dark hair says, her gaze directed at me.

I keep my expression neutral, but my senses sharpen. The bartender with white-blonde hair moves toward me, and some-thing... shifts. The air around her feels different—charged with an energy I've rarely felt outside the fae realms. My fingers tighten around the glass as a thin layer of frost begins to form where my skin makes contact.

I relax my grip immediately. Control. Always control.

When she's finally right in front of me, I find myself staring into the most remarkable pair of eyes I've ever seen on a human. Blue, like the deepest parts of the winter lakes. But there's something else there, something hidden beneath the surface.

"Rough night?" she asks.

"You could say that." I hold her gaze, curious about what she'll do next. Most humans can't maintain eye contact with me for long. There's something about fae eyes that unsettles them, even when they don't understand why.

But she doesn't look away.

"Lucky for you, I have just the thing." She reaches for a silver shaker. "This one's on the house."

I watch her work, fascinated despite myself. Her hands move with a fluid grace that speaks of natural talent—or something more. There's a rhythm to her movements that feels almost... magical. Not the controlled, calculated magic of the Winter Court, but something wilder, more intuitive.

Water magic. Untrained, unconscious, but unmistakably there.

"Aren't you a bit young to be serving drinks?" I ask, probing for information. If she's truly fae—a changeling as Ghost seems to think—she'd be older than she appears.

"I'm eighteen," she replies easily. "I make the best drinks in Maine. So, as long as I don't drink the drinks, the restaurant lets me make them and serve them."

The drink she places before me is a soft pink—delicate, almost innocent in appearance. Nothing like what I'd normally choose. My ice magic stirs within me, responding to my quiet amusement.

"Do I seem like a man who orders pink drinks?" I raise an eyebrow, testing her reaction.

"You must not be from around here," she counters confidently.

No, indeed. Not from around here at all.

"I'll take it as a compliment that I don't seem like I'm from a small town in Maine." I allow myself the ghost of a smile.

"People come here from all over. But I always remember a face. And yours..." She trails off, her cheeks coloring slightly.

Interesting. I need to provide a reason for my presence without arousing suspicion. "I lost my cat," I explain, the half-truth coming easily. "Ended up finding him nearby, and this place seemed busy, so I figured I'd check it out."

"Your cat?" she repeats, clearly skeptical.

"Correct." I lean back, letting my power subtly fill the space between us—not enough to be noticed, just enough to test if she senses it. "His name's Ghost."

No reaction. Either she's exceptionally skilled at concealing her abilities, or she truly has no awareness of what she is.

"And where's Ghost now?"

"He's waiting outside." My attention catches on the bracelet adorning her wrist—a delicate silver chain with a sapphire pendant. The stone pulses with a faint magic, old and protective. Someone wanted to keep her hidden. "That's a beautiful bracelet."

"My mom gave it to me." She forces a smile that suggests there's more to that story. "So, are you going to try the drink?"

"Depends," I say, allowing myself to play along. "Are you going to tell me your name?"

"I'm Sapphire." She glances down at her bracelet. "Like my bracelet."

"Except you're far more beautiful." The words slip out before I can stop them—not calculated, not strategic.

I need to distract her. Pull her focus away from the crack in my armor.

So, I lift the drink to my lips and take a sip. The taste explodes across my tongue—sweet at first, then warming, with a surprising complexity that speaks of skill far beyond what any human should possess. As the liquid touches my throat, a surge of calm strength flows through me, easing the constant tension in my shoulders.

Potion-making talent. Rare even among the fae. My suspicions crystallize into certainty—this girl, whatever she believes herself to be, is not human.

And she might be exactly what I need.

For a moment, the noise of the bar fades away, and I'm acutely aware of her presence, of the potential she represents. The Winter King could be saved. The court could be stabilized. And all because Ghost led me to this unassuming establishment in a forgotten corner of the human realm.

"What about you?" she asks, her voice pulling me back to the present. "What's your name?"

Before I can answer, the door slams open with enough force to draw the attention of everyone in the room. A young man strides in, radiating the particular brand of aggressive energy that only human males seem to perfect. His emotions are written plainly across his face—jealousy, anger, possession.

"Larkin!" someone calls out to him, but he ignores it, pushing through the crowd toward us.

He barely glances at me as he steps around the bar to stand possessively next to Sapphire.

"Sapphire." His eyes roam over her in a way that makes my fingers itch with frost. "We need to talk."

Frost forms inside my boots as I resist the urge to freeze him where he stands. That would certainly complicate matters. Instead, I observe the interaction carefully, noting the way Sapphire's posture changes—tense, guarded, yet resigned. The water in glasses across the bar ripples almost imperceptibly.

She doesn't even realize she's doing it.

"Now's not really a good time," she tells him, but he reaches for her wrist, his fingers closing around it with a possessiveness that makes my jaw clench.

I set my drink down silently, frost creeping along my fingertips. The temperature around me drops several degrees, though no one seems to notice. No one except Ghost, who would be growling if he were here—I can feel his agitation even from outside.

"Please," the boy—Larkin—pleads, desperation edging his voice. "It's the last few minutes before the new year. I don't want to end it like this."

Sapphire's eyes dart around, taking in all the spectators— including me. I keep my expression carefully neutral, though my magic coils inside me, responding to my growing distaste for this human and his presumptuous hands.

"Fine." She pulls her wrist free with a sharp motion. "Talk."

His pause suggests he didn't expect her acquiescence. Interesting —he seeks to dominate, yet falters when given what he wants. Typical human contradiction.

"I want us to have a fresh start." He leans closer, invading her space. "Come home with me. Tonight."

"I'm not moving in with you." Her voice is weary, as if they've had this conversation countless times before. "I'm not ready."

"You're never going to be ready."

His hand slams against the bar with enough force to make the glasses jump, and I straighten imperceptibly, my magic surging in response to his aggression. But before I can decide whether to intervene, there's a loud crack from the service sink behind the bar, and water sprays outward in a sudden, powerful jet.

Not an accident. Her magic, responding to her heightened emotions.

"Great," she mutters, rushing to the sink as water soaks her shirt and jeans.

I watch with fascination as she works to stem the flow, her movements instinctive, her connection to the water evident in how quickly she finds the right valve setting. This is exactly the kind of raw, untrained talent I've been searching for—someone who can manipulate elements without even realizing they're doing it.

"Let me help," Larkin says, his anger apparently forgotten as he moves to take over.

Before he can reach her, Sapphire twists the valve shut, cutting off the spray. Water drips from her sleeves, her wet clothes clinging to her skin. Even soaked and frustrated, there's something undeniably captivating about her.

"I didn't realize how handy you were," Larkin says, his tone a strange mix that sets my teeth on edge.

"It's been happening a lot lately," she explains, attempting to dry her hands on her already soaked jeans. "We really need a new sink."

His expression softens, and I recognize the manipulation before he even opens his mouth. "You know I just want us to be together," he says, his voice gentler now. "I love you. I always have, and I always will."

Ice-cold irritation—or maybe something else, something I'm not sure I've ever felt before—floods through me. Because that's it. I've heard enough. If I stay here for much longer, the man who I presume is Sapphire's boyfriend is going to become a popsicle by the end of the night. And if that happens, my chance of getting her to help me might lessen considerably, and it will *definitely* complicate my plans.

The countdown to midnight begins, humans raising their glasses with manufactured excitement.

"Ten... nine... eight..."

I drain the last of my drink, setting it down silently.

"Seven... six..."

I slip away from the bar, moving through the crowd with the silent grace that marks me as something other than human. No one notices. They never do.

"Five... four..."

I cast one last glance toward Sapphire. Larkin's hands are on her waist now, his body pressing close to hers. The possessiveness of the gesture makes my magic pulse cold against my skin.

"Three... two... one..."

He kisses her as midnight strikes, and I turn away, a strange, unfamiliar feeling twisting in my chest. Not jealousy—royalty of the Winter Court doesn't indulge in such petty emotions. Strategy, perhaps. Irritation at an unnecessary complication.

"Happy New Year!" The humans erupt in celebration, their voices rising in a way that grates against my senses.

Outside, Ghost waits in the shadows, his massive white form nearly invisible against the snow. His eyes meet mine, questioning.

"Yes," I tell him as I approach. "You were right. She's the one we need."

I cast one last look at the bar behind me, plans already forming in my mind. I'll find her again. After all, a human male is hardly an obstacle for a prince of the Winter Court.

And Sapphire—with her undiscovered magic and innate talent—will help me save my father, whether she realizes it or not.

The Winter King's madness will be cured. The court will be restored.

And this remarkable changeling with the sapphire bracelet will be the key to it all.

RIVEN

I STARE out at the raging storm beyond the wall of ice I've created to barricade the cave, searching for any sign of Ghost in the swirling white chaos. The howling wind carries no trace of him. Nothing. My familiar has never been gone this long before, and the gnawing worry in my chest grows with each passing minute.

Ice spreads beneath my fingertips where they rest against the cave floor. I try to breathe evenly, to maintain the composure expected of the Winter Prince, but Ghost's absence tears at me in ways I can't control. My magic responds accordingly—thin layers of frost forming and melting in rhythm with my breaths.

I sense Sapphire's approach before I see her. The subtle shift in the air as she moves closer, the warmth of her presence cutting through the chill I've wrapped around myself like armor. I expect her to keep her distance. After everything that's happened between us, she has every reason to stay away.

But she doesn't. She settles beside me instead, close enough that I can feel her warmth, yet far enough that we don't touch.

The relief I feel when she doesn't walk away is embarrassing. Weak. I shouldn't need her presence like this, but I do.

"Tell me about Ghost," she says, her voice soft in the stillness of our shelter. "How did you meet?"

The question catches me off guard. Not because she's asking about Ghost, but because of the genuine curiosity in her tone. Not pity. Not manipulation. Just... interest.

I remain silent, weighing how much to reveal. Vulnerability has never served me well—not with my father, and not at court. Showing weakness is an invitation for others to exploit it. Yet with Sapphire, the walls I've built seem to crack without my permission.

"I was eight," I finally say, still watching the storm rather than looking at her. "Lost in the forest at the edge of Winter Court territory after sneaking out of the palace. I was angry at my father. I thought if I ran far enough, I could leave it all behind."

The memory surfaces with painful clarity—the biting cold of that winter night, the fear that clawed at my throat as darkness fell, the childish belief that I could somehow escape my birthright by simply running away. I'd been naive enough to think freedom was something I could find if I just went far enough.

"What happened?" she asks, and her voice draws me back to the present.

My fingers trace patterns in the frost beneath us, unconsciously forming the same spirals of ice magic I'd released that night, desperate to find my way home once I realized how foolish I'd been.

"Ghost found me. He appeared through the trees, like he was made of snow itself." The image is still vivid—Ghost's powerful form emerging from the darkness, his eyes gleaming with intelligence that felt ancient even then. "I thought he was going to eat me."

Despite the worry, a faint smile tugs at my lips. I'd been certain I was going to die that night, torn apart by a predator I had no hope of fighting. Instead, I found the only companion who's ever truly known me.

"But he didn't," Sapphire says, drawing me out of the memory.

"No." The smile remains, genuine in a way few of my expressions ever are. "He just... walked up to me. Sat there, staring like he was trying to figure me out. Eventually, I stopped shaking long enough to reach out, and he let me touch him. That's when the bond formed."

"The familiar bond?"

I nod, feeling the phantom echo of that connection snapping into place—the rush of ancient winter magic, the sudden awareness of another consciousness linked to mine. Ghost has been the one constant in my life since that moment. Unlike everything else in my world of political maneuvering and court intrigue, my snow leopard's loyalty has never wavered.

"He led me back to the court," I continue. "Saved my life. I've never doubted him since. No matter what, Ghost has always been there. Always."

I say it as much to reassure myself as to tell Sapphire. Ghost has survived countless dangers over the years. A storm, even one as fierce as this, won't stop him from finding his way back to me. It can't.

"He found you once," Sapphire says, and I hear the effort she's making to be encouraging without offering false hope. "Which means he can most likely find you again."

"He'd better." I force a chuckle, trying to lighten the moment. "He's my only friend. The only one who doesn't care about titles or politics. Who sees me, and not my crown."

The words slip out before I can stop them—more honest than I intended to be. I don't look at Sapphire, not wanting to see pity in her eyes. I've revealed too much already, shown too much of the loneliness that has shaped me.

When I finally risk a glance at her, there's no pity in her expression. Just understanding. Maybe even something like recognition.

"I always wanted a pet," she admits, the wistfulness in her voice tugging at something deep inside me. "Something to care for. But Aunt Martha refused. She couldn't stand the thought of an animal 'dirtying' our home."

"Ghost isn't a pet." The correction comes automatically, but there's no anger behind it. Just the need to make her understand what Ghost truly is to me. "He's my constant. The only one who's always been there—who hasn't become lost to me."

The words hang in the air between us, heavy with everything they don't say. My mother, gone. My father, slipping further into madness with each passing day. I've watched everyone I've ever cared about disappear in one way or another.

If I lose Ghost, too...

The thought sends a surge of panic through me that cracks the icy barrier I've maintained over my emotions.

"We'll search as hard as we can," Sapphire says, and then she does something completely unexpected.

She reaches for my hand.

Her fingers are warm against mine, and the simple contact sends a shock through my entire system. Touch has never been freely offered in my world. It's always been calculated, political—a means to an end. But there's nothing calculated about the way Sapphire's fingers intertwine with mine. Nothing political about the comfort she's offering.

I look up and find myself caught in her gaze. Those impossible blue eyes hold a depth of understanding I've never encountered before. She knows fear. She knows what it means to worry about those you care for.

"Sapphire," I whisper her name, barely trusting my voice not to break. Her name feels like a confession torn from somewhere buried deep—a place I've kept locked away for so long I'd forgotten it existed.

My gaze trails from her eyes to her mouth, then to the curve of her neck, memorizing every detail as if I might never get this chance again. I want to move, to close the space between us, but years of restraint hold me back. I've spent my entire life being taught that wanting makes you weak. That needing someone else is the surest path to destruction.

My father's voice echoes in my mind: *Never reveal your desires. They become weapons in the hands of others.*

But she steps closer, erasing that final trembling inch between us, and the moment our bodies touch, the breath I've been holding rushes out in a stutter. I close my eyes briefly, overwhelmed by the sensation of her against me, by the collapse of every wall I've ever built. My carefully constructed defenses—years of practiced detachment, of holding everyone at arm's length—crumble in an instant.

I lean in before I can stop myself, capturing her lips in a kiss so careful I'm barely breathing. Every movement is measured and restrained, asking permission with each subtle shift. The Winter Prince reduced to silent pleading with each press of my lips.

When she responds—when she winds her arms around my neck and presses herself against me—something primal surges through my veins.

"I've dreamed of this," I murmur against her lips, words I never meant to reveal slipping out. "Of you. Every night since the moment I saw you." My hands slide down her sides, leaving trails of frost that melt against her heated skin, my magic responding to the war between desire and fear. "Even when I told myself I shouldn't want you—couldn't have you—my body betrayed me every time I closed my eyes."

I meet her gaze, knowing she must see the fever in mine—the desperation, the edge I'm balancing on.

"You don't have to fight it anymore." Her palm finds my cheek, and I lean into it, starved for the touch, for the warmth that no one has offered me since my mother died. "You don't have to pretend you don't feel it. Because I've wanted you, too."

"You shouldn't want someone like me," I say hoarsely, the truth scraping my throat raw. Years of my father's lessons, years of watching what love did to him when my mother died, years of believing love was weakness flashing through my mind. "But gods help me—I need you like I need air. And I'm not strong enough to keep pretending I don't."

I kiss her again, harder this time, hungrier—memorizing the taste of her, the feel of her lips, the warmth of her body. Because some part of me is certain this can't last. That the universe will snatch her away like it's taken everything else I've ever cared about.

"If you want to stop—" I force myself to say, even as every cell in my body screams in protest at the thought. I search her eyes, needing her to understand that despite what I want—what I crave—I won't take what isn't freely given.

"Don't you dare," she breathes, pulling me closer. Her water magic surges around us, droplets dancing frantically in the air, mirroring the chaos inside me. "I want you, Riven. All of you."

Something breaks in me then. Not just desire unleashed, but the walls around my heart cracking open. Not the calculated prince trained since childhood to control every emotion, not the cold warrior who's killed without hesitation. Just a man who's been fighting so hard not to feel this, not to need this, and failing miserably.

I lift her against the cave wall, my hips grinding into hers, my hardness pressing against her through our clothes. The gasp she releases sends a shudder through my body. The temperature between us fluctuates wildly—ice crystals forming and melting as my control starts to fracture.

"I've made mistakes. But you've changed me," I confess, the truth spilling out as my hands slide under her shirt, fingers tracing the delicate skin over her ribs, up to the swell of her breast. "From the moment I saw you, you've been breaking down every wall I've built. You're making me want to be better. For you."

Emotion tightens in her throat—I can see it, the shimmer of tears in her eyes. "You've always been enough, Riven. You just never saw it."

I pull back just enough to look at her, stunned by her words. No one has ever seen beyond the icy mask of the Winter Prince. No one has ever bothered to look. Naked vulnerability rises inside me—a terrifying openness I haven't allowed myself since I was a child.

"With you, I want to believe it," I whisper, my voice rough with emotion I can barely contain. "I try to."

My hand slides lower, slipping beneath the waistband of her pants. When my fingers part her, finding her wet and ready for me, I nearly come undone. I stroke her with all the precision and focus I've honed in battle, watching every reaction, every flicker of pleasure across her face. My eyes never leave hers—I can't look away, captivated by the trust I see there, the vulnerability she's offering.

"You're so beautiful." Awe threads through my voice as she moves against my hand. Ice crystals form in the air around us, suspended and glittering, responding to the surge of emotion I can't contain. "Let go for me. Let me see you come apart."

When her release hits, it's like watching a storm break. Her water magic erupts around us, droplets suspended in the air before cascading down the cave walls in rivulets of shimmering blue. I watch, transfixed, chest heaving as I fight for control of my own body, my own magic. My jaw clenches against the need pulsing through me, demanding release.

"Do you have any idea what you do to me?" I ask, my voice rough with the emotion I'm struggling to contain. Even now, part of me is terrified—of feeling too much, of losing myself completely, of what comes after. But even though I should, I can barely think about the after. All I can think about is this moment, with Sapphire, and the need to know what it's like to be one with her, fully and completely.

My hands find the hem of her shirt, urgent now. She raises her arms, and I peel the fabric away, my breath catching as more of her is revealed. For a moment, all I can do is look at her—drinking in every curve, every shadow, and every detail.

Inside me, a war rages. The prince I was raised to be—cold, calculated, and detached—is fighting against the man I am with her. The man who wants to let her in, who's desperate to be hers, who already belongs to her in ways I'm only beginning to understand.

"Your turn," she murmurs, fingers reaching for my shirt.

I help her strip it away, exposed now in more ways than one as her gaze travels over my bare chest. For the first time in my life, I'm being seen—not as the Winter Prince, not as my father's son—but just as Riven. And it leaves me trembling.

We undress each other with growing urgency—hands roaming, unfastening, sliding across bare skin as more and more barriers fall away. When the last piece of clothing drops to the cave floor, I exhale shakily and lower her down, my body following, covering hers. The muscles of my abdomen brush against the softness of her stomach, my hips settling perfectly between her thighs, hard and ready against her entrance. The press of her against me sends electricity racing through my veins, my core aching with need. Every muscle in my body draws tight with restraint, trembling with the effort not to thrust forward, to claim her completely.

"If we do this—" I stop, struggling to find words for what I'm feeling. How do I tell her this isn't just physical desire? That what I feel for her has become so much more? "I don't think I can go back to before. To pretending you're just—"

She presses her fingers to my lips, silencing me. "I don't want to go back, either."

Something flickers to life inside me—that desperate, haunted hope I've spent a lifetime crushing. The belief that maybe, just maybe, I could have this. Have *her*. That she might not be taken from me like everything else I've ever loved.

"I've spent my whole life guarding myself," I confess, the admission costing me, scraping against years of training, years of believing vulnerability was weakness. "And then you came along and just—" I make a gesture with my hand, ice crystals forming and shattering in the air, a perfect reflection of what she's done to every defense I've ever built. "You broke through. Like it was nothing."

My words hang between us, raw and exposed. I've never been this honest and open with anyone. The terror of it nearly chokes me.

"I'm glad I did," she whispers, pulling me closer until our foreheads touch.

I kiss her then—wild and hungry, like I'm trying to pour everything I can't say into the press of my lips, the slide of my tongue. Like I'm trying to crawl inside her skin, to lose myself where I know it's safe. For the first time since my mother died, I'm not afraid of what I feel. Not when I'm feeling it with her.

She arches beneath me, hips lifting to welcome me, to take me in. But I catch her waist with my hand, holding her still. There's one more thing I need—one truth I have to know before I can surrender completely.

"I need to know this is real," I murmur, my forehead resting against hers. "That it's not just another thing that'll be taken from me."

The vulnerability in my words strips me bare, more naked than my unclothed body ever could. I'm revealing the deepest fear that's haunted me since childhood—that everything I love will eventually be lost. My mother. My father's sanity. Ghost, in the storm. And now, potentially, her.

She cradles my face in her hands, forcing me to meet her gaze. "It's real," she promises, blue eyes steady on mine. "I'm here. I'm not going anywhere."

I stare into her, searching for the hesitation—for the doubt—and finding none. Only certainty. Only truth. And something in me settles. Steadies. My breath trembles out as I shift, lining us up, the tip of me pressing against her entrance.

Slowly, I push inside.

The sensation is exquisite—tight heat enveloping me inch by inch. I grit my teeth against the urge to thrust fully forward, to claim her completely in a single movement.

She gasps, back arching, body clenching around me, drawing me deeper. The grip of her around me is almost too much to bear.

"Sapphire," I groan, eyes fluttering closed as pleasure washes over me. When I open them again, I know they're blazing with heat—an emotion so different from the ice I normally wield. "You feel like coming home."

I draw out slowly, then push back in, deeper this time—a smooth, grinding thrust that makes her gasp again. Each movement is deliberate, controlled, the last remnant of the discipline that's been beaten into me since childhood. But now that discipline serves a different purpose—ensuring that her pleasure, her comfort, comes before my own.

I move like I'm committing her to memory. Like I want this carved into me. Like it might be the only time I ever get to have this —to have her—and I can't waste a single sensation.

She wraps her legs around my waist, pulling me deeper, matching my rhythm. Our bodies move together in a harmony that feels both new and somehow ancient, like some part of me has always known how to love her.

Our magic responds to our mounting passion, forming a tempest around us. Where my frost meets her water, something new emerges —a shimmering, ethereal phenomenon that feels like our elements recognizing what we ourselves haven't fully admitted. Ice fractals dance in the air, catching the light as they form and dissolve. Water droplets float and freeze, creating a crystalline canopy above us.

"See that?" I say, my voice strained but filled with wonder. "That's us. That's what we are together."

She cups my face, dragging me down into a kiss that makes me shudder—a full-body tremor that breaks my rhythm, forcing me deeper inside her. I find a new pace then—faster, deeper, driving into her with a force that makes her cry out, her nails digging into my back, marking me as hers.

"Come apart for me again," I breathe, the words a rough plea, ice crystals forming and shattering with each thrust. "Let me feel you."

I slow just enough to build the pressure unbearably—grinding deep, deliberate, watching her face as pleasure builds. I shift my angle, finding that spot inside her that makes her gasp, and focus there, determined to feel her come undone around me.

Her body convulses around me, clenching hard as she cries out my name. Her magic explodes outward in shimmering waves that ripple across the cave walls, water and ice merging in a display so beautiful it steals my breath as her climax ripples around me, tight pulses that drag me closer to the edge of my own release.

I still, my breath hitching as I watch her unravel, her face transformed by pleasure. My hips jerk involuntarily, grinding deeper, and I feel the pulse of my own release building, catching fire at the base of my spine.

But I stop it. Force it back. My entire body seizes with the effort, every muscle locking, thighs trembling, a choked sound tearing from my throat as I pull back from the edge through sheer willpower alone.

"No," I grit out, forehead dropping to her shoulder. "Not yet. I need—" My arms shake with the strain, breath coming in shallow, broken gasps. "I need to feel you do that again."

"Riven," she whispers, cradling my face, brushing her thumbs across my cheeks. Her touch is so gentle it threatens to break me. "You're safe with me. You don't have to hold back."

My eyes squeeze shut. My jaw clenches. I stay buried deep inside her, fighting against the pleasure that threatens to overwhelm me. I can feel her body still fluttering around me, each small movement sending shocks of sensation through my entire being.

"Let me give this to you," I whisper, opening my eyes to meet hers. This isn't about control anymore—not the way she might think. It's about giving her everything I am, everything I have. Showing her that her pleasure matters more than my own. That I'm more than the cold, insufferably arrogant prince she first met. "And then I'll let myself fall."

She nods, throat working with emotion, and that's all I need.

A groan tears from deep in my chest as I pull out slowly—the drag of her body around mine nearly my undoing—and thrust back in with a precision honed through years of discipline. Every stroke is calculated to bring her the most pleasure, grinding against that spot inside her that makes her gasp and tremble.

I pin her with my weight, one arm braced beside her head, the other hand sliding between our bodies to find her most sensitive point between her legs. I circle it slowly, in time with my movements, and she cries out—the sound sending a surge of satisfaction through me that's more powerful than any release could be.

She claws at my back, hips rising to meet every thrust, every touch. I can feel her building again, faster this time, her magic responding in kind—water droplets forming and rising around us, suspended in the air like tiny stars.

"I can't—" she gasps, voice breaking.

"Yes, you can." I drive into her with the full force of my need, jaw clenched against my own building pleasure. My fingers work in tandem with my thrusts, drawing her closer, tighter, until she's trembling beneath me.

A cry rips from her throat as her body convulses a second time, inner walls fluttering, clenching around me so hard that a shudder runs through my entire body. Her magic lashes out—water bursting from her in a radiant surge that arcs across the cave ceiling, catching the light like liquid diamonds.

The sight of her undone—the feel of her pulsing around me— finally breaks the last of my control. A groan tears from somewhere deep inside me, from that wounded place I've kept hidden for so long. My rhythm falters as I bury myself deep inside her, my release overtaking me in waves of pleasure so intense that ice magic fractures across the floor in wild, uncontained bursts as I spill myself inside her, hips grinding against hers as I ride out the aftershocks, my breath coming in harsh gasps. My arms tremble with the effort of holding myself above her, my body wracked with pleasure so intense it borders on pain.

When it subsides, I collapse onto her, burying my face in her neck. I don't pull out. Don't move. I just hold her—arms locked tight around her, like she might disappear into thin air if I let go.

"I'm yours," I whisper against her skin, the words torn from the deepest part of me. "Always, Sapphire. Yours."

But my voice shakes, betraying the fear still lingering beneath the surface. I clutch her tighter, unable to stop myself. Some part of me is convinced that this is temporary—that like everything else good in my life, she'll be taken from me. That I'll wake up tomorrow and find this was nothing but a dream, or worse, that she'll regret what we've done.

"You're not going to lose me," she says, as if reading my thoughts.

My breath stutters in my chest—hope warring with a lifetime of disappointment, of loss, of learning that nothing good ever lasts.

"Even if you think this was a mistake tomorrow?" I ask. "Even if you wake up and wish you hadn't..." I trail off, unable to finish the thought. But the fear is there, trembling through my body, the need for reassurance I've never allowed myself to ask for.

She cups my jaw, turning my face toward hers, forcing me to meet her gaze. "Do you really think I could feel everything we just felt and walk away like it meant nothing?"

I stare at her, disbelieving and desperate. The guards I've kept up around my heart for my entire life are gone now, leaving only raw truth exposed.

"I don't think I could take it if you did," I admit—a whisper, a confession, a breaking point.

She tightens her legs around me, keeping me locked inside her. Holding me there. Grounding me in her.

"You don't have to take losing me," she says, steady and certain. "Because you're not going to."

I go still, her words cracking something open inside me—something that's been sealed shut for so long I'd forgotten it existed. Hope. Real hope, not the desperate kind that comes before disappointment, but something solid. Something I might actually be allowed to keep.

I raise my head just enough to look at her—really look at her. Searching her eyes for any hint of doubt or uncertainty, and finding none.

My hand cradles the back of her neck, thumb brushing over her jaw as I claim her lips again—slow, steady, and breath-stealing. I kiss her like I'm drowning and she's air. Like if I pour enough of myself into it, she might understand everything I can't say. Everything I'm afraid to believe.

When I eventually pull back, it's only far enough to rest my forehead against hers. My breathing is still ragged, my voice barely a whisper when I speak.

"Don't let go."

It's not a command. It's a plea—one I've never allowed myself to make before. Not to anyone.

"I'm not going anywhere," she promises, soft but sure.

And in the quiet that follows—just our breathing, our heartbeats, and the slight shifts of our bodies still joined—I feel something change. Not in the world around us, but in *me*.

Because the ice that's encased my heart for so long is beginning to thaw, melting away under the warmth of her touch, her gaze, and her promise. For the first time since I lost my mother and watched my father shatter under the weight of his grief, I allow myself to believe that maybe—just maybe—love doesn't have to end in loss.

That maybe, with Sapphire, I've found something worth the risk of breaking.

TRIAL OF HEARTS
FAE BOUND: VOLUME TWO

The second volume in the *Fae Bound* series, *Trial of Hearts*, is out now! It's my favorite book I've ever written, full of twists that will break your heart in the best way possible. Seriously—there's so much intensity between Sapphire and Riven that even I was on the edge of my seat while writing it.

Get *Trial of Hearts* now:
mybook.to/TrialOfHearts

ABOUT THE AUTHOR

Michelle Madow is a *USA Today* bestselling author of fantasy romance novels filled with forbidden love, elemental magic, and epic twists that readers never see coming. With over three million books sold and translations in multiple languages, her addictive stories have captured hearts around the world.

She wrote her first novel in college and never looked back. Now, with over fifty books published, she spends her time dreaming up magical realms and devastating romances that keep readers hooked from page one.

Originally from Maryland, she's lived everywhere from Florida to New York City. After a winding journey, she's back in NYC, where the city's magic rivals anything she could dream up on the page.

When she's not writing, she's likely getting lost in the magical world of reading, plotting her next big twist, or reminiscing about her travels to all seven continents.

Never miss a new release by signing up to get emails or texts when Michelle's books come out:

Sign up for emails: michellemadow.com/subscribe
Sign up for texts: michellemadow.com/texts

Connect with Michelle:

Instagram: @michellemadow
TikTok: @michellemadow
Facebook: facebook.com/MichLMadow
Email: michelle@michellemadow.com